Darynda Jones has won several awards, including a 2009 Golden Heart in the Paranormal Category for *First Grave on the Right* and the 2012 RITA award for Best New Book.

She lives in New Mexico with her husband of more than 25 years and two sons, the mighty, mighty Jones boys.

Visit Darynda Jones online:

www.daryndajones.com
www.facebook.com/darynda.jones.official
www.twitter.com/Darynda

Praise for Darynda Jones:

'Hilarious and heart-felt, sexy and surprising, this paranormal has it all ... An absolute must read – I'm already begging for the next one!'
J. R. Ward, No.1 *New York Times* bestselling author

'From its unique premise to its wonderfully imaginative characters, Jones's award-winning Charley Davidson mystery series ... will continue to attract and delight a broad spectrum of readers'
Booklist (starred review)

'Jones perfectly balances humor and suspense ... will leave readers eager for the n

By Darynda Jones

First Grave on the Right
Second Grave on the Left
Third Grave Dead Ahead
Fourth Grave Beneath My Feet
Fifth Grave Past the Light
Sixth Grave on the Edge
Seventh Grave and No Body
Eighth Grave After Dark
The Dirt on Ninth Grave
The Curse of Tenth Grave

The Curse
of Tenth
Grave

Darynda Jones

piatkus

PIATKUS

First published in the US in 2016 by St Martin's Press
First published in Great Britain in 2016 by Piatkus

1 3 5 7 9 10 8 6 4 2

A CIP catalogue record for this book
is available from the British Library.

ISBN 978-0-349-41142-2

Printed and bound in Great Britain by
Clays Ltd, St Ives, plc

Papers used by Piatkus are from well-managed forests
and other responsible sources.

MIX
Paper from
responsible sources
FSC® C104740

Piatkus
An imprint of
Little, Brown Book Group
Carmelite House
50 Victoria Embankment
London EC4Y 0DZ

An Hachette UK Company
www.hachette.co.uk

www.piatkus.co.uk

For Jennifer,
part-time superhero,
full-time purveyor of awesomeness and badassery,
and editor extraordinaire.
Thank you.
So very, very much.

Acknowledgments

First and foremost, thank you so much to every single one of Charley's fans and to all those voracious readers who can't get enough of the written word. You make so many authors' dreams come true. We can only hope to return the favor.

Thank you to my amazing agent, Alexandra Machinist, my wonderful editor, Jennifer Enderlin, and to everyone at ICM, St. Martin's Press, and Macmillan, including the insanely talented Lorelei King, a.k.a., the voice of Charley Davidson. My gratitude knows no bounds.

Thank you to our publishers across the pond, Piatkus/Little, Brown, Milady/Bragelonne, Círculo de Leitores, and all the others. Thank you for introducing Charley to readers across the globe. She totally loves to travel.

Thank you to Netters and Dana, who crack the whip and keep me sane.

Thank you to Dana, Theresa, Jowanna, and Trayce, who made this book so much better than it would have been. Seriously, sometimes the stuff I put on the page could fertilize a potted plant. These fantastic women catch so much of that and turn fertilizer into fruitcake. (That's the best we can hope for with Charley.)

And thank you to the newest member of the team, Beth, for all your crazy hard work.

Thank you to my Ruby Sisters for the camaraderie and support.

Thank you to my family and friends for liking me despite everything you know.

And thank you, Lenee from the RSS Winter Writing Festival, for the "lotion" line. I still crack up.

And for aspiring writers everywhere, to blatantly steal a line from one of the best movies ever, *Galaxy Quest,* I encourage you to: Never give up! Never surrender!

Keep reading.

Keep writing.

Keep pushing yourself.

And never stop learning! We writerly types have to stick together. (Mostly because everyone else thinks we're "weird.")

The Curse of Tenth Grave

1

Charley Davidson:
Maybe she's born with it.
Maybe it's caffeine.

Ignoring the dead girl standing next to me, I crossed my bare feet on the cool windowsill, took a sip of piping-hot coffee, and watched the emerging sunrise from my third-story apartment window. A soft yellow scaled the horizon and stretched across it like tendrils of food coloring suspended in water. Ribbons of pinks and oranges and purples quickly followed, the symphony a slow, exquisite seduction of the senses. Or it could have been if there weren't a dead girl standing next to me.

She jutted out a tiny hip, anchored a fist onto it, and let loose a lengthy sigh of annoyance for my benefit. I continued to ignore her. There were few things in life more irritating than other people's children. Hell, perhaps. Been there, done that. But for the moment, the only thing complicating an otherwise serene morning was a tiny blond-haired, blue-eyed beast in Strawberry Shortcake pajamas.

"Are you going to read it to me or not?" she asked, referring to our recent ventures into Harry Potter land.

I stopped what I was doing, which was basically trying not to drool into my cup. As a master mixologist, I felt the need to experiment from time to time on my morning elixir. To liven it up. To create new concoctions of greatness to which others could only aspire. This morning, however, I'd done good just to push the right button on Mr. Coffee. At least I think I pushed the right button. I could have started a nuclear war, for all I knew.

"I've already read it to you 7,843 times."

She pursed her bowlike lips, causing dimples to emerge on either side of her mouth. But these weren't happy dimples. They were dimples of disappointment. Dimples of frustration and irritation and fury.

I hung my head in shame.

Just kidding!

I turned back toward the window and ignored her.

"You've read it twice."

"Which is two times too many in my book," I said, focusing on the spectacular display before me, realizing that, to the everyday passerby, my apathy toward the tiny creature might've seemed cold. Aloof. Cruel, even. But I'd just come from an all-night stakeout that involved a woman, a.k.a. my client, who swore that her husband was sneaking out at night and meeting his personal assistant for some *very* personal assistance. She wanted proof.

After showering, the only thing I wanted was to drink the key to life itself, enjoy the colors bursting before me, and figure out how to tell my client that her husband was not cheating on her with his personal assistant. He was cheating on her, in a sense, with the college kids who rented out their above-garage apartment. He snuck out to play video games and enjoy a little plant-based medicinal stress relief. After getting to know his wife, I could hardly blame him. She turned high maintenance into an extreme sport.

Now I just had to figure out how to tell her what her husband was up to. Even though there was nothing sexual about her husband's exploits, a woman like that would still feel betrayed. If, however, I could put just the right spin on it, I could lessen the sting when I gave her the news. So, instead of my original plan of saying, "Your husband is escaping you for a few blissful hours of recreation because you are cra-cra and he needs a break," I figured I could say something like, "Your husband is sneaking out to tutor the struggling college kids who rent out your apartment. He counsels them on how to stay focused no matter what life throws at them (or who throws it), advises them on how to shake off a bad day (or a bad marriage) and push through. He even cautions them about the dangers of illegal drug use."

Yeah. I nodded my head, quite proud of myself. That's the ticket. By the time I was finished with her, she'd see her husband as a paladin of the pawn. A defender of the downtrodden. A savior of the suffering.

A *hero*!

I took another sip, ignored yet another sigh coming from the irreverent beast beside me, and let myself slip. Just a little. Just enough to see the other side. The supernatural one. Because there was nothing more spectacular than watching the sunrise in the mortal world, the tangible one, from the vantage of the immortal world. One seemed to affect the other. The raging, powerful storms of the supernatural realm grew even more vibrant. Even more brilliant. As though somehow our sunlight spilled into the domain of the preternatural.

Made sense. Preternatural inhabitants tended to spill into our world as well. On occasion.

The marvel that I could shift from one realm to the other was not lost on me. For a month, I'd lived on the crux between the two worlds, having no idea I could control where I stood in each.

In my own defense, I had amnesia at the time. Had no idea who I was. What I was. The fact that I was a god from another dimension who'd volunteered to be the angel of death in this one, to be its grim reaper, was the furthest thing from my imaginings, and even as an amnesiac, I was pretty darned imaginative.

Now that I had all my memories back—both good and bad—I saw my mission as a celestial version of the Peace Corps. Volunteer work for the good of another people and, in turn, for the good of all.

That was a week ago. I'd been back in Albuquerque a week. I'd had my memories back for a week. And still I felt disoriented. Unbalanced. Like a Weeble that wobbled but wouldn't fall down. That *couldn't* fall down. I had too much to do.

My best-friend-slash-receptionist, Cookie, was worried. I could tell. She put on a happy face every time I walked into her office or strolled into her apartment unannounced, an action my uncle Bob, a.k.a. her new husband, did not appreciate. But one of the advantages—or disadvantages, depending on one's point of view—of being from the supernatural side of things was that I could feel others' emotions. And I could feel the worry that ate at her every time she looked at me.

She was right. I hadn't quite been the same since I got back, but for good reason. Three, actually. Three main ones, anyway.

First, my daughter had been taken from me when she was barely two days old. It was for the best. To keep her safe, we had no choice but to send her away. But that didn't make it any easier. Probably because the fault lay at my feet and my feet alone.

I was apparently made of this bright-ass light that lured the departed, those who did not cross when they died, to me. Cool beans, right? I'd always considered the light a pretty nifty side effect of being grim. But that was before I had a child who was destined to defeat Satan and save the world. Now that same light worked only to lead our vast and powerful enemies straight to me. And in turn, straight to my daughter.

Thus, it wasn't so much that we had to send Beep away to be safe. It was more that we had to send her away from *me* to be safe. Her mother. Her matriarch. The woman who bore her. At the bottom of a well, no less. Long story. So the torment of heartbreak I felt was a constant weight on my chest and, unfortunately, my mood.

Second, in an attempt to restore my memories, my departed father crossed through me. When people cross, their lives flash in my mind. When my father crossed, I was flooded with memories of myself through his eyes. I saw the love he felt every time he looked at my sister and me. I felt the pride that swelled his heart to twice its normal size. But as wonderful and surreal and life affirming as all that was, I'd still lost him. He was now safely tucked on the *other* side of this dimension, a realm to which I had no access. None that I knew of, anyway.

But his crossing was only the predecessor of the second reason for my melancholy state. When my father's life flashed in my mind, he also made sure I saw what he'd learned since he died. In an instant, I learned secrets of an underworld I never knew existed. Spies and traitors. Anarchists and heretics. Alliances lost and nations won. And wars. A thousand wars that spanned a million years. But the most salient thing he wanted me to see was the fact that Reyes—my husband, my soul mate, and Beep's father—was a god as well.

A god.

But not just any god. He was one of the three gods of Uzan. Three brothers who knew only death and destruction. Who devoured millions. Who ate worlds like others ate corn chips. Worse, he was considered the most dangerous of the three, the most bloodthirsty, before Satan tricked him, trapped him, and used the god's energy to create his son, Rey'aziel. Otherwise known as Reyes Alexander Farrow.

So my husband was a god—an evil god—who'd destroyed worlds and obliterated life wherever he went. Who was known across a thousand dimensions as the Razer. And I was married to him.

But there was still so much I didn't understand. I'd had no idea I was a god. Not really. Not until I learned my celestial name. When that happened, all the memories I had as a god came rushing back to me. I wasn't supposed to learn my celestial name until my earthly body passed. Until I died and took up my reapery duties. But an unfortunate

series of events forced a friend to whisper my name into my ear. Now I
had the power of creation itself at my fingertips and only an inkling of
what to do with it or how to control it, a fact that set Jehovah, the
God of this dimension, a little on edge. This according to His archangel
Michael.

Michael and I don't really get along. He tried to kill me once. I refuse
to be friends with anyone who's tried to kill me.

But Reyes has heard his celestial name. He's even met the other two
brothers. Was lent out by his father to fight with them side by side during
a particularly nasty war between two realms. Does he know he is a god?
Does he know the most important ingredient his father used while creating him, the one that made him so powerful, was a god? Even if he
doesn't, how much of the god Razer controls Reyes's actions? How much
of him is god? Demon? Human?

In a nutshell, is he good or evil?

All evidence would point to the latter. It was hardly his fault. He was
forged in the fires of sin and damnation. Did that affect him? Did the evil
that forever burned in his home dimension leach into him as he grew up?
As he fought to survive the cruelties of being raised in hell by a bitter fallen
angel? As he rose through the ranks to become a general in his father's
army? To command legions of demons? To lead them into war and sacrifice?

After all this time, after everything we have been through, I thought
I knew my husband. Now I wasn't so sure.

One thing I was sure of was the fact that I needed to learn his true
godly name. It couldn't be Razer. That term had to be an interpretation
of his true name. Or perhaps a nickname. If I knew Reyes's godly name,
I could do what Satan did. I could trap him, if need be, in the god glass I
kept with me always.

I shifted back onto this plane, patted the pendant in my sweats pocket, and turned to the girl beside me. The one who clearly had no intention of leaving.

After forcing my biggest and brightest fake smile, the one made of irritation and paint remover, I asked, "Why don't you have Rocket read it to you?"

Rocket was a mutual friend who'd died in a mental asylum in the fifties. He was also a savant who knew that names of every human being on Earth who'd lived and died. Ever. Strawberry crashed with him and his sister, Blue, though I'm not sure the departed actually sleep. I hadn't seen Rocket in weeks, and his place was first on my list of places to hit for the day, now that my one and only case was almost over.

Strawberry crossed her arms over her chest. "He can't read it to me."

"Why not?"

I was expecting her to say, "Because he's dead, and he can't turn the pages." What I got was, "Because he can't read."

I finally leveled a semi-interested gaze on her. "What do you mean, 'he can't read'? He writes the names of the departed all over the walls."

That was his main gig. Rocket scratched thousands and thousands of names into the walls of the abandoned asylum, all day, every day. It was fascinating to watch. For about five minutes, at which point my ADHD kicked in, and I'd suddenly have places to be and people to see.

She rolled her eyes. "Of course he can *write* names. Duh. It's his job. Doesn't mean he can *read* them."

That made about as much sense as reality TV.

"They aren't there for him to read, anyway," she added as she picked at the sleeve of my T-shirt that read MY BRAIN HAS TOO MANY TABS OPEN. "They're for her."

As intrigued as I should've been, intrigue was not as intriguing as one might imagine at six o'clock in the morning. Especially after pulling an all-nighter. I took another sip. Studied the steam rising out of the cup like a lover. Wondered if I should use my powers over the next twenty-four hours for good or evil. Evil would be more fun.

Finally, with the patience of a saint on Xanax, I asked, "For who, hon?"

Her large irises bounced back to mine. "For who what?"

I shifted toward her. "What?"

"What?"

"What did you say?"

"For who what?"

I fought the urge to grind my teeth into dust and asked, "If not for Rocket, for who—whom—are they written?"

She pursed her lips and went back to lacing tendrils of my hair into her tiny fingers. "For whom is *what* written?"

I'd lost her. And I suddenly had a raging desire to sell her on the black market. It would do me little good, though. Poor thing drowned when she was nine. Not many on Earth could see her. My luck I'd have to take her back and give the buyer a refund. Then I'd have to mark the perv's soul for hell for trying to buy a child on the black market. Seriously, what the fuck?

I took another sip for strength and then explained as simply as I could. "The names Rocket writes on the walls of the asylum. If he can't read them, who are they for?"

"Oh, those!" Suddenly excited, she tried to disentangle her fingers and took half my scalp with her. She spread her arms like wings and began running in circles around the apartment making engine sounds. No idea why. "Those are for Beep."

I paused mid-scalp-rub. "Beep?" A tingling sensation racing over my skin. "My Beep?"

She stopped just long enough to shoot me a look of exasperation before flying around the apartment again. Not literally. "How many Beeps do you know?"

I blinked at her for a solid minute with my mouth slightly agape. Drool slipped from one corner as I tried to wrap my head around what she'd just said. If only I had more brain cells at 6 A.M. They didn't even begin to amass until around 7:12, and the all-nighter didn't help.

As I sat pondering Strawberry's statement, the son of Satan walked in from our bedroom wearing only a gray pair of pajama bottoms and a sleep-deprived expression. The bottoms rode low on his lean hips. The expression darkened an already dark face. Black hair sat at charmingly unnatural angles. Thick lashes hooded sparkling brown irises. The boy defined the popular phrase *sex on a stick*.

But I had to remember what he was. It was bad enough that his father was public enemy number one, but to be an evil god from another dimension? That was a lot of evil to pack into one body, no matter how succulent.

I should have guessed long ago that he was more than met the eye. Even barely awake he had a powerful stride. Sleek. Graceful. Like that of a big cat. I slipped into the outer edge of the supernatural realm and saw the darkness billowing out of him like a cloak to cascade over his shoulders. To wash down his back. To pool at his bare feet.

The fire that bathed him in yellows and oranges and blues licked over his smooth skin like a layer of sin. It dipped between the valleys of hard muscle. Shifted with every move he made. As though it were as alive as he.

Strawberry noticed none of that. Her harried little mind, like her body, spun in circles as though she hadn't just dropped a bombshell on me. Why would those names be meant for Beep? It made no sense.

"What do you mean, hon?" I asked her, suppressing a giggle when Reyes spotted the little beast coming in for a landing near his rubber tree plant. It wasn't like she could actually knock it over.

Instead of answers, I got, "I love cotton candy. I'd marry it if I could." She swooped in for a landing, taxied just long enough to catch a second wind, then took off again. "I can smell it sometimes. There was a house on fire once, but I couldn't smell it. I can't smell perfume or paste or oranges, but I can smell cotton candy. Only sometimes, though. All pink and fluffy. Do you like cotton candy?"

I'd been busy watching my husband head for the kitchen, trying not to let the soft grin he tossed me ease the turmoil roiling inside me.

"Cotton candy daiquiris," I said, unable to take my eyes off him.

We had fallen into a continuous series of short conversations and awkward silences. And I had no idea why. No idea what I had done. For a man who could barely keep his hands off me a week ago, this new form of torture was disconcerting.

Did he know that he was a god? More important, did he know that I knew that he was a god?

Such knowledge could certainly put him on edge. Then again, why? I was a god. Why shouldn't he be one as well? Maybe there was more to this than I knew. Or perhaps his recent disinterest had nothing to do with any of that.

Maybe it was due to the fact that I had done exactly what he had predicted I would. I forgot him. When I learned my celestial name, I forgot him. He'd said I would. No, wait—he'd said I would leave him, and then I would forget him. Two for two. But amnesia was a really good excuse for not remembering someone. And it's not like I'd done it on purpose.

The fact that he was so drop-dead sexy did not help anything. The pajama bottoms did absolutely nothing to hide the fact that he had the most perfect ass I had ever seen. Steely. Shapely. Deep divots on either side. Solid, rock-hard muscle. The kind of ass no heterosexual woman could resist. Damn him.

I craned my neck to watch him walk into the kitchen and pull the carafe out from the coffeemaker.

"I just made it," I said, referring to the coffee.

"What do you think brought me in here?" There was a softness to his voice despite the darkness surrounding him. A humor. It was nice and more reassuring than it should have been.

"Sometimes I eat it for breakfast," Strawberry added, then pointed to Reyes from the space between a slate coffee table and a creamy sofa. "Does he ever eat cotton candy for breakfast?"

He stepped around the counter to face us, lowered his gaze, and took a sip from the black mug in his hands.

"No," I said. "He's very much like the Big Bad Wolf. He eats little girls for breakfast."

He spoke from behind the cup, his voice deep and as smooth as butterscotch. "She's wrong. I eat big girls for breakfast."

A tingling sensation fluttered in my stomach.

Strawberry stopped at last and crinkled her nose in thought, our playful banter going over her head, thankfully.

"Did you catch the bad guy?" Reyes asked, pinning me with his powerful gaze.

I turned around in the chair I'd pulled up to the window and sat on my heels to savor the view. "No bad guys this time. Just a man trying to make it through the day."

"Aren't we all?" he asked, and I paused to study him.

He studied me back, his lashes narrowing as he took me in, and I wondered if he really understood, on even the basest level, what he did to women. A man just trying to make it through the day? Uh-huh. Right.

Strawberry landed again, plopped onto the coffee table, and let her feet dangle beneath her. "I like what you've done with the place."

Reyes grinned and ducked back into the kitchen, hopefully to make me the breakfast of champions, whatever that might entail. I took the opportunity to once again scan the vastness of what used to be my microscopic apartment. I hadn't seen it for over nine months, eight of those having been spent at a convent—long story—and the other one spent as an amnesiac waitress at a café in Upstate New York.

At some point during our recent adventures, Reyes had renovated the apartment building. The entire thing. The exterior remained relatively unchanged. A few fixes here and there, a good cleaning, and it was good to go.

The interior, however, had been completely overhauled. Each apartment had been updated as students graduated or long-term residents moved into one of the newly renovated ones while theirs received the same treatment. But the third floor, the top one, had received a little extra attention.

It now had only two apartments, ours and Cookie's, each consisting of over thirteen thousand square feet of absolute luxury.

The rooftop storage units had been opened up so the ceilings in half of the apartment were now over twenty-four feet tall. Metal rafters zigzagged across our ceiling. Two adjoining gardens sat on the flat part of the roof outside, complete with lights and a pond and real plants. The whole place look positively magical.

Reyes kept only one room locked and had refused to open it when he brought me home for the first time in months, but locked doors were never much of a problem for me. The day after we'd arrived home, I took advantage of the fact that he left earlier than I did and broke in. I'd flipped the light switch and stopped short. The room had been decorated in mint green stripes and pastel circus animals and equipped with a bassinet. It was Beep's room, and the fissure in my heart had cracked a little more.

"I'm going to see if Blue wants to play hopscotch."

She disappeared before I could get out a good-bye. Or good riddance. Either way.

I looked past where she'd been sitting toward Reyes's plush creamcolored sofa. He didn't get it at a garage sale like I'd gotten my previous sofa. Her name had been Sophie, and I often wondered what happened to her. Was she lamenting the days away at a dump site? Sure, she'd only cost me twenty bucks, but she'd been with me a long time. I hated the thought of her being destroyed.

Then another thought hit me.

Speaking of discarded items, "Hey," I said, suddenly concerned, "where did you put Mrs. Allen and PP?"

PP, a.k.a. Prince Phillip, was an elderly poodle that had once fought a demon for me, doing his darnedest to save my life. He and Mrs. Allen had been living down the hall since I'd moved in, and if anyone had a right to live here, to have one of these sparkly new apartments, it was those two.

Reyes lowered his head. "Her family had to put her in a nursing home."

My spine straightened in alarm. "What? Why?"

He bit down. "A lot's happened since we've been gone."

"You should have told me."

"It happened last month. You wouldn't have known her."

I paused to absorb that. He was right. Didn't make it any easier to swallow. "Where is she?"

"At a retirement home in the North Valley."

I made a mental note to visit her. "What about PP?"

"PP?"

"Her poodle. The one that saved my life, I might add."

He fought a grin. "He's with her. The home where she is allows animals."

"Oh, thank goodness." I slumped in the chair and put my chin on the back. Reyes was right. A lot had changed. Including the state of my cup.

"I'm going to make another pot if you want more after your shower," I said, hopping up and heading that way.

He lifted a wide shoulder, studying his own cup. His bare feet were crossed, his other shoulder propped against the opening to the chef's kitchen, and I slowed my stride to take it all in.

"I'm not sure I want to shower today," he said.

"What? Why?"

A panty-melting grin as wicked as sin on Sunday slid across his handsome face. "Your aunt Lillian keeps . . . checking in on me."

I stopped midstride, finally becoming intimately acquainted with true, paralyzing mortification.

He stifled a chuckle as he set his cup aside and started for the bathroom.

"Aunt Lillian!" I yelled, summoning her to me instantly. Aunt Lillian had died in the sixties. She'd been elderly at the time, but she didn't let that stop her from enjoying the flower child generation complete with love beads and a floral muumuu. I'd always figured a hit of acid at her age could not have been good.

"Pumpkin head!" she said, her tone as hollow and insincere as her dentureless mouth. She wasn't even looking at me. Her gaze instantly sought out the son of evil. Locked on to him like a laser-guided missile.

He tossed her a wink as he strode past, and I thought she was going to melt right then and there.

"Aunt Lillian," I whispered accusingly. "I thought you didn't even like my husband that much."

"Oh, pumpkin, I've seen him naked. What's not to like?" She wiggled her brows, and I gaped, appalled. Appalled that, for once in my life, I had no argument. No sarcastic comeback. No snippy comment. Because she was right as rain on a scorched desert.

I looked my husband over once again. Watched his back muscles ripple with each step he took. Our apartment was much bigger now, so it took a lot of steps to get to the bathroom. A lot of rippling.

One of those ripples was inside me. A ripple of unease. So much had changed. Way more than I was comfortable with. Which brought me to the third, but far from final, reason for my gloom. My husband hadn't touched me in days. Since we got back, in fact. Normally, he had trouble touching anything *besides* me, but he hadn't offered his services in over a week. A very long, very lonely week, made even lonelier when I'd been blindsided by a receipt I stumbled upon. He'd made a payment to the Texas Child Support Division.

He was paying child support.

He had another child.

I closed my eyes again, trying to figure out if I ever really knew the man I married.

2

You can't control everything.
Your hair was put on your head to remind you of that.
—MEME

Just as Reyes was about to disappear into the bathroom for a visit with
George the shower, the front door crashed open. It banged against the
wall, and I jumped all the way to the twenty-four-foot ceiling. At least it
felt that way.

Reyes, completely unalarmed, paused to watch Cookie, a curvy
thirtysomething goddess with short black hair and a challenged sense
of accessories, and her lovely daughter, Amber, a tall, slender, thirteen-
going-on-seventy-year-old with long, dark locks and delicate, wing-
shaped eyebrows, practically stumble over themselves to get inside. A
quick glance told me Reyes found them amusing, if the sexy tilt of his
mouth was any indication.

I, on the other hand, was still searching for my heart. I glanced back
up at the ceiling. No heart there, but the blond boy dangling his feet where
three thick metal beams converged was still there. He'd been hanging out
since I got back a week ago and had yet to talk to me. Or anyone, for that
matter. Had he always been there and we'd just never seen him? Stuck in

the storerooms on the roof? Had he died there? No one found a body during the renovations that I knew of, but that didn't mean he couldn't have been killed there and dumped somewhere else.

Once Cookie and Amber settled in front of me—Amber's face full of excited intrigue, Cookie's full of horror, but that was pretty much her morning look until she got some rocket fuel in her—I tore my attention off the boy and offered it to them.

They started talking at the same time, each interrupting the other over and over until it was impossible to tell who was speaking at any given moment.

Cookie started it off with a "There's something you have to see."

Then Amber chimed in. "It's everywhere."

It went downhill from there.

"You won't believe—"

"I think you should—"

"So many hits—"

"It's crazy—"

"You'll be—"

"You'll be—"

"—famous."

"—exposed."

"This is awesome!"

"This is so bad."

I finally reached up and gently placed a hand over each of their mouths. They hushed instantly, then Cookie mumbled, "Fine. Amber can tell you."

Appeased, I lowered my hands. Amber giggled, risked a quick glance at the hotness walking back our way, then shoved her phone into my hands.

"You'll just have to see for yourself."

I took the phone, leaning in for a quick hug in the process. She kissed my cheek and curled me into her long arms for a solid five seconds. She'd been doing that since D-Day, the day I got back. She hadn't been allowed to go to New York to babysit my pathetic ass. Or to try to knock some sense into my amnesiaced brain. Whichever way one wished to look at it. And the moment we got off the escalator at baggage claim, she ran past her mother and tackle-hugged me. All the way to the ground.

She hadn't seen her mother in a month, but she'd been talking to her every day. Me, she'd had no contact with for a month, and her exuberance was proof that she liked me. Her tears were proof that she *really* liked me.

Which was kind of wonderful. I *really* liked her, too.

"Okay," she said, pulling away. "Take a look. You're going to die!" She clapped her hands over her mouth excitedly.

Cookie seemed to grow a little paler.

Reyes shifted for a better look, and I couldn't help but notice where Amber's eyes landed: at the waistband of his pajama bottoms. The waistband that hung low enough to show an inkling of the dip between hip and abdomen. That sweet spot that turned women to jelly.

It didn't concern me that Amber was only thirteen. What concerned me was that she was thirteen and I was pretty sure her sweetheart, Quentin, had a similar dip. Hopefully she didn't know that. Yet.

I lifted the phone, angled it so Reyes could see, and pressed PLAY.

The video read: UGANDA, AFRICA. POSSESSED GIRL AND EXORCIST.

Okay. A bit dramatic, but who was I to criticize?

Then a young African girl materialized onto the screen. A girl I recognized from my time in the Peace Corps. The shot was a close-up of her face with a night-vision camera. Her skin was covered in scratches. Her lips, cracked and bleeding, pulled tight over gnashing teeth. Her eyes solid white. Drool slid from the corners of her mouth as the camera pulled back to reveal her neck arched. Head thrown back. Chest heaving in furious pants.

She lay on a pallet on a dirt floor, her wrists and ankles bound by a very concerned, very loving father. Faraji. He'd been helping us dig a well for his village, and when I'd first met him he was distant. Wary of us newcomers. It was not unusual. Many villagers on our journey had welcomed us in an almost celebratory manner. But others, mostly men, were not so keen on having us invade their territory, Peace Corps or not. Faraji had been one of them.

I'd taken note of him instantly, not because of his standoffish behavior, but because of the deep sorrow that emanated out of him.

No, not sorrow. Fear.

Terror, actually. So much so that I found it hard to breathe around him, and digging a well without the ability to fill one's lungs was not an easy way to dig a well.

We'd been in the village about three days when I finally followed him home one night. Or at least, I thought I was following him home. I found out later it was an abandoned hut, and he and his family had been in hiding. I felt the reason long before I got to the ramshackle hut. Like needles on my skin. Like acid in my mouth.

I'd never felt anything like it. And when I stepped inside unannounced, I'd never seen anything like it, either. His twelve-year-old daughter, Emem, lay in the throes of a heated battle with whatever had taken up residence inside her. Nkiru, Faraji's wife, sat beside their daughter. Pressed a cool cloth to the girl's head. Rocked back and forth in prayer.

She looked up when I stepped under the eaves of their hut that amounted to little more than a well-fortified lean-to.

"Faraji," she said, her voice shrill and harsh. Eyes like saucers, she glared at her husband. "Get her out." She spoke in her native language, believing I wouldn't understand. "The elders will take our daughter." She tightened her grip on the child's forearm. "The elders will kill her."

Faraji had turned and was staring at me in horror, unable to believe that I'd followed him. Or that I'd been able to follow him without being detected.

I'd wondered how long the situation had been going on. The girl looked skeletal. Dehydrated to the point of emaciation, except for her beautiful, scar-covered face. From various markings on the floor, I got the feeling they had been consulting a shaman-type healer. And why wouldn't they? This was no medical condition. Whatever was in her burned my lungs and seared my eyes.

I crept forward, but Faraji stepped in my path. I felt the turmoil rise within him. He had a choice to make.

At first, I thought he was weighing the pros and cons of allowing me to try to help him. He wasn't. I soon realized he was trying to decide if he should let me go and risk the village finding out about his daughter or kill me. I got the feeling he was leaning toward the latter. Mostly because he'd tightened his grip on the machete he'd been carrying. Steeling himself to do what had to be done.

"May I see her?" I asked. In his language. I swallowed back my heart before it jumped out of my chest. He could've killed me before it managed another beat. I was hoping that speaking to him in his language would give him pause. It did.

I didn't go around touting my ability to understand and speak every language ever spoken on Earth, even to my comrades in the Peace Corps. Too difficult to explain, first of all, and then too difficult to deal with. Once someone found out, they were constantly having me *prove* it. So I'd had yet to speak Bantu in the village even though I understood everything everyone said.

But the decision to reveal that little gem did exactly what I was hoping it would. It surprised him enough to reconsider my impending doom. Good thing, because I didn't think I could've outrun him, and that machete was as sharp as a scalpel and sat in the hands of a very skilled hunter.

I glanced past him toward his wife, her expression on the verge of hysteria.

"I don't know if I can help," I said to her as calmly as I could, considering my heart had been relocated. "But I can try."

The girl had been possessed. That much was painfully evident, though my only references were Regan from *The Exorcist* and Stan Marsh from *South Park*.

For some reason, most likely desperation, Faraji's wife nodded, and I stepped past him to kneel beside their daughter.

The video began there. It showed the girl for only a second before pulling back and showing me kneeling beside her. I'd had no idea what I was doing. At the time, I hadn't known demons existed, and I still doubted it after that encounter. Still, whatever it was had left an impression.

But who'd filmed it? There'd been no one else there. Had someone followed me as I'd followed Faraji? Where had the footage come from?

I'd spoken to whatever was inside the girl in Latin at first, then in Ancient Aramaic. It just seemed appropriate. It was the Aramaic that got its attention, because soon after, the hut started tumbling around me.

According to the video, however, the hut hadn't moved. I was being tossed around like a rag doll. Nkiru screamed and scrambled back. Faraji dropped the machete and held his wife in horror as I was flung from floor to ceiling and everywhere in between.

I didn't quite remember it that way, but okay.

Thankfully, the attack was short-lived. It screamed, the thing inside her, the moment it left the girl to give me a what for. I'd lost all sense of direction as the floor had been snatched out from under me, so I'd never actually seen it. But its screams had filled the space between my ears to splitting precision.

To anyone watching the video, however, the only sounds that would be heard were the thuds of me hitting this or that and my groans of agony. Everything else would have been silent. Even to Faraji, Nkiru, and

Emem, who lay still on the floor, unconscious. But the screams had grated over my nerve endings at the time. A blinding darkness had enveloped me. A blistering heat had burned my throat and lungs.

Then it stopped. As unexpectedly as it started, it just stopped.

Unfortunately, I'd been on the ceiling at the time. I fell. Face-first. Bounced up a bit. Then fell again. When I'd finally settled into a prone position, I spent the next few moments whimpering into my armpit and asking no one in particular, "Why?" Sadly, the camera caught it all.

I gripped the phone tighter as Reyes watched me reenact *The Poseidon Adventure*—me being the *Poseidon*—but the way my head bounced off the packed earth was kind of funny. A giggle slid out of me before I could stop it, while Reyes struggled to contain his anger, anger being the predominant emotion at the moment. It was hard to tell with him sometimes, he was so tightly packed.

The next thing I remembered about that particular night was hearing a soft cry. Well, one other than my own. Then a throat-wrenching sob as Nkiru scrambled back to her daughter. She and Faraji cradled her, Nkiru wailing, her shoulders shaking, but the emotion that had been emanating from her was elation. Utter elation and crushing relief.

The video stopped there, but I remembered struggling to my feet and hobbling off to let them celebrate in private.

I also remembered getting lost on the way back to camp. It had taken me what seemed like hours to find it, but I'd been pretty banged up. Turned out, I had only been gone a total of two hours. Another Peace Corps volunteer had found me. Samuel was his name. Was he the one who'd recorded the event?

It had to have been one of my Peace Corps associates. The villagers didn't even have running water, much less a video camera.

"What are we going to do?" Cookie asked as I pressed REPLAY. That last bit was too funny not to watch again.

"Two hundred thousand," Amber said just as I was thrown to the ceiling. "Last night Quentin said it only had a few hundred hits, and now it's over two hundred thousand. It's going viral."

"This is so bad," Cookie said, repeating an earlier sentiment.

The angle at which I bounced off a sidewall, my foot punching through the straw before being jerked—shoeless—back out was worth the price of admission.

"This is so awesome," Amber said, her voice full of awe.

And my face slams into the packed earth, bounces back up, and slams again. I laughed softly before catching myself. Reyes stood deathly still. He rarely found the humor in things I did.

"I'm sorry, Uncle Reyes," Amber said, believing she'd made some kind of mistake. "I didn't mean—"

"He's fine." I turned to him, but he continued to stare at the phone.

He bit down. Lowered his head. Stalked off.

"I'm so sorry, Aunt Charley."

I watched him go, only a little concerned. He did that. Got angry at the strangest things. He was probably mad that he hadn't been there to save me from the big bad monster. But what could he have done even if he'd been there? Gotten tossed around with me?

"He'll be fine, hon. But, seriously, did you see the look on my face?"

I played it again, and Amber and I burst into laughter at last, doubling over as it shook us to the core. Cookie stood there. Speechless. Sadly, her astonished expression only served to prod us deeper into the darkest caverns of amusement, and my belly started hurting.

"Charley," Cookie said, "what are we going to do?"

"Wait," I said, holding up an index finger while I tried to gather myself.

Amber anchored her arm against me and sobered first. "Sorry, Mom. It's just . . . she bounces."

We crumpled into a heap of giggling Jell-O on the floor.

3

What does it mean if the holy water sizzles when it hits your skin?
—ASKING FOR A FRIEND

Once I was able to form complete sentences again, I promised Cookie I'd think long and hard about the possible ramification of that video. I'd made a similar promise to my high school principal when he told me to think about my actions that day. Who knew a wolf call would cause John Burrows to run Hailey Marsh over with his shiny new 'Stang? It was a pretty car. And a pretty boy. And Hailey's legs totally healed after six months of leg braces and another six of physical therapy. Though her dream of the Olympics was pretty much over. I did feel bad about that.

I had to admit, however, I was very curious who'd posted that video.

"Quentin and I will find out," Amber had said, her chin jutting proudly.

"Quentin and you will do your schoolwork," Cookie replied. She'd drawn her eyebrows into a stern line, but her voice fell a few inches short of the intended emotion. Quentin did that to her. Turned her all soft and mushy.

"We will, Mom. Then we'll find out who posted that video." She gave me a thumbs-up. "We're on it."

Knowing those two, they'd do it. I thought about putting my friend Pari on it, too, just in case. That woman was a hacker extraordinaire. But I'd give them first crack at it.

In the meantime, I had to get dressed and get to work, because going to work in my pajamas was apparently the definition of unprofessional. Cookie's words. I looked it up, though. She was wrong. *Webster's* mentioned nothing about pajamas.

The bulk of Reyes's anger seemed to have evaporated, but not his sudden . . . what? Insecurity? Was that what I'd felt wafting off him since we got back? Surely not. He was about as insecure as a jaguar in the jungle.

As he was leaving, wearing jeans and a white button-down with the sleeves folded up to his elbows, he turned back to me and leaned against the doorframe to the bathroom, where I was pulling my hair into a ponytail. He lowered his head, his dark hair falling forward.

"I'll see you for breakfast?" he asked, hesitant.

"I don't know. I've kind of been seeing someone for breakfast on the side."

One corner of his mouth lifted. "And who would that be?"

"Her name is Caroline. I'm in love with her."

"Is that right?"

"She makes the best mocha lattes I've ever had. She splashes in a touch of heavy whipping cream. Makes all the difference in the world."

"So, your breakfast is a mocha latte?"

"Yes."

"Mine's better."

Damn it. He was right. As much as I loved Caroline and her amazing mocha lattes, few things on the planet compared to Reyes's huevos rancheros. He knew what chile did to me. He knew what he did to me, decadent creature that he was. He totally should have been a master chef. Or a male stripper. Or an exotic dessert. Reyes à la mode. I'd eat every bite of him and lick the plate clean.

Without another word, he pushed off the frame and left, but not before I caught a hint of his earlier anger. It was a protective type of thing, and I couldn't help but wonder if he was hiding anything else. Did I miss a vital detail in the video?

I guess I could do something crazy like ask him. We worked in the same building, so the journey wouldn't be long. He had the restaurant on the bottom floor, and I had the offices on the top, and they both sat about fifty feet from our apartment building.

It was a great arrangement most of the time. But as I was trying to get back into the swing of things, the closeness only emphasized the distance I'd been feeling from him. The chasm.

Thankfully, during the fifty-foot walk to my office and the dozen or so stairs and the welcome mat I somehow managed to trip over every single day, I had an epiphany.

Cookie had beaten me to work, which was a good thing. I needed to announce my epiphany and proclaim my inevitable victory.

"I am going to seize this day," I said to her when I walked over to her desk.

She was on her knees going through a cabinet, so I actually said it to her butt.

"Good for you," she mumbled from inside the cabinet. "You can start by telling me where you hid the staples."

"I'm serious, Cook." I peeled off my jacket and tossed it toward a hook on the wall, missing by about twelve feet. But not even that would stop me. "No more wallowing," I said as the black jacket crumpled to the ground like so many of my exes. "It's time to take action."

"Stapling is an action."

"The way I see it, there are two kinds of people in this world."

She paused her search and straightened to give me her full, undiluted attention. "This should be good." She was still on her knees. It was kind of like being worshipped.

"There are those in this world who, when they have to get up in the middle of the night to pee, turn on the light. And there are those who leave it off." I graced her with my best look of absolute determination. Jaw set. Shoulders straight. Eyes narrowed—just a little—as I anchored my fists onto my hips and looked off into the distance. "I pee in the dark, baby."

"Which explains why you stub your pinkie toe so often."

"I am the definition of adventurous."

"Not to mention accident-prone."

"I am getting my daughter back."

A knowing grin slid across her. "Attagirl."

Beep, or Elwyn Alexandra, was currently being cared for by Reyes's human parents. The same parents he'd been stolen from as an infant. They were wonderful people, and I couldn't have been more grateful for their willingness to help us, but giving her up for good had never been part of the plan. Not my plan, anyway.

She was also surrounded by a veritable army of both human and supernatural protectors, any one of whom would give up his life for her. Again, my gratitude knew no bounds. But, again, my own need to protect her, to care for her and watch her grow, was stronger than anything I'd ever felt in my life. It was a constant clash of wills, a continuous struggle as though the devil that sat on one shoulder was forever battling the angel that sat on the other, and their arena resided right in the middle of my chest.

I drew in a deep, determined breath just as the emptiness of my cavernous stomach hit me. "Now that that's settled, when is lunch?"

She bent back to her task. "We just ate. But we can play Find the Staples until then."

"Fine." I looked around for something to do. "I'll just sharpen pencils." Pencil sharpening sounded important. Right up there with Pilates and solving world hunger. I started for my office, which was a hairbreadth past our reception area, a.k.a. Cookie's Domain.

"And hunt for staples?" she asked.

"Bottom right-hand drawer of your desk."

"I've already looked there."

"They're under your copy of *Man Parts*."

"What?" I heard a soft bang and then a drawer opening and papers rustling as I started a pot of coffee. "I don't subscribe to *Man Parts*."

"Oh, you do now. I forgot to tell you."

"Charley," she said with a gasp. "You're subscribing me to porn magazines?"

"Only one."

Before she protested too much—because the girl loved man parts as much as I did—the door opened, and two men walked in. Men with man parts, most likely. Coincidence?

I decided to pour all my energy into the art of making coffee as Cookie saw to our guests. We hadn't had much action since we'd gotten back, so I doubted it was a potential client. They were probably selling vacuum cleaners or Ping-Pong balls or toothpaste. Wait, I needed toothpaste.

Fingers crossed.

Cookie stepped to the threshold of our adjoining door and announced the fact that there were two men in her office who'd like to see me immediately. If possible.

It was all very formal, very professional, like we were a real business again.

A giddy sensation rushed through me. I turned on the Bunn, hurried to sit behind my desk, and nodded to Cookie. "Show them in, please, Cookie."

"Right away."

Sadly, the first guy through the door was a jerk ADA named Nick Parker. No idea who the other guy was, but how great could he be with a friend like Nick Parker?

I stood but didn't offer my hand in greeting. Nick didn't take offense.

He wasn't about to offer his, either. He didn't seem to like it when I proved people he was trying to prosecute innocent of the charges he filed against them. And I'd only done it to him once. Man could hold a grudge.

"This is Charley Davidson," he said to his friend, an older man with an aging suit that had seen perhaps one too many decades.

For him, I held out my hand.

"This is Geoff Adams," Parker said to me, and if the feeling of utter desolation weren't enough to bowl me over, taking his hand and having that emotion injected straight into my heart via a handshake came close.

They were both upset, actually, but Mr. Adams was more so. Devastation had shredded him from the inside out. Someone had died. I'd have bet my last nickel-plated Glock on it.

"Please, sit," I said, gesturing for them to do that very thing.

I sat as well and then took in Nick Parker, wondering if he was playing me. It was hard to get past the emotions of the older man, but I felt several coming from Nick the Prick, a nickname I'd given him the first time I met him. He'd ordered a drink from me. We were at the bar when my dad owned it, and he knew damned well I wasn't a server. Yet, he snapped his fingers at me, an arrogant smirk on his face. I'd been itching to break those fingers ever since.

"What can I do for you?" I asked as coldly as I could.

Nick eyed me a long moment, then looked at Mr. Adams. Sensing he'd have to take the reins, he cleared his throat and said, "Mr. Adams's daughter was murdered last week, and the main suspect is her boyfriend, a freelance artist named Lyle Fiske."

"I'm so sorry, Mr. Adams," I said as I jotted down names with a pink pen I'd stolen off Cookie's desk.

I seemed to repel pens. I could never find one when I needed one. Unfortunately, I did not repel the departed, as was evident by the Asian woman—the one only I could see—who seemed very irritated with my desk lamp, if her tone was any indication. I could hardly blame her. That lamp was always causing problems.

I focused harder on the potential clients sitting before me. Another wave of grief crushed Mr. Adams, slicing into me as well, as though I were made of butter. I clenched my fist around the pen but didn't block the flow of energy. I needed to feel everything they were feeling. Clients often lied to me. They often lied to themselves, so I rarely took offense.

But those lies, the ones that were so rehearsed the speaker believed them himself, were harder to detect. While the grief Mr. Adams suffered was painfully real, raw and cutting and visceral, I also caught a hint of guilt wreaking havoc on his frayed body. It shuddered through him with every breath he took, like an undiagnosed form of pneumonia rattling his lungs.

I didn't know the case personally. I'd been out. But I did hear a smidgen of it on the news a couple of days ago.

"So, you want me to make sure the boyfriend goes to prison for the rest of his natural-born life," I said.

It wasn't a question, but Parker shook his head, anyway. "No. Lyle didn't do this. He couldn't have. We want you to do the exact opposite. We want you to prove his innocence and find who did this."

I hadn't expected that. I leaned back in my chair and tapped the pen on my chin. "Why don't you think he did it?"

"I just know," Mr. Adams said, his voice hoarse and hollow. "He—he couldn't have." His glassy, red-rimmed eyes met mine. They were filled with absolute conviction. He wasn't guessing. He knew the guy was innocent.

Had he killed his own daughter? It was hard to miss the guilt wafting off him. But there was no mistaking the grief, either. If he did kill her, he felt really bad about it.

Or he and the boyfriend had been very close. They would have to have been for him to be so certain. And I couldn't imagine a father, especially one so loving, could do what they did to Emery Adams. The inside of her car had literally been painted with her blood. Whatever happened, Emery's death had been a very violent affair.

"We went to college together," Parker said. "I knew him well. He could never have done this. Never."

He knew him in college? That was the best he had? He was a prosecutor. Surely he knew how little weight that held.

"I thought the police had yet to find her body," I said. "Why are they so sure she was murdered?"

"The amount of blood found in the car," Parker said. "There's simply no way she could've survived the attack."

"And all of it was hers?"

"Every drop," Mr. Adams said, his voice cracking. "Every precious drop." The pain that welled up inside him stole my breath. It was so apparent that even the Asian woman stopped trying to hit my lamp and looked at him. He sobbed into a handkerchief, and I couldn't stop the welling of tears if I'd superglued my tear ducts shut.

I took a deep breath as Parker placed a hand on Mr. Adams's shoulder. I had no idea the man had a tender bone in his body.

"There was nobody better," Mr. Adams said. "Not in this whole world. She was everything to me. But I—I wasn't the best father. She deserved so much better."

He broke down again, his shoulders shaking so hard I thought he'd shatter. We gave him a moment, but when he couldn't stop, he stood and strode out of my office, not stopping until he was outside on the front balcony.

It would give me a chance to grill Parker in a less delicate manner.

I leaned forward. "Why are you here, Parker?" I said, my tone accusing.

He let out a long, resigned sigh. "Because you get the job done, Davidson. No matter what I think about you or your methods or your . . . habits—"

What the hell?

"—you do what you set out to do. You prove people innocent when they are destined for the needle. You see evidence where no one else does. You see the good when others only see the bad. I need you on Lyle's team. He didn't do it, but the evidence against him would strongly suggest otherwise."

He handed me the case file, and even though I didn't trust him as far as I could drive him down a golf course with my dad's nine iron, he presented a good argument. Then again, he was a prosecutor vying for the DA's corner office. And he was just young and ambitious enough to get it. Someday.

"Where's Lyle now?"

He relaxed, though just a tad. "They're holding him for questioning."

I perused the folder he gave me. "They must have something good. They wouldn't have arrested him without a body unless they were convinced there was a murder and that he did it."

"I know. It's unprecedented. But, just between you and me, they're hoping for a plea bargain. A confession is just what this case needs."

"Will they get one?"

He glared up at me. "No, Davidson, they won't."

Fair enough. "Did you know Emery Adams?"

He shook his head. "No. I'd never met her, but from what I understand, she was a very good person." He dropped his gaze, his expression hard. "She didn't deserve this." When I said nothing, he refocused on me and continued, "Look, I know we don't exactly get along, but everyone is right about you."

"Everyone?" I asked, knowing precisely what he was going to say.

"You solve crimes. You close cases."

"That I do," I agreed, putting the pen down and bracing myself. The woman finally gave up on the lamp and noticed me. She gazed longingly. Lovingly. Wanting to go home. Wanting to see her family again. I wanted that for her, too. I really did. Just not at that precise moment. But she was going to cross, and she was going to cross now, and there was nothing I could do about it.

I stood and walked around my desk to buy myself a few seconds. "Who's prosecuting?"

He cleared his throat and shifted uncomfortably. "I am."

"Come again? I thought Fiske was your friend."

"He was. Still is."

What game was he playing? "Then you need to step down. You'll be fired. Hell, you could be disbarred if they find out, not to mention the fact that it will cause a mistrial and cost the state tens of thousands."

"You let me worry about that."

"Parker—"

"Look, no matter what I think of you or what the rumors say about you—"

"Rumors?"

"—Lyle didn't do it."

"What rumors?"

"You have an uncanny ability to get the guiltiest person who walked the face of the earth off when they have everything stacked against them. Prove to me it's not just blind luck."

"That could be a bit difficult. Luck plays a big part in my daily life. And I don't get guilty people off, Parker."

He stood, too, and rounded the desk until we stood toe-to-toe. Ballsy.

"I need this case solved," he said.

"I'm getting that."

"Quickly and quietly."

"I'm not really the quiet type. But you still need to step down."

"No," he said, a sly grin curving his mouth. "I'm the contingency plan."

"The what?"

"The contingency plan. You fuck this up, I'll make sure things go our way from my end."

Even saying something like that out loud was so damning—in the legal sense—I got light-headed. I whispered my next words, worried someone would overhear. "You're going to throw the case?"

He lifted a shoulder. "I'm going to make sure Lyle Fiske is acquitted."

"On purpose?"

Without responding, he waited for my reaction, his expression calculated.

"Isn't that against your code of conduct or something?"

"Very."

"And what makes you think I'll go along with it?"

Again, his only response was the barest hint of a smile.

Son of a bitch. He had something on me. He was way too confident and way too smart to just drop something like that in my lap, something that could end his career and possibly send him to prison, without having some kind of insurance. A backup plan to make certain I'd play nice.

The woman stepped closer, my desk no hindrance to her whatsoever. I stepped back, and Parker thought I was shying away from him. He took another step closer. Other than his spatial boundary issues, he was daring me to threaten to go to the DA.

This required finesse. Unfortunately, I didn't have an overabundance of the stuff, but I knew who did. I'd keep quiet for now. Let him think I'd joined the team. But I would get to the bottom of whatever he had on me. Hopefully it wasn't actually my bottom in, say, a compromising position. It'd been ages since I'd compromised my ass.

"And what if he really is guilty?" I asked. "If I find evidence contrary to your opinion, how far are you going to take this?"

"I'm not worried in the least."

"But what if I do. How far?"

"You won't, so all the way."

"What makes you so certain, so convinced, that you're willing to risk your entire career for this guy?"

And there it was again. That niggling of guilt that I'd felt the second he walked in. I'd felt guilt from both of them. Had they conspired on something and it backfired?

Before he could answer, I held up an index finger, pulled a tissue out of the box on my desk, and coughed softly into it. Then I braced my palm on my desk. Took a sip of coffee. Coughed again. All the while, the woman's life flashed before my eyes.

She had worked the rice paddies of Jamuna, Nepal, her entire life, surviving floods and earthquakes to gather food for her family. After Amita married a man she didn't love, her girlfriends at the fields became her salvation. They laughed together. Raised their children together. And talked about their husbands from behind cupped hands and hushed giggles.

But her feelings for her husband grew. Sijan was mysterious to her. *Rahasyamaya*. With silvery eyes and a guarded smile. He was raised in a village to the west, and when he felt her distrust of him, he left to become a Sherpa guide. It was a skill his father had passed down to him. Treacherous and foolhardy, Amita thought. But it would bring in money. And she began to look forward to his return.

When he did come home, he would not tell her about his adventures, and all the girls would try to guess. It must have been glamorous, they would say, getting to know the rich Westerners, but Amita knew better. Sijan's body was battered when he returned. The elements on the mountain were the most unforgiving kind. He'd slimmed to unhealthy proportions, and it took her a month to fatten him up again. Yet he grew stronger every year. More beautiful every time he came home.

And then she asked him. It was all she had to do. He would tell her whatever she wanted to know. Were the Westerners nice to him? Did they respect him? Were the white women pretty? Sijan told her everything and gave her every rupee he made. He brought their children presents and gave her exquisite gifts she didn't need but cherished.

He and Amita became something of celebrities, though she still worked the paddies every year. As did her children. For years and years she carried on the tradition, because one year Sijan didn't come back.

With a broken heart, she worked until she died, still waiting for Sijan to come off the mountain. She could not cross, knowing he was up there alone. But the moment she crossed through me, I felt her joy at seeing him and two of their children again. Hardships forgotten, she fell into his arms and crushed her children to her, and I swallowed a lump in my throat.

I collapsed in my chair while Parker grew more and more agitated.

"Are you okay?" he asked.

"Sorry. Dizzy spell."

"Yeah, I heard you've been having some . . . balance problems."

He sat across from me again and gave me a moment. I took the opportunity to bask in the fierce love Amita had for her husband. I knew how she felt. Those dark mysterious types did it every time.

After taking a deep lungful of air, I opened the file and perused it while Parker gave me the rundown of the case they had against Lyle Fiske. It didn't look good. I could see why he was just desperate enough to come to me.

On paper, the guy was as guilty as they came. He'd been found at the crime scene with Emery's blood all over him. His fingerprints were inside the car, and he had her phone in his hands. Not only that, according to the first officer on scene, he'd been so belligerent, they'd had to subdue him. If Fiske was really innocent, he was probably more distraught than belligerent.

But if he had done it and was at the crime scene, where was the body? His prints hadn't been found on Emery's steering wheel, and they'd taken his pickup apart. Beyond the usual contaminants one would expect a girlfriend to leave in her boyfriend's vehicle, there was no trace evidence to suggest he'd used it to move her body.

Their case, purely circumstantial, definitely had holes. I would just have to find a way to punch a few more. To cast enough doubt for a jury to acquit him, if he really was innocent.

4

I tried to start a gang once.
It turned into a book club.
—MEME

When I walked back into Cookie's office, she was just hanging up the phone. I instantly felt something awry. A depression weighing on her, perhaps. The same depression I'd been feeling for days.

"How'd it go?" she asked me, watching as Parker shot me one last warning glance before closing the door behind him.

I flipped him off—because I was twelve—then turned to Cook. "Peachy. But what's up with you? What's wrong?"

"What do you mean?"

"You've been moping since we got back."

"I'm just worried about you. You know me. The perpetual worrier." She fluttered her fingers around her head. No idea why.

"I get that. I do. But I get the feeling there's something you're not telling me. I'm kind of intuitive that way."

"Nope. Not me."

"You know you can tell me anything."

"Charley, you've had so much on your plate. My problems are stupid in comparison."

"What?" I asked, shocked. "What problems? What's going on?"

Cookie sat back in her chair, a sadness weighing down her movements. "Amber has decided she wants to finish out the semester at NMSD."

"*The* NMSD? The School for the Deaf in Santa Fe?"

Amber's squeeze, Quentin, went to NMSD, which made sense since he was, in fact, Deaf, but Amber was far from it.

"That's great," I said, trying to sound positive. "I think. But isn't she missing something? Or maybe *not* missing something?" When Cookie questioned me with a raised brow, I added, "She hears really well. You know, to go to a school for Deaf children."

"Oh, right. They actually allow some hearing children to go. Mostly siblings of their Deaf students or children of teachers there."

"So, they're letting girlfriends go now? That's very forward thinking of them."

"Not exactly. Because Amber has become so active at the school, they've agreed to make a special exception. Apparently she's made quite an impression. Everyone loves her. The teachers. The students. The staff. That man in the cafeteria has fallen head over heels. He keeps sending homemade salsa home with her."

"Oh yeah," I said dreamily. "He's kind of fantastic."

"Right?"

"But, as awesome as that sounds, you don't want her to go?"

"It's not that I wouldn't love for her to go. I mean, what an experience, right? To be immersed in the culture so fully? But she wants to get everything out of it she can. The full Monty."

"I don't think that's what that means."

"She wants to live in the cottages with the other students. During the week like they do."

"Oh." I could see where Cookie would be distressed over something like that. "She would stay in one of the girls' dorms during the week? A dorm that would be right next to the boys' dorm?"

Cookie only nodded, her expression the epitome of worry.

"Yeah. I think I'm with you."

"They would practically be living together," she said. "Amber really wants to go, and this is a great opportunity. But I'm just not sure I'm ready. She's so young. They both are."

"I gotta agree with you on this one. I know they are *in love*," I said, adding air quotes, "but this is huge, Cook. This is bigger than her boobs, even."

"She doesn't have big boobs," Cook said. "They're actually kind of—"

"No, I mean, when she got boobs. It was kind of a big deal. That whole bra thing traumatized her. And now this? Maybe I can talk to her."

"Would you?" she asked, her face filled with hope.

"Of course. I mean, she could take the Rail Runner and go to day school there. She doesn't have to live in the dorms, right?"

"Right. Maybe, if she really likes it, we can talk about it again this summer."

I patted her back. "Sounds like a plan."

"So," Cookie said, satisfied I would be able to convince Amber to take her foot off the gas pedal, just for now, and rev it down a notch, "since we're baring our souls, what's up with you?"

"What?" I scoffed. "Nothing."

"Charley, I know something's bothering you. You can't hide anything from me either, remember?"

"Seriously. I'm good. Everything is good. The sun is semi-out. The skies are almost blue with only a strong hint of gray, which, as you know, is my favorite. What could be wrong?"

"You can tell me anything. Surely you know that by now."

"Yeah. I kind of forget how awesome you are sometimes. There's just been so much going on lately. A lot happened in New York."

"I know. I was there, remember?"

I laughed softly. "I know, but there's a lot I didn't tell you."

She leaned forward. "Yeah? Like what?"

"It just seems like, ever since we got back, Reyes has been pulling away from me."

"What? Oh, honey, you are wrong."

"No, it's true. He hasn't touched me in a week. I knew I should have taken up vaginal weight lifting when that homeless guy gave me a fifteen percent off coupon." I did the face-palm thing and crumpled onto Cookie's desk.

"Charley, I don't think vaginal weight lifting is the answer to . . . well, anything."

"But there's more." I peeled my face off her desk. "Remember that night that Kuur tried to kill me?"

Kuur had been an emissary sent from Lucifer to kill me. Or, more accurately, trap me in the god glass. Thanks to his arrogance and my father's sacrifice, I'd trapped him instead.

"Oh yes, you told me that part," she said with a negating wave of her hand. She wasn't keen on hearing the story again.

"Right, but what I didn't tell you was that my father crossed that night. That's how I was able to remember everything again."

"Wait, he crossed in the hopes that it would give you your memory back?"

I nodded.

"And it worked?"

'Nother nod. "And when he crossed, I saw the loveliest things, Cook. Things I never knew he felt. He loved me. Despite his poor spousal choices, he really loved me."

"Of course he did, Charley. Did you really doubt that?"

"I don't know. I guess not. But it was nice to see, anyway."

"But he crossed," Cookie said, her voice soft. Knowing. "He's really gone now."

"He's really gone." I fought a tightening in my throat. "But I learned so much that night. He showed me so many things. Things that I'm not sure how to tell Reyes."

"Like what?" She glanced around, checking for the aforementioned entity. "What more could there possibly be? You are so incredible. A supernatural being beyond anything any of us ever expected. There can't be anything left."

I let a sad smile lift one corner of my mouth. "You might be surprised."

She folded her arms at her chest. "No. Not possible. Nothing would surprise me. I'm sure of it. I am unsurprisable at this moment in time."

"You're absolutely sure?"

She grew wary. She knew full well not to assume such a thing. I had to razz her a little, though.

I reached into my pocket after a furtive glance around myself, just to make sure there were no gods close by, and brought out the pendant. To her, it would simply look like a necklace. Like a beautiful, aged pendant from an era long past, but a pendant nonetheless.

To me, however, it was like a galaxy inside another galaxy wrapped in an opal. It sparkled and shimmered and lured me closer every time I looked at it.

Cookie gasped. "That's beautiful. Did your father give that to you somehow?"

I shook my head. "No. This was a gift from Kuur."

"Well, that was nice of him," she muttered, not sure how to address that one.

"Right? It's not every day a guy gives a girl he's trying to kill a beautiful necklace. Especially one from the 1400s."

"The 1400s?" she asked, sucking in a soft breath of fascination. "You're really lucky. If he hadn't been hired to kill you, I'm sure he would've been a great guy."

"But, Cook, this isn't just any necklace."

"Of course it's not. It was given to you by an evil assassin from another dimension. It can't just be any necklace." She filled her lungs and girded her loins, metaphorically. "Okay, hit me. What is it? I can take it."

"Inside this innocent-looking pendant with this innocent-looking jewel and these innocent-looking carvings is another dimension."

Cookie had started to reach for it. Just to touch it. She stopped and slowly pulled her hand back.

"And it's not just another dimension. It's a hell dimension. Kuur was sent to trap me inside it for all eternity. The bad part is I sent him, a demon-like being from another dimension, into a hell dimension in which dozens of innocent people have also been sent. And now I have to get them out, one by one, all while leaving him inside. And to make matters worse—"

"It gets worse?" she asked, her face turning an ashen white.

"I have no idea how to do any of that." I had regained all my memories as a god, but for some reason, things didn't work quite the same in my human state of affairs. I still had to learn everything.

"Well, we all have our little problems, right? Of course this one makes mine sound a little pathetic in comparison."

"Don't you dare say that. Amber's growing up, and it's hard to see that happen. She's just a little girl in our eyes."

"Charley, you had to send your daughter away before you even got to know her. My problems are ridiculous in comparison."

"They most certainly are not. Of course, I didn't tell you the best part yet."

"There's more?"

"Cookie, don't you know me by now? There's always more."

"In your world, yes, there is. I'm ready. Whatever you got, I can handle it."

"Okay, one of the things I learned when my father crossed was that Reyes, my beautiful, breathtaking husband, is a god."

I figured I'd give her time. She clearly needed it. She was now gaping at me, her mouth hanging open far enough to cause a triple chin. When I'd given her long enough—we did have cases to see to, after all—I said, "He's one of the gods of Uzan."

"Wait, aren't they bad?"

"Very."

"Oh, Charley. I'm not sure I understand."

"Join the club. I don't even know if he knows. Satan tricked one of the three gods of Uzan. He trapped him using this jewel." I brushed my fingers over the glass covering the gem, the dimension, inside. "It's called god glass."

She leaned closer but still kept a safe distance. "Why—how are there innocent people inside?"

"Long story involving an evil priest. Suffice it to say, it's very powerful, and from what I could tell when this pendant was open, very big."

"I—I don't even know what to say."

"Don't say anything yet. It still gets better."

Her eyes rounded, but I plowed forward.

"Let's say, for argument's sake, I can stop the gods of Uzan. Let's say I can stop Reyes if I have to, using this glass."

"Stop him?" she asked, panic-stricken.

"If I have to," I reiterated. "And let's say Michael—you know, the archangel?—let's say he lets me live."

She paled further, but I kept going. Best to just get it all out there.

"Let's say I can get Beep back, and we can, I don't know, save the world or whatever we're supposed to do."

Cookie nodded, right there with me.

"There's something even worse."

"Than a hell dimension in a necklace?"

"Yes."

"Than the fact that an archangel tried to kill you?"

"Only that one time, but yes."

"Than the fact that your daughter is destined to battle Satan for control of Earth?"

"Yep."

She shook her head, at a complete loss. She leaned forward and put a hand on mine. "Charley, what?"

"Reyes is paying child support."

She stilled. Blinked. Furrowed her brows. "What?"

I fought the wetness springing between my lashes. "Reyes—*my* Reyes—is paying child support. I saw a receipt."

"Okay," she said, taking a moment, "let's just say that, yes, Reyes paying child support is worse than all that."

"I don't understand your point."

"Who is he paying? I mean, is it to an old girlfriend?"

"You think he has old girlfriends?" I asked, sniffing.

"Charley, you have old boyfriends, right?"

"Yes, but—but I wasn't in prison for ten years. And he couldn't have been terribly fertile going in. He was, what? Twenty?"

"Old enough to get a girl pregnant. Trust me."

"But what makes you think he even knew any girls?"

"Have you seen that boy?"

"I mean, he was really shy growing up."

"Because that's such a chick deterrent."

Damn it. She was right. Hot, sexy, shy guys? Like a blazing inferno to an ovulating moth. "How many old girlfriends do you think he has?"

"I'll look into it."

"Like, a guesstimate. Five? Ten?"

"I'll look into it," she said, but this time she had her soothing I'm-here-for-you voice on. It helped.

"You will?"

"Absolutely. Besides, there has to be an explanation. He would have told you if he had a child."

"Maybe he just found out. He hasn't been paying it long. Three or four months, I think. Either that or his other child is only three or four months old, which would mean he got someone else pregnant before I conceived Beep."

"No," Cookie said, shaking her head. "There's no way. Charley, he is crazy about you. He crossed the badlands of a hell dimension just to get to you. He waited for centuries for you to be sent to Earth. He gave up everything, even his memories, to be born a human just so he could see your smile."

"When you put it that way . . . but let's face it, Cook. I'm not the easiest person to live with on a daily basis."

"Like he is?" When I dropped my gaze, she added, "Charley, you're amazing, and you know I think the world of you, but perhaps we should focus on more pertinent details of all this."

"Right," I said, straightening my shoulders. "Exactly. It's not about when. It's about whom. And did he love her?" I gasped when the next thought hit. "Does he *still* love her?"

"Well, I actually meant along the lines of the fact that Reyes is an evil god hell-bent on destroying Earth and an archangel wants to kill you. But we can start with that."

I drew in a deep, cleansing breath. "No, you're right. I need to just put on my granny panties and deal. We have a case. No more thongs for me."

"We have a case?" she teased.

"A real one," I said with a nod. "And according to Nick the Pri—Nick Parker, an innocent man could go to prison if we don't figure out who really killed his girlfriend, Emery Adams."

"See? It's good to keep busy. Keeps your mind off all the other, total-annihilation-and/or-death-by-an-angry-celestial-being stuff."

"But you'll still look into it, right? The child support?"

"You know I will. Now, go do private-investigator-y stuff. I'll see what I can dig up here."

I nodded. Throwing myself into my work would keep my mind off the other things. Like Cookie said, the total-annihilation-and/or-death-by-an-angry-celestial-being things. Not to mention the most pertinent of our problems: Reyes's other child.

What I did not place in that category was the Beep thing. I didn't ever want to stop thinking about her. Not for a minute. I'd been there, done that in New York. It would not happen again.

Not that I was worried about the possible outcome of that scenario. I was going to get my daughter back. No god in this dimension or the next was going to stop me.

5

My love is like a candle.
Carry me with you and I'll light your path.
Forget me and I'll burn your fucking house down.
—T-SHIRT

I heard footsteps in the hall outside my office where a balcony overlooked Calamity's, Reyes's restaurant-slash-bar. The creaking of floorboards stopped on the other side of the door.

I walked to it and waited, knowing who stood on the other side. I could feel the emotions cording through him like the center spirals of a tornado. Also, I could smell red chile. Gawd, I loved that man.

"Are you going to let me in?" Reyes asked from the other side. Not, like, *the* other side, but . . .

"Depends. Do you know the secret password?"

"Chile."

I swung the door wide. "Holy green chile, Batman. You're good."

"I like to think so," he said, his eyes sparkling. He was holding two plates, but when I stepped back to let him bring them in, he stayed in the hall. "You have to invite me in."

I narrowed my lashes. "Is your middle name Dracula, by chance?"

"Close." But he still didn't come in.

So, I swept my arm in a grand gesture and said, "You are officially invited into my humble abode."

Humble was taking things a bit far, because while we were away, he'd had the entire top floor of this building remodeled as well, and yet he kept the restaurant exactly as my father had left it. As though to preserve the memory for my sister and me. But my office now resembled a posh Manhattan apartment, minus the dining room table, all soft colors and smooth lines.

He still didn't step inside. I glanced around, suddenly self-conscious. Did I have offensive material up? I didn't see any but, admittedly, my tastes ran a little west of the norm.

I turned back to him, and his expression had changed. He'd grown serious in the space of a heartbeat.

"Are you sure you want to do that?"

"What?"

"Invite me in."

He'd lost me. "Of course. I mean, you do own the building."

"We," he said, his voice hard. "We own the building. And that's not what I asked."

Without another word, he stepped forward, and while still holding a plate in each hand, he bent down and put his mouth on mine. I raised half-closed fists to his chest and melted into him. Most of me did, anyway. Some of me melted into my panties.

He hadn't kissed me, really kissed me, in a week. His mouth, like fire against mine, grew more demanding instantly. He ran his tongue over my teeth then plunged it deeper, and I had to curl my fingers into his shirt to keep from unbuttoning his jeans. The heat that perpetually surrounded him scalded my lips, soaked into my hair, brushed flames over my skin, pushed between my legs.

Even with all that, the niggling in the back of my mind nudged its way forward. That part of me that worried about how much control the

Razer had over him. Over my husband. Would he be a threat to our daughter? Would the god of destruction someday take over? Or was the god in him—like the one in me—a part of who he was now? A part of his makeup? Ingrained into his DNA?

I was Val-Eeth, the god Elle-Ryn-Ahleethia. But I was just as much Charley Davidson. We were not two separate beings. Two separate personalities. Was it the same with Reyes, the last and youngest god of Uzan? Was it simply who he was now? Could a being made of absolute evil change when melded with something good? I had high hopes that it could.

Then there were the child support payments, and suddenly I was in the tenth grade, wondering how many girls my boyfriend had kissed before me. How many he'd groped in the backseat of his father's Buick. How many bases he'd stolen before he got tagged out.

Reyes had to sense my hesitance. Was that it? Why he'd been pulling away?

He tensed, and I knew that he felt my concerns. I sucked in a sharp breath of arctic air between our mouths. It was like ice on my teeth. It startled me, and I broke off the kiss, wondering where the cold air had come from.

A sad smile lifted one corner of his mouth. He licked his lips slowly as though to savor our encounter, then said, "That's what I thought."

I blinked at him. He'd told me he could no longer feel my emotions. Not since I'd learned my celestial name. Not since I'd dematerialized my human body and come into my powers more fully. Surely he couldn't sense my dilemma now. "I don't understand."

He lowered his head. "Then I can't help you."

"Reyes—"

"Eat," he said, pushing the plates into my hands. They were scalding hot, as though they'd just been taken out of an oven, and I wondered if he'd done that. "I'll send Valerie to pick up the plates."

He turned and left a half second before I said, "Valerie?"

But he kept walking, taking the stairs three at a time, his movements quiet, lithe, and powerful. After a moment, I went back inside and took Cookie her plate, because while Reyes may have been raised in hell, I did not quite have the aptitude for scalding heat like he did.

"Hot," I said, my voice breathy as I practically dropped the plates on her desk.

"You can't ply me with food." She didn't even bother to look up from her computer.

"Reyes made it."

"Oh!" She jumped out of her seat to get forks and napkins, then headed for the Bunn to refuel.

I sat across from her chair. We often ate in the reception area. It let potential clients know we were human, too. We had to eat. And hydrate. And dehydrate in the form of pee. Just because they wanted us to stake out their wandering spouses at the most ungodly hours known to man did not mean we didn't need a potty break every so often. There were laws, even! We had rights!

Just kidding. We ate in the reception area because it had the best view of the UNM campus. People watching was fun *and* educational.

"We have a new case," I said when she came back with a full cup.

"So you said, but what about our old case?"

"Oh, I solved that last night. I just have to work up the nerve to meet with Mrs. Abelson."

Cookie's face fell. "Her husband is cheating?"

"Worse. He's been hanging with a group of college kids, playing video games and experimenting with cannabis."

"And how is that worse?"

"Have you met Mrs. Abelson?"

"Oooooh," she said, drawing out the syllable in understanding. "Gotcha. Want me to set up a time to meet?"

"No."

"Great, I'll call now."

"I don't think I can deal with her."

"Well, somebody has to deal with her, and it's not going to be me."

"No."

She picked up the phone and was dialing the woman's number through my protests.

"Please, no?"

"Rip off the Band-Aid," she said, punching numbers in with her pen.

"I don't want to."

"Of course you do."

"I like the Band-Aid right where it is."

"You'll feel better."

"Bandages make me look noble."

"Just rip that puppy off."

"It'll hurt."

"So will a lawsuit when Mrs. Abelson finds out you made her suffer with doubt longer than she had to."

I gasped. "She can't sue me."

Cookie's brows inched heavenward. "Have you met Mrs. Abelson?"

I caved, crestfallen. With wilted shoulders, I held out my hand for the receiver.

After setting up a meet for later that day, I decided to pester my assistant. Well, pester her more than I already was. "What are you looking at?"

"Nothing."

She reached up and turned off her monitor. So, naturally, I reached over and turned it back on.

"I was working, I swear," she said through a mouthful of tortilla, eggs, papas, and red chile. "Then, a few clicks later, I was lost in the devil's lair."

"You got lost in our apartment again?" I filled my own mouth, paused to let the fact that I'd just eaten a tiny piece of heaven sink in, then leaned closer to examine the photograph on the screen. "It's fake."

She'd been looking at strange and unexplained photos from the past. All black and white. All admittedly creepy. I'd fallen down that rabbit hole a few times myself. It was hard to blame her when the majority of our workdays of late had consisted of sharing cute cat videos and clips of *Ellen* on YouTube.

"Why were you so upset about the video this morning?" I asked her.

"Because, what if—wait, how do you know it's fake?" She squinted at her screen. "These pictures defy explanation because they can't be explained. That's the whole point."

The photo she was looking at was of a little girl with a fairy on her shoulder. "Seriously?"

"Okay," she said, caving, "but what about this one?"

It was an image of a man in a straitjacket, levitating off a bed.

"Fake."

"So, levitating crazy men aren't real, but grim reapers are?"

She had a point. " 'Parently." I took another bite.

"Fine, but this next one truly defies—"

"Fake," I said the second she clicked the next photo. "Just what, exactly, do you think will happen?"

"I don't know. What about this one?"

"Fake." It was of a little boy sitting cross-legged and hovering inside an old Radio Flyer wagon. "And I think you do know."

"You could be exposed," she said at last.

"I've exposed myself before. It's never bothered you."

"Not your normal one-too-many-margaritas exposed. And how do you know?"

"I don't know. You've never told me it's bothered you."

"No, I mean about the picture."

I pointed from around my fork at the picture. "Can you see the little boy floating?"

"Of course. That's why it's strange and unexplained."

"People don't float. Not live ones. If he were really floating, he'd be incorporeal. Or an incorporeal entity would be lifting him up. If you can see him, he's not incorporeal. And if I can't see an incorporeal entity lifting him up, there isn't one. And so what if I'm exposed? A little exposure never hurt anyone. It's not like the grim reaper police are going to arrest me."

She clicked again. "I guess, but you don't know who, or what, that video could attract. Do you think that's why the Vatican has a file on you?"

"What, that video?" I took another bite. "According to their watchdog, they've had a file on me since the day I was born. So, probably not." In the next photo, a boy was covered in scales. "Fake."

She didn't bother to ask before clicking again. "What if the wrong forces get ahold of it, though?"

"Like what forces? Unless you mean the armed forces, because that could get fun. All the other forces know what I am. And I'm a freaking beacon, so they also know *where* I am. I don't know how a person could be less hidable. To the supernatural world, anyway. Fake . . . fake . . . fake . . . just creepy . . . fake . . ."

"But what about someone in *this* world? Someone who doesn't know but would be very interested? I mean, very, very interested."

I could feel her anxiety level rising. "Cook, who cares? What will something like that mean to anyone?"

"But—"

"First of all," I said, totally interrupting, "nobody will believe it. They'll think it was wires or CGI."

She shrugged one shoulder as she studied the next photo.

"And second, even if someone did take note, I ask you again, what could they do?" I glanced at the next picture. "As fake as the day is long."

"You know, you kind of take the magic out of this stuff."

"I know. Sor—" I'd started to apologize, but the next image on her screen stopped me mid-grovel. I leaned forward. Squinted. Then stilled. "What is that?"

Cookie stilled, too, her fork halfway to her mouth. "Don't even tell me that little girl could really remove her head like that."

"Oh, no, that's totally fake, but that in the background." I pointed closer. "That little boy. What's he doing?"

In the background of a ridiculous picture of a little girl holding what looked like her own head by her long blond locks was a little boy pointing to a storefront window.

"That little boy?" She pointed to the one in the street, as there were several in the background. He wore vintage clothing. Short pants. Knee socks. Suspenders. A newsboy cap on his head. He was looking straight at the camera and yet pointing at the store window.

"Yes." I put down my fork, pushed my plate aside, and leaned all the way over the desk, flashing my cleavage, but Cookie never took the bait. Damn it. She coulda been a contender. "Print that."

"Ooooh-kay," she said slowly, her voice wary. "Do I need to be freaked out?"

"I don't know." I hurried over to the printer and grabbed the image before it was done printing, so I played tug-of-war with the printer until it gave in. Then I sat back down and pointed again. "Look at that store window. What do you see?"

"Dirt. Well, mud, actually."

"Like in a pattern? Like in a strange font or perhaps pictographs?"

"Not really. Just splotches of mud. It's all pretty Rorschach-y. Why?" When I continued to study the picture without answering, she said, "Charley, what? What do you see?"

"That little boy standing there in vintage clothing? His hands are muddy, like he wrote on the plate glass window. It's what's on the window that caught my attention."

"What's on the store window?" Cookie said, growing more fascinated, and more wary, by the second.

"It's angelic script."

"Angelic script? Is he an angel? The boy?"

I almost laughed. "Not exactly. At least, I don't think so."

"Can you read the script?"

"Oh yeah," I said, dread slithering up my spine like a snake made of ice.

"And?"

This was unreal. It didn't make sense.

Cookie reached over and put her hand on mine to draw me back to her. "What does it say?"

"It's a message, but how?"

"From who?"

"If I'm not mistaken, that little boy is Rocket."

"Rocket? Our Rocket? From the asylum Rocket?"

"Yes." I looked closer at the round face and the boyish features. He would have been a boy right about that age at the time.

"What does it say?" Cookie leaned closer, trying hard to see what I was seeing. "I don't understand. How do you know it's him?"

"First, it looks like him, only younger. And second, it says, 'Miss Charlotte, what's bigger than a bread box?' "

She looked up, still confused.

"He's the only one who calls me Miss Charlotte. But I have no idea what he means and how on earth he got a message to me. He wouldn't have died for another twenty years after this was taken. And I wouldn't meet him for over fifty more."

"The store is a bakery. It's painted to look like a bread box."

"Okay." I'd have to take her word on that.

"My grandmother used to have one just like this. See, there's the handle."

It did begin to resemble a bread box with a handle across the top. And over that was a sign that read MISS MAE'S BREADS AND CONFECTIONS.

"So, then, what's bigger than that building?" I asked. "I don't get it."

"Me neither. And how is that even possible?"

"Well, actually, there are a lot of things that could be bigger than that building."

"No."

"A bigger building, perhaps?"

"I didn't mean—"

"A skyscraper?"

"Charley." Cookie was trying just as hard to figure it out as I was. "This picture has to be from the forties or something."

"It's the thirties, to be exact." I studied him harder and became more and more convinced that Rocket was sending me a message from the past. "I need you to find out everything you can about this picture."

"You got it, boss. Boy, the creep-factor in this room just spiked tenfold."

"That's because your husband is about to walk in."

She looked around and then back at me in awe. "You really are psychic."

"Yeah." I didn't have the heart to tell her I'd seen a shadow pass, so I looked up to see his blurred image slide across the glass on the picture behind her desk. It would ruin the moment, though why anything about me would surprise her at this point, I had no clue.

I jumped up to grab my jacket. "First, find out all you can about our murder victim, Emery Adams."

"Right."

"And then figure out who my husband is paying child support to."

"On it."

"And then—"

"Go," she said, still studying the photo. When the door opened, she looked up at my ramshackle of an uncle.

I dived in for the first hug, making him horridly uncomfortable. Which was exactly why I did it. He patted my back and then almost, almost hugged me back, his tall, only slightly overweight frame the epitome of male etiquette. Men didn't hug. It was against their code of manly conduct unless they were in the throes of frat party. Or an even manlier event. Like touch football. Or backyard grilling. It was okay to hug in American guydom as long as one or both of the participants had grilling tongs in hand.

They also didn't hasten to their wives to plant big wet ones on them, which was exactly what Ubie did.

I would have waited until they came up for air, but there were only so many hours in the day. I decided to risk it. "I forgot to ask, Cook. Who's Valerie?"

She flipped me off. She literally gave me the naughty finger while she molested my uncle. I was so proud. Even prouder than she was that time she got food poisoning and lost seven pounds in two days. But I took that as my cue to slip out. There was only so much PDA I could handle when a relative was involved. Especially one who manhandled my BFF in his spare time.

I stepped out to what had become a dreary, misty gray day. My very favorite kind. Clouds had rolled in from the northeast and were hovering low over the Sandias, spilling over the peak, making the entire mountain look like a witch's cauldron. One would think that image alone would lift my spirits. Or the fact that the entire mountain was covered in sparkling white snow would at least garner a smile, but I had a lot on my mind. I was afraid. So very, very afraid. It curled around me and slipped into my lungs, making it impossible to breathe.

I stopped halfway to Misery, my cherry red Jeep Wrangler. Why was I afraid? I'd been afraid before, but not like this. Not like deathly afraid.

Yet fear swirled like a fog around me. I took inventory. Looked myself over. Patted my pockets and my jacket and my girls. Nope, not me. So, if it wasn't my fear nigh paralyzing me, whose was it?

I glanced around. There weren't many people in the alley. Many businesses on this part of Central had a back entrance, and with the college right across the street, the area got quite a bit of traffic despite the alley status, but there were only a couple of students cutting through the alley on their way to campus.

I started walking, trying to home in on the source, fighting the urge to sniff like I was searching my kitchen for an odd odor. It happened.

When I rounded a Dumpster, I spotted it. Or her. A young homeless girl, actually, and most likely a runaway. Her fear hit me full on, and concern lifted the hairs on the back of my neck.

The girl sat cross-legged, her black sneakers as tattered as the dingy once-pink blanket wrapped over her shoulders. She had pixielike dark hair, spiked but in more of a bed head kind of way, and pale youthful skin. She couldn't have been more than fourteen. Fifteen at the most. She was fiddling with the lid to a yogurt cup with granola. A plastic spoon sat next to her along with a cup of juice. Her fingers were shaking, and she couldn't get the wrap off.

"Can I help?" I asked, softening my voice as much as I could.

Her head jerked up, anyway. Her gaze, wild with surprise and fear, paused on me for only a second before it darted around, wondering if I were with anyone. God only knew what she'd gone through, being a very young, very pretty teen. And God only knew what, or more likely who, sent her to live on the streets. What had pushed her to such a rash decision.

Satisfied we were alone, her gaze raked over me, but mine had drifted back to the snack in her hands.

"Where did you get that?" I asked, suddenly more curious about her food than her circumstances. If she'd panhandled, she probably wouldn't have bought anything quite that healthy. Most kids lived for chips and pizza, and that had come from Boyd's Mini Mart on the opposite corner of our building.

She had no intention of answering me, but her eyes answered for her. She glanced ever so quickly toward Boyd's, and I had to tamp down a spike of anger.

"Mr. Boyd? Did Mr. Boyd give that to you?"

Her brows slid together, and I almost scoffed aloud.

"I bet he said you could stay in his storeroom, too. You know, if you ever need a place to sleep? To get out of the cold for a while?"

She volunteered nothing, but I felt recognition flood through her. She had the wherewithal to know she'd been had and the intelligence to look sheepish.

"Dude's a perv, hon, through and through." I stepped closer, and she stiffened again. Probably due to the edge in my voice. "Stay away from him," I ordered, because that's what a homeless kid on the run needed. More adults ordering her around. Telling her what to do. Trying to run her life. Or, more to the point, taking advantage of her.

She rose slowly, and I realized I'd gone too far. I was going to lose her.

I held up both hands, showing my palms. "Wait—"

But she rabbited. Bolted down the alley, leaving her belongings and her breakfast behind.

Good job, Davidson.

I watched as she knocked over a trash can, rounded a corner, then headed toward Central before I gathered up her belongings and stashed them behind the Dumpster. She'd be back. And our encounter wasn't a total loss. I'd caught her . . . *scent,* for lack of a better phrase. Her emotional fingerprint. Her frequency. I could feel her. If she didn't come back, I could use that to find her. I was a bloodhound. Through and through.

6

I can never remember if I'm the good sister or the evil one.
—T-SHIRT

I stepped over to Misery. She now had her own carport, another upgrade thanks to Mr. Farrow. It was funny how much I'd enjoyed seeing her again when we got back. All red and shiny and ready to do my bidding. I'd had another object that fit that description perfectly back in college, but it vibrated. And fit in my pocket. And its name was most definitely not Misery. It was rather appropriately named Han Solo.

I drove to the station in Misery. The Jeep. And possibly a little of the emotion.

Parker had already cleared me to interview Lyle the Boyfriend, and though the detective on the case was a little surprised, he didn't argue. He simply led me back to an interview room where a very distraught, very devastated Lyle Fiske sat waiting.

And, not to my complete surprise, the man was as innocent as a freshly driven snowplow. He may have been a bit dirty underneath the hood—did snowplows have hoods?—but he'd been driven hard. Without regular oil changes.

He sat cuffed to the table in the interview room. I wondered if they'd had to subdue him again.

When he looked up at me, his pale caramel eyes didn't quite seem to comprehend the situation. He was somewhere else. His dark auburn hair hadn't been slept on, and from what Parker had told me, they'd arrested him the night before. He'd probably paced the entire time, a sure sign of innocence. Only the guilty slept after being arrested.

"Mr. Fiske," I said, holding a hand out. "I'm Charley Davidson, a private investigator and consultant for APD. I've been hired to look into your case."

He didn't take my hand at first. He stared at it instead for a solid thirty seconds before he finally took it into his.

"You were hired?" he asked, trying to wrap his head around everything that had happened to him in the last week.

I stopped to take inventory myself. His girlfriend had been murdered in her car sometime between 6 and 11 P.M. just under a week ago. According to the report Parker gave me, Lyle was going to propose to Emery Adams the night she was killed. He miraculously found her car in the middle of nowhere and had called the cops himself. His fingerprints were found all over the car, and Emery's blood was all over him. Oh, and just to add insult to injury, the couple had been spotted arguing the day before.

This was not going to be easy.

"Yes, the people who hired me"—the same ones who didn't want Lyle, or anyone else for that matter, to know they'd hired me—"believe quite strongly that you are innocent of the charges against you."

He laughed softly, the sound containing no humor whatsoever. "Like that makes any difference."

I hadn't figured him for a cynic when I walked in. Something had happened to him. Something had set him against the universe.

"Can you tell me what happened that night?"

"My girlfriend was murdered, and they think I did it. Isn't that why you're here?"

"But you didn't?" I asked, just to gauge his reaction for the record.

Instead of answering, he leveled those hauntingly pale eyes on me and asked, "Does it really matter?"

His cynicism sparked a burning curiosity. I needed to look deeper into his background, much deeper, to try to understand his animosity. I got the feeling he was a good guy. Then again, he'd been friends with Nick Parker. Maybe my feelers were wrong this time.

"Mr. Fiske," I said, trying to get him to trust me if only a little, "try to think of me as your best friend. I am here for you, and if anyone can prove you didn't do this, it's me."

"I already have a lawyer. I heard he's the best public defender taxpayer money can buy."

"Christianson. He's good," I assured him. "He'll give us some leeway as far as asking for more time and what have you."

"More time?"

I folded my arms on the table. "Before it goes to trial."

"So, you want me to sit in here longer than I would anyway? It's not like they granted me bail. It's not like I'm twiddling my thumbs in the comfort of my own home, so what does it matter?"

"I just don't want the state to rush this." Now I was worrying about Parker's career. If this did go to trial, he would be risking everything for his friend. "I'm hoping to thwart their case long before it comes to that, so let's hope for the best."

He scoffed. "You people are all the same. Relying on hope. Believing that just because someone is innocent doesn't mean they won't spend their life in prison."

Okay. No more talk of hope. He wanted straightforward, he'd get it. "The state is going to offer you a deal. You plea no contest, and they'll probably take the death penalty off the table. Or some such. Then they'll give you a certain amount of time to respond. Yada yada. Standard operating procedure. If we have to, we can get them to hold off on even offering the first deal until I can get this sorted out."

"You're going to sort this out?" he asked, as skeptical as I was the time a group of boys from the playground told me they'd caught a turtle in the trees. It was a trick to get me to follow them in, and I knew it. He thought he was being duped as well, and I wasn't sure how to convince him otherwise. I'd just have to get the charges dropped. Maybe he'd trust me then.

"I'm just saying, don't sign anything until you hear from me."

"If you believe I didn't kill Emery, why would you think I'd take their deal in the first place?"

"Once they make that offer, they probably won't offer again, and this will all go to trial. You could be facing the death penalty. Taking that off the table is a good incentive to take the money and run. Just don't be tempted."

"I'll try to keep my enthusiasm at bay."

"Okay, first question: How did you find Emery's car?"

"I told them already, I have an app on my phone. That's how I found her."

"So, her phone was at the crime scene?"

"Yes. Plugged in to the charger. And hers is the kind that continues to charge even when the car is off. I found it the same night she disappeared."

I shuffled through the papers. "Right. So you have the Find a Friend app. The one that lets you know where she is at all times." When I glanced up from underneath my lashes, his anger soared.

"It was her idea. She wanted me to put it on my phone. Thought it would be fun or something, I don't know. I didn't fucking ask."

Geesh, he was touchy. "Did she have one for you on her phone as well?"

"Yeah, I guess. I don't know."

"But you can see how that looks."

His gaze snapped back to me. "I don't give a fuck how it looks. I was not stalking her. It was her fucking idea."

"Lyle," I said, trying to calm him down. "I swear to you, I'm on your side. I'm just trying to stay one step ahead of the detective on this case, because he's good. Make no mistake about that."

He sat back in his chair, his eyes watering before he squeezed them shut and rubbed them with his thumb and index finger. I could feel the frustration rolling out of him in waves.

"Lyle." I used my mommy voice. When he looked at me, I said, "I am your best bet of beating these charges. It's what I do. The people who hired me know that, so cut the bullshit and let me help you."

His mouth thinned into a straight line, but he scrubbed his face with his fingers, the chains clinking with his every move, then nodded. "I wasn't even supposed to be in town."

"That's right. You were supposed to be at your father's wedding in Florida, but you decided to stay?"

He took a moment more to calm down, then explained. "I couldn't go. I went to the airport, parked my truck, caught the shuttle. I had every intention of going, but when I went inside, I just couldn't. Something didn't feel right."

Now we were talking. "What?"

"Emery. She'd been upset maybe? Distant? I don't know how to describe it, but for about two weeks before she disappeared, she hadn't been herself. She swore nothing was wrong, but I could feel her pulling away."

I knew the feeling.

"Besides, that was my dad's fifth marriage. There comes a time when a son has to put his foot down."

I grinned. "I agree. Parents," I said, rolling my eyes.

Now that we were getting somewhere, he let me question him for the next hour with no further outbursts, though he did mention that he was going to strangle me when I cleared him of all charges, just for the principle of it. I did have a tendency to push people to mayhem and violence.

But he explained everything. Everything I could see Detective Joplin throwing at Parker, Fiske could explain. I couldn't help but feel like Joplin jumped the gun on this one. Open and shut isn't always wide or tight. There are subtleties in every case. Discrepancies that can sway a jury to one side or the other. I was certain that even with all the circumstantial evidence against Fiske, his lawyer could get him acquitted. But he would definitely need more than a public defender. If Parker was serious about helping his friend, he should have started there.

"They're going to move you to the detention center soon. I'll come out when I know more."

He nodded.

"One last thing," I said just before the guard showed me out. "How long ago did she ask you to download the Find a Friend app for your phone?"

"A little over two weeks ago. When she started pulling away almost to the day."

Interesting.

"I was going to propose," he said, stopping me again. "When I left the airport, I was going to propose, but I couldn't get ahold of her."

"How many times did you try to call her?"

"At least a dozen. I left message after message and texted her more than that. They said that was my motive. That I couldn't find her so I thought she was cheating, hunted her down, and killed her." His voice broke on the last word.

As did my heart.

I stopped in at Uncle Bob's office to give a shout, but he was in a meeting. So I left a message on his desk asking him to call me. I wanted to ask him what he knew about the Emery Adams case. Reports were one thing, but a seasoned detective's gut instinct was another.

I finished up my message by drawing little hearts all over a piece of paper that, about halfway through the fifth heart, I realized was an arrest warrant. An arrest warrant I calmly folded and pushed aside before writing the same message on an actual memo pad. Who knew he'd have something like that on his desk?

Afterwards, I went in search of the first officer to respond to Lyle Fiske's call after he found Emery's car, only to find out his shift didn't begin until later. Still, I had plenty to get me started. I left the station more determined than ever to find who killed Emery Adams. It could be the only way to get the charges against Lyle dropped. And I was headed to do that very thing when I saw Garrett's truck in the parking lot. With him in it.

Garrett was a former soldier turned bond enforcement officer turned certified member of Team Beep. He'd been with us through hell and high water, and I owed him so much. Mostly, a thank-you.

I walked over to him and had to knock on the window even though he clearly saw me. It was spitting snow, and I got the feeling he was enjoying what it did to my hair.

He finally grinned and rolled down the window.

"What are you doing here?" I asked, suspicious. "Are you following me?" We'd been down this road before.

"Not this time, sweet cheeks." He graced me with a lopsided grin. Asshole. He knew what that grin did to people. Mostly people of the female persuasion.

"But you are on a stakeout, yes?"

"Sort of."

He no longer worked for the bonds company unless it was a special request or Javier, his old boss, was just shorthanded, so I asked, "For whom?"

"Your mama," he said, flashing me the same grin.

"You can talk to dead people, too?"

A soft chuckle rolled out of his chest. "Not hardly."

Uncle Bob walked out then with two uniforms and a perp in cuffs. Garrett zeroed in on them, and I wondered who the perp was. He'd clearly already been arrested, so what was there to watch?

That fact nudged something inside me as not being quite right, but I decided to drop it. If he had wanted me to know, he would've told me. If I had wanted to know, I would've bombarded him with questions until he caved. I did that.

"I'm glad I saw you," I said instead.

He gave me a suspicious glance. "Yeah?"

"Yeah. I just—I thought—I wanted to thank you."

That time he laid the full power of his silver gaze on me. "For what?"

"For, you know, New York."

"Well, you're welcome, but I haven't given it to you yet."

That time I laughed. "You were there for me, and I'm really grateful."

He stared a long moment, one wrist resting loosely on the steering wheel.

I broke the silence first. "I just wanted to thank you."

"You're welcome, beautiful."

My heart swelled at the appreciation I saw in his eyes. He'd put up with so much, been through so much since meeting me, and though he could be a pain in the ass, he was such a good guy.

I rose to my toes and still didn't stand a snowball's chance of hitting my target, so he leaned toward me so I could place a soft kiss on his stubbly cheek. But at the last second, he turned his head and my lips landed on his.

I kissed him, anyway, the scoundrel, short and sweet.

When I lowered myself to the ground again, he looked at me in surprise before ducking his head. "You just tell that demon of yours to keep a close eye on you."

"I will." I wouldn't, of course. Reyes didn't relish the fact that he was part demon. I preferred to think of him as part fallen angel. It sounded so much more exotic. Exoticer?

A part of me couldn't help but notice that Garrett and Reyes had been working together a lot lately. Much like Osh and Reyes. And, hell, even Angel and Reyes. I could only hope he was paying Garrett what he was worth—his weight in gold.

I offered him one last wave and then jogged to Misery. I had a few more people to thank, not the least of whom was my FBI friend, Kit. And my sister, Gemma. And Uncle Bob. I saw him every day now that he lived right across the hall, but I had yet to really thank him for everything he did. Just like Garrett and Osh, Ubie and Cookie had put their lives on hold to be with me in New York. I owed them all so much.

I decided to call Kit on my way back to the office. I let the Bluetooth blast the sounds of her voice all through Misery's innards.

"Special Agent Carson," she said when she picked up. She was such a professional. I could be professional. Hadn't Cookie and I just been professional that morning? Wasn't that proof?

"Hey, SAC," I said, ditching the professionalism.

"Hey, Davidson, how you doing? I haven't heard from you since you got back."

"You mean since you stopped that guy from blowing my brains out in New York?" That guy really liked his shotgun.

"Yeah, well, you saved that family, so let's call it even."

"Deal."

While we were talking, I heard a woman screaming in Dolby 5.1 Surround Sound, and I couldn't figure out if it was coming from Kit's office or from Misery. Misery didn't usually scream in a feminine voice. She usually just rumbled, and at a much lower octave, unless I was jamming to Halestorm.

"Where are you?" I asked.

"You called me, remember? I'm in my office. And next time you call, you might not want to tell the operator you're a Top Ten wanting to turn herself in."

"Got your attention, didn't it?"

"Yeah, they take that kind of thing pretty seriously around here. Lucky for you, we don't have a woman on the Top Ten Most Wanted right now."

"Shouldn't be a big deal, then, huh?" I glanced around Misery, checking all the nooks and crannies just to be certain. The screams were definitely coming from the general vicinity of Kit's office. "Hey, who's screaming?"

"Screaming?"

"In your office. Who's with you?"

"What do you mean?"

"Someone is screaming. Loudly. You can't miss it. Unless . . ." Clearly there was a departed woman in Kit's office. One who was utterly pissed at someone named Louie. "Who's Louie?"

The next time she spoke, her voice was soft and a bit muffled as though she were covering the receiver with her hand. "The only other person in my office is Special Agent Louie Guzman. He's here on a case from D.C. Why?"

I could hear the curiosity in her voice. This was getting fun. I narrowly missed a white Honda that had decided it had the right of way. The driver flipped me off. What the hell? I was going straight at the intersection, and she was turning left. And she had the right of way just because the light turned red just as we entered the intersection?

"I still had the right of way!" I yelled, flipping her off back, but she'd hightailed it across six lanes of traffic before those who actually had the right of way T-boned her.

"Sometimes I can't believe you still have your license," Kit said to me.

"Right? It's a mystery."

"So, the screams?" she said again, all hushed like. "Agent Guzman is on the phone."

"Then whoever he's talking to can really project. It's like she's right there in your office." I was teasing, of course. If no one but me could hear the woman, she was departed and yelling at the other agent.

"Yeah?" Kit asked. "What's she saying?"

"She's threatening, mostly. Telling Louie to get his head out of his ass and find her body. And she's doing it all in a Southern accent, so it's kind of funny. Mucho grande mocha latte. Extra whipped cream. Extra hot," I said to the barista on the other side of the counter. I'd stopped for sustenance.

Kit seemed to perk up. "Where are you?"

"Satellite."

"Can you swing by?"

"Sure."

"And bring me one of those, too."

"You got it."

7

It is inhumane, in my opinion, to force people
who have a genuine medical need for coffee to wait in line
behind people who apparently view it as some kind of recreational activity.
—DAVE BARRY

I had to go through the usual red tape to get to Kit's office. Metal detector. Pat down. Strip search, but only because I'd asked for one. Guy was hot.

By the time I got past security, Kit's extra-hot venti mocha latte was no longer extra hot. It was more Skywalker warm. Luke Skywalker warm.

A nice woman in a crisp suit showed me to a conference room instead of Kit's office. I stepped inside and almost ran face-first into a woman with a chef's knife. She was pissed. Screaming. Waving the knife. Threatening to call someone's mother, but only as a last resort because she detested the woman.

Kit was keeping Special Agent Guzman busy while I got a feel for what was going on. I thought the woman might notice me standing there, but she was way too into her rant to pay attention to little ol' me, so I walked over and handed Kit her coffee.

"Davidson," Kit said, pretending to just notice me. She took the cup and pulled me into a big hug.

The other agent stood back with a congenial smile on his face as Kit showed an unprecedented amount of emotion. I felt it quake within her.

When she pulled back, her eyes shimmered with it as well. "I'm glad you're doing so well."

She meant it. It took me a moment to recover from the shock. Also, I was kind of lip-reading, so I was only guessing at what she said. That departed woman had a set of lungs that went on for days. Kit could have said, "I'm mad you're going to hell," but I didn't know why she would say something like that to me. As far as I knew, she didn't have that kind of insight.

She cleared her throat and straightened her shoulders. "This is Special Agent Guzman," she said before physically turning me to face him like one would a child. I tried not to crack up.

It was hard to actually see Special Agent Guzman. The woman was in his face. Like in his face. Yelling. Screaming at him. But a hand popped out of her lower back, so I took it, praying it was the agent offering a greeting. It was hard to tell at that point.

"Nguyen," Kit said as her partner in crime walked in. Agent Nguyen and I had never bonded.

The two male agents shook hands, then it was my turn. Agent Nguyen's gaze landed on me. I waved a tight hello and got the feeling Nguyen was warming up to me. His smile held less acid than the ones he used to offer me, but that was all the warmth I'd get from him.

I chose a chair and started to sit down.

He pulled the chair out from under me and took it for himself.

Oh yeah. I was totally winning him over. The Discovery Channel had a special that said punking their friends was how the FBI genus showed affection. Their mating rituals were stranger still.

Kit and Guzman took a chair, too, so I walked around Agent Nguyen, who was only slightly glowering at me, and sat opposite, well, everyone. This wasn't intimidating at all.

All three of them looked at me. Kit expectantly from behind her cup. Nguyen impatiently. And Agent Guzman curiously.

"So," I said, clasping my hands together and probably speaking a tad louder than necessary, "I bet you're all wondering why I called this meeting."

Kit fought a grin while the new guy glanced at her in question.

"Davidson is a private investigator," Kit told him. "She does some work for us from time to time."

"You hire private investigators?" he asked, surprised.

"Hire would imply payment," I corrected. "This is more of a volunteer thing."

"Ah." He nodded, pretending to understand why we were all sitting there.

"Mrs. Davidson recently came into some interesting information about your wife's disappearance," Kit said, and I had to force my smile to stay put.

Not that I hadn't figured the woman yelling in his face was a skeleton from the guy's closet, almost certainly a departed wife, but I wasn't sure how Kit wanted this to play out. Did she suspect the guy of killing his wife? And since when did she call me Mrs. Davidson?

"I don't understand," he said, looking as perplexed as I felt.

Mrs. Davidson.

"Are you having her look into Mandy's case?"

Mrs. Davidson.

Kit shook her head. "No, I think this information just kind of landed in Mrs. Davidson's lap."

It was one thing to know I went by Mrs. Davidson.

"How does information about a missing persons case in D.C. just happen to fall into a private investigator's lap in Albuquerque, New Mexico?"

It was another thing entirely to hear it spoken aloud.

"Is there a reason you're getting defensive?"

Maybe I should hyphenate.

"Is there a reason you think I should get defensive?"

Davidson-Farrow.

"You tell me."

Mrs. Davidson-Farrow.

"Is that why I'm here?" The young agent bolted out of his chair, his movements sharp and on the ragged edge of violence. "Is that why they brought me here?"

Agent Nguyen had risen, too, readying himself to subdue his volatile colleague. But it was around that time that I noticed something else. The woman had stopped screaming. She was staring at me, almost as curiously as the agent had.

"Finally," she said, crossing her arms, the knife resting across her rib cage. She tapped her toes and waited.

"Well?" Kit asked me, waiting as well.

I dug deep for a nonchalant smile, hoping for a cue from Kit. Any cue.

"Oh, my god," the woman said, throwing her arms up. "She doesn't know any more than anyone else."

I focused on her. "Then tell me."

"If I had a nickel for every time someone had new information on my case . . ."

She still had no idea I could see her, and she didn't seem to give a rat's ass that I was bright enough to sear the retinas from her eyes. Most departed noticed the fact that I hemorrhaged light like a trophy wife hemorrhaged money right off the bat. That usually led to them wanting to cross. I was the flame. They were the moths.

Maybe her antennae were broken.

"Tell me what happened," I said softly. It was hard to miss the blunt-force trauma to her head, or the blood that had saturated her hair and pale pink robe.

Everyone had stopped and was staring at me, including the woman.

"Tell me what happened," I repeated.

"You—" She took an involuntarily step forward and was now standing with her hips halfway inside the conference table. "You can see me?"

I nodded.

"How?" she began, but changed her mind. "Why would—? Wait, no." She bent her head to think a moment, then looked back up. "What are you?"

I glanced around at our audience. "That's hard to say at the moment."

"Who is she talking to?" the agent asked.

Agent Nguyen sat back down and glared at his fingernails. Kit grinned and took another sip of her latte.

"Do you know where your body is?"

The woman blinked at me, turned to look behind her to make sure I was talking to her, then refocused on me and nodded.

"Do you know who killed you?"

"A psychic?" the agent asked, angrier than ever.

"Not a psychic," Kit said, so calm and pleased with herself, I almost giggled. "A prodigy."

"In our backyard. And, no, he didn't do it," the woman said before I could ask. Then she turned to her husband. "His psychotic, freakazoid sister drugged me, then bashed in my skull with my Miss Kentucky trophy. I can't believe nobody noticed it was missing."

I knew I'd detected an accent.

"He's, like, the worst investigator. I've been trying to tell him who killed me for two effing years." And she was off. "Two mother-effing years. I tried to defend myself." She waved the knife at me.

I encouraged her to continue with a nod.

"But it's hard to fight off batshit crazy, ya know? Woman is effing batshit."

So, *shit* was okay, but *fuck* was not. She had to be Southern Baptist.

"Batshit. With a capital *B*. And then she moves in with him to help him take care of the house. Moves right the fuck in."

Or maybe Catholic.

"Like she owns the place. And there I am, pushin' up daisies. And I know what you're thinking." She leaned her face toward mine. "But I mean that literally. I am literally pushin' up daisies."

I decided to relay the current bits of information while she got it out of her system. "Your sister did it," I said.

To say that he had his doubts about my ability would have been an understatement. The sneer on his face could've scoured the rust off metal.

"She planted them over my dead body."

"And she buried your wife in your backyard."

"It was her way of having the last laugh even though she already had. I mean, hello. I'm dead, aren't I? But no. That's not enough. She just can't let things alone. She has to throw in that final 'fuck you.'"

"Your sister didn't happen to put in a daisy garden when she moved in with you, did she?"

I knew I'd get the agent's attention eventually, but his expression when I mentioned the garden didn't quite go as planned. Instead of a dawning of understanding lighting his features, he turned a lovely shade of purple. I'd never seen that particular hue on a person before and wondered if I could get a picture without him noticing. For research purposes.

"This is beyond unacceptable," he said.

"See!" she screamed, pointing the knife at him. "He. Will. Not. Listen."

"Agent Guzman," I began.

"Oh, don't even bother," she interrupted. "He won't listen. He is the most bullheaded, stubborn at-shass I've ever met."

I scanned my extensive repertoire of verbiage and got nothing. "What's an at-shass?" I asked her.

She let out a lengthy sigh. "It was something we said. Louie swore I called him that on our first date. I wouldn't know. I got shitfaced and was apparently trying to call him an asshat. It came out at-shass and stuck."

As she explained that she used it as an inside joke when they were around friends to signal to her husband that his bullheadedness was rearing its ugly bull head, I couldn't help but notice the one-eighty Guzman did.

His face paled when I said that word aloud. Alas. The lovely purple was gone. But Agent Guzman was coming around.

I glanced at Kit. "Can you give us a moment?"

"Oh, hell, no." She put her mocha latte aside like she was ready to get down to business. "This is my favorite part."

"You have a favorite part?" I hadn't realized we'd done this often enough for her to have a favorite part.

"Yep. You talk to yourself for a few minutes, try to negotiate with the air around us, beg and plead sometimes, and then come up with these mind-boggling revelations. Then you send us in directions we never would have thought to go, and suddenly the case, whatever that case may be, is solved. Like magic. Oh no, honey. I wouldn't miss this for early retirement."

"And now," Mandy continued, her rant only just beginning, "he's going to sit there and pretend he doesn't know I'm here. Just like before. Just like always. Everything and everyone else comes first. Trying to get his attention is like trying to pull teeth from a lion's mouth. I've even stabbed him in the face."

I snapped back to her. "You've tried to stab him in the face?"

"Not tried." She waved a negating index at me. Girl had spunk. "Did. Many times." She looked at the knife she carried around. "This thing is as useless as it was the day I picked it up. I tried to stab Cin in the face, too. Didn't even come close, but I did get her in the shoulder."

"Well, in your defense, you'd been drugged."

"True."

"If you'd been in your right mind, I'm sure you would have stabbed her in the face. Many times."

"You think so?" she said, sniffing.

I patted her back to console her. "Her face could've doubled as a colander."

"Aw, thanks."

"Are you getting anywhere?" Kit asked, but that was when I noticed Guzman's reaction.

"Mandy always said she would stab me in the face if I ever ignored her. It became a joke."

I thought about mentioning the fact that the joking days were long gone, but he didn't need to know she'd stabbed him in the face. Several times. Thankfully, her knife was as incorporeal as she was.

"Look," Guzman said, calming even more as his mind raced, "my sister was out of town."

"The perfect alibi," Mandy said. "No one even checked. Like, seriously. She was never even a suspect."

I looked back at Guzman. "Did you check to make sure?"

"What? No. Why would I check my own sister's alibi?"

"That's it," Mandy said, right before she dive-bombed him. She flew right through him, but she came back kicking. And screaming. And stabbing.

If she tried that with me, it was going to hurt.

"Mrs. Guzman!" I said, trying to get her attention. "You have to give him some time. This is not going to be easy."

She looked up from her last efforts to puncture his esophagus, blew her bangs out of her face, and said, "Two years. Two effing years."

We were back to the *effing* thing. "I know, hon. But—"

"I'm out of here," Guzman said, rising from his chair.

I rose, too. "Just check it out. Check out your sister's alibi. And check her credit card records. She drugged your wife first, then hit her with her Miss Kentucky trophy, which, by the way"—I looked at Mandy—"congrats on that."

"Thank you," she said, her face one solid, Southern smile. All sparkly eyes and beautiful teeth. "It was so long ago, really." She took one hand from her husband's throat to smooth down her hair.

"Well, it's quite an accomplishment."

This time when Guzman's face paled, I honestly thought he would fall. Nguyen did, too. He jumped up and helped the man back into his chair.

"I haven't seen that trophy since—"

"Since your wife went missing?"

Guzman's mind raced, his eyes scanning the table in front of him as he played and replayed the investigation. The events of that day. Every second he could recall, all of which, I would bet my bottom dollar, were burned into his mind. What could he have done differently? What did he do wrong? Was she abducted? Did she leave of her own accord?

So many questions were playing out in his mind, and the pain of them showed on a face that was too young to be as lined as it was.

He stood, walked out, turned around, and came right back in. "Why? Why would Cin do this?"

That was a great question. Mandy had been watching her husband, her face alight with all the love she felt for him. "It's not his fault. Not really. He's an amazing investigator. No one suspected Cin. No one, least of all me, knew what she was capable of."

"Do you know why she did it?"

Mandy smiled. "She saw us, the way we acted toward each other, the way we spoke to one another, and decided I wasn't the right girl for her brother. He'd been a star quarterback. The president of his senior class. He was destined for greatness, but she hated me. Thought I didn't love him." She reached up to touch her husband's cheek as everyone waited with bated breath for my answer. "She was wrong. We always talked to each other that way, but it was just our way. We weren't being mean or belittling one another. That was just how we showed affection."

I decided to paraphrase. "Your sister did it because she's batshit crazy."

Mandy snorted.

"She didn't understand your relationship," I said, editing as I went. "She didn't understand that the way you spoke to one another was how you showed affection."

"What?"

"The little digs? The innuendos? You were just playing. Your sister didn't understand that."

"That's just how we are. How we were. I loved Mandy more than anything."

"Even football?" she asked, and I fought a sad smile.

"She's—she's gone?"

I hadn't realized until that moment that he'd been holding out hope. All this time.

"I'm so sorry, Agent Guzman."

"The necklace," Mandy said as a new thought came to her. She explained, and I relayed.

"You gave your wife a necklace the morning you left for a conference. You were going to miss your anniversary, so you gave it to her early. Your sister has it in her jewelry box. It came off when she—during the attack."

I felt pressure build inside the agent. He didn't want to believe. He fought it with every ounce of strength he had, but I simply knew too much. He couldn't deny that.

"Wait," his wife said. "There's something else. I was going to tell him when he got back from his trip." For the first time, tears sprang to her eyes. She lowered her head, suddenly unable to talk.

I'd done enough of these to know exactly what she was going to say, but that didn't make it any easier. I put my hand on hers. "I'm so sorry, Mandy."

"I'd just found out. I was going to make a doctor's appointment that day to make sure before I told him, but I knew. We'd been trying for so long. And I knew."

I closed my eyes and felt Guzman stiffen. "What?" he asked.

"I'm so sorry, Agent Guzman, but she—your wife was—you were going to have baby."

In Guzman's eyes, I'd gone too far. Anger rocketed through him before he got it under control and the truth slowly and painfully set in. "She told you that?"

"Yes. You'd been trying for a year. It finally took."

"No." He shook his head, not sure if he was the victim of a horrible prank or witnessing the impossible. He decided to give it a shot. "How do I do this? How do I justify digging up my backyard because a crazy woman told me to without looking crazy myself?"

Kit smiled. "Anonymous tip. Works every time."

"You know, you can cross if you'd like," I said to Mandy. "It's what I do. I'm a ticket straight to the other side. Straight to your family and friends who are waiting for you."

"Are you kidding? And miss seeing Cin's face when my husband arrests her skank ass? Not likely, sister."

I nodded and glanced at Nguyen. He may not have been warming up to me, but I got the feeling he was becoming a believer. He didn't offer me any praise or anything, but he didn't glower at me when he stood and walked out. I felt like we were making progress.

"You know," Kit said as I was leaving. "You never told me why you called."

"Oh, right. So, yeah, thanks."

"Thanks?"

"You know, for New York."

"You helped to save a family."

"But you believed in me. Even in amnesiac me. It means a lot."

"Oh yeah? How much?"

"How much?" I asked. She had slipped into negotiation mode. "How much we talking?"

She lifted a shoulder. "Just a little information. Nothing earth-shattering."

"What kind of information?"

She stopped and leveled a serious gaze on me. "How do you do what you do?"

Kit knew a lot. Much more than the general populace, who dismissed any notions of the supernatural as bogus. But she did not know my many titles, and I planned to keep her virginal in all things Charley Davidson as long as possible.

"Ancient Chinese secret," I said.

"I'm pretty sure the Chinese culture as a whole would find offense in your using them like that."

"True. And they know martial arts and stuff."

"Yep." We'd started for the front entrance again, but she stopped me with a hand on my shoulder. "One day, I'm going to get to the bottom of you, Charley Davidson."

I had no idea she was into anal. "Okay, but buy me dinner first?"

8

I'm not a ride-or-die kind of girl. I have questions.
Where are we riding to?
Why do I have to die?
Can we get food on the way?
—MEME

On the way back to the office, I took the long way around and drove past the Fosters' house. Mrs. Foster was the woman who, since there was really no way to sugarcoat it, abducted Reyes when he was a baby. When they were on the verge of being busted, they basically sold him to the monster that raised him: Earl Walker.

Since I'd been back, I made a point of driving through their neighborhood, checking for Mrs. Foster's car, making sure they were still in the vicinity. I'd also been keeping tabs on their online activity. They had yet to be charged with not one but two abductions, and I'd need all the ammunition I could get when the time came for me to present my case to Ubie. And now that I was working with an assistant district attorney, I could include him in the fun.

Mrs. Foster was home when I drove by. I'd never actually seen her before, but I made the turn onto her street just as she was walking inside with an armful of groceries. I hated her. Seeing her didn't change that.

Instead of taking the outside stairs when I finally made it back to the office, I pulled Misery into her carport and walked to Reyes's restaurant, planning to enter via the back door. A soft rain, almost warm against the crisp day, misted around me and left me damp and a tad frizzy when I strolled inside and made my way Reyes's office.

He sat behind his desk doing paperwork and didn't look up when I walked in. So, I took the opportunity to peruse his office. It looked exactly as my father had left it, including all the family photos that lined the shelves and punctuated the other paraphernalia on the walls. Mostly cop stuff. A map here. An award there. A set of old handcuffs that sent my mind reeling in the wrong direction.

I had to get a grip. Either Reyes was affecting me even more than usual, or my fallopian tubes were about to be invaded.

I glanced over my shoulder to make sure Reyes hadn't noticed me noticing the handcuffs. He was pretty deep in thought, though I had little doubt he not only knew I was there, but also knew where my mind had wandered.

Refocusing on his office, I scanned the photos he still had up. I'd been surprised the first time I walked into it last week after being gone for so long. Everything else in our lives had been upgraded, but the bar and grill he'd left exactly as my father had kept it. Still, it was one thing to leave the restaurant the same. It was another to leave the office the same.

Then I noticed one tiny change. He'd actually removed several of the pictures my dad had scattered here and there. The only ones remaining were the ones with me in them. I didn't even have to be the focal point of the picture. I could've been in the background, as I was in a beach photo we'd taken in SoCal when I was in grade school.

The picture was supposed to be of my sister, Gemma, showing off her lopsided sand castle. But there I was in the background, pulling my mouth as wide as I could with my fingers and sticking out my tongue. Oh, and my eyes were crossed. No photobomb was complete without crossed eyes. Not my best look, but Reyes seemed to like it.

"Come to shower me with ice again?" Reyes asked.

I turned back to him. He was still poring over a stack of papers and hadn't looked up.

"Shower you with ice?" When he didn't answer, I asked, "What are you working on?"

"My will."

I walked around the desk in alarm. "Your will? Why do you need a will?"

He looked up at last. "Surely, you're joking."

I started to argue, but he was right. We did lead a rather hazardous life. To deny that would be ludicrous. Then again, ludicrous was my middle name.

"I have a plan," I said, steering the conversation away from places I was not comfortable going.

"Does it involve my death? If so, you might want to wait another day or so. I need to get this back to our lawyers."

"We have lawyers?" That was cool. I'd never thought of myself as a lawyer-y type person. "Never mind that. I have a plan to get our daughter back."

He finally gave me his full attention. He put down the pen he'd been holding and sat back in his chair. The movement was so small, so everyday, and yet it sent a tiny rush of excitement spiraling over my skin.

He'd rolled up his sleeves, exposing his corded forearms. His strong hands. His long, capable fingers.

He noticed me noticing for sure that time, but instead of reaching out to me, instead of inviting me into his personal space, he waited. He simply waited. For me to speak? For me to act? I had no idea which, so I went with the former.

"Yeah, so, for this plan to work, we are going to need a dozen syringes, a case of nitrous oxide, a serial killer, and a tank."

He didn't respond, and I stood a little confounded when he didn't mock my shopping list. He didn't even question it, so I clarified the last item on my list.

"You know, from the military."

"Yes," he said, his voice low and smooth. "I know what a tank is."

"Right. I just thought you might be leaning toward a fish tank or a septic tank."

"No, I got it." His gaze shimmered as he took me in, and I could see the interest sparkling in their dark depths. I wanted to shift, just a little, to straddle the other plane and see him in his supernatural form, but I got the feeling he knew when I did that, so I stopped myself.

"Do you think it'll work?" I asked.

"Your plan?"

"Yes."

"I haven't actually heard it. I've only heard the physical requirements for it."

"Oh, of course." I tried to shake out of the carnal desire racing through my veins and pooling with zero regard to my sanity in my abdomen. When I failed miserably, I walked to the other side of his desk and sat opposite him. To put some distance between us. And a large piece of wood. It didn't help. Probably because I knew what he could do to that piece of wood to get to me if he wanted to. Clearly, however, he didn't want to.

I took a deep breath, but instead of relaying my plan to him, I asked, "Can you tell me what's bothering you?"

He didn't move. His expression didn't change in the least. He simply stared, his long lashes making his irises shimmer all the more in the low light.

"We have company."

"And that's bothering you? The little boy in the ceiling?"

Before he could answer, Osh, or Osh'ekiel as he was known in the

celestial realm, walked into Reyes's office. Just strolled in like he wasn't
supposed to be somewhere else.

"Osh," I said, alarm rocketing through me. "Why are you here?"

He bowed his head a moment and stuffed his hands in his pockets. As
usual, he was wearing a short black top hat over his shoulder-length black
hair. But today he also wore a long duster, just as black as the rest of his
attire, and heavy motorcycle boots.

Reyes stood and waited for his answer as well.

"We had to move her."

A blast of heat scalded my skin as Reyes lost control of his emotions.
My emotions, however, took a different turn. They pushed my heart into
my throat and poured adrenaline by the bucketload through my nervous
system.

"Where is she?" I asked, stepping closer to him.

He pulled his shoulders up to his ears and jammed his hands deeper
into his jeans pockets. "You know I can't tell you that."

I was on him before I even had the thought. No matter that he was
the deadliest Daeva—lower-level demon trained for fighting—that hell
had ever seen. To me, he was a nineteen-year-old kid who knew more
about my daughter than I did, and I suddenly found the situation intoler-
ably unfair.

I had him against the wall with one hand around his throat. He held
my arm with both of his hands but didn't try to stop me.

Reyes was at my side in an instant. "Dutch," he said softly, placing a
hand over the one I had wrapped around Osh's throat, but unless he
planned on helping me choke the life out of the kid, he was of no use to
me at that moment. So my free hand went to his throat. He raised his chin,
almost as though he welcomed the contact.

I needed to know where my daughter was. Why they had to move her
was one thing, but not knowing where she was gave me few options
should I need to help her.

Valerie, who Cookie told me was one of Reyes's servers, stopped wiping off a table, glanced inside the office, then scurried off, presumably when she noticed her boss's ire.

"Dutch," he said again past the tightness in his throat. I'd slipped to the other plane and looked on as Osh's aura spiraled like vapor around me. He didn't fight me in the least. He still held my arm with one hand but had moved the other to my shoulder. He was lightning quick and just as deadly, so I had little doubt he was forming a plan.

The darkness surrounding Reyes billowed around him. The flames that perpetually bathed him leaped out at me. Normally, they would have scorched. Blistered. Seared. But today they only annoyed.

"Where is my daughter?"

Osh simply shook his head, carrying out his orders, obedient till the last. And it was about to be his last; that much I could guarantee. My anger shook the walls around us, and I heard a high-pitched scream from the kitchen. Probably Valerie, the server.

"Dutch," Reyes said, "he can't tell us. You know that."

"Then he'll die wishing he could."

If I'd been paying closer attention to my husband, I would have seen the sideways glance he offered Osh a microsecond before my face was planted into the wood floors of his office. They had turned the tables so fast, I hadn't seen them move.

They'd slowed time.

And I'd stood there like a lunatic on too much lithium. I could only hope I didn't drool.

"Do you understand?"

I blinked, groaning under their weight, trying to remember what they'd said. Whatever it was, I felt *yes* would be the appropriate answer.

"Yes," I said from under a ton of limbs and torsos. Holy cow crap, they were heavy.

"What did I say?" Reyes asked. Damn him.

"That the two of you are going to get the fuck off me, and Osh is going to tell me where my daughter is."

"Wrong."

The weight multiplied, and I groaned, the agony of defeat almost too much to bear. As were its muscle mass and bony elbows. They had to weigh like five hundred pounds. Each.

They had my arms locked behind my back, several knees lodged there for good measure, and one arm—Reyes's, I assumed—was wrapped around my neck while the other one held my head down, keeping my face planted hard against the floor, so close I could see every splinter in the wood grain.

And, sadly, I was going nowhere fast. If I could've spoken more clearly, I would've cried uncle. As it stood, I couldn't even get enough air in my lungs to cry, period.

"We are going to let you up if you promise not to kill anyone." When I only groaned, I received another fifty pounds per square inch of pressure on my midsection.

"Okay," I half groaned, half squeaked.

Slowly, as though to make sure I didn't lose it again, they eased their weight off me but kept my face planted to the floor. Probably hoping I'd germinate. Sprout roots. Why else plant something so thoroughly?

A soft feminine voice penetrated the fog of oxygen deprivation. "Is— is everything okay?"

"No—" I started to say, but a strong hand clamped over my face.

"Yes," Reyes said. "Thank you."

A deep laugh came from behind Valerie. It had to be Sammy, the head cook. Also known as the traitor. I was clearly being subdued against my will, but did he care? Hell, no. Like the men holding me down, he probably belonged to the League of Extraordinary Assholes.

"It's okay, Valerie. They do this sort of thing all the time," he said. Completely overstating the fact.

"Oh," she said, unsure.

I saw feet through my tear-blurred vision as Sammy led her away.

Then I was up. I took a lungful of air, grateful for the fact that Reyes had pinned me to the wall as a precaution. I would have fallen otherwise.

"No fair slowing time," I said, leaning my head back and panting.

"You did it first," Osh replied. He was doubled over, one hand on a knee, the other massaging his throat. Testing it with hesitant pokes from his long fingers here and there.

Reyes had pressed his entire body against mine. It was the most action I'd seen all week, and I basked in the feel of it. The warmth as the tips of his flames licked across my face and saturated my skin.

Then I realized what I'd just done. I'd threatened the life of one of my best friends. One of the few beings on Earth who could help protect Beep. One of the even fewer beings on Earth who would give his life to do so.

Guilt rocketed through me. I'd never lost control like that. Or had I? Was that why the archangel Michael had tried to kill me in the diner in New York? Did I truly have no control over my powers?

Osh coughed and then straightened, falling back against the wall kitty-corner to me. He rested his head on the wood paneling as well. Closed his eyes. Drew in long, deep breaths.

"I'm sorry," I whispered to Reyes.

He wrapped his long fingers around my neck and buried his face in my hair. He smelled like a lightning storm. His emotions electricity. His body the desert after a rain. Fresh. Starkly beautiful. Dangerous.

"Are you okay?" he asked, his breath warm on my neck.

"I am now."

He pulled back, took one look at my face, then stepped out of my embrace and turned away from me. I lifted a hand to my cheek and whirled around to face a picture, trying to see myself in the reflection of the glass, but I could only see a blurred outline of my features. Still, they looked pretty unremarkable. What was so wrong with me that my own husband would turn away?

"Your eyes," Osh said, practically reading my mind.

Reyes growled at him, but he'd never seen my husband as much of a threat. I wondered how he would feel if he knew he was a god. Then again, he may already know. He was there, after all. When Lucifer created his one and only son, siphoning the energy from a god to mold him, using the fires of hell to temper him. To make him strong. To make him indestructible.

Before I could ask about my eyes, I heard Cookie tearing down the stairs. She rushed through the restaurant, stumbled into the office, took one look at me, and knew something was wrong.

"What happened?" she asked, a hand over her heart.

"That's what I'm trying to find out."

I stepped over to Osh, and he stiffened. Guilt flooded every molecule in my body, dousing it in acid, the taste bitter in my mouth. What had I done?

"I'm sorry," I said to him. I reached up and put my hand on his throat. He didn't fight me this time, either. In fact, he practically leered.

"Oh yeah?" he asked, completely ignoring the man behind me. The one I was married to. A slow grin raised one corner of his mouth. "How sorry?"

He took hold of my shirttail and pulled me closer, and even though he was deflecting, drawing attention away from the fact that I'd just attacked him, I raised my arms and pulled him into a hug.

"Very," I said into his ear.

He wrapped his arms tight around me. "I'm sorrier," he said, and he meant it. He truly did wish he could tell me where my daughter was, but we'd decided. No one would know her location but Osh and, naturally, the Loehrs, since they were her caretakers for the time being. Beep's guardians knew, too, of course, her army of the ragtag sort, but they were never to leave her side.

And her side was a sight to see. She had my dimension's version of an archangel, the man I used to call Mr. Wong, a skilled warrior and leader. She had the three bikers who swore loyalty to Reyes and me. And she had twelve huge, ruthless, and completely adorable hellhounds known as the Twelve.

She had an army, and still they'd had to move her.

My chest tightened again with the thought, and I tamped down a wave of dizzying anxiety.

I slid out of his hold and wrapped an arm in Cookie's. "Okay," I said to him. "I won't ask where she is again. For now. But can you at least tell me why you had to move her?"

Reyes stepped behind me, and I inched back until we were touching.

"The signs were all there," Osh said, eyeing Reyes as though he'd personally fucked up. "Bodies started showing up, one by one. The first ones were two counties over. Then they started getting closer, like something was homing in."

"The bodies?" I asked Reyes.

"Is this about Beep?" Cookie asked.

I nodded. "They had to move her."

Cookie's worried expression mimicked the fear thundering through me. I led her to a chair and sat her in it before sitting in the one Reyes held for me. "What do bodies have to do with anything?"

"You want to tell her?" Osh asked Reyes.

He took a knee beside me, and I wondered if he thought I'd lose it again. I wondered even more if I would.

"We have something of a checklist. An outline of things to keep a lookout for. It's how we know the gods are getting close. And one of the signs is dead bodies. But how did they look?" he asked Osh.

"I wouldn't be here if they didn't fit the criteria."

Reyes bit down and cursed under his breath before coming back to me. "A supernatural entity can't just shift onto this plane carte blanche.

It doesn't have that kind of authority. In order to be able to interact within the parameters of the plane, it has to be able to shift fully. And the only way to do that, as you may have noticed, is to inhabit a human."

"But," Osh said, "a human's body is too fragile to hold a god for more than a few hours. It begins to decompose instantly and at a much faster rate than normal."

"But demons can do it," I argued. "They've possessed people for years at a time. They've even kept an injured or sometimes a dead body going for months."

"Yes," Reyes said. "A demon can do that. Pretty much any supernatural entity from any dimension that can find its way onto this plane can possess a human to shift fully."

Osh pushed off from the wall and turned to look out a high window. "But while a demon can keep a human body in a state of animation for an eternity, a god is simply too powerful for a vessel as fragile as a human to hold."

He turned back to Reyes. Let him take over. "A god can only keep a body animated for a little while before its cells eventually begin to disintegrate and meld into one another. Until it no longer looks human."

"And what happens to the person it possessed?"

"Nothing that hasn't already happened. He or she will have died the instant the god hijacked the body. It's like putting the core of a nuclear reactor inside a human and watching the person melt around it."

Cookie's hands curled into fists around the fingers I'd laced into hers. She was shaking visibly, her pretty brows drawn into a severe line.

Osh didn't notice. "If there is a god in the area and he is using and discarding bodies at will, he is onto Beep's scent. And like any good bloodhound, he won't give up until he has his prey firmly between his jaws."

Cookie inhaled sharply, and Osh finally realized how distressed she was. I think, in fact, my worry for her was keeping my own stress-induced hissy fit at bay. I wanted to rant and rail and crush a few larynxes until somebody came up with the location of my daughter. But I couldn't do it in front of Cookie. I couldn't upset her any more.

"And the bodies?" Reyes asked him. Still kneeling beside me, he had one hand on my leg and one around the arm of the chair. The arm cracked with the pressure he was putting on it.

Osh nodded. "They're . . . decomposing at an unnatural rate. Not to mention the fact that the hounds were getting restless. Pawing the ground. Sniffing the air. Itching to hunt."

"But what could they do against a god?" I asked.

"Buy us time."

The direness of the situation had me light-headed. "You got Beep out of there before you needed them, though?"

He nodded again. "She's at a new safe house with the Loehrs and most of the Sentry."

That's what we were calling Beep's army. The Sentry. "Most?"

Osh dropped his gaze. "Your man, Donovan. He stayed behind to keep an eye on the area. To let us know if any more bodies showed up."

I blinked, astonished, and so grateful that he would do such a thing that a lump formed in my throat. "Is he still there?"

The beautiful kid before me, who was actually older than Reyes by a couple of centuries yet looked like he was in his late teens, nodded, his mouth a grim line. "He's trying to get ahead of it. To track it down and figure out its next move."

I shot to my feet. "By himself?"

"He insisted the other two go with the Sentry."

"Osh, he's only human." I stepped closer to him, and Reyes stood as well. Took hold of my arm in warning. I shook it off. "What's he supposed to do if he does find it?"

"Call," Reyes said, taking my arm again.

"Call?" I asked, appalled. "And would that be before or after the god hijacks his body?" When no one answered, I said, "I need to go to him."

"And do what?" Reyes asked, his ire pulsing through the room like a bass drum. "Be the guiding beacon that leads him straight to your friend?"

"You must not like him very much," Osh teased.

They were right. I would only get him killed faster. As would Reyes. His darkness was very much like my light. I'd found that out when I learned to shift between planes. He was like a great void in the landscape. A dark chasm. Just as I was a portal to heaven, he was a portal to hell. And any supernatural being could see it from a thousand miles away.

"Can I ask, what makes you think there's only one god in the area?"

"That's how they work," Reyes said. "They split up until one finds its prey, then the other two join it."

Reyes really had no idea he was one of the three gods of Uzan. That there were only two out there.

"If this were any other world, they would've just destroyed it."

"What's stopping them?" Cookie asked.

Osh answered her. "The God Jehovah. It's part respect and part self-preservation."

"The last thing they want is a war with another god."

"So, they're cowards as well as mass murderers."

"Pretty much," Osh said.

But my husband was the furthest thing from a coward. He was truly nothing like his brothers at all. "What can I do?" I asked first Reyes then Osh.

"Go back to work," Osh said.

Reyes agreed. "Go about your day as normally as you can. They could have spies."

"Spies?" Cookie said, paling even more than she had.

"They could be trying to smoke us out," Osh explained. "If you panic and start checking on Beep and the Loehrs, trying to track them down to make sure they're okay, the spies could lock on to their location."

"We would be doing all the legwork for them."

"So, I'm just supposed to go about my day, knowing—"

"Knowing Beep is okay," Osh insisted. He stepped to me and brushed his fingers under my chin. "I promise. We've already moved them to a secure location."

"Secure for now," I said.

Unable to argue, he offered another nod and then started to head out. He stopped at the door and added, "I almost forgot to tell you. I killed another emissary."

Reyes, who until only recently saw Osh as a lowly Daeva, an entity beneath him that was more foe than friend, walked over to him and gripped his forearm. Osh took Reyes's in turn, solidifying the brotherhood that shared a common goal: protect and serve, at all cost, Elwyn Alexandra Loehr, the girl who would battle the pestilence of the world. The girl who would save humanity.

I hadn't told Reyes that Osh was also destined to fall in love with our daughter. No need to rock that boat just yet.

I pushed my hand inside my jeans pocket and wrapped my fingers around the god glass. It was our only hope against the two gods of Uzan. The only one that I knew of, anyway. Should I tell Reyes?

In order to trap a god, or any spiritual entity, in the hell dimension, one had to know its name. Its true name. But I didn't know the gods' true names, much less Reyes's. Not his godly name. If I told him about the god glass, would he use that against me when he found out his true origins?

It had only been a week. I'd known he was a god for a week. I could hold on to that tidbit for a while longer. Just until I had more information. Just until I knew for sure that I could trust the godly part of my husband. The part that was supposedly as evil as they come. Which sucked.

9

When I was a kid . . .
No, wait, I still do that.
—T-SHIRT

I wondered when I left how many of the bad twelve, the emissaries sent from Satan himself, were left. If I was counting correctly, I guessed nine, but there was no way to be certain without calling them all in for a roll call. That could work, actually. We could do a sting and tell them they'd won a TV like they do with criminals who jumped bail. If only I had their addresses. How could I send them a letter announcing their wins if I didn't have their addresses? And did demons even watch TV?

Beep was safe. I forced myself to say it over and over in my head, Beep was safe, while Cookie and I pretended our day was going beautifully. We began looking into Emery Adams's background as well as Lyle Fiske's.

While Cookie pulled up Emery's credit report and phone records in a feat that I slid into the "don't ask, don't tell" category, I met with Mrs. Abelson and told her what her husband was up to, trying to push the superhero angle on her.

She didn't buy it, and my heart went out to the guy. He was about to have a very bad day. I think it was the pot thing that sent her over the edge. What would her church group say?

I couldn't help but wonder why the church group would say anything unless she told them, but there was no arguing with her. Not that I was in the mood, anyway. So, I sat there and let her jump to her own conclusions. Listened to her rant and rave about how she'd been betrayed. About how unfair he was being by hanging with a bunch of kids and relaxing.

I was doing really well with the whole thing, staying calm and collected despite the odd looks we were getting in the Frontier, one of my favorite restaurants on this crazy rock. But then she started in on her husband, and I lost it. I told her how lucky she had it to have a husband who could enjoy himself despite her incessant nagging and high-maintenance marriage plan.

She sat livid for a solid minute after I'd finished, then walked out, her face a bright scarlet, her back ramrod straight. There was just no way to dislodge the stick up her ass. Her husband was cursed.

After the meeting, I scratched Mrs. Abelson's name off my Possible Repeat Customers list and hustled back to the office with a to-go pint of salsa verde. Quite frankly, we'd be lucky to get paid on this one.

Way to go, Davidson.

Wait, no, Davidson-Farrow. Hmmmm . . . it was growing on me.

But the case was over, and that called for a celebration of salsa verde and tequila. Of course, the latter would have to wait until tonight, but salsa verde, much like salsa dancing, could be enjoyed anytime. Not, however, before I went to pay my old friend Rocket a visit.

I hadn't seen Rocket since I got back, but I was still completely intrigued by the bombshell Strawberry had dropped while invading the air space in my living room. The names that he wrote on the walls were meant for Beep? They were chosen specifically for her?

First, how?

Second, why?

And third, come again?

It boggled my mind, but getting information from Rocket was even harder than getting information from Strawberry. Rocket was like an overgrown child who'd died in a mental asylum in the fifties. He was a savant of sorts, and if he'd had his gifts while he was alive, I could only imagine how they treated him. Electroshock therapy came to mind. Anything to control him.

I pulled up to the abandoned asylum I now owned, thanks to my sugar daddy. Not that I had any idea what my husband's net worth was. And not that I wanted to. I had zero interest in looking at his will. Ever. I figured I'd go first, anyway. I seemed to have been born with a flashing hazard sign duct-taped to my back.

After trying several combinations on the keypad, I finally found one that worked.

The combination didn't work on the front entrance, however. I wondered if the keypad needed a battery or something. It had worked before.

No big. I would just do what I did before Reyes bought the building. I'd sneak in.

I walked around the east side and found my usual entrance, a basement window, but a vicious Rottweiler tackled me to the ground before I could get inside.

Artemis must have been hanging out at her old stomping grounds. Though the house where Donovan and the gang used to live had been torn down, that apparently didn't keep her from seeking out a familiar environment.

I let her lick my face, her stubby tail wagging at the speed of light, for several minutes before I realized we had an audience. A little boy was watching me try to wrestle the ninety-five-pound dog, to get the upper hand and bury my face in the folds of her neck.

But Artemis was incorporeal. She was my very own personal guardian, and while that was all well and good, to the little boy watching me, I was basically wrestling air.

I cleared my throat and waved to him. "New exercise routine. It's going to take the world by storm. Mark my words. It's called . . . Grassercise," I said as I picked dried grass out of my hair.

Then, with an air of nonchalance, I stood and walked to the basement window.

"Rocket!" I said, calling out to my old friend as I wiggled inside.

Stuffing my ass through a tiny window used to be easier. When I toppled over the sill and landed headfirst on a table that I hoped had already been broken, I called out again.

"Rocket! You here?"

I took the flashlight out of my jacket pocket and shined it toward the stairs leading from the basement.

Nothing had changed in all the months I'd been away. The area was still strewn in trash and debris. A decrepit, three-wheeled gurney sat in one corner of the basement and an old rusted bathtub decorated another.

I loved this place. Creepy things gave me a sense of nostalgia. I blamed my upbringing. And my stepmother. She hadn't been so much creepy as a bona fide creep, but still. It warmed the cockles of my heart. If I'd ever taken art, I would draw stuff like this. The stuff of my dreams. The stuff of others' nightmares, if the plethora of horror movies set in abandoned asylums and hospitals was any indication.

Still receiving no answer from Rocket, I headed upstairs. I ran my fingers along the hundreds and hundreds of names he'd carved into the walls. What had Strawberry said? That the names were meant for Beep? How? What did she mean?

Maybe it was simply her nine-year-old imagination taking hold, but somehow I doubted it. Why would she come up with anything like that?

Just to test out a theory, I decided to see the names from a different vantage. I stopped in one particularly graphitized area and shifted. My celestial vision instantly picked up on things my human vision simply could not. The storms that plagued the intangible world raged around me, whipping my hair into a frenzy, scorching my skin.

The walls of this building were still there, but I was straddling both worlds. Both planes. I had yet to shift completely. Not consciously, anyway. I was terrified of getting lost in the other realm. Of being unable to find my way back to this one. So when I shifted, I did so hesitantly. Cautiously.

But it was enough to see something I'd never seen. The names Rocket carved fairly glowed in the burning edges of this world. As though they were on fire. As though his writing them set them on fire. Was he assigning the names? Or was he simply writing the names already destined to . . . what? What did the names mean? What did they have to do with my daughter?

The chicken-and-egg conundrum would get me nowhere. I needed to talk to Rocket. And I would just as soon as he stopped crushing me and put me down. One minute I'm standing there, minding my own business, and the next I'm being lifted off the ground by an ox. A strong one.

"Rocket," I said through the sound of my ribs cracking. I'd snapped back to the tangible world the moment he picked me up, so the names had stopped glowing. But his bright, bald head hadn't. It was as pale and shiny as ever.

I hugged his head and kissed it while he got the pleasantries out of his system.

"Miss Charlotte," he said, his words muffled by my girls, Danger and Will Robinson. I had a feeling he was doing more than just greeting me.

"Rocket," I said, kicking out to loosen his grip. "Are you molesting me?"

He still held me high, but he looked up, his eyes shimmering with elation. "I missed you, Miss Charlotte."

I hugged him to me again. Thankfully, he didn't need to breathe. "I missed you, too."

We stood like that a long moment. Me with the hugging. Rocket with the accosting. At least he didn't motorboat me. I didn't know how Danger and Will would take to being manhandled in such a way.

Who was I kidding? They'd love it.

When he finally dropped me—literally—I peeled myself off the trash-strewn floor and gave him a loving punch on the arm. "How have you been, handsome?"

He still wore the hospital attire that he'd died in: dingy slippers and grayish-blue pajamas that resembled scrubs.

"Where have you been, Miss Charlotte? Everyone is very upset."

"Really? Because I've been gone for so long?" That was so sweet.

"You've been gone?" he asked. He looked up in thought.

"Not that long," I amended. "But if not for that, why is everyone upset?" I wondered who "everyone" was, but I didn't want to stump him this early in the game.

"Everyone, everyone," he said, throwing his arms up, utterly exasperated with me.

I had that effect on people.

Then he leaned in, his round face full of intrigue. "Can I see it?" he whispered.

"Of course," I said, hoping he didn't want to see anything X-rated. No way was I playing doctor with him. "What would you like to see?"

"It," he said. "The gate."

"Okay," I said, looking around. The only gate I could think of was at the front entrance. "You mean the gate out front?"

"It's outside?" he asked, appalled. "Where anyone can see it?"

"Well, yeah, I mean, it's a gate."

"No, no, no, no, Miss Charlotte. You have to hide it. No one can just see it for no reason just 'cause. Everyone is very upset."

I got the feeling we were talking about two different gates. Then it hit me. The god glass. The portal to the hell dimension I had sitting pretty in the pocket of my jeans.

"Rocket, who is everyone, and why are they upset? Is it about the god glass?"

He clasped his fingers together over his mouth like a child hiding his excitement, his irises dancing with glee.

"They are very upset," he said, almost giggling. Which was odd. Normally, if the supernatural world was upset, Rocket was upset.

"I know, I know. I broke the rules."

"You didn't break the rules," he said, shaking his head, suddenly serious. "You broke *the* rule."

Figured. I was always breaking some celestial being's rules. They could bite my ass. Every last one of them. I was doing the best I could with what they gave me. If they wanted me to do better, they should have graced me with the *Girl's Guide to Grim Reaperism*. Instead, I somehow ended up with Harry Potter's map, where I had to solemnly swear I was up to no good before it would show me anything. And I couldn't lie about it, so I had to constantly be up to no good. It was exhausting.

"Whatever," I said, ignoring his scandalized gasp. "If I show you the god glass, the gate, will you tell me what these names mean?"

His brows cinched together in confusion. "You know what they mean. They are those of good spirit who have passed."

"Yes, you've told me that. But what else do they mean? Are they somehow connected with my daughter?"

He gasped again. "That is another rule you broke, Miss Charlotte. They'll tie you to your bed."

I'd forgotten that whole banging of Mr. Farrow and the pregnancy that followed seemed to have caused quite the uproar in the floor one level up. Another thing they could all bite me over. "The only person who's going to tie me to my bed is Reyes."

At the mention of Reyes's name, Rocket turned his back to me. "You should stay away from him."

"We're married, hon. That would be difficult."

"The sun can't marry the moon. It makes no sense. The heavens will fall." He turned back and pleaded with me. "Everything will fall, Miss Charlotte."

I reached up and put a hand on his pale gray cheek. "Nothing is going to fall, hon, except maybe this building if you don't stop carving into the walls like this."

He glanced around. "I have to write the names or they burn my brain. I have to get them out when it's time."

"You have to write them when the person dies?"

He nodded as he studied his works of art.

"But why these particular names? What do they mean?"

"They're in the waiting room, and their names have to be written down before they can be called. Otherwise, the doctor will never see them."

"And how do you know who is who? Can you read them?" He'd led me to particular names before. He had to have been reading them.

"I don't have to read them, Miss Charlotte. They tell me who they are when I ask."

I'd known it would be a long shot before I came, but I'd hoped for at least a little more. An inkling of what Strawberry had told me. In fact . . .

"So, Strawberry told me the names are important for a reason. That you're writing them for my daughter. For Beep—Elwyn. Is that true?"

He blinked as though I'd stumped him. Stepped closer to a wall. Ran a chubby finger over one of the names he'd carved. But he didn't respond, and I didn't want to push him too far.

"Okay, Rocket," I said, stuffing a hand down my pants. Well, the pocket, anyway. "I'll show you the gate."

"Everything," he said, his voice suddenly far away. "Everything."

I left the god glass be, walked to his side, and examined the name he was tracing. It was in Arabic, a language I knew but couldn't read. The next was in Spanish. The one underneath that Korean.

"Everything?" I asked.

"What will happen when he finds out what you've done?"

"Who? No, wait. What'd I do?"

"The son," he said, his voice sad. Despondent. "The sun cannot marry the moon."

"Rocket." I turned him to face me. It was like turning a Zamboni. Not with the steering wheel, but by standing on the ice in front of it and pushing. "When you say the sun cannot marry the moon, do you mean like the sun in the sky?"

He shook his head. "No, Miss Charlotte. He is the son and the brother and the father. He is the destroyer and the darkness. He is the everything."

"So, I'm not the sun in your metaphor?" I asked, more than a little disappointed. "I'm the moon?" I'd just figured the sun was in reference to my bright-ass light. How on earth did I rate the moon? Then I remembered I loved the moon, and I was happy again.

Rocket placed his hands on my arms. "Don't tell him what you've done, Miss Charlotte."

The guy had never known his own strength. His fingers bit into my skin, and when he shook me, my teeth rattled.

"Don't ever tell him. The son is the most dangerous of the three."

"The three?" I asked from between clattering teeth. "The three gods of Uzan?" I gaped at him. "Is that who you're talking about?"

"He is the most dangerous, Miss Charlotte. He will scorch the world and everything in it. He will turn the mountains to ash and the seas to salt. And there will be nothing left but the dust in the wind."

Aw, I loved that song.

He let go of me, and I knew the moment he did what was going to happen. He disappeared. I shot forward to try to grab him, to try to keep him with me a bit longer, but he was gone by the time I realized I may have overshot my mark. I stumbled forward and caught myself on the opposite wall. With my face.

My face had been through a lot already, and the day was still relatively young.

I rubbed my cheek and replayed what Rocket had said. None of it boded well for the world, but Reyes would never do that. His daughter lived on this world. He would never burn it to the ground. He would never destroy it.

Unless . . . I'd been heading back down to the basement to make my escape, singing "Dust in the Wind," when I stopped halfway down the stairs. Unless he found out what I did.

I covered my mouth with a hand, suddenly worried he'd find out the truth. Then I remembered I had no idea what that truth might entail or why Reyes would care. Did it have something to do with the god glass and the fact that I was carrying around an entire dimension in my pocket? I didn't do anything but trap a minion of evil inside a hell dimension. How mad could he be?

Rocket didn't even look at the god glass, and he'd been so excited. I felt like I'd ripped him off in some way. Like I'd cheated him out of a little excitement.

Next time.

It wasn't until I'd scurried out the basement window that something else he'd said hit me. The moon. In my original language, my celestial language, there was a word that sounded like we would say "the moon." It sounded a bit more like *dtha-muhn*. It would be like comparing Luke, as in moon, to look, as in *muhn*. Could that have been what he was saying all along? The words were similar, but the meanings were worlds apart.

The word *dtha-muhn* in my language could be used in a number of ways, but it all boiled down to one simple concept: the idea of a single omniscient overseer of life. And, more specifically, one who takes it at will. Like a slayer. Or an assassin. Or an executioner. In the celestial realm, the only comparison I could come up with would be the angel of death.

But I was none of those. Gods didn't take life. They gave it. Created it, even. Or at least that's what I'd grown up believing. But then I looked at the gods of Uzan. They seemed capable of nothing but death and destruction. Surely that wasn't what Rocket meant.

I dropped off the salsa to a very grateful Cookie and tried to dismiss the idea, but it lingered in the back of my mind all the way to the station, where I had a certain cop to harass. Two, actually.

At least Beep was safe. I could be grateful for that. Right?

10

I think senility is going to be a fairly smooth transition for me.
—TRUE FACT

Beep is safe.

I repeated that mantra over and over, certain that if I said it enough, I'd believe it.

"Hey there," I said, making my voice as deep and sultry as I could. Officer Taft looked up from the paperwork he'd been filling out on his computer. Or playing Pac-Man. It was hard to tell. I'd caught him just as his shift started, knowing that would probably be the only time I could before he ventured out to make our streets a safer place.

"Davidson," he said, glancing around to make sure no one noticed me talking to him. He was so touchy about his rep. And, quite frankly, it wasn't that great. "Is she here?"

Strawberry Shortcake, a.k.a. Rebecca, was Taft's little sister. I'd been playing messenger for some time, and while I loved the position, the benefits sucked.

"I want a raise," I said, sitting uninvited in the chair beside his desk.

"I don't pay you."

"Exactly."

His mouth thinned across his face as he went back to what he was doing. He wasn't bad looking. Not at all. He'd filled out, in fact. Had started lifting weights. Or eating more doughnuts. It was hard to say. Either way, he looked good. Older. More coppy. Especially with his sharp blue eyes and dark military cut.

"She's fine," I said in answer to the burning question he wanted to ask.

He gave me his attention again. "Really? She's not, you know, lonely?"

"Please. That kid never met a stranger, even in the afterlife, and there are definitely beings she should avoid there."

"Is she in danger?" he asked, alarmed.

"No, Taft. She's perfectly safe and playing up a storm with Rocket and the gang." I'd noticed a photo sticking out from underneath a form. "What are you working on?"

He followed my gaze and scooped up the pile of papers before I could get a better look. "Nothing."

"Fine. So, I'm working the Adams case, and I noticed in the report that you were the first officer on scene."

"You're on the Adams case? Did the boyfriend hire you?"

"Taft, you know I can't tell you that. You look good, by the way."

He sat back in his chair and crossed his arms over his chest. "Okay, let me have it."

"What?" Some people were so suspicious.

"The only time you tell me I look good is when you want something."

"That is so not true." It was, actually, but I could argue with a parking meter. "I just want to get an idea of what you think of the case."

"Do your own legwork, Davidson."

He went back to punching keys, chomping dots and fruit and following it up with a discreet fist pump. I was almost impressed. "I didn't even glance at your legs. I've been hired. For reals. They're going to pay me and everything." I hoped. "And I have permission from the higher-ups to interview you."

He stopped playing and leveled a dubious smirk on me. "How high?"

"High-ish. Mid-level-y?"

"Why don't you bug your uncle?"

"Not his case. It's Joplin's. Joplin hates me."

"I can't imagine why."

"Right? So, the car?"

"Fine, what do I think?" He handed me a file folder, put his elbows on the arms of his chair, and clasped his fingers. "I think a beautiful, smart woman suffered a horrible death at the hands of her jealous boyfriend."

"Really?" I opened the file. It held his report only. But I had yet to read it, as it wasn't in the file Parker slipped me. "You're liking the boyfriend for this?"

"Who else? Have you seen the mountain of evidence against him?"

"I haven't seen any of it." And I hadn't. Not literally.

"His fingerprints were in the car."

"They were dating."

"The prints were in the blood, Davidson. After the incident occurred. In more than one place."

"He found the car. He opened the door and touched the blood, which was apparently everywhere, when he searched for her."

"What's there to search? He opened the door. She wasn't in the car. The car was drenched in blood. He was drenched in blood."

"There was a sleeping bag in the backseat. He thought she might be in it. He crawled inside to check it."

"So he crawls through buckets of blood to check a sleeping bag he could have checked by going around to the other side and opening another door?"

He had a good point, but there was an explanation. I just wasn't telling him what it was. Ammunition should this go to trial. That door handle was tricky and would only unlock with the remote. The interior door locks didn't work on it. If they didn't figure that out on their own, they would look incompetent, and that always helped.

I handed the file back to him. "That's all circumstantial."

Taft leaned forward and played his trump card. "He's done it before."

After taking care to guard my surprise, I gauged his emotions. He wasn't lying. "What do you mean?"

"Have you even checked into this guy's background? Did three years. Man two."

Manslaughter? Damn it. Parker didn't mention that part. It would make my job harder, but not impossible. I didn't care what the guy did in his past life. He was innocent of killing Emery Adams.

"So, that's why you guys are jumping on the arrest so fast."

"Pretty good reason, if you ask me. Once a murderer—"

"Manslaughter is a far cry from murder."

"He was directly responsible for another person's death. If that's not murder . . ."

Feeling more ill equipped to handle this case than I had, I flew back to the office to check on Cookie's progress and to do a few background checks of my own, all the while trying to figure out how to get close to a god without being detected. If one or both of the gods of Uzan were hijacking humans and discarding their dead bodies willy-nilly, they needed to be stopped sooner than later. This wasn't just about Beep anymore.

Well, it was mostly about her, but people were dying, and I couldn't help but take a little of the blame. We'd been warned, Reyes and I. We'd been told not to consummate our relationship, though admittedly we weren't warned until the deed had been done. Several times. In more than one location. And on a variety of surfaces.

"I'm glad you're here," Cookie said, rushing over to me. She handed me a file on Lyle Fiske. After my conversation with Taft, I dreaded looking at it.

"So," I said, regarding her hopefully, "thumbs-up or thumbs-down?"

"It's debatable. I will say after what you told me about him, take everything you read here with a grain of salt."

"Will do."

I read for several hours from the plethora of info she'd dug up on both Lyle Fiske and Emery Adams before doing my own investigation on a third cog that just didn't quite fit. Why was Parker so convinced of Fiske's innocence? Or was this about something else? And why did he purposely leave the man two conviction out of Fiske's file? I was certain he did that on purpose.

Cookie took off to pick up Amber from school while I read late into the afternoon. Fiske was a fraternity president at UNM. A kid died in a hazing accident on his watch, and it happened to be around the time fraternity hazings were under fire from the media, activists, and politicians. To make an example of him, the judge sentenced him to five years for negligent homicide. He got out early for good behavior.

His record would make it more difficult for a jury to acquit him no matter how much Nick Parker tried to sabotage the case. And his career in the process.

A search of the shady ADA's digital footprint showed that he had been in the same fraternity as Lyle. He did say they were old college buddies. He failed to mention the frat connection. Or the hazing accident.

A general background search didn't reveal a whole lot on Emery's grieving father other than the fact that he'd made a couple of bad business investments over the years. Who hadn't? I still couldn't believe Martian Barbie didn't take off.

I did find out Emery had wanted to become a nurse when she'd started college. Specifically, a trauma nurse. She ended up getting her doctorate in medicine but went on to get a Ph.D. in hospital administration.

She drove the speed limit. Paid her bills on time. Even finished reports early.

I sat back, suddenly realizing what was going on. How could I have been so stupid? Emery Adams was a robot sent from an alien world to study our strange ways. Clearly she was missing the point of being human.

I texted Cookie to let her know I was going to check out Emery's car. I almost stopped in the restaurant to check on the rascally son of Satan, but I stopped myself. It wouldn't do any good, so I drove back to the station.

I began my investigation by harassing a couple of cops at impound, then headed to where they were keeping Emery's car. The one supposedly drenched in so much blood, they couldn't decipher the true color of the interior until they looked up the car title.

I would visit the actual crime scene later. It was getting dark, and the car was found in a remote area. One thing about New Mexico: we had our fair share of remote areas.

Squaring off against a curmudgeonly guard who had zero intention of letting me see the car, I fought the urge to recommend trying Rogaine. The CIB had already gone over the car with a fine-toothed forensics kit, so it wasn't like I could contaminate the evidence.

Fortunately, Parker had arranged for me to have full access to everything, so the guy had no choice but to let me see it.

Unfortunately, it didn't take long for blood to spoil.

The officer shrugged his round shoulders, found the keys, and led me to the car as slowly as he possibly could. The smell hit me long before the reality of it did. I wasn't even close enough to see inside. I had to stop, put my hands on my knees, and take a deep breath.

"You sure you wanna do this?" the officer asked. I got the feeling he didn't want to get any closer to the car than necessary, either.

I nodded, filled my lungs, and held my breath as he unlocked the car and stepped back, not wanting to be anywhere near it when I opened the door.

I scanned the interior from where I stood, hoping Emery would still be inside just waiting for someone who could see the departed to show up so she could tell them who killed her. Was that too much to hope for?

'Parently.

She was nowhere to be found. Had probably crossed the moment she left her still body.

Speaking of which . . . if the killer left all this blood out in the open, clearly having killed someone inside, why take the body? Lyle discovered the car that night around midnight. Maybe the culprit had planned to come back for the car and dump it. Why else leave it out in the open like that? Unless the body had some kind of incriminating evidence, but if the killer was so worried about evidence, surely he would know that the car would be covered in incriminations of every size and shape.

Yet there was none. CIB found no evidence pointing to anyone other than Lyle Fiske. No other fingerprints. So suspicious fibers or stray hairs. I couldn't walk to my kitchen without leaving some kind of incriminating evidence behind. I could find hair in places I'd never visited in my life. And yet there was none in the car. Not even from her dad? Her best friend? A coworker?

Besides the blood, the car was pristine.

So, naturally, anything Fiske had touched or shed would seem highly suspicious. And Taft said he'd done it before. He'd killed before.

I bit my lip, fought a wave of nausea, and stepped even closer. I wasn't wrong. Fiske did not do this. But whoever did knew a lot about crime scene investigation. Enough to do a bloody good job of framing him.

I opened the door. Perhaps it was because I hadn't eaten in a while or I'd been stressed about Beep or I'd been manhandled by a large child, but my face once again headed straight for the ground. This time all on its own.

"You okay?" the officer asked as he held out a paper cup.

We were in a cage that held weapons and ammunition and file cabinets.

It smelled like metal and dust and gunpowder, which was way better than Emery's car had smelled. I feared Eau du Death would never take off. The mere thought of it caused my stomach to clench yet again, and I fought the heave with everything I had. I failed.

The officer kicked a metal trash can over to me as I fell to my knees and made the most humiliating retching sounds I'd ever heard from man or beast. They echoed off the metal that somehow muffled and amplified the sounds at the same time.

Ignoring the laughter coming from outside the cage—there were several cops hanging around—I wiped my mouth on a sleeve and sat back on the chair. At least now I'd have some interesting fodder next time I played Never Have I Ever.

Cookie texted me saying she was taking some files home and to pick them up from her when I got in.

Mr. Adams had mentioned that Emery was very close to her grandfather. If someone was stalking her or if she'd received any threats, he might be the only one she'd tell.

Even though it was getting late, I drove out to the Morningwood Retirement Community—which sounded like it had been designed by a horny botanist. Oddly enough, Mrs. Allen from the complex was now living here, too, with her poodle, Prince Phillip, a.k.a. PP.

I stopped at the office to let the administrators know who I was and what I was doing there, though the residents had their own apartments. This was assisted living, but not like a nursing home, so that was nice.

The receptionist drew my route on a map to point me toward Mr. Geoff Adams Sr.'s apartment. I asked about Mrs. Allen as well, but she told me Mrs. A. was in the actual nursing home on account of the fact that she liked to take PP for walks and would sometimes end up on Alameda Boulevard in her nightie and socks. To see her, I'd have to come back during visiting hours and sign in at the next building.

I made a mental note to come back ASAP and then headed toward Mr. Adams Sr.'s place.

I'd originally thought the name of the retirement center odd, but driving through the housing units confirmed it. I entered on Morningwood Lane. Turned left at Pussy Willow Drive. Right on Peter Pepper Place. Left on Cockscomb Court. And finally right on Wang Peonies Way.

Oh yeah, this community was definitely planned by a horny botanist.

A part of me hoped Emery would be with her grandfather. If they were as close as Mr. Adams said and her grandfather was elderly, possibly even sickly, she could've stuck around for him. No such luck.

Mr. Adams Sr. was a hardy man in his early seventies who only lived at the center because he didn't want to take care of a yard anymore.

"They do everything," he said, handing me a cup of coffee, the liquid threatening to spill over the top with his shaking.

Grief had covered him like a cloak. I worried he'd go downhill now that his granddaughter had passed away.

He tried so hard to make everything look normal. Like he wasn't crumbling inside. "They do all the yard work. All the cooking. We have to go to the cafeteria, but the food's not half-bad. All the cleaning. It's— it's great here."

As he fell silent, his mind consumed with sadness, I studied him further. He had a full head of silvery-gray hair and a farmer's tan. He wore shorts in the winter and a country club sweater. And his grief was so all-consuming, I had to block it before I passed out. Again.

He snapped back to the present and raked a hand over his face. "There's a golf course and tennis courts right down the road."

I nodded. "Mr. Adams, did Emery say anything to you about being worried? Maybe someone was following her or calling and hanging up?" I let a wave of grief wash over him as he fought back tears with all his strength before continuing. "Anything that would suggest she was in danger?"

His shoulders shook, and he coughed into a handkerchief.

"She didn't—no, not that I know of," he said when he'd recovered. "She never mentioned anything to me."

"Did she seem worried or anxious lately?"

At first he shook his head, then he thought about it. "Actually, yes. For the last few weeks, she'd seemed distracted. Upset, even."

"Did she say why?"

"No, and I didn't push it. She just said she was having some issues at work."

"At the hospital."

"Yes. She was the administrator." His face softened with pride. "Youngest in their history."

"I read that. You must have been so proud of her."

"Honey, that girl made me proud every time she took a step. She was the perfect kid, which was something considering her childhood."

"Her childhood?"

"Oh, you know. Just everyday stuff, I guess. Need a refill?"

He was changing the subject, especially since I hadn't touched my coffee yet. "Mr. Adams, anything you can tell me, no matter how minor or seemingly inconsequential, may help me find who did this."

He hung his head. "It's my fault, really. I should have been harder on the boy."

"The boy?"

"My namesake. My son. He doesn't have the willpower that Emmy and I have. I worked hard for what I have. I wanted a better life than I had for my boy. Figured out I had a head for business and was very successful at a very young age. So, Junior grew up wanting for nothing. I think—well, my wife, God rest her soul, warned me over and over to stop indulging him, but I was so busy, and it was just easier to give in."

"So, he grew up privileged."

"He grew up spoiled. Never had the resoluteness that Emmy and I had. It was always one failed venture after another. I finally quit sinking money into his schemes. His marriage had fallen apart. Then Emmy's mother died."

"She died?" I asked.

"Breast cancer. She was a good woman. A bit hardheaded, but it was a good head. Emmy was the best of both of them. Smart and creative. A good problem solver. She wasn't afraid of risk, but she always weighed her options and came up with a plan. A thinker, that one. A real thinker."

"Which was why she made such a great administrator."

He nodded. I rose from the chair to look at the photos on his mantel while he struggled with another wave of grief. He had several pictures of Emery growing up. She was beautiful. Long, dark blond hair. Wide inquisitive eyes. His grief was affecting me, pouring into my rib cage and dissolving my bones.

"Can you think of any other reason she might have been upset lately?"

"Like I said. The boy."

"Her father? He had upset her?"

"He always upset her. Again, he's not the most stable person. Their roles were switched most of her life. She had to be the responsible one while he went off half-cocked on this adventure or that. She didn't have a childhood, really. Had to grow up entirely too fast. And through it all, through everything Emmy had gone through, she never asked me for anything."

"She was independent, even growing up?"

"Oh yes. She wouldn't let me do any extra for her. When she was in Girl Scouts, every year she would only let me buy three boxes of cookies, like everyone else who was addicted to Thin Mints. She would not accept favors. When she was in high school, her dad managed to buy her a car. I remember her face. She was so excited, but God only knows how illegal that transaction was."

Mr. Adams's face grew somber.

"And yet when he lost everything two months later in a Ponzi scheme and had to hock it, she wouldn't even come to me. She wouldn't even ask for help to get her car back. Two thousand dollars. He lost a fifteen thousand–dollar car for a two thousand–dollar debt. I carry that much in my front pocket."

Alarmed, I asked, "Are you sure that's safe?"

He cast me a warm expression. "You want to know the worst part?"

I nodded even though I kind of didn't.

"She wasn't even upset. She wasn't disappointed. A junior in high school lost her car, and she wasn't the least bit agitated. She'd never expected to keep it as long as she had, she was so used to being let down. She was so used to being disappointed. She was so used to coming second to everything else in his life."

"Why was she like that?" I asked, more troubled than I thought I would be. "Why wouldn't she accept money from you? You're family."

"I asked her that once. She told me that she saw how I looked at her dad, at my son, and she never wanted me to look at her that way."

His last words were so broken they were hard to decipher. He broke down. His shoulders shaking. A strong hand over his eyes.

I let him grieve, knowing that was my cue to leave, but there was one more thing that I didn't quite buy.

When he recovered enough to continue, I asked him, "Mr. Adams, this is going to be a very indelicate question, but if you have so much money, why are you living in this tiny apartment in a retirement center? I'm not sure I buy the yard work argument. You could afford a hundred gardeners."

"About two years ago, right after Emmy got her job at the hospital, I decided I didn't want to waste another nickel on myself and my stupid spending habits. I retired and liquidated everything. I scraped together every penny I had and put it in a trust fund for Emmy. On the day I die, she was supposed to get millions. I wanted it all to go to her." He broke down again, and it took him a moment to say, "I never expected to out-live her. How is something like this even fair?"

It wasn't.

After I walked Mr. Adams to the center's dining room for dinner, I thanked him and headed home. It was late, and smelling the food in the dining room seemed to help my appetite find its way back to me after its recent hiatus. I think it went to Scotland.

Mr. Adams was a wonderful man, and I would be checking on him every time I came to see Mrs. Allen.

11

*If one door closes and another one opens,
your house is probably haunted.*
—BUMPER STICKER

I walked into the apartment knowing full well Mr. Farrow was there. I felt him as I was walking up the stairs even though we now had an elevator.

After putting my bag down, I sought him out. "I think we should talk about what's going on."

He almost looked up from his desk. "Why? What's going on?"

"Nothing. That's kind of the problem."

I wasn't used to being ignored. Well, actually I was, but not from Reyes, and yet Reyes had been doing that very thing for several days. It was eating at me in the same way a person on bath salts eats at the flesh of others. Strangely and disturbingly.

"Are you seeing someone else?"

I'd shocked him. The look on his face, which I had to rely on because I could no longer decipher his every emotion, told me so. Perhaps that bothered me more than I'd imagined. That I could no longer read him as precisely as I used to. Like an electrical field was fucking with my sensors. Giving me false readings.

"I did have amnesia. I figured you might have found someone else in that time. You know, someone less work and more fun." My thoughts went to Mrs. Abelson. I'd made fun of her because she was so high maintenance, but maybe I was, too. Maybe Reyes just needed to play video games with his friends and smoke a little weed. To relax. To get over the stress of living with yours truly. I was exactly like her.

"Look, you know if you ever just need to play video games and smoke pot, you can tell me, right?"

"Are you on medication?"

"No. I'm serious. I know . . . I know I can be a little much at times. I would understand if you just needed a break."

"Okay. Well, thanks for the offer, but I'm good."

"Then what's bothering you?"

"Nothing."

"Fine. Okay, then why haven't we . . . you know." I shrugged so he would get the picture.

"Why haven't we shrugged?"

"No. Had sex. Why haven't we had sex? I mean, a week ago you couldn't keep your hands off me and now—oh, my god." It hit me. In the solar plexus. Hard enough to knock the wind out of me.

"You liked me better as an amnesiac."

"Did I?" he asked, amused.

"Only you can answer that. Why haven't you—? Why aren't you—I?"

"Happy and content? I am."

I blew a stray hair out of my eyes. "Let me get this straight. You have no intention of telling me what's wrong. You don't want to talk about whatever is wrong. And you're going to let me continue to believe I've done something horrible before you'll open up. Even if, say, I restrain you? Force it out of you?"

"The only thing you are going to force out of me under the confinement of restraints is an orgasm."

Finally! "So, you'd be open to my restraining you for my own sexual pleasure?"

"Wide open."

"And, it would be something you'd enjoy?"

"Who wouldn't?"

"Then why haven't we—? I mean, what's stopping us from—?"

This was getting me nowhere. I wasn't a shrinking violet. I knew how to speak my mind. A little too well. I couldn't remember the last time I'd used my internal filter. It had been so long, I'd forgotten where I stashed it. But when it came to Reyes Alexander Farrow, I lost all sense of uncouth. I turned couth. It was just so unlike me.

I took a deep breath and started over. "Why haven't you touched me?"

He reached over and poked my elbow.

"Funny, but you know what I mean."

"I'm giving you time."

"Time for what? Origami lessons?"

"I'm giving you space."

"Space for what? The elephant I've been trying to adopt?" I looked around. "He'll need a pretty big play area."

"I'm sure."

"Just tell me what's bothering you." Did he know? Did he know he was a god and that I knew he was a god and that I had the only thing in the universe that could trap him for all eternity? Fingers crossed he didn't.

After a long moment of contemplation, he released the breath he'd been holding. "Nothing is bothering me, Dutch."

"That's it," I said, putting my foot down and girding my loins. Metaphorically. "If you won't tell me, I'm moving in with Cookie."

"Again?"

I ground my teeth, stomped to our bedroom, took down an overnight bag, and stuffed it with a toothbrush, a few mismatched articles of clothing, and a nightshirt that read DRIVE IT LIKE YOU STOLE IT. Then, without another word, I marched to the door, opened it, and had every intention of slamming it so hard the shock wave would shake the building, when I heard him say, "Don't let the door hit your ass on the way out."

Appalled, I stopped mid-swing. Or I tried to. I'd put so much energy into the door thing that it kept coming despite my wishes. Only I'd turned back to Reyes. And that was when my face found yet another object to slam into.

"I'm moving in," I said, marching past Cookie when she opened her door.

"Again?"

"I mean it this time, Cook. That man is impossible." I pointed in the general direction of our apartment in case she didn't know who I was talking about.

But before I could form another word, I noticed a particularly mouth-watering scent in the air. "What's that smell?" I asked, sniffing.

A nervous laugh bubbled out of her. "What smell? There's no smell." She eased toward the kitchen as though to block me. She may have been bigger, but I could tackle a 225-pound tight end given the right motivation.

Then it hit me. The truth. The betrayal. I gasped. And gaped. And glared. For, like, a really long time, until she crumbled like the cowardly traitor she was.

"I was hungry," she said, her shoulders deflating in shame.

"Really?"

"You were off doing whatever it is you do."

"La Satilla?"

"And I didn't feel like cooking."

"You got chile rellenos from La Satilla?"

"Only a few."

"And you didn't feel the need to mention it?"

"I was going to. I swear. But it all happened so fast."

"You know what their chile rellenos do to me."

She finally let a saucy grin slip. "I got stuffed sopapillas, too."

I dropped my bag and rubbed my hands together. "Looks like I moved in at just the right moment."

She laughed as we went to her kitchen and started arranging the feast. Amber strolled in with a dimple-faced Quentin in tow, the two of them as charming as ever.

"Hey, Aunt Charley," she said, giving me a quick hug. "Did you move in again? I saw your bag."

"Yes, I did."

"Sweet." She signed the entire time she spoke for Quentin's benefit, then she turned to him and explained, her movements quick and silent.

Quentin laughed and said I had a screw loose. Like literally. He signed, "Screw loose." I pounced, attacking him for his insolence, using that as an excuse to give him a great big bear hug. He hugged back, wrapping his long arms around me. He was a really good hugger.

After the reunion, the two of them made a plate and headed for the family room.

"Should I talk to her tonight?" I whispered to Cook.

"Nah. We have some time to decide how to go about it."

I nodded.

"Oh!" Amber shouted back from over her shoulder. "We're still working on the video. We have a lead we're checking out now, but it has over eight hundred thousand hits."

"That's so great!" I shouted back.

Cookie closed her eyes in horror. "That's so bad."

I chuckled and waited for Uncle Bob to walk in. He was in a mood. I could feel him the moment he got out of his car three stories down.

"Hey, you," I said when he walked in and hung up his coat.

"Oh, hey, pumpkin. Moving in again?"

For the second time in as many minutes, I grabbed the first hug. "Yeah. I've named your sofa Fabio."

"Fantastic. It looks like a Fabio."

"Right? Blond and inviting with hills and valleys in all the right places."

"But you know we have seven thousand guest rooms now. You don't have to sleep on the sofa." He walked around the island to give his wife a hug. And a kiss. A really long kiss that may or may not have involved tongues.

I fought my gag reflex and finally interrupted. "So, what's going on?"

"Not much."

"You seem agitated."

He tore his gaze off Cook to look at me. "Nope. Is Amber home yet?"

I'd thrown Cookie with the agitated comment, but she recovered quickly. "Yeah. She and Quentin are eating in the family room. They're working on a case."

"A case, huh?"

"The video."

"Ah," he said as he made a plate.

"Is she in trouble?"

He stopped and looked up at me. "Why would she be in trouble?"

"I don't know. You just seem agitated. And she's a teen. Fits."

"No, Charley, Amber is not in trouble. The day that kid gives us a minute of trouble will be the day I hang up my badge."

I snorted and was on the verge of giving him a greatest hits compilation of the adventures of Amber Kowalski when Cookie cleared her throat and glared at me from behind Ubie's back.

"Oh, right," I mouthed. Thankfully, Ubie was studying the fare. I gave her a thumbs-up sign and changed the subject. "Did you grill Joplin yet?"

"Why would I grill Joplin? This smells incredible."

"Because he's the detective on our case."

"Exactly. Your case. You grill him."

"He hates me."

"He hates everyone."

"True."

He was calming down. Cookie did that to him, but it didn't make his earlier agitation any less concerning. Whatever had his hackles in an up-roar could wait. It was probably work related, anyway.

He cleared magazines off the table, and we sat down to eat. The three of us at the table. The kids in the family room investigating a video of a possessed little girl. We were like the fallout of a nuclear family. I only felt a little guilty for eating without my love nugget. Then again, he was a spatula away from being a bona fide chef. He could fend for himself.

Amber came back in for seconds and gave him a hug. "Hey, Ubie." She'd started calling him Ubie because calling her stepdad "Uncle Bob" sounded wrong on all kinds of levels. I agreed wholeheartedly.

She gave him a kiss on the cheek, grabbed another chile relleno along with more chips and salsa, and headed back to the family room. Before she got ten feet, she pulled a U-ey and stuck her head through the door-way. "I almost forgot. A blogger who goes by the name of SpectorySam would like an interview with you."

"With me?" I asked.

"Yeah. About the video. He wants to do a whole feature and is pretty sure he can get it on *Huffington Post*."

If I didn't think Cookie would pass out, I'd have said yes. "That's okay. Tell him I'm not giving interviews right now and to contact my agent. It'll make me sound important."

"Okay," she said with a giggle as she pranced off.

"That girl should be in show business," I said to Cookie.

"Oh, hell, no."

"Not in a child-star capacity. Those poor kids. But more like an extra in a Tide commercial."

Her brows formed one continuous hard line. I fought the urge to cough and say "unibrow" from behind my fist. It was so juvenile. The real trick was to do that during a sneeze. Sneezes were harder to fake.

"I'll think about it," she said. She was lying.

"So, what do you think he's doing?" I asked.

Uncle Bob looked at his watch. "Damn it." He took out a five and put it on the table.

Cookie snatched it up and displayed it between her fingers, making it dance and do flips like she'd won the lottery.

"What's going on?" I asked.

"You beat your record by five minutes," he said.

"I told you." Cookie squirmed with excitement in her chair.

"What the hell?" I asked, pretending to be offended.

"Last time you didn't start asking about him, wondering what he was doing, begging for us to go borrow a cup of sugar to check on him, for a whole thirty-*five* minutes," he explained.

"You broke your record," Cookie said, tearing up. "I'm so proud of you."

"Oh yeah, you guys are a riot. A laugh a minute." I stabbed my relleno and shoved a huge piece into my mouth right before I said, "No, really, what do you think he's doing?"

No matter how much I begged, neither of them would go across the hall—it was like ten feet—to check on my beloved. And I refused to sink to stalking, which I could very well have done incorporeally, but I felt like that would be cheating. Also, I was pretty sure he'd know if I were floating around the apartment, following him. Because that's not creepy at all.

So, I got ready for bed and landed in the arms of Fabio.

He wasn't nearly as cooperative as I remembered. Last time I slept with him, he curled around me, pushed his folds into my hips, let me ease a hand between his cushions. This time he was cold and hard, and there was a metal rod between the cushions I was trying to anchor myself to. I tossed this way and that, wishing I'd taken Ubie up on more hospitable accommodations. Not that I could've slept, anyway.

As I lay there contemplating the case and Emery Adams and the gods of Uzan and Beep and my cantankerous husband, I realized I'd forgotten to tell him I was being followed by three men in a minivan.

Oh, well. They were in a minivan. How dangerous could they be?

12

I love asking kids what they want to be when they grow up.
Mostly 'cause I'm still looking for ideas.
—MEME

I woke up to the smell of coffee brewing and bacon sizzling, but nature was calling. I wandered into the little girls' room to answer it and brush my teeth. When I walked into the kitchen, Cookie was still in her robe, checking e-mail on her phone.

I smacked my lips and then headed for the Keurig. "I don't know how this happened, but I think I just ate lotion."

"My ex is such a douche."

"How is it I've never met him?" I grabbed a coffee cup from the coffee cup cabinet. It was like a magic box full of devices specifically made to hold the blood of my enemy. Or coffee. They were equally capable of both.

"He said no."

"How dare he," I said, currently in the role of support personnel.

"I mean, I'm pretty hesitant myself, but he just flat out said no."

"We could sue," I offered, stepping into the role of legal advisor. I rested against the counter and took the biggest drink I could manage—of coffee, not the blood of my enemy—without requiring medical attention for third-degree burns in my piehole.

"It's going to break Amber's heart."

I straightened and slipped into the role of BFF for life. "Oh, hell, no. Where's your baseball bat? He has kneecaps, right?"

"It might come to that. It's like he says no to things just to punish me. He uses his privilege of shared custody as a weapon against me, completely uninterested in what it does to Amber."

I stepped over to her. "I'm sorry, hon. What's going on?"

"I told him about NMSD and how Amber wants to go. He said no. Period. He will not allow her to be exposed."

"Exposed?" I asked, completely offended, and I wasn't even Deaf. "Exposed to what? A culture rich in history and traditions? A proud and powerful group of people who have to put up with more shit in one day than we have to all year? I mean, have you even tried to order a pizza through relay? Nightmare."

"Exactly. She could learn so much."

I put on my best mafioso and asked, "You want I should talk to him?"

She laughed softly. "No. I'll do it. I can do it. Besides, the last time you helped, *Fredo,* there were dead fish showing up all over town, only these were gift wrapped and delivered by Pappadeaux. Cost us a fortune."

"Hey, at least I got the message out. You do *not* want to mess with us. And we got some lovely thank-you cards in return."

"I don't think that's how it works."

"Wait, why Fredo?"

"I'll talk to him myself."

"Isn't he shot in the head on orders from his own brother?"

"I'll probably have to cave on something else he wants. God only knows what that might be."

"What?" I asked, suddenly very interested. "So he manipulates situations like this to get his way with other things?"

She looked up at me and blinked. "That's what marriages are based on."

"Okay, but didn't you divorce him?"

"Not the point."

" 'Cause, if not, we should mention that to Uncle Bob."

"Are you kidding me? I have plans for that boy. He will never be the same after I'm done with him."

I laughed. "I don't doubt that for a microsecond."

"He left early, by the way."

"Uncle Bob? Yeah, I heard him."

"No. Mr. Farrow."

"Ah yes. Mr. Smexy. The bane and bliss—mostly bliss—of my existence."

"You know, you could do something crazy and talk to him. Open up a bit. Tell him about the you-know-who and the you-know-what."

No idea what she was talking about. "I tried that. Last night. He is the stubbornest, most unwavering, bullheaded—"

"All synonyms of the same concept. One that, I daresay, applies to you as well."

I gaped at her.

"Only sometimes," she added. "Like yesterday when you ordered a burrito and they brought you a burger. You were totally flexible."

She had a point. I had stretched before going in. Did a few lunges to warm up. I'm always more flexible after a good warm-up. I could even do the splits if the situation demanded. And it was amazing how often the situation actually did demand.

I felt eyes on the back of my neck as I walked to the office.

I got that a lot. Those prickly feelings that someone was watching me. Odds are, someone was. It could have been the Vatican guy. I hadn't checked up on him since being back. I thought, perhaps, the Vatican had fired him. His cover was blown, after all. But now I wondered. The person wasn't familiar to me, so I knew it wasn't Garrett. I could feel him when he was close. I could feel Cookie and Ubie and Gemma. They had a very distinct vibration. A distinct essence that I now recognized. No, this was someone else. Perhaps more than one.

I finally found the source. The three amigos were back. Their lime green minivan sat about half a block away. I got the feeling they didn't have a lot of money to throw at their stalking hobby. Or experience tailing people.

Before I could do anything about it, I felt a more familiar presence. I spotted the homeless girl I'd seen the day before down the street. She was leaning against Boyd's in the same clothes, but she had her stuff with her. She'd gone back to get it, thankfully. I was worried someone else would get to it first.

Mr. Boyd came out then. In the sea of people bustling here and there, mostly college students trying to get to class, he'd singled her out. Walked over to her. Tried to hand her another yogurt and juice. He also had an apple, and I couldn't have come up with a more appropriate metaphor if someone had paid me.

Without saying a thing, I slowly walked over to them. I knew Mr. Boyd flirted with the college kids, the younger the better, all day every day. But this was different. This kid couldn't have been more than fifteen. And honestly, the guy was in his early fifties with a huge black mustache and a belly Jabba the Hutt would be proud of. What on earth made him think any of these young girls would be interested in him? Was he truly that delusional?

I slowed when the kid shook her head at him, pulled the strap of her backpack over her shoulder, and turned to walk away. She'd turned in my direction and spotted me instantly, but I was too busy giving Mr. Boyd the evil eye to offer her a hello.

"What?" he asked, taking a step in my direction.

I lowered my head and took another one in his. Then another until I was between Boyd and the girl. If he wanted a confrontation, he would most definitely get one. I'd been waiting for an opportunity to give him a piece of my gray matter. All squiggly and covered in slime.

Before it came to that, he noticed a couple of people noticing us. Things could get sticky fast for a perv preying so close to a very forward-thinking college campus. He backed down, throwing his hands up and walking back into his store.

When I turned to check on the girl, I'd expected to see her backside hustling down the street, putting as much distance between us as she could. Instead, I found her right where I'd left her. Her black jacket and black hair made her look more Goth than I guessed she was, considering she carried around a pink blanket and backpack.

"This from you?" she asked, pulling a ten out of her front pocket. It was all the cash I'd had yesterday when I stashed it in her things.

"Nope." I pushed my bag higher on my shoulder. "I don't carry cash."

Her lids narrowed as she studied me. "Thanks," she said anyway, not buying it.

I'd totally have to work on my sales pitch. Nobody was buying what I was selling these days. Maybe I'd lost my touch. Or left my touch in New York. Darn. I'd have to go back for it.

Road trip!

"You hungry?" I asked, pointing out the fact that the Frontier was a mere two blocks.

She looked back and then shrugged a shoulder. "I could eat."

I wondered why she hadn't already bought herself something to eat. She was shaking with hunger. Or fear. It could have been the fear causing her slim body to quake.

"Come on. I'm starved."

Thankfully, even though I'd already had a lovely breakfast compliments of Cookie Kowalski-Davidson of runny eggs and burned bacon,

I'd left room for Reyes's homemade chips and salsa. Just in case a basket happened to end up in my arms as I took a shortcut through the restaurant, turned down the scenic route through the kitchen, then headed up the stairs. It was odd how often that kind of thing happened to me.

We ordered breakfast and then navigated the maze that was the Frontier to find a quiet table in the very back room. By the time we found a spot, our number popped up on the screen.

"I'll get it," I said, hoping she wouldn't change her mind and bolt out the back door that stood ten feet from us.

She was uncomfortable but hungry. Her gaze had darted from plate to plate as we'd stood in line to order.

"Well, this looks amazing," I said when I got back. I handed her the orange juice and #1 breakfast plate while I nibbled on a side of carne adovada with a side of carne adovada. One could never have too much carne adovada.

"It does," she said, her wary expression doing a one-eighty and sliding headfirst into lust.

I liked her.

"So," I said, taking small bites. Mostly because I wasn't the least bit hungry. "Got a name?"

She hesitated, then gave me her real name. I was worried she wouldn't. "Heather."

"It's nice to meet you. I'm Charley."

I reached over and took her hand for a formal shake. She let me and then went back to tearing into her food.

"Can you tell me what's going on?"

"Going on?" she asked, stuffing a huge bite into her tiny mouth.

"Why are you living on the streets? There are safer places to live, you know."

"Right." She swallowed and gulped half the juice in one round.

"Then can you tell me how old you are?"

"Eighteen."

I gave her a moment, then asked, "Can you tell me how old you really are?"

She paused and looked at me from underneath her lashes, trying to decide if she could trust me.

"I guess I should have mentioned something before I invited you to breakfast. I have a superpower."

She put her fork down and readied herself to bolt.

"I can feel other people's emotions." When she only squinted at me, trying to figure out my game, I continued. "I can tell when someone is afraid. Or when they are guilty of something. Or when they're mad."

"I'm not mad."

"But you are afraid. I could feel it from a block away."

"For reals?"

"For reals." I spoke as unthreateningly as possible, keeping my tone light and my actions slow, as though totally uninterested in the fact that she was constantly about half a second away from rabbiting. "And you're not eighteen."

"What's it to you?" she asked, suddenly defensive.

"You're making it hard for me to breathe."

"What?"

"When someone is as scared as you are, all the time like you, it tightens my chest and crushes my lungs. It makes it hard to breathe."

"Like asthma?"

"Very much like asthma," I agreed, even though I was certain asthma was a thousand times worse, but it was a good analogy. "Your food's going to get cold."

She scoffed. "Cold food is still food."

"Good point," I said, laughing softly.

It was enough to set her at ease. She picked up her fork and continued eating.

"Nine?" I guessed, purposely insulting her.

She shook her head. "Twelve."

Damn. Even younger than I'd thought. The thought of a twelve-year-old alone on the streets of Albuquerque shocked me.

"So, this superpower," she said as she stabbed at an egg. "You use it for good or evil?"

Oh yeah. I liked her a lot. "It kind of depends on the day. I vacillate between the two depending on the weather. I will say evil is more fun."

She laughed, the sound a little too breathy, her voice a little too husky, like she'd recently been ill.

"Now on to the tough stuff. Why are you scared?"

"I'm not," she said, her barriers rocketing into place around her.

"My lungs don't lie, and you're on the verge of suffocating me." I grabbed my throat with both hands. "Seriously. Not. Much. Time."

As I slowly sank into my chair, she frowned. Took another bite. Then asked, "Are you messing with me?"

"Nope." I straightened. "Maybe a little, but I won't lie to you. Go ahead. Ask me anything."

She sat back, gave me a thorough once-over, then nodded toward another patron. "What's that guy feeling?"

I looked at him. He was an everyday sort, a nerdy college student but handsome as heck with a body to match, and the girl he was sitting with was more beauty queen than science geek. They were studying. He was most likely tutoring her. "He's into the girl."

"Too obvious," she said, disappointed.

"Give me a sec. I'm working here."

She grinned and waited.

"He's *really* into her, but what I bet he doesn't know is that she is even more into him."

"Get outta here."

"Totally."

The woman leaned into him as he showed her how to find the area between two curves, whatever the hell purpose of that was. The odd thing about that situation was that she wasn't learning anything. Like she already knew what he was teaching her.

"Holy SpongeBob," I said, blinking in surprise when I got the whole picture. I leaned into Heather and whispered, "She doesn't even need his help. She hired him because she's in love with him. I can feel it oozing out of her."

"No way," Heather said, as shocked as I was.

But the more I looked at the guy, the more I understood. He was a doll. "They are going to make beautiful, smart babies together one day."

"You can see the future, too?"

"No. That's just an educated guess."

"Oh," she said, even more disappointed than before. She'd started playing with her food, her mind a thousand miles away.

"There's something else I didn't tell you. I'm a private investigator."

She looked at me, and I saw panic set in.

"Nobody hired me to find you," I hurried to explain. "My office is right down the street. Like I said, I can feel your distress, and I have resources. Whatever, or whoever, is frightening you, I can find a way to help."

Her laugh, more like a scoff, sent her into a fit of coughs. When she recovered, she said, "Nobody can help me. It's too late."

Concern shot through me. Was she dying? Did she have a disease? Or worse, cancer?

"Can I at least try?" I asked. "I'm really good at helping people."

"You'll think it's stupid and send me back."

"Back?"

She bit down and slumped in her chair. "To the home. I'm number ten. I'm next, and I'm going to die soon."

13

I guess I should've been thankful we were getting somewhere, but her imminent death was a tad disturbing. Did she have access to an assassin's hit list? A serial killer's project board? A psychopath's scrapbook? How could she know such a thing?

"What makes you say that, hon?"

Her fist tightened around her fork, and I could only hope she wasn't the violent sort. I eased back just in case. I liked the number of holes in my face at the moment.

"It's the curse," she said, coughing again. "I got sick like all the others."

"The others?" I asked. This was going nowhere good.

"I live in a children's home. Nine other kids have gotten sick and died. Nine in the last seven years. And now I have the same symptoms. That's why I ran away." Tears threatened to push past her thick lashes. "We call it the Harbor House Curse, and I'm next, and there's nothing anyone can do about it." She looked up at me. "Not even you."

Fear so palpable, I could taste it pour out of her. I reached out and put my hand over hers. She didn't pull away, which surprised me.

"There are three things wrong with your theory."

She pulled away after all. "I knew you wouldn't believe me. Adults never do."

"First," I said, reaching out to bring her back to me, "remember the whole superpower thing? I know you're not lying."

I didn't mention the fact that I could only sense when someone *knew* they were lying. If she believed she was cursed, right or wrong, she wouldn't be lying.

"Second," I said, letting go of her hand but staying close, "you've never met me. You have no idea what I am capable of." Hell, I didn't know myself, so I was fairly certain she didn't. "I have a way of finding out how to solve the most impossible of problems. Even the ones that nobody believes they can do anything about."

For the first time since she sat down, hope shone on her pretty face.

"And third," I said, lifting her chin until her gaze met mine again, "whoever thinks they can put curses on kids and get away with it has never met me, either."

She swallowed hard and asked, "You really think you can stop it?"

"I will do everything in my power to stop it, and I have a lot of power."

She smiled and sat back in her chair, her future suddenly not as dire as she'd previously thought.

"I mean, I can't fly or anything. Or stop a bullet. Though I did stop a knife once. With my leg. I still have the scars if you wanna see."

That finally got another giggle out of her. Soft and hoarse, much too raspy. I really wanted her checked out by a doctor, but I wasn't sure how to go about it without drawing unwanted attention. Surely, there were alerts out all over the state.

And no way could I leave her to fend for herself. Nor could I take her to the station. They'd send her back to the home before the ink dried on my arrest papers because then I'd have to kidnap her. Not an option.

Until I had time to look into her story, she was not going back to

Harbor House, which sounded like the setting for a horror movie. Why was it all the evil places in horror movies had such promising, uplifting names?

But all this raised the question of where to put her. With the case we already had and everything going on with Cookie and Amber and the ex, I didn't want to burden Cook any more than was absolutely necessary. A runaway could not be good for the stress levels, no matter how sweet.

Then it hit me, and a slow smile spread across my face. "Will you trust me?" I asked her.

"I already do. That's dumb, huh? I don't even know you."

"Not dumb at all. I just want you to stay with a friend of mine. She's a bit quirky and keeps odd hours."

"I like quirky," she said, putting on a brave face but jumping at the chance to get off the streets. I should have known. She was scared and alone.

"Perfect," I said, already going over my to-do list where Heather was concerned. "But first, what do you say we split one of their infamous sweet rolls?"

Her face brightened, and she nodded enthusiastically. Girl had good taste.

I had a plethora of people to interview on the Emery Adams case, and I had the perfect solution to keeping Heather both off the streets and safe. Ish. Hoping my solution would agree, I found her, a.k.a. my tattoo artist friend Pari, sleeping—which would explain why she hadn't answered my texts, or phone calls, or her door when I pounded for ten minutes. Luckily, I knew where she hid the key.

After leaving Heather downstairs in Pari's office with computer, a soda, and a half-eaten bag of chocolate chip cookies I found on a desk, I made my way upstairs, hoping Pari had gone to bed batching it. There were just some things I didn't need to see.

Her apartment sat above the tattoo parlor she had on Central. I opened the door slowly, really slowly, to get the full effect of how badly the hinges needed to be oiled. Just below the headboard sat a patch of thick brown hair, so either her unruly locks would need a thorough brushing when she got up, or she'd gotten a cat.

I tiptoed to her side and turned on a lamp. It was a bit early for her. She kept late hours, sometimes working until two or three in the morning. But I needed to get Heather taken care of quickly and quietly.

"What the fuck?" she screeched when she realized I was standing over her. Staring. Wondering how best to rouse her. "Turn off the fucking light!"

She buried her head deeper in the covers as I reached over and turned off the lamp, knowing it would do no good. Pari'd had a near-death when she was a kid. She'd seen apparitions ever since. Not really people like I could see, but mists and fogs where a departed might be.

But with me, she got the full effect.

"I swear to God, if you don't turn out that—"

I think it hit her who I was. Probably because I'd started to giggle.

She threw the covers off and bolted straight up. "Chuck!" she yelled before covering her eyes and falling back. "Oh, my god. Find my sunglasses. The industrial-strength ones."

Like I knew which of her sunglasses were industrial strength.

She snapped and pointed to her nightstand. "Purse. Side pocket. Hurry before my retinas disappear completely."

With another laugh, I fished out her glasses and put them in her outstretched hand.

She slid them on and then bolted upright again. "Chuck! Where the hell you been?"

"What do you mean?"

Her hair was flat on one side and Texas big on the other. "You've been gone for, like, a year."

"Really?" I said, perplexed.

Scrambling up for a hug, she grabbed hold of me and pulled me onto the bed with her.

"This is kind of sudden," I said, giggling again, "but okay."

"Holy hell, I missed your face."

"You can't actually see my face. You told me it's just a bright white blur even with your shades on."

"Then I missed your blur. How long have you been back?"

"A week."

She settled beside me, snuggling closer against my side.

"And while I love the whole reunion thing," I added, "like, I'm totally into it, for reals, but you sleep in the nude."

"That I do," she said, her "pretty if not a little road-worn" face morphing into a full-on smirk. "That I do."

She wrestled her way off the bed and found a robe while I struggled to sit up.

"And you have a water bed," I said, perplexed for real that time.

"One of my boyfriends left it, and it's too heavy to move, so I just gave in to the inevitable. I'm a water creature, anyway."

"You're a creature, that's for sure."

"Oh, man, Chuck." She beamed at me, and I'd forgotten how much I missed her until that moment.

I stood and hugged her again, and I could feel emotion welling inside her. Like, real emotion. Pari wasn't exactly the emotional type except when it came to her love interests.

"Hey," I said, setting her at arm's length. She was about a foot shorter than I was with a killer body and an attitude to match. "What's this?"

"I wanted to go. To be there."

"What?" I hugged her again. "Stop it. I was a mess. I couldn't even remember my own name, much less yours."

When she looked up at me again, I fought the urge to giggle for the thousandth time. She looked like a bug with her huge *industrial-strength* sunglasses. But her distress was real.

"I thought we'd lost you," she said. "And you are way too special to lose."

"I feel the same way about you."

"Okay." She stepped back and sniffed. "What do you need?"

"What makes you think I need something?"

She pursed her lips and waited me out.

"Okay, I need you to watch a twelve-year-old homeless girl who is trying to outrun a curse that will kill her soon if I don't stop it."

Fingers crossed.

It took her a moment, but she finally nodded. "I can do that on one condition."

"Name it," I said, elated.

"The curse. It's not contagious, right? I have enough shit on my plate without death looming over my head."

"It looms over all our heads," I reminded her, bringing her in for a hug.

"I suppose it does."

"Also, I need you to hack into ADA Nick Parker's computer, both work and home, and see what he has on me."

"Of course you do."

"I feel a blackmail situation coming on. And I need you to get ahold of that sexy doctor dude. The one who lost his license for prescribing Oxy to his patients and then buying it back from them."

"Okay, but I don't think he can get ahold of any more."

"I don't need Oxy, but thanks. Heather's been sick, and I need to know what's going on with her as soon as possible."

"Aye, aye, Cap'n. Sure you don't want to crawl back into bed with me for a while? I'll make it worth your while."

"I'm sure you would." Her offer didn't sound half-bad, actually, with my recent forced vow of abstinence, but I preferred outies over innies. "What happened to Tre?"

"Oh, he's still around. But he doesn't consider my relationships with women cheating."

"That's very pervy of him."

"That's Tre for ya. By the way, who's Heather?"

After I got Heather settled and explained that I was going to have a doctor come look at her while I looked into her situation-slash-curse, I left her in the capable-ish hands of Pari.

They'd hit it off beautifully once Heather found out Pari had not only an Xbox but a PlayStation as well. They would have a ball.

I swung by the office before heading out to interview some of Emery Adams's friends and associates as well as look at the scene where her car was found. Cookie filled me in on what she'd found that morning over lunch—a.k.a. my third meal of the day, and it wasn't even noon yet. But the minivan boys were back, and I wanted them to follow me inside the restaurant. To familiar ground.

Also, Reyes was there, so I was basically leading the lambs to slaughter should they try anything. Valerie brought our plates as I read the report on Geoff Adams Jr., Emery's father, that Cookie had given me.

She was still absorbing the Heather dilemma and having a hard time with it. "Twelve?" she asked, heartbroken. "How is that even possible? How has she survived?"

"I don't know, hon, but we'll find out. He's had a very eclectic career."

She nodded. "And she's been sick?"

"Yeah, poor kid. That's why I need you to find out everything you can about Harbor House. Pari's hacking their files, but I want to know what they project to the community. And who does the projecting. If nine children have really died there in the last seven years, I want to know why there hasn't been an investigation."

"Of course. She could stay with us, you know."

I turned to the next page. "I thought of that, but we have so much going on. Who would keep an eye her? A racetrack? Really? He tried to open a racetrack?"

"Yeah, that fell through. Aren't you going to eat?"

"Oh, right." I took a bite of my nachos and went back to reading. "An upscale billiards room."

"Failed."

"A chain of restaurants."

"Failed."

"This guy sank a ton of money into one venture after another, and yet they all failed miserably before they even got off the ground."

"He certainly doesn't have the head for business his father did."

Every few sentences, I'd look into Reyes's office. He'd been on the phone since we got there, pacing back and forth like a caged animal. His gaze would lock with mine occasionally, at which point I'd duck my head and start reading again.

Cookie had collected a ton of articles on Mr. Adams. He hadn't struck me as a man this careless. This wasteful and sloppy and irresponsible. He'd struck me as being rather intelligent.

"I just find it interesting that his father, who is as savvy as they come, would sink money into a venture that had no chance of paying out. And then do it over and over again."

"Why haven't I seen her on the news?" she asked, unable to drop it. I should have brought Heather by to meet her at least.

Reyes finally ended the call. He eyed me a long moment, then strode behind his desk, combing through some papers, his movement agitated.

"I'll be right back," I said as Cookie was asking about Heather's parents. "And that is another thing you are going to find out for me."

She nodded, still in a daze, as I navigated the twists and turns of tables and chairs to get to Reyes's office.

"What's wrong?" I asked.

"Nothing," he said without looking up.

"Of course there's something wrong. I can feel the heat rolling off you like the flames from a forest fire." I curled my fingers into the front of my sweater, right over my heart. "Is it Beep?"

"No. Everything's okay. Just an issue with one of our vendors."

He was lying. I couldn't feel it, not from him, not anymore, but I knew he was lying. My own anger spiked.

"If it's Beep, I have a right—"

"It's not," he said, his voice deathly quiet.

I curled my other hand into fist at my side. "It's like I don't even know you anymore."

He stopped and looked up at me, his gaze curious. "You no longer know me? Or you no longer wish to?"

"What? What does that even mean?"

"Nothing. I have to cook. Sammy called in."

He stepped around the desk and walked out, pausing slightly as he passed, then disappearing into the kitchen. He left me frustrated and more confused than ever. What had happened on our way home from New York? I'd played the entire month we were there over and over in my head. When we left, everything seemed fine. Perfect almost, aside from the fact that I'd just found out he was created from an evil god. Also, I had trapped a demon from another dimension inside a hell filled with innocent people. And I'd lost a friend while in New York. A very good one.

But on the way home, I could feel him pulling away. And now I was just frustrated and worried and wondering about our future more and more.

14

Just when you think you have all your ducks in a row,
someone comes along and teaches you the recipe to
duck à l'orange, and you realize you can live without a duck or two.
—MEME

I walked back to our table and realized there were two, actually. Two
groups of men were following me. I got the feeling they weren't together.
But they seemed to have similar goals. Follow me around and record my
every move.

One team was very good at their job. The other, Crew Minivan, was
not. I'd spotted them yesterday, but I had no idea how long the second
crew had been following me. They were definitely not from the Vatican.
I hadn't seen the Vatican guy in a while. They could have replaced him
since he'd been made, but I rather doubted it.

No, these guys had ulterior motives, but quite frankly, I was tired of
being followed around. And EMFed. I passed by the Crew Minivan and
heard static coming from one of the guy's laps.

Either he had serious bladder issues, or they were EMFing me. I'd never
been EMFed before. Not in public, anyway. I couldn't decide if I should
be insulted or flattered.

I stopped at their table. Gave them all a thorough once-over. There were three and a tail. The three were men around my age, so old enough to know better but young enough not to care. They were your classic nerds. One even wore a pocket protector in his button-collar shirt. I thought those went out in the eighties.

Two of them had dark hair and looked similar enough to be brothers. They were pudgy and cute. The kind of guys that set your mother at ease when picking you up for a date, only to be the decoy for your real date, the bad boy from down the street who raced his motorcycle through the neighborhood at midnight. Or that was my experience, anyway.

The third one had been the driver every time I'd spotted them. He had light brown hair, too long in the front, and a bit of an overbite. He was also the one wearing a pocket protector. I'd have called him PP if the name hadn't been taken by a poodle.

I stood at their table for over a minute, waiting for them to look up at me, absorbing the panic that was rushing through their veins. They clearly had not expected contact.

Finally, in unison, they looked up at me, their mouths slightly open, and I couldn't decide if they were afraid of me or in awe.

"Are you EMFing me?" I asked.

The meter was going crazy underneath the table, and Pocket Protector was trying frantically to shut it off. Either that or he was playing with himself. Neither was acceptable.

"Tristan," one of the brothers said. "Just—" He shook his head, telling his friend to give up the game.

Tristan, though I liked Pocket Protector better, brought out the meter that measured electromagnetic fields. Ghost hunters liked to use it to detect ghosts, believing they put out electromagnetic frequencies that could be detected. After some fumbling, he got it turned off, then had the decency to look sheepish.

"Why are you here?" I asked, though I was pretty sure I knew the answer.

"There's a video," Tristan said, his voice trailing off when he saw my expression.

"Ah. Right. Well, it's amazing what they can do with special effects these days."

"We know the guy who posted it," one of the brothers said.

"And you are?" I asked.

He jumped up, and the other two followed suit. "I'm Isaac. This is my brother, Iago, and our fearless leader, Tristan."

I didn't shake their outstretched hands. They turned to each other in discomfort, then offered me a seat.

"Please, join us," Isaac said.

Cookie shrugged when I looked at her, wondering what I was doing. I held up an index finger and decided to join them.

"So, you know the guy who posted it?"

Tristan nodded. "He saw it firsthand. He said he was there when it happened and that he's been obsessed with supernatural phenomena ever since."

I was starting to understand what it was like to be a rock star. They all gazed at me, their faces full of awe and reverence.

"Is that how you found out where to find me?"

"No," Iago said. He seemed quieter than his brother. "He wouldn't tell anyone. He said he's been keeping an eye on you and is going to have a documentary soon."

Motherfucker. "Can he even do that?" I asked, so offended it was unreal.

"I don't know," Tristan said. "He's going to try."

"If he wanted me to be kept a secret until he could put out this documentary, why did he post the video in the first place?"

"I don't think he expected anyone to recognize you."

Iago nodded in agreement. "He was trying to build buzz. And now that you've been identified, he's really upset."

My ire rose several notches with each word out of their mouths. "Do you have the name of the guy that I'm going to have to kill?"

They all gaped, believing me.

Tristan snapped out of it first. "Just his online name. He goes by SpectorySam."

Motherfucker. Again. He was e-mailing Amber trying to get an interview with me? No. No way. If he knew so much about me, he knew exactly how and where to find me. He was e-mailing Amber for inside information. Probably tricking her into saying this or that. I'd have to get on top of it and fast. He could try to meet with her.

"So, let me get this straight. You guys are here to make money off me, too?"

Their eyes went so wide, it was almost comical.

"No," Isaac said. "Never."

Tristan leaned toward me, wanting me to understand. "We're more like urban explorers. We don't change anything. We don't do anything that will affect the future."

"I don't get it," I said. "What's your angle, then?"

Tristan laughed softly. "Burning curiosity."

"But most are hunters," Iago said. "Not explorers. They aren't like us." His gaze darted to the table of the other hunters I'd spotted earlier. "Most are in it for the money and the glory."

"Mostly the glory," Tristan said. "There's not a lot of money in this, unless you have a great subject." He dropped his gaze, embarrassed he'd said such a thing. I felt it burn through him.

"Look, what makes you think I'm the real deal? That guy is lying. I guarantee it."

"You put out an electromagnetic field," Tristan said.

I played it off with a laugh. "Doesn't everyone?"

All three shook their heads as though they'd choreographed it.

"Oh."

"We won't tell."

"Um, thanks? But you can't follow me around, okay?"

"We weren't—"

I stabbed them with my best glare of skepticism. Their faces fell, but they nodded, disappointed.

"Just be careful," Tristan said. "The other team members aren't professionals like we are."

He was a doll. I didn't have the heart to tell him he had a tail. A shadow. A departed who'd taken it upon himself to follow the guy around. The entire time we'd been talking, the departed man, who was in a straitjacket no less, stood behind Tristan, staring down at him, his face full of rage. But he didn't say anything, and I didn't want to strike up a conversation just then.

"Don't worry about me. I can take care of myself."

"Yeah, I've seen the tape."

I figured I should say good-bye. Reyes had glanced out the kitchen door several times, wondering what was going on, so I wished them my best and decided to pay the second team a visit while I was at it.

Unfortunately, they didn't have the sense to be worried when I stopped at their table. They had a completely different feel entirely. They were polished, clean cut, with expensive haircuts and even more expensive gadgets, especially in comparison to Tristan's team.

I stopped at their booth. Looked them over. Found them lacking in spirit and character.

Tristan and the brothers were passionate about what they were doing.

These guys, on the other hand, all four of them, were privileged. Expectant. And in it for the money. I could see the hunger of the hunt in their eyes. They wanted to catch me doing something so bad they could taste it. Then what? Sell it to the local news station? Who would even pay for something like that? Something that would make them look like idiots?

They weren't the least bit surprised that I'd stopped, but I was. The more I looked, the more surprised I became.

"You're SpectorySam," I said to the one sitting closest to me.

He'd been hiding underneath a baseball cap. He took it off and let me see his face. My jaw dropped. It all made sense now.

"You douche," I said to him.

One of the team members immediately took out a small camera to film our interaction. I narrowed my lashes, and he put the camera down, but I wasn't stupid. He'd already hit RECORD and was angling it just enough to capture anything I did or said.

"Douche?" he asked, his French accent still as thick as I remembered. I wondered if they were all French. Sam was the only one I recognized. But back then I knew him as Samuel. "That's not very nice."

My temper rose so quick and so fast, Reyes stepped out of the kitchen. I saw him in my periphery. He was wiping his hands on a towel, assessing the situation before him with what looked like only a slight interest. In reality, he was on guard. Completely alert. His muscles tense and ready to move should the need arise.

I forced myself to calm, then leveled my best glare on Samuel. "You recorded that video."

During my stint in the Peace Corps, we often encountered teams from other countries or even visitors who flew to the region once a year to help in any way they could. Samuel was on one such team. His parents had made him join. I remembered him talking about it. He talked about a lot of things when I was around, certain I couldn't understand him.

"I did," he said, quite pleased with himself.

"Why? Why would you even follow me?"

"You were . . . how do you say?" He lifted his napkin and touched the sides of his mouth before he continued. "Unique. I knew you were different from the moment I saw you."

"I'm just like any other girl, Samuel. I told you that then, and I'm repeating it now."

"And I knew better, *cheri*. I followed you often. Watched you talk to no one. Saw you drop to your knees when they came close."

"Myself. I was talking to myself. Crazy people do that."

"You were talking to apparitions. To those who have passed and still wander the earth. And when they come close to you, it is like ecstasy."

"I guess I'm not the only crazy one in the room."

"I have it on camera. You were talking to nothing and then you told the——" He leaned into his friend and asked him for the English equivalent of *elders*. His friend answered, and Samuel came back with, "Ancestors of town."

Close enough. He meant the village elders. I knew exactly where this was going.

"You tell them where to find the body of old woman. You say you find it. Is accident. You, Charlotte, are liar."

"Or maybe you're just a sore loser?"

He bit down, his turn to know where I was going.

"You tried to kiss me. I said no. You kept pushing it, so I slapped the shit out of you. I think perhaps you were a little resentful?"

"You mistake your value. It is what you Americans do."

This was getting me nowhere fast. I scooted into the booth next to him so we would be at eye level. They had to squish together to fit me in.

"So, what's this all about, Sam? What are you trying to accomplish?"

He shrugged. "I decide to make film. Documentary, yes? You are big business."

"You think——?"

"I do," he said, a sharp edge to his voice. If he wasn't careful, he'd cut his own throat with it.

"I wasn't finished. I meant to ask you if you think you'll live that long."

The other three men in the booth tensed and looked at their friend a little more worried than they had been.

"All we need is interview, and we will leave."

"I think not."

"We know who you are," Samuel said, his words broken around the edges.

His thick accent was almost impossible to understand at times. Now was not one of them, though. I was getting every word. Every syllable.

"We know *what* you are."

It was a threat. Give them an interview or else. But, seriously, or else what? What could they do? Throw me into ghost-hunter jail?

Still, a threat was a threat, and it stung. This wasn't about me anymore, however. He had been talking to Amber. Manipulating her into giving him information.

Despite the anger pulsing through my veins, driving the blood through my body faster and faster, I smiled. Put my elbows on the table. Leaned my head on my clasped hands. And said in the softest voice I could manage, "If you knew who I was, you wouldn't be speaking to me in broken English."

At last, his smile faltered. Just a little.

I leaned closer, going in for the kill. "If you knew *what* I was, you wouldn't be speaking to me at all."

Then I put my mouth on his. I wasn't sure why until I did it, and then I knew. I showed him. What I was. What I was truly capable of.

He couldn't move as I pressed images into his mind. Things I'd seen. Things I'd done. Things I'd do to him given a good enough reason.

I showed him just enough to put the fear of God into him. I felt his body lose all its energy, all its life force, as he watched the atrocities play out in his mind, unable to close his eyes to them as though they'd been injected straight into his brain. Then I felt him lose control of his muscles, but he stayed locked against me, unable to move, until I heard a whisper in my ear as though from miles away.

"Dutch," it said. Soft. Unhurried. "You're killing him."

I felt my face being pulled off Samuel's. Turned. And another's lips taking the place of his. Scalding. Sensual.

The kiss did what I had just done to Samuel. It stole my energy. It siphoned my will, but I fought back. I showed the intruder images. Of things I'd seen. Things I'd done. Things I'd do to him given a good enough reason. But these images were not morbid or horrific or atrocious. They were a visual representation of all the feelings I had for him. My husband. My dark, cryptic, mystifying man.

He deepened the kiss. Drove his fingers into my hair. Breathed fire into my mouth as his tongue pushed past my teeth and he drank his fill. Passion overrode all other thoughts. A warmth pooled in my abdomen as his heat leaped out and swallowed me. He put a knee on the bench. Wrapped a hand around my throat. Pressed into me.

And then he took control. He pushed his thoughts into me, pushed his energy into me, constricted and released, deep and sensuous, until wetness flooded my panties. My legs parted involuntarily. Wanting more. He pulsed through my veins like electrical energy. Tugged at my inner core. Drew me closer to the brink of orgasm.

And then we were no longer in the restaurant.

Then we were no longer in the city.

Then we were no longer on Earth.

Star systems rocketed past us. Creatures from other dimensions swam around us. And suns collided. Exploded. Showered us with a billion shards of light.

I gripped the table so tight my fingernails broke against the wood. The pleasure of pain brought me spiraling back to the present. Reyes was bent over me. His breath ragged. He pulled back, and his face showed the same surprise I felt to the marrow of my bones.

Then I remembered where we were. What I'd done. I turned back to Samuel. His hands were clasped tight on the table in front of him. To steady himself. To try to keep his hands from shaking. But his entire body shook, so it did little good. A combination of tears and sweat streamed down his face.

I stumbled to my feet. Reyes helped me, his movements as unsteady as my own. Then I glared at every man at the table, taking my time with each, making sure the threat was clear.

Ignoring the wetness between my legs, I leaned into Samuel to make sure he got the message and said just below my breath, "If you e-mail or try in any way to contact Amber Kowalski or Quentin Rutherford, I'll stop your heart from ever beating again." I leaned in closer. Put my mouth to his ear. "Then I'll rip it out and shove it down your throat."

I straightened and almost lost my balance. Reyes caught me, but his gaze was on Samuel's crotch. From the looks of it, he'd wet his pants. I knew how he felt.

Cookie rushed over, and the two of them took me into the kitchen. I glanced over my shoulder to see if Tristan and the crew had noticed that last exchange. Their saucerlike eyes would suggest that they had. As had every woman in the place. The awe on their faces, the longing, and the hush that had come over the entire restaurant would suggest I might've taken it a bit far.

Reyes had leaned me against a prep table while Cookie grabbed me a glass of water, and nobody said anything. I was in shock. Cookie didn't know what to think. And Reyes . . . who knew about Reyes? What he must think of me? I literally possessed the kiss of death. What would have happened if he hadn't stopped me? Could I really have killed Samuel? Would I have?

"So," I heard a voice say from beside me. "That was pretty intense."

I turned to see Angel, my thirteen-year-old investigator. Or at least he'd died when he was thirteen.

"I thought you were on assignment." I glanced at Reyes to make sure he was okay with Angel shirking his duties. His attention had been dragged to a shortage of corn tortillas by Valerie.

"I am, and it's great and all, but damn. That was hot. I almost came, and I'm dead."

I glowered at him. Now was not the time. "What are you doing here?"

He raised his palms in surrender. "Just updating the boss."

"Why?" I asked, softening my voice. "Who are you watching?"

He leaned close enough for me to see the peach fuzz on his face. "If I told you, I'd have to kill you, and since you're a god and all, well, you see my dilemma, *belleza*."

Damn. So close.

15

I miss being able to slam the phone down in anger.
Violently pressing END CALL just isn't the same.
—MEME

That afternoon, I interviewed several of Emery Adams's friends and co-workers. They all had glowing reports. She was a hard worker. She was professional and smart and kind. She looked out for the little guy. She didn't take shit from doctors.

From everything I could tell, Emery was the most liked woman in the history of mankind. Then who would want to kill her? Somebody either hated her or her passing was a random act of violence. She was the squeakiest clean I'd ever encountered. Besides, perhaps, Cookie Kowalski.

But nobody was liked by all. It was a statistical impossibility. She was a hospital administrator, for goodness' sake. They had to make some pretty tough decisions. Someone had a beef with her, but was it enough of one to kill her?

The more people I talked to, the more it appeared to be random. Could Emery really have been viciously attacked for no reason?

I gave up on interviewing her colleagues and went in search of the supposed scene of the crime. While Emery lived at the foot of the Sandias, her car had been found miles from there off Highway 313 between Albuquerque and Bernalillo, in a deserted field.

The land was privately owned, but the owners had been on a cruise when Emery was killed. Were still on a cruise, hitting beaches up and down the coast of South America. Tons of Facebook updates confirmed it.

So, what looked even worse for Lyle Fiske, the man I was fighting tooth and nail to prove innocent, was that he'd found her car in the rural area, even though he'd explained that she'd had a tracking app installed on her phone.

Cookie called while I was stuck on I-25. Traffic crept forward, and I realized I could be there awhile. Thank God for Cheez-Its, though only He knew how long they'd been in the back of Misery.

"Hey, Cook," I said through half a mouth of crackers.

"Hey back. Are you feeling better?"

"You mean since I almost kissed a guy to death? Peachy."

"I'm sorry, hon."

"I really need to learn to control my shit, but how can I control it if I'm not really even sure what my shit is capable of? It was one thing to be a god from my very own dimension, but it's like those rules don't apply here. Here, I'm the grim reaper. Why would anybody in their right mind give someone like me this kind of power?"

She laughed, but I got the feeling she agreed with me.

"So, what's up, chicken butt?"

"You aren't going to like it," she said.

"Do I ever?"

"A reporter from KOAT wants to do a story on you."

"Like, a real one?"

"It could be KRQE. I'm so bad with letters."

"But he's legit?"

"Then again, what's that other one? No, wait, that's KOB. Only three letters. I'm pretty sure there were four."

"Okay, but—"

"And there's always KASA."

"Cook," I said, launching an intervention. "Come back to me. Is this guy a real reporter?"

"Apparently. He's left three messages."

"Sounds legit to me. So, he wants an interview, huh? Is it because of my reaper status?"

"No."

"Is it because I'm a god from another dimension?"

"No."

"Is it because I solve so many cases for APD, they want to give me an award and a year's supply of oven cleaner?"

"No. It's because of the video."

I heard the "told you so" dripping from her voice. Or that could've been my guilty conscience projecting for dismissing the video so carelessly. "That old thing? I was, like, twenty-two."

"I told him you weren't available for comment."

"Oh, hell, yeah. We're sounding more and more important all the time, Cook. More celebrity-like. Next thing you know, we'll get special seating at the Macaroni Grill."

"You think?" she asked, intrigued. "I love the Macaroni Grill."

I snorted. "Who doesn't?"

"Oh, and that bakery in the creepy picture? It was owned in the thirties by a Mae Dyson. Mae L. Dyson, to be exact. Ring any bells?"

"Not even a Tinker."

"Okay, I'll keep digging."

"Thanks. And I'm at the scene of a violent crime."

"Where? What happened?"

"No, no. It's nothing. I just came to check out the scene where they found Emery's car."

"Oh. Okay." She breathed a sigh of relief.

The area was starkly beautiful with gnarled trees and tall grasses. I saw the crime scene tape and headed that way, careening over bumps and through ravines. Thank goodness Misery was made for that shit. "It's beautiful out here."

"Oh, I know. My dad used to go hunting in that area before Albuquerque expanded as much as it did. Hey, what did you find out about Ms. Adams?"

"As squeaky as my dishes after Reyes washes them."

"I figured. I can't find anything. She's never filed a police report. Never filed a grievance at work. Never filed a report of any kind while at college. Had perfect attendance and perfect grades. The word *Stepford* comes to mind."

"And yet," I said, "according to her grandfather, her dad was not the best. I don't doubt that he loved her, but he has some serious issues. And a horrendous head for business. Cost his father a lot of money and him his marriage."

And yet when I'd met him, he'd seemed so normal. But he was clearly a man continuously living beyond his means. Or was there something more? A bad business investment was one thing, but to do the same thing over and over for years—decades, even—would suggest a deeper problem. Though I had no idea what that might be.

"Having an irresponsible parent could explain Emery's strong need to project a perfect image."

"Exactly what I was thinking. She's overcorrecting."

"I did that once," Cookie said. "You know that huge dent on the side of Olive Garden?"

"No," I said, aghast.

"Yep."

"It's like I don't know you at all."

"Oh, I checked out the Harbor House," she continued, unfazed. "Charley, she's right. Heather is right. Nine residents have died there over the last seven years, but not all of them died on the grounds, and they all seemed to die of completely different causes. It doesn't seem malicious, and yet the sheer numbers would suggest otherwise."

"I agree. Keep digging. I'll head back to town in about twenty."

"Will do. Be careful."

"Careful's my middle name."

I stepped out of Misery and onto dry pastureland. Crooked trees surrounded me, bare and hauntingly beautiful against the landscape. Many vehicles had been in the area recently. The ground was covered in tracks, so it must've been raining the night Emery's car was found.

I walked the area, not sure what I was looking for, until I'd crested a ravine about a hundred yards away and saw it. More tracks, but these were separate from the others. The vehicle had been stuck. Deep ruts had dried. The vehicle had been sitting in the rain awhile before the driver tried to rock it out. It looked like the tires spun for quite some time before catching.

It could've been guys out having fun, four-wheeling their way across the area, but there were better places to go four-wheeling.

Could this have been the vehicle that took Emery's body? If so, why would they kill her, leave her blood-soaked car to be found by anyone, and take off with her body? She had to have been killed somewhere else, her body dumped in one place and her car dumped in another.

Just in case, I texted Parker and told him to check out the tracks if they hadn't already.

On my way back to town, I received a call from another of Emery's co-workers. From all accounts, he was her closest friend. They went to lunch often, and I'd wondered how Lyle Fiske handled their close relationship. Until I heard him on the phone.

"You're gay," I said, stating the obvious.

"As a blue jay on a sunny day." I imagined he normally delivered that line with a great deal of enthusiasm and gusto. But today it lacked energy.

"And you're a poet," I said sadly. Diageo's sexual orientation would certainly explain why Lyle didn't have a problem with their relationship.

"I try."

"I'm sorry to bother you, but I've heard from a couple of people now that Emery had been upset for about two weeks before her . . . disappearance." I almost said *death,* but I couldn't imagine someone like Diageo would accept such a sentence without physical proof.

"She was, but she wouldn't tell me why. I do know it involved her father."

"You're certain?"

"Ninety percent of the time she was upset, which wasn't often, it involved her father. But this was different. She wasn't mad at him. Or anyone, for that matter. She was hurt. Hurt like I'd never seen her."

"Hurt? Not worried? Or scared?"

"Not that I could tell. The girl told me everything, but not this time. She tried to hide it, but she was upset."

"And you don't have a guess as to why?"

"Not without making shit up."

"I appreciate the honesty. You have my number. Call me if you remember anything else?"

"Of course. I want this guy caught as much as anyone. Probably more so."

"You mean Lyle? Emery's boyfriend?"

He laughed softly. "Lyle Fiske doesn't have a violent bone in his body. Trust me. I've studied it at great length. From afar, naturally. I know good, and I know bad, and that boy is one hundred percent good."

"I'm glad you think so, too."

"And I thought this one was the one."

"The one? Lyle and you?"

"Oh, no, honey, Lyle and Emery. She liked him. She really, really liked him. For a while, I even thought she was pregnant."

My pulse jumped in reaction. "Why?"

"She'd almost passed out during lunch one day. I had to grab her bag and help her to her car where she promised to sit and wait for Lyle to come get her. But I saw iron supplements in her purse. You know, like pregnant women take. At least I think they do."

"It depends," I told him, mulling over that last bit. As far as I knew, she wasn't pregnant when she died. "Thank you so much, Diageo."

"No problem, sweets. I'll let you know if I think of anything else."

I walked into ADA Nick Parker's office determined to find out two things from him: Why did he withhold pertinent information about Lyle Fiske's conviction, and what exactly was his stake in all this?

Getting the answer to the first should be fairly easy. I could guess, actually. He left that out so I wouldn't see it and would be more likely to take the case. It was the second one I was most interested in.

"Excuse me," his receptionist said as I stormed past her and into his office. I'd wanted to do that since the first time I saw it in a movie.

"I want answers," I said to him. Only it wasn't him. It was an elderly gentleman in a sharp suit with a woman on her knees in front of him. "Oh, gosh, I am so sorry."

I started to back out. The woman raised her head. She was holding a measuring tape and had pins sticking out of her mouth. He was being fitted for said sharp suit.

"It's lovely," I said to him before closing the door and trying the next office.

"You'll have to set up an appointment," the receptionist said, hurrying behind me.

I shoved open the next door. Broom closet.

"I'm calling Security," she said just as I reached the right door. I totally needed to stop and read a sign here and there.

I shoved open his door. It banged against a bookcase, and I tried not to cringe. I straightened my shoulders and hiked my chin up a notch. "I want answers," I said for the third and hopefully last time. He was looking out the window of a much smaller office than I'd expected.

Without even turning to see who'd barged in, he held up an index finger to put me on hold.

"I'm sorry, Mr. Parker," the receptionist said. Just like in the movies. He held up a finger to her as well.

I snorted. "Looks like we both got the finger."

She glared.

"Sorry. I saw it in a movie once and wanted to do it."

"If I had a nickel for every time someone said that to me. I swear there is something in the water here." She turned and left us alone, closing the door behind her.

"Davidson," he said, turning to me at last.

"Parker."

"How's it going with the case?"

"Peachy keen, Parker. Thanks so much for asking."

He motioned for me to sit down. I ignored him.

"Why didn't you tell me about Fiske's priors?"

"Prior," he said, raising a brow. "Singular. Please sit down."

I walked around a black leather chair and sat. He joined me. Not on my chair, but he sat in his.

Parker could have been good looking if he didn't have such a rigid stick up his ass. He was so uptight, it actually made others around him uncomfortable. A trait like that probably came in handy during a trial.

"Why did you leave it out of the folder you gave me?"

"You act like I did that on purpose."

I did my best deadpan in which I channeled a sarcastic Christopher Walken.

"I didn't think you'd take the case if you knew about that."

"No shit."

"But I can explain."

"Let's hear it."

He leaned forward and started shuffling and straightening papers, unconsciously forming a barrier between us. The guilt I'd felt before came cascading down around him.

"He was one of those people everyone loved, you know? The girls chased him nonstop. The guys couldn't help but like him. He was that rare combination of nice guy and killer looks that everyone wanted to be around. To absorb."

I could see that. The guy was probably a doll when he wasn't being accused of murder. Especially one he didn't commit.

"He had offers from schools all over the country. Could have gone to graduate school anywhere. He had his whole life ahead of him."

"So did that kid, I suspect."

He nodded, the guilt like fire roiling out of him. "It was rush week, and a hazing went bad. The kid went into anaphylactic shock. El did everything to save him—"

"El?"

"Lyle. It's what we called him. Anyway, the kid died. El took the fall. Did three years for negligent homicide." He shifted in his chair, the guilt eating him alive. "It was my idea, but because he was the president, he took the fall. He took the fall for all of us."

"A kid died during a hazing at a fraternity of which he was the president. He was ultimately responsible."

"Yeah," he said, pasting on a sour smile. "That's what he said. But he wasn't responsible. I was."

"Directly?"

"Yes." He coughed into a fist and then left it pressed to his mouth as the memory of what must have been a horrible night overcame him. "We would kidnap our pledges, put sacks over their heads, put them in a van, take them to the seedier side of Central, and kick them out. They were all in their underwear at the time, of course. But Lyle said it would be too dangerous to leave them there like that, so we did doughnuts awhile and then drove onto the middle of campus to drop them off there."

"Sounds like standard operating procedure."

"It would have been if I'd just done my fucking job. I was supposed to check the medical records of the pledges, but I'd had a big exam that day and didn't get around to it."

"This can't be good."

"One of the pledges was allergic to peanuts, and the bags we used were from a peanut plant."

"Damn," I said.

"I didn't know someone could have an allergic reaction like that. I mean, I thought you had to actually ingest whatever you were allergic to."

"That's a hard way to find out."

"They told us later his throat swelled shut so fast, he couldn't even call out for help." He turned to look out the window. "I killed him, but because Lyle was the president and the media was all over the DA's ass, he was convicted of negligent homicide."

And here I thought the guy had no conscience.

"Okay, you feel guilty. I can certainly see why, but what does that have to do with this case?"

He gave me a fierce look, one of utter determination with jaw clenched and lids narrowed, and said, "He will not go down for something else he didn't do, Davidson. That ain't happening."

"The evidence is pretty compelling." Then again, the evidence is always compelling. That's why people came to me. I was their last hope. Their last-ditch effort. Not that I was going to tell Parker that.

He leaned forward. "Trust me, you do not want this to go to trial. Either you un-compel the fuck out of the evidence, or I'll cop to the murder myself."

I sat back in my chair, almost wishing he would cop to it. It would ease the guilt he felt for the guy. Allow him to move forward with his own life.

"What if I can't?"

He slammed a hand on his desk. "He didn't do it, Davidson, and you damned well know it. You have a sixth sense about these things."

"I know he didn't do it, but how did you know? The evidence says otherwise."

"I know. I'm the one sifting through it to make sure we have enough to prosecute, remember?"

"Ah yes. The smoke and mirrors."

"Pretty much. So, the case?"

I shook my head. "No. Let's get back to me. What exactly do you have on me? I'm not fond of being blackmailed."

"Extorted, actually. What I'm doing is extortion."

"Either way, what is it?"

He narrowed his eyes, as though trying to decide if he should trust me or not, then he reached over and grabbed an evidence bag with a bloody knife in it. "This was found in a wall at a cold case crime scene a few weeks ago. It was used to murder a woman in the South Valley."

"Okay," I said, growing a tad wary.

"It has your fingerprints on it."

I felt the blood drain from my face. "I have never seen that knife before."

"Yeah?" He stood and leaned forward. "Not even when you killed Selena Ramos?"

"What?" I asked, my mouth falling open. "I have no idea who you're talking about. I've never——"

"Just kidding," he said, laughing harshly as he fell back in his chair.

I gaped at him, speechless. If I hadn't been so shocked, I would've been able to tell he was lying.

"This old guy in Corrales slaughtered his neighbor's pig. Said he was hungry. He's being charged with theft and cruelty to animals."

After I could fill my lungs with air again, I scowled at him. "You're an ass."

"Exactly. How do you think I got this far? So, don't even try to fuck with me."

I was beginning to seriously wonder about ADA Nick Parker. "Did you even try to intervene on Lyle's behalf?"

"Of course I did. But according to campus bylaws, the president takes the fall for whatever happens in his house. I'm paraphrasing. And——"

When he dropped his gaze again, I prodded him with a "Yes?"

"I think my dad intervened."

"Ah. The state's attorney."

"At the time, yes. Anyway——" He stood and went back to the window. "How is the case coming?"

"Well, I'm actually a little surprised you guys moved forward with an arrest. Everything, just about all the damning evidence, can be explained and backed up."

"That's not good enough," he said to the window. "I need you to find who killed Emery Adams to be sure El is cleared of all charges."

"I'm working on it."

"Work harder," he barked.

I lifted an unconcerned shoulder. "I need access to the ME's records."

I needed access to investigate the deaths from the children's home, but he didn't need to know that.

"For what? There's no body."

"He still examined the scene. Tested the blood."

"I can get you an updated repor—"

"I'll get it myself, thank you."

"Fine. I'll have Penny set it up."

"For this afternoon."

"Anything else?"

"Yes. What about the other thing?"

He turned back around. "The other thing?"

"I've taken the case. Hand over whatever you have."

That time he shook his head. "When you clear El, you'll get the file."

"You have a file?" I asked, getting up. "How odd. So do I."

He sat down again, leaned back, and clasped his hands behind his head. "And just what's in your little file, Mrs. Davidson?"

I let a slow, satisfied smile—it was more of a smirk, really—widen across my face as I pulled out my phone from my jacket pocket. "This conversation, for one thing."

That time the blood drained from his face, his gaze superglued to my phone.

"It's in the cloud, so don't even think about it. Do you think I'm an idiot, Parker? I don't appreciate being blackmailed. Or extorted, for that matter."

He started to get up, but I motioned him to sit back down. "Go ahead and keep whatever you have on me. But just remember, games are much more fun with two players."

I turned and walked out the door, feeling slightly vindicated from the stunned look on Parker's face. He shouldn't have punked me like that. A woman's wrath and all. I hadn't thought far enough ahead to actually record the conversation, but he didn't know that.

He could keep whatever he had on me. I wouldn't be the one losing sleep tonight.

Or so I thought.

16

I went straight to the Office of the Medical Examiner from Parker's office. Wade was a friend of mine, but without clearance, he would never have let me look through his files willy-nilly.

"Hey, Charlotte," he said.

"Hey back." One of his assistants walked in. I had no choice but to take advantage. "How's the chlamydia?"

The assistant chuckled.

"Oh, don't worry. You won't shock her. The moment Parker called, I told everyone all about you and your . . . creative sense of humor."

"Man. I was so looking forward to humiliating you."

"I know. I was looking forward to being humiliated. So, anything, huh? How'd you rate that?"

"Haven't you heard? Parker and I are now besties."

"I didn't think Parker had any friends."

"Well, he does now, thank goodness. That stick up his ass was getting longer and straighter."

He laughed and led me to a computer. "Okay, so you look up the files here, and then, depending on how old the case is, you may have to take the call number to the dungeon."

"Wade," I said, surprised. "Last time you had me in the dungeon, we got the cops called on us."

Wade looked over his shoulder at a lab tech who'd walked in to grab a file. "Nope. Told him, too."

"Dang it. You're no fun since you got married."

"Hon, I've been married longer than you've been alive."

"That's a long time."

"Call out if you need any help."

"Are you off to perform an autopsy?"

"That's the plan. Want to come in?"

The smile I offered was part in-your-dreams and part surely-you-jest. "No thank you."

One would think that, with all the corpses at a morgue, the place would be filled with the walking dead, wandering about, trying to find their bodies. It didn't work like that, thankfully. I didn't need a sudden influx of life stories to hit me all at once. That had happened to me in my late teens. I've never been the same.

I sat at the computer, which was perched on a lab table, and started looking at the names Cookie had texted me along with the dates of birth. The OME may not have gotten all the kids here, but surely they'd had to autopsy a couple. A child dying was not an everyday occurrence.

The first one popped up on the screen immediately, and unfortunately her files were in the dungeon. I wrote down the number and went on to the next name. By the time I got to the bottom of the list, only two names were not in Wade's system. Seven were, with all those residing in the basement/dungeon. I always got the feeling Wade was a big D&D fan.

I told a tech I was headed into the pits of despair. He smiled and nodded. I could have walked out with a corpse at this point and no one would care. But why would I? Probably why security wasn't terribly tight. Like, they didn't have an armed guard or anything like Parker did.

I made my way down to the basement, which was actually a rather well-lit room on the lower level. I'd forgotten it had vending machines. I totally would've dug through my furniture for change.

By the time I'd finished grabbing all the files and going through them, I came to one insurmountable conclusion. Someone was killing kids at Harbor House.

"How's it going?" Wade asked.

"Pretty good. Can I ask you about a few cases?"

"Absolutely." He'd hit up the vending machine for coffee and powdered sugar doughnuts. I loved vending machine coffee, so I looked at it longingly.

Wade grinned. "Would you like some coffee?"

"Sure!" I grabbed his and took a sip. "Mmmmm."

"I was going to get you your own."

"That's okay. Yours is fine. So, do you remember any of these cases?"

He wiped his hands together and then took the files from me. "Oh, sure do. I autopsied this one. And this one."

"They all died of different causes." And they did. A couple had been in and out of the infirmary for months. Taken to the hospital multiple times. But their illnesses were all over the place. The doctors couldn't find an underlying cause for either of the cases. This was all in the notes Wade had made. Then a couple died violently. One hit by a car that was never found. One was struck by a blunt instrument.

If there was a single person killing those kids, he was doing a damned good job of covering his tracks.

"Well, yeah," Wade said. "Blunt-force trauma to the head and suicide by rat poison are considered to be vastly different causes of death."

"But look where they all lived."

"Oh, that's right." He nodded as he looked through all the files. "I remember your dad looking into these cases."

"My dad?" I asked, taken by surprise.

"Yes, yes. He suspected a connection, but since nothing ever came of it, I guess he couldn't prove it. Have you been hired to look into Harbor House?"

"In a way, but I don't have a lot to go on. There's no pattern. No common ground. Did Dad tell you anything about the case other than he was looking into it?"

"No. Sorry, hon. But since you're on official business, I can have my assistant make you copies if you'd like."

"I would most definitely like. I need more time to study them. To find a common thread."

"Well, I sure hope you see something your dad didn't. This case really bothered him."

"I can see why. I hope so, too."

As I sat waiting for the files to be copied, I wondered who'd set Dad on this case in the first place. Surely someone had assigned him the case, but who'd noticed the pattern, or lack thereof?

Wade's assistant didn't really want to copy all those files right then and there, but I wasn't taking no for an answer. Heather Huckabee was sick, and I had a feeling it was related to all the cases.

I walked out of the OME with an armload of case files and another cup of joe. Wade had turned his back on me. Great guy but far too trusting.

When I walked out the front door, I ran smack-dab into the middle of a building. I didn't remember them putting a building there, but there it was nonetheless.

I looked up at Ubie, who was busy staring down at me. "Hey, Uncle Bob."

"Hey, pumpkin. What are you doing here?"

"Oh, you know. Little of this. Little of that. You?"

He flashed me a saucy grin. "'Bout the same. While I have you, I need to know who hired you for the Adams case."

"Really? You need to know?"

"Yeah. You know, for our records."

"Ah yes, those pesky records. Did you ask Cookie?"

"I did." His jaw jumped. "She wouldn't tell me."

"That's weird."

"Very," he agreed. "So?"

"Oh yeah, sorry. I can't tell you."

"Bullshit. You always tell me who hired you."

"Wait. Are you catching heat for this?"

"Nothing I can't handle."

"From Joplin?"

"He *is* the lead detective on the case."

"Really? I had no idea."

"We were just talking about that fact yesterday."

"Were we? What does he know?"

"You're really not going to tell me."

"I'm really not. But it was great to see you," I said, bouncing off to be pelted by icy wet sleet.

"That you've been hired," he called out to me. "But he doesn't know by whom. Kind of like me. Your favorite uncle."

"My only uncle," I called over my shivering shoulder.

"The one who saved your life and gave up everything for you."

Okay, the saving-my-life thing, I could see, but . . . "Everything?"

"Well, a lot."

He had me there. "And I'm totally grateful." I stopped and turned back to him. "More than you will ever know or understand, Uncle Bob. You're the only family I have left."

"What about Gemma?"

"You and Gemma are the only family I have left. You have done so much for me."

"I have. I really have," he said above the sound of the sleet firing little cannons of razor-sharp glass. "You could repay me by telling me—"

Before he could finish that thought, I ran back to him and threw my arms around him. Or, well, one arm. The other was holding a plastic bag with all the copied files and my nigh-frozen coffee. Wade's assistant had put the files in the bag, not wanting all her hard work to go to waste.

He wrapped large arms around me and hugged back.

"I love you so much." After I said it, I couldn't remember another time when I told him that. Surely I had, because it was true. I loved him.

"Hey, what's this? You okay, pumpkin?"

"Yes." I stepped back. "It's just, you've done so much for me, and all I seem to be capable of doing in return is almost getting you killed and/or fired."

"Well, then. It's a good thing I love you, too."

I gave him another hug, refused to tell him who hired me when he asked for the third time, then hurried to Misery before I became a coffee-flavored Popsicle. The weather wasn't totally unusual for Albuquerque, but I was suddenly glad it never lasted long.

After I'd climbed inside, I took another look at something I thought I'd seen through the sleet. Garrett's truck was parked down the street, and I almost came unglued until I realized I hadn't seen him all day until now. Maybe he wasn't tailing me, but then who?

I turned back and watched Uncle Bob through the glass door. He was talking to Wade, laughing about who knew what. Was he following Ubie? Why on earth would he follow Ubie? Weren't they on the same side?

Having yet to check on Heather and Pari other than the occasional text in which Pari would ask things like, *Is eating only beef jerky for 24 hours straight harmful?* and *Quick! What continent has the fewest flowering plants? Don't blow my lead!*

Was she kidding?

I snuck in through the back door of Pari's place and called out.

"We're in here!"

"Where?" I walked through the maze that was her shop until I was standing in the tattoo room where she did tats, and almost passed out when I saw Heather in Pari's chair, her arm covered from shoulder to wrist in a full sleeve.

"What do you think?" Pari asked.

She slipped on her shades while Heather held up her arm for my inspection. "It didn't even hurt that bad."

I covered my mouth with both hands. This was it. I was going to prison.

Heather cracked first. Laughter bubbled out of her a half second before it bubbled out of Pari as well.

"Told you," Pari said. "So gullible."

I rushed forward to inspect her arm. The artwork was gorgeous. But underneath there was no swelling, no bleeding, no signs of trauma at all. Temporary.

I almost passed out again, this time in relief. After giving Heather a quick hug—and hoping we were at the hugging stage or that was just really awkward for her—I offered Pari the same treatment.

"I can't thank you enough," I said.

"Oh, please. This kid is an angel. And, dude, she seriously likes beef jerky."

Heather pointed to a series of shelves. "We organized all her paints, and Pari is teaching me to draw." She reached over to grab a sketchbook and opened it to the first page.

"Wow," I said, completely impressed. It was the beginnings of a dragon, and though the scale was a little off, for the most part it was fantastic.

"You, Heather Huckabee, are going to be a star," I said to her. "I've done some drawing. I drew a duck once. It was a great duck except that it was supposed to be an eagle."

Heather laughed, and I was floored by her transformation. She turned to watch one of Pari's artists tattoo a young man's calf. He was getting a steampunk clock that was melting down his leg.

"So, what did the doc say?"

Pari motioned for me to join her in the front parlor. Two young girls were perusing the photo albums.

"He didn't find anything, but he said her pallor is too yellow and her white blood cell count is high. She told him she gets stomach cramps sometimes and feels nauseated and has to swallow a lot." She leaned in closer. "Chuck, he thinks she's the victim of chronic, low-dose poisoning."

I closed my eyes. "Son of a bitch. Why hasn't another doctor picked up on this?"

"I don't know. He said he only suggested that because I told him she could be the victim of a crime, and all the signs are there. Unfortunately, without a thousand tests, there's no way to know what she's been poisoned with. If at all."

"But we have her now, and the dosing has stopped. Will she get better, or do we need to get her to a hospital?"

She shrugged. "He's coming back in the morning. Said he knows a guy who knows a guy who can run some very basic tests on the side, if you want to go that route. It'll cost around five hundred."

"That's fine. Anything."

"And I wish I had better news, but you were right about Nick Parker. He has a file on you on his home computer. It seems like more of a personal project than an official one."

"You're kidding me. Did you get a look?"

"I did." She handed me a manila envelope. "This is a copy of everything he has on you. Charley, he knows you had a baby and that the baby is gone. He suspects foul play."

I'd started to open the envelope but stopped and stared at her a solid minute. "This is about Beep?" I asked, the edges of my vision darkening.

"He's been going around to hospitals, showing your face, asking if anyone in the maternity ward had seen you. And I think he found the doctor Reyes hired. Somehow figured out he knew something. Threatened him."

I closed my eyes. "This is not happening. Not with everything else."

"I'm afraid it is. And this is serious stuff. He could bring you up on all kinds of nasty charges. Bizarrely enough, from what I could tell from his notes, he stumbled upon the pregnancy while investigating Reyes."

I had to sit down. Pari grabbed a visitor's chair and pushed it under my shaking knees. "Reyes?"

"I guess he can't just let it alone. Some people feel like there was something fishy about his release from prison and exoneration of all charges. He's looking into both of your financials, too. And he's been e-mailing the authorities in Sleepy Hollow, New York, asking about your stay there."

"How the fuck does he know about Sleepy Hollow?"

"He's following the money, Chuck," she said, cupping my face and turning me toward her, "you have to get in front of this."

"I know. You're right. I have no choice. He is going to push too far."

"No," she said, hardening her gaze. "Don't let it come to that. Tell Reyes. He'll know what needs to be done. More importantly, he'll be willing to do what needs to be done."

"Pari, we can't kill him."

"I know," she said, but I wasn't sure she did. "I don't mean kill him. Just, you know, put him in the hospital for a few days. Or years. Whichever."

If the situation hadn't been so dire, I would have laughed.

"Can I get a soda?" Heather had searched us out and was standing in the door to the front room.

"You absolutely can have a water. You know where they are."

"Okay," she said, disappointment lining her fragile face.

Well, either way, dealing with Nick the Prick Parker was going to have to wait until I could find out more about Heather and the home.

"Heather," I said before she went back to the tattoo room, "who told you that what you had was the curse? Anyone in particular or just a general consensus among the ranks?"

She thought back. "Just the kids, I guess." Her breath wheezed when she took a breath. I stepped over to her and felt her forehead and neck, just in case things were taking a turn for the worse. She let me, like it was an everyday act. Her temp seemed normal. "They were all talking about me like I was next. My friend Amelia freaked. She doesn't want me to die."

"How odd," I said, teasing her. "I don't want you to die, either."

She ducked her head, hiding a shy smile, just as my phone rang.

Cookie's name flashed on my screen, along with my favorite picture of her. I took it after she'd accidentally put pure cinnamon oil on her face instead of frankincense. I had no idea why one would put frankincense on one's face, but I did learn that pure cinnamon oil was like acid on the skin. It burned her face instantly, and before she could get it washed off, it turned the brightest red I'd ever seen on human skin.

I snuck the shot as a memento so that I would never forget the lengths Cookie would go to for my entertainment. Or for flawless skin. Before I met her, I had no idea you could even put milk of magnesia on your face. Or why on earth you'd want to.

Actually, I still didn't know that last part.

I answered with a "Charley's House of Ill Repute."

Heather giggled and went in search of water as Cookie's alarmingly sexy voice wafted toward me thanks to the miracles of technology.

"When will you be back?"

"I can be there in ten if you need me to make sweet love to you."

After a long—very long—pause, she said, "No. No, I'm good."

"Are you sure? I'm cheap and relatively easy."

"I'm pretty sure, but thanks. So, are you sitting down?"

My butt immediately sought out a chair. "I am now."

Pari questioned me with her brows. I couldn't actually see her eyes due to the ginormous shades, but lines appeared on her forehead over them. I shrugged.

"I'm not sure if this is good news or not," Cook said, "since I have yet to be able to explain it, but the child is the wrong age."

"Does the kid know that?"

"The one Reyes is paying child support to. The one in Texas."

I bit down, hoping beyond hope that Cookie's news was good. "What do you mean the wrong age?"

"It's a boy, and brace yourself for the name."

I tightened my muscles and clenched my butt cheeks. It seemed like the right thing to do. "Okay, hit me."

"Damien." When I said nothing because I was a little more than surprised, she added, "Damien Ledger Clay."

"Could that name be any more appropriate?" I asked, heartbroken.

"Clay is the mother's maiden name. But the father's name isn't listed."

"If Texas is going to go after Reyes for child support, there has to be some kind of proof that he's the father. What about on the kid's birth certificate?"

"Nope. It says 'Unknown.'"

"That's a weird name." I was trying to lighten the suddenly very heavy mood. "Why is he paying child support to a woman who didn't even list him as the father?"

"That's just it. I'm not sure he *could* be the father. Charley, Damien is five years old."

I slumped back in my chair in relief. "Reyes was in prison five years and nine months ago."

"Exactly. I mean, I'm not saying it's impossible, but it's just very highly unlikely that he fathered a child while in prison. Do they even allow conjugal visits in Santa Fe? And don't you have to be married to even be considered?"

"I don't know, but I do know who to call to find out. Then again, the rules of regular folk don't always apply to my husband."

"That's true, but I like to think of this as a ray of sunshine." Her voice, filled with empathy, softened.

"I'm all for sunrays," I said, absently fondling the god glass in my pocket. "Give me permanent skin damage and a little radiation any day."

"I love how you see the bright side of everything."

"Right? Okay, I'll let you know what I find out."

"The second you find out," she said.

"The second I find out."

17

The man who invented chocolate vodka
more than makes up for the bastard who invented pantyhose.
—KATIE GRAYKOWSKI

I said my good-byes to Pari and Heather and headed to Misery to make a call. Neil Gossett would probably be off work already. The sky had darkened, and the clouds that still hung low had changed from a beautiful murky gray to an ominous, rich black. If only every day could be so serene. And the icing on the *Playgirl* centerfold? The roads were clear. I was worried with all the sleet we'd had I'd be driving on solid ice.

Gotta love New Mexico.

Grateful to have Neil's cell number thanks to a resourceful Cookie who'd pretended she was a reporter wanting to do a story on him for *Santa Fean,* I let it ring until voice mail picked up. Then I disconnected and called again. And again. This went on for several minutes before Neil picked up, sounding annoyed as hell.

"Yes," he said, his tone ice-pick sharp.

"Hey, Gossett!" I said as happily as I could. "How's it hanging?"

"Same as always."

"Ah, a little to the left?" I didn't really know that, but how could I pass up such an opportunity?

"Who is this?"

I was hurt. I really was. Or I would've been if Neil and I had been friends. We were more like old high school acquaintances who had zero need to communicate except when we did. Like now.

"It's Charley . . . Davidson . . . We went to high—"

"I know who you are, Charley. How'd you get this number?"

"Oh, that. So my assistant called your assistant and pretended to be a reporter—"

"Never mind. What's up?"

"Did Reyes have conjugal visits while he stayed at your establishment?"

He cleared his throat and softened his voice. "How is he?"

"Free."

I really did like Neil. Not in high school, but he'd grown up a lot. I had to give it to him. He'd always had a soft spot for my man while he was in prison for a crime he didn't commit. He'd kind of had his back as much as a deputy warden could have an inmate's back. But he knew Reyes was different. Special. Destined for bigger things.

If he only knew the half of it.

"May I ask why?"

"He's paying child support on a child who is five years old, so unless you released him for the occasional boys' night on the town, he was having conjugals."

"He wasn't," he said to the sound of a sizzling grill in the background. "Not exactly."

I frowned, suddenly worried. "What does that mean?"

"It means that he didn't have any conjugal visits."

"So, he could have? New Mexico allows them?"

"Not anymore. They were offered for about thirty years, but the state did away with them in 2014. And there were strict requirements. Most inmates had to be married before their conviction to even be considered, then there was a lengthy application process. So, I can assure you, Farrow didn't have conjugal visits."

"But?" I really felt a *but* coming on.

"But . . . yeah, that doesn't mean the child can't be his. There was a situation with a female CO."

"What?" I asked, taken aback.

"Three, actually, but this one in particular . . . oh, and a female former deputy warden, so four, I guess, and those are just the ones that I know of."

"This isn't real."

"But from what I understand, he didn't initiate contact. If that helps."

"Oh, my god," I said. "My husband was a manwhore even in prison."

"In his defense——"

"Gossett," I said from between clenched teeth.

"In his defense," he continued, charging forward like he did in football, "I'm not sure there was ever any sexual contact. Relationships between COs and inmates were strictly prohibited, not that it didn't happen, but Farrow kind of kept to himself. He got plenty of attention, from both sexes, but from what I could tell, he didn't seem all that interested."

"Really?" I asked, that ray of sunshine hitting me in the gut.

"Then again, it's hard to keep an eye on them 24-7."

"Thanks." Disappointment threatened to rip out my heart.

"No problem."

"Okay, let me just ask, were there any situations where an inmate got a female CO pregnant?"

He hesitated long enough that I knew the answer before he said anything. "Female COs got pregnant and took maternity leave all the time. Most of them were married. But there was one. We'd heard a rumor she'd been seeing an inmate. When we questioned her, she confessed that it was an inmate who'd knocked her up, but refused to give us a name."

"What was her name?" I asked, my heart sinking deeper by the second.

"Davidson, I can't give you that information. You know that."

Damn. I thought I had him.

"My mushrooms are burning. Are we finished?"

"I guess. Wait! Can you at least tell me when it happened?"

"Davidson," he said in warning.

"Come on, Gossett. For old times' sake."

"You hated me during those old times."

"I didn't hate you. I just found you exceedingly annoying."

"I intimidated you, didn't I?"

I snorted. "Stop trying to change the subject."

"Oh, man," he said, his voice whinier than usual. "I can't remember exactly. I'd say maybe five, six years ago? They all blur together. There was this one time . . ."

He started to tell me a story about an inmate who'd accidentally severed his own artery with a spoon, but he'd lost me at "five, six years ago." My husband had another child.

I lay draped over a bar, my head resting on an arm thrown across it. It had been comfortable until the bar started spinning. I curled my fingers around its edges. I'd never been fond of merry-go-rounds.

Caroline walked over to me with my next mixed drink. She announced last call and then started to set it down. She hesitated. I lifted my head, tried to focus on her face, but there were just so many of them.

Caroline was an adorable redhead with a short bob and a button nose. Or at least she was adorable until she said, "I think you've had enough caffeine for one night," and took my drink away.

"What?" I asked, the depth of my outrage knowing no bounds. "I've only had five."

"Mmm-hmm," she said, taking the grande mocha latte, extra whipped cream, extra hot away.

A male voice met my ears then. Bryan. That boy could brew like he'd been conceived and incubated in an espresso machine, and he was my second-favorite person on earth. Or he would've been if he'd given me my drink.

"Tell her I'm okay, Bryan. I have a strong heart. I can take it."

He grinned. "I called her husband."

"You know Reyes?" I asked, my words slurring but just ever so slightly. "He's the son of Satan."

"Oh no," Caroline said as they cleaned up for the night. "Did you guys get into a fight?"

"I bet they did. I've called my boyfriend worse," Bryan said.

"Just one more. I promise I'll get help in the morning. I'll go to counseling and support groups and—"

"What stage is bargaining?" Bryan asked.

"It's somewhere in the middle," Caroline said, and then straightened, her face brightening. Only one guy did that to every girl and every other guy I knew.

It was him. He was here.

"Thanks for calling," Reyes said, his voice like smooth bourbon.

I'd gone back to resting my head on the bar. It had gotten so heavy over the last couple of hours. So all I could see when the son of evil incarnate walked up was his crotch. The same crotch that got Miz Clay pregnant. The same crotch that I craved like a heroin addict craved, well, heroin.

"You ready to come home?"

"No." I held up a finger. No idea why. "I'm hanging out with my friends Caroline and Bryan. And I have no idea who you are. I already told you that once today."

I heard the humor in Reyes's voice when he said, "Dutch, do I need to bend you over my knee?"

When he took my hand and started to drag me off my barstool, I yelled to no one in particular, "Stranger danger!"

Sadly, both Caroline and Bryan were too busy passing flirtatious glances Reyes's way to call the cops. Damn them. No, damn him!

He stopped and lifted my face off the bar. "Are you actually drunk?"

"I think she may have been doctoring her mocha latte," Caroline said, her face all soft and sparkly. "We aren't supposed to have alcohol on the premises."

He searched my pockets, causing a stir deep in my belly, and found my flask. "Sorry about this," he said.

Just kidding. I didn't have a flask. Like a tiny flask would get me drunk. I'd had to stop by a package store and buy a fifth of Jack. I downed half before I even walked in, then I smuggled the pint that had come with it in my jacket.

"Oh no. No problem," Caroline said, waving off the very idea. "I think she's had a hard day."

"You, my friend," I said, pointing at her, "have no idea. First, I find this homeless girl who's been cursed and is going to die soon. Then I find out not one, but two ghost-hunting teams are following me. Stalking me. EMFing me."

"Is she going to be okay?" Bryan asked Reyes.

"I feel so violated."

Reyes didn't respond to Bryan's question. He was looking at me with his brows drawn, concern lining his face.

"Then," I continued since I still had the floor, "I find out the ADA has a secret file on me and my husband and my baby." I stopped and looked at them, a sadness falling over me like a shadow that blocks the sun. "I had her at the bottom of a well."

I'd fallen down it. The well. And since I'd been close to popping, anyway, the fall sent me straight into labor.

"It's much trickier to have a baby at the bottom of a well than one might think. First, there's all this dirt you gotta deal with. Then you gotta boil water. No idea why. Then—"

Before I could even finish act 1 of my tirade, I was haphazardly tossed over a shoulder—admittedly a wide one—and carried out of Satellite Coffee like a sack of potatoes. Only I'd never actually seen anyone carry potatoes like that.

Reyes strapped me into Misery, his movement sharp and aggressive and just plain sexy. I started to turn the key and floor it before he could get in the other side, but my steering wheel was gone. Someone stole it! How on earth was I supposed to drive home without my steering wheel? Then it hit me. Maybe that was part of my powers.

I concentrated really hard, and Misery purred to life.

Oh, hell, yeah.

The only thing I remembered from that trip home was pretty lights reflecting off the windows, sliding past as we drove the streets of my hometown. They glittered in his eyes and reminded me of Christmas morning. He would be the present in this scenario.

I woke up days later on Fabio and wondered how I'd gotten there.

"I take it you're awake?" It was Cookie. She sat beside me on the sofa. "You were supposed to call me the second you found anything out."

"I know," I said, turning away in shame. "I was so surprised and hurt and suicidal."

"Oh, sweetheart," she said, pulling me into a hug. Kind of. She'd actually pulled my face into her cleavage, and while it was great cleavage, I started having difficulty breathing.

I patted her shoulder.

"Now, now," she said, rocking me.

I patted again and tried to talk from between her breasts to no avail.

"You just rest. It'll be better tomorrow." She tightened her hold. "If you live that long."

Okay, she was pissed. It didn't happen often, but it did happen.

"I'm sorry," I said, my voice muffled. "I was upset."

"So, instead of calling me, you sit in a bar—"

"In a coffee shop."

"—at a bar in a coffee shop and get wasted? Were you planning to drive home like that?"

"Of course not!" I said, aghast. I shot up to look at her. "It just kind of happened."

She rolled her eyes. "You didn't drive home, Charley. Reyes drove you home, and Robert drove Reyes's Cuda."

I brightened. "I bet he enjoyed that."

She giggled. "Made his day. First thing he said when he walked in the door: 'That thing has so much power.'"

"Uh-oh. You don't think he'll get the bug, do you?"

"I hope not. But you know what?" she said, changing her mind. "He deserves to have fun. Let him get a muscle car. Or a sports car."

"Or a Harley?" I asked, teasing.

"No. No motorcycles."

Cookie'd had an aversion to motorcycles ever since she banged a biker on one in her younger days. She fell off and burned the shape of Indiana on her calf, the tailpipe was so hot. She'd been scared of them ever since.

"I wouldn't have driven home," I told her. "Surely you know that much about me." Driving drunk never ended well. "It's just—it's his. I think the boy is his."

Cookie gaped at me until the whole exchange turned uncomfortable and then asked, "Your friend from the prison told you?"

"He may as well have."

"Wait," she said, holding up a finger, and I could feel panic set in, "he was married? He got conjugal visits?"

I shook my head. "No conjugals. But it seemed there were several incidents involving female corrections officers and even a female former deputy warden."

"Oh, my heavens. I hadn't even thought of that."

"Okay, so Gossett didn't say Reyes got a guard pregnant or anything. He just said it was possible. But the one did quit because an inmate had knocked her up. And guess when that was."

"Oh no."

I nodded. "Five or six years ago."

"I'm so sorry, hon."

"No." I stood and paced the floor, which was only slightly wobbly. "You know what? I have decided I am okay with it. I'm okay with it all. We can bring little Damien home and raise him as our own."

"Like a wolf found in the wild."

"This will be great. We can go get him this weekend."

"Isn't that called kidnapping?"

"He'll love it here. Especially once I adopt that elephant."

"I have a feeling his mother might not appreciate that."

"Oh, right. He might be scared of elephants."

"No, I mean the part where you go and get him. She will probably want a say in that."

"Oh yeah, huh?"

"You know what?"

"You're a chicken butt?" I sat beside her again, Fabio forming to our asses. Caressing them.

"Let me do a background check on her. It will take me five minutes once I get to the office tomorrow to see if Miz Clay worked for the New Mexico Department of Corrections."

"That's a great idea. Or we could do it now."

She laughed. "I'm cooking dinner. And you are in no shape to go over there by yourself. You'll fall down the stairs again."

"Dude, I wasn't drunk when I did that."

"My point exactly."

"So how many days have I been out?"

"Um . . ." She checked her calendar on the wall. "About thirty minutes."

"What?" I shot up to look at the calendar with her. "I've only been here for thirty minutes?"

"Close to it."

"But we've been talking for ten."

"Yep."

"How did I sober up so fast?"

A mischievous grin that showed off one charming dimple spread across her face. "It was probably that kiss."

"Kiss?" I asked, intrigued. "We made out, you and I?"

"Not you and I. You and Reyes. Oh, Charley, when he put you on the sofa, and I don't mean he just plopped you down there. He eased you onto it like you were the most fragile thing on the planet." She walked into the kitchen, tossed a few spices into a stew she was cooking, and stirred, her gaze a million miles away.

That's when I remembered I hadn't eaten dinner. My stomach gurgled in reflex to the mouthwatering aroma drifting my way.

"And then he leaned over you," she continued, the stirring slow and steady as she thought back, "his powerful body flexing as he bent and put his mouth on yours. It was like Sleeping Beauty all over again. Like his kiss healed you."

"Seriously?"

"And then he touched your face. Pushed a lock of hair off your cheek. Brushed his fingers over your shoulder."

"Cookie, you're really turning me on right now."

"Sorry," she said, snapping out of it. "He's just so—so—you know?"

"Yes." Boy, did I. "Also, I'm hungry."

"Oh, darn," she said, turning the stove low to let the stew simmer. "I don't think there's going to be enough for you."

"What?" I pointed to the pot, which was only slightly smaller than my bathtub.

"Sorry. You'll just have to go to your own place to eat."

"Ah," I said, going back to Fabio. At least he understood me. "Not on your life. I'm here to stay, Cook. I'm calling the movers tomorrow. You may as well just adopt me now. This is my new forever home."

"That's it," she said, marching to a closet off her kitchen. "You leave me no choice."

"What?" I asked, growing nervous.

She pulled out a box. *The* box.

"Oh, Cook, no."

"Oh, Charley, yes."

"Not that," I said, shaking my head and backing away from her. "Anything but that."

She stopped short in front of me. "This is happening, so you may as well deal with it."

"It's cruel and unusual, and he'll never agree to it."

She smirked. "Want to make a wager on that?"

I didn't. I really didn't. I had a strong suspicion I'd lose.

18

Things we hated as children:
naps and being spanked.
Things we love as adults:
naps and being spanked.
—MEME

When Cookie marched me over to my apartment, box in hand, I was surprised she wasn't dragging me by my ear. I felt like a child being led to my punishment. Or utter humiliation. Either way.

We walked in, and Reyes stopped what he was doing, which was basically cooking something—the scent almost dropping me to my knees—and regarded us with one sexy brow arched in question.

"We are settling this once and for all," Cookie said matter-of-factly.

"Okay." He said it cautiously, not sure how we were settling it, or possibly even what *it* was.

She headed to the living room and started rearranging the furniture. I rose slowly to my toes, trying to see what Reyes was cooking. It was definitely rich, definitely spicy, and definitely worth a slap on the wrist to risk a bite. Just like the chef himself.

He tilted his head as he watched Cookie work as I inched closer. Then he cast the same questioning gaze in my direction. I stopped and shrugged, pretending to be as flummoxed as he was. But Cookie took this stuff pretty seriously. We'd have to play along if only to appease her. I just wanted to know if I could eat first.

"Over here," Cookie ordered, standing back to admire her setup. "Both of you. And you might want to turn off that stove, Mr. Farrow, before you take off your shoes."

That answered that.

She only called Reyes *Mr. Farrow* when he was in trouble. Or at least I figured she only called him *Mr. Farrow* when he was in trouble. He'd never been in trouble before, and she'd never called him *Mr. Farrow* with quite that tone before, so I put two and two together. I was so good at math.

Reyes stepped from around the counter, already barefoot, and took in the scene. He didn't seem particularly worried, but he'd probably never had this form of punishment before. He had no idea what he was getting himself into. It was excruciating and required the utmost concentration.

"Places," she said, using her referee voice. She sat on our sofa, took her board, and spun the little arrow.

I slipped off my boots and shuffled over to the plastic tarp. The tarp, otherwise known as a torture mat, was covered in rows of bright circles. I stepped into my designated spots and waited for my opponent to do the same.

The moment of truth was upon us. Would Reyes scoff and refuse the game? Or would he take the challenge?

With humor playing about his full mouth, he stepped to the opposite side of the tarp and took his place among the circles.

He wore a gray T-shirt, loose except for the shirtsleeves, where his shoulders, the ones you could land a 747 on, and his biceps, the ones you could build a shopping mall on, stretched the fabric tight. The muscles in his forearms flexed as he lifted the hem of his shirt to hook his thumbs in his front pockets.

Cookie spun the arrow on her board and called out, "Left foot, red."

We both stepped onto the next red circle with our left feet, Reyes turning his back to me, and waited for the next challenge. His wide shoulders tapered down to slim hips, the loose jeans curving around the half-moon of his ass. Even the backs of his arms were sexy.

"Left hand, green."

Again, we both accepted the challenge, which was by no means easy for either of us. I grunted a little but stayed the course despite my most recent state of inebriation.

"Twister?" Reyes asked as though trying not to laugh.

"Long story," I said. Twister was Cookie's way of getting Amber and her cousins to stop fighting when she was younger. There was something about the challenge of trying to balance and twist and turn without falling that got them giggling like, well, children, and magically the fight would be over.

But what Reyes and I were going through was far worse than anything Amber and her cousins had fought over. We were way beyond Barbies and hair clips. At least Reyes was. I still had a tiny thing for both.

"Left hand, blue."

We moved our left hands again, the position taking some of the strain off my medulla oblongata. Or whatever that tendon between the heel and calf was called.

"It looks like we are going to have some time if you want to explain," he said, not even winded yet.

"I'd rather ask why you won't talk to me."

"Right foot, yellow."

This was getting awkward. I felt like an orangutan at a gymnastics competition during a floor routine. But Reyes looked as though he were completely in his element. A predator sizing up his foe. A panther readying to strike. His eyes shimmered from underneath his long lashes. His muscles shifted and rolled with each movement. His long fingers steadied his weight, but just barely, as though he were balancing the lion's share on the balls of his feet.

"I talk to you every day," he countered. The deep timbre of his voice sent a shudder through me that shot straight to my abdomen and tugged between my legs.

"Left foot, green."

"So, you're not going to tell me what's bothering you?" I asked, fighting my body's natural inclination to let gravity take hold.

"You first."

"Right hand, green."

"Nothing's bothering me. You're the one who barely speaks."

"Left hand, red."

I almost lost it that time, my fingers slipping when they landed in the circle. Balance was apparently not my thing.

"Dutch, if you are going to lie to me, why bother talking?"

I sucked in a sharp breath of air, then had to let it out again because I'd already started the heavy breathing thing. This game was so much harder than it looked. "I'm not lying. Why do you think something is bothering me?"

"Left hand, red."

"Again?" I whined, trying to move my hand to a red circle within my reach, but Reyes beat me to it. I had to practically reach under him to get to a circle, our arms touching. I looked like I was ready to crab race. He looked like he was training for an MMA fight. His jeans fit snug across his waist. His loose gray T-shirt fell over a rippled abdomen, the hills and valleys creating soft shadows across the landscape of his torso.

He regarded me for a long moment before saying what was on his mind. "We haven't talked about what happened in New York."

"True," I said, pretending not to struggle for air. "But I haven't talked about it because you haven't wanted to talk at all."

"Right foot, red."

"Seriously?" I had one chance of doing that without falling, but Reyes was closer to the circle I needed.

And yet he waited, giving me a chance to claim the circle first. That left him with no choice but to practically straddle me to get to the next one. By the time he finished, his face was so close to mine, I would hardly have to move should the next command be "Mouth, mouth."

"Right hand, yellow."

Damn.

"What makes you think I don't want to talk?"

I decided to come squeaky clean. There was no sense in beating the bush to death any longer. We were married. If we couldn't talk, we didn't stand a chance. "I don't know," I said with as much of a shrug as my haphazard position would allow. "You pulled away. On the plane, I felt you pulling away."

"We were on a plane. How far could I go?"

"Right foot, green."

"Emotionally," I said, sounding like all those women on reality TV shows who whine to their husbands about how they never open up. They never share their emotions. They never let them in.

No. I wasn't that woman. At least I didn't think I was until tonight.

"So, we are in a plane thirty thousand feet in the air and you feel me pulling away."

"Left hand, yellow."

My extremities were visibly shaking, and I wasn't sure if it was the game or the company. "Something like that."

"And what were your indications?"

"You were sulking."

Hovering half over me, his powerful arms on one side of me, he tilted his head. "I'm the son of Satan. Sulking is in my blood."

"This was different." I thought back. I'd given him the window seat so I'd have to lean over him to look out. To breathe him in. To rub my shoulder against his. He'd stared out that window the entire trip. "You got quiet."

He frowned, thinking back as well. "How would you know? You slept through the entire flight."

"I went to sleep when I felt you pulling away. I couldn't face it at that time."

He froze, and while we weren't quite as close physically as we had been, we were still close enough for our breaths to mingle. "Again, what were your indications that I was pulling away?"

He asked, but I couldn't answer. I honestly didn't know. Instinct? A gut feeling?

When I didn't answer, he said, "Maybe you were projecting."

"Projecting? You mean, maybe I was the one pulling away? Reyes, I had just gotten you back. I wanted to grab hold of your hair by the roots and never let go."

I felt a ripple of emotion course through him. My closest guess would be abashment?

"What?" I asked.

"I didn't want to push you."

"In what way?"

"You'd been through a lot. Losing your dad."

"True, but—"

"A difficult delivery."

"Most deliveries at the bottom of wells are."

"Losing your stepmother."

"Now you're just reaching."

"Having to give up your own child."

I stared at him a long moment. "That one killed. I'll be honest. But I wasn't the only one who had to give up a child that day. And it wasn't your fault."

"Of course it was. Partly."

"No, Reyes, it wasn't. And that can't be what I felt on the plane. What else? What made you distance yourself from me?"

"Fuck, Dutch. I don't know," he said, growing frustrated. "We'd been through so much, I wanted to give you some time to think about everything."

"Like what?"

"Us," he said point-blank. "I wanted you to be able to reevaluate us without having me crowd you. Suffocate you."

What the hell was he even talking about? Was this one of those "it's not you, it's me" lines? "And by reevaluate, you mean our relationship?"

His jaw flexed, but he said nothing.

"First, why would I want to? And second, even if you were suffocating me, you know I'm into erotic asphyxiation."

He was over me at once. Like a predator. Like a powerful cat preparing to devour its dinner. His heat soaked into every molecule in my body. Fueling it. Nurturing it. He wrapped an arm around me and lowered me to the ground. I looked over at Cookie. Or where Cookie should have been.

"She left."

"Oh."

He braced himself on an elbow, keeping one hand on my hip, as we sank to the floor. I collapsed underneath him. Reveled in his gaze. Basked in his presence, because it was quite a sight.

"So, back to this," I said, dragging myself out of my musings. "Why would I want to reevaluate our marriage?"

He dropped his gaze to my stomach. He'd lifted the hem of my sweater and splayed his fingers across my abdomen. His touch sent tiny quakes of pleasure shooting through me.

"Because you saw me."

"Come again?"

He curled his fingers, digging the tips softly into my flesh, causing another quake of pleasure deep in my gut. "You saw the real me, and I realized how I must look to you."

His full mouth, the exotic angles of his face, a curl resting along a cheek. These were the things artists craved to paint.

"What are you talking about?" I asked, my voice thick. "I see you every day."

"No." He ran his fingers up my shirt and under my bra, brushing the tips over a nipple.

A sting of arousal spiked inside me.

"In New York," he continued. "When you first saw me after you lost your memory." He lowered his hand, brushing it back over my abdomen. Pulling away again. "You were horrified."

Lifting my own hand, I ran my fingertips over his sensuous mouth. "If that's what you believe, then you don't truly understand the word *horrified*. I could never be horrified by you."

He graced me with a sad smile. "And yet you were."

I rose up onto my elbows. "Reyes, I woke up with no memory of who I was or what I could do. The first departed I saw almost caused me to seize. I was terrified."

He winced but recovered quickly. "I can imagine."

"But that first time you walked in, Reyes Farrow . . ." I lay down again, draped an arm over my forehead, and thought back. "My god. You honestly have no idea how magnificent you are, do you?"

He scoffed and lay on his arm beside me, but kept his hand on my abdomen, lowering it ever so slowly, leaving heat trails across my skin. "Your expression would've suggested otherwise."

"You're right." I turned over to face him and laid my head on my arm, too, the plastic crinkling beneath us. "And you're wrong."

"I'm talented that way," he said, sliding his knuckles over my belly button.

"You walked in, and because I couldn't quite control the shift from this plane to the next, I was straddling both at that time. All I see is this darkly fierce, insanely powerful being that is not entirely human, but not entirely otherworldly, either. He's like a panther and an otherworldly assassin all rolled into one. He oozes power and stealth and grace and"—I lowered my gaze—"and sex, so much so that I'm afraid of what I will do around him. Around you." I pulled my bottom lip between my teeth. "My attraction to you was so instant and so visceral, like I had a rope inside me, and it had been anchored to you the whole time. And the minute I saw you, something tugged it. Pulled it tight. The world spun around me, and I was so afraid I would melt into a puddle." I let my gaze wander back to his. "Reyes, I was awestruck."

"Really? 'Cause you looked horrified."

I laughed softly. "It's a statistical truth that women are better at non-verbal cues and reading people than men. Maybe you should leave that stuff up to me from now on."

He dropped his gaze again. "Horrified is pretty hard to mistake."

"I've been wondering if it was something else," I said, ignoring him. Horrified, my ass. "Well, a lot of something elses but one in particular."

"And what would that be?"

"I'd forgotten you." When he didn't say anything, I explained. "You'd predicted months earlier that I would forget you when I learned my celestial name, and you were right."

"I knew you would. It was no surprise."

"But I didn't forget you like you made it sound like I would forget you. Like I would grow out of you. Like I would get over you and just not love you anymore and move on."

"True. But in a way you did. You almost grew out of yourself."

"That was a lot of power to give to a down-to-earth girl from New Mexico whose only aspirations included trips to coffee plantations around the world and eating orange Popsicles without getting juice on her chin. When I find out whose idea it was . . ."

A gentle laugh softened the sharp edges of his tightly wound emotions.

"But the thought of not loving you anymore? Reyes, I can't breathe when you aren't near me. I can't think straight."

"I'm glad to hear that." He smoothed his thumb over my belly button, causing another tingling sensation between my legs. "And I'm grateful, but you've had a lot on your mind as well."

"No, I'm good."

"Ah." He nodded in understanding. "So I have to tell you all my secrets, but you won't share yours?"

A snort escaped me before I could stop it. "Reyes Alexander Farrow, I know damned good and well you have not, and will not ever, tell me all your secrets."

His gaze suddenly bored into mine. "I might surprise you someday."

"Yeah?"

"But you have to go first."

He was right, to a degree. We had to communicate. Wasn't that what the experts said? Communication was key?

I decided to start with the one that hurt the most at that moment in time. I closed my eyes like a coward and said into the darkness, "You have another child."

"Do I?" he asked, his voice fused with humor. "Thanks for letting me know."

I looked at him again, mouth slightly agape. "How is this funny?"

"No idea. But trust me, it is."

"Reyes, you have a five-year-old son in Texas."

He cinched his brows together and then released them when understanding dawned. "Right. Damien. I'd forgotten I fathered him. And while I was in prison, no less."

"So, that's your excuse? You couldn't possibly father a child while you were in prison?" When he only stared, fighting a grin, I said, "Ha! I already know how it happened, *Mr. Man*."

His brows shot up, completely intrigued.

"You impregnated a female corrections officer."

"Ah." He nodded, thinking back. "Oh, right, well, thank goodness it wasn't a male corrections officer. Talk about a hard labor."

He was laughing at this. Scoffing. Dismissing it willy-nilly. I lay there appalled and flabbergasted and stunned. Speechless. "How can you take this so lightly?" Well, not entirely speechless.

He slid his hand around my waist until his fingertips rested on my spine. "Because you, Mrs. Davidson, are hilarious."

He was taking this really well. Maybe a little too well. "Are you insinuating that Damien Clay is not your son?"

"Please tell me you didn't waste valuable time and resources investigating this when all you had to do was ask me."

"I most certainly did not. Cookie did. I'll have a talk with her tomorrow. So, fess up. Yay or nay on the paternity test?"

"Dutch, if I ever have another child, I promise, you'll be the first to know. Probably because you'll be in the throes of labor, screaming. Damien Clay is your boyfriend's son. He never married the mother."

I blinked in surprise. "My boyfriend? My new one? You know about Fabio?"

He didn't bother answering. Apparently it was beneath him to comment on Cookie's sofa.

Okay. My boyfriend's son. Great. "Well, it's awfully nice of you to make his child support payments for him. It's very avant-garde. Very nuclear family. In a postapocalyptic way."

"It was part of the deal," he said with a shrug. "I wanted extra eyes I could trust on our daughter, and he was extra eyes I could trust."

I snapped to attention and rose up on my elbows again. "What does Beep have to do with any of this?"

"I hired your boyfriend. Actually, all three of them." When I gaped in confusion, he added, "Your biker friends, remember? They keep an eye on the Loehrs and, in turn, Elwyn. Only I didn't want a paper trail. They are, after all, wanted fugitives."

"Donovan?" I asked, stunned. "Of course. You hired Donovan and the guys to watch over Beep."

They were perfect. And he was right. They were wanted for a bank robbery thing. It didn't matter that they were blackmailed into doing it. They were good guys, and when it came to hiring strong arms to protect Beep and the Loehrs, Reyes had brought them in.

"So," he continued, "part of the deal was that they use only cash and the credit cards I send them and that I make his child support payments so there will be no trace of his whereabouts online."

I was still gaping at him, but this time in absolute awe, even more in awe of him than when he'd first walked into the Firelight Grill, the diner in New York. "That's amazing, Reyes. I had no idea you did all that for them. For Beep."

His full mouth thinned. "Sometimes your lack of faith in me astounds."

"Not lack of faith." I shook my head, adamant. "Never lack of faith. I just tend to underestimate that brain of yours." I tapped his temple and then brushed a lock of hair back and tucked it behind his ear. He totally needed a trim. "I keep forgetting your IQ is higher than my bank balance."

"That's not saying much."

"It's kind of too bad, though. I was going to rescue Damien, bring him home, and raise him as my own."

"Like a wolf in the wild?"

I could swear I'd heard that before.

"I doubt his mother would have appreciated that," he said, being all logical.

"Yeah, Cookie said the same thing."

"Okay," he said, "next. Now that we're getting everything out in the open, what else has been bothering you?"

"Nope, the last one was mine. It's your turn. What else has been bothering you?" I'd let my fingers linger. Traced his jaw. Delighted in the feel of his stubble. "What other secrets are you hiding behind those sparkling eyes?"

He grinned. "You have my heart. That's where I hide all my secrets."

"Then I guess I don't have the key."

"Are you kidding? You forged the key." He kissed the tip of my nose, lay back, and tugged on one of my belt loops until I was tucked safely at his side. Folding one arm behind his head, he stared at the ceiling. I followed his line of sight, wondering about the little boy hanging out up there, then returned to Reyes's magnificent profile.

"You haven't really talked about what happened to you in the warehouse in New York."

"You mean before you got there?" I asked.

He nodded, and I thanked God he could no longer read my emotions. That was where I got the god glass. That was where I found out my husband was a god of Uzan. And that was where I got the means to trap said husband should the need arise.

"There's not much to tell. Kuur tried to get me to tell him where Beep was. I wouldn't. He got mad. Chaos ensued."

"Chaos always ensues when you're around," he said, his voice full of humor. "Nothing else happened?"

"Not that I can think of."

"Then why do I think you've been hiding something from me ever since that night?"

"No clue. Why do I think you've been hiding something from me ever since that night?"

"No clue."

I rose onto my elbow and put my chin on his chest. "Let's make a deal."

"Okay."

"Let's not keep any secrets from each other anymore."

"That's kind of radical, don't you think?" He was teasing. Humor tugged at one corner of his mouth.

"I hear it's all the rage."

"No secrets between married couples? You're going to start a revolution if you keep thinking like that."

I squinted in thought. "Maybe more like, no secrets unless the other person knows you're keeping a secret. You know, full disclosure."

"I'm not sure you've grasped the concept of full disclosure. It would imply, you know, full disclosure."

"True, but work with me here." I got excited. This could be just the ticket. "I could tell you I have a secret that I couldn't tell you, but then you'd know I had a secret so it would all be out in the open and no one would feel guilty or left out of the loop, et cetera, et cetera."

"You don't think that would defeat the purpose of revealing a secret?"

I shook my head. "I don't think so."

He cleared his throat, and I had a sneaking suspicion he was trying not to laugh. His hand, the one he'd slipped under my sweater again, slid up my spine, his splayed fingers scorching my skin, infusing it with warmth. "Okay, let's give it a shot."

I wiggled closer in excitement. I thought about the things I'd been keeping close to my heart. The first secret, the super-big biggie, the monstrosity of all monstrosities, was of course his godly status. I was keeping it because, well, he was created using the energy of an evil god, so I wasn't sure what would happen when I told him. And the second was the god glass. Similar reasons. Different outcome. Besides, the god glass was the heart of my backup plan.

Now that I knew what he was, I understood so much. I could feel his power. It pulsated out of him in waves. It was raw and turbulent and dynamic. He was so much more than *just* supernatural, and now that I knew, it made sense.

He was a force. A maelstrom. A nuclear reactor. And such power was often wild. Unpredictable and uncontrollable. I simply needed to know more. Unfortunately, there was only one entity I could think of who grew up in the same neighborhood, who knew more about Reyes than anyone else on this plane: Osh'ekiel.

I would tell Reyes eventually, but I needed to do a little digging first.

"All right," I said, swallowing hard, "I have two secrets I can't tell you." I fell back and spread my arms, one landing on his face. Quite on purpose. "Whew. Boy, do I feel better getting that off my chest. Oh, wait." I thought a moment. Technically the fact that I hadn't told him that Satan had somehow trapped him when he was in evil-god mode could count as a third secret. "Cancel that. I have three. Sorry."

He bit the arm that was still lying across his face softly, making me giggle like a schoolgirl. I rolled closer.

After I nestled beside him again, he said, "Three, huh? That's a lot of secrets."

"True, but at least now you know I have them and that I'll tell you when I can. The minute I can. No, the microsecond I can. So, what about you?"

"Hmmm," he said, thinking aloud. "I guess I just have one. No." He thought again, drawing it out until I was on the verge of chewing my nails off. "Two. Yeah, technically I have two."

I stared, crestfallen. "You're keeping two secrets from me?"

He laughed out loud. "You're keeping three from me."

"But—" I rose onto my palms. "But what are they? Why are you keeping them from me?"

For the barest hint of a moment, sadness flashed across his face. It was mostly in the eyes. The tiniest slip. The barest hint. But he recovered instantly and grinned again. "I knew this wouldn't work."

Dread spread through me. Reyes didn't get sad. Reyes got mad. He became stone. He plotted and planned and worked until no matter what the problem was, he knew how to solve it. But sadness? Was it something he couldn't control? Something he could do nothing about? Inevitable?

But the whole reason for this was to form a stronger bond. To trust one another even when we couldn't tell the other, for whatever reason, what that secret may be.

"No, you're right. It'll work. Thank you for telling me." I lay back down and focused on the hand at my back. At least he was touching me. "I was worried," I said, reveling in the feel of him.

"About what?"

"The fact that you haven't touched me in over a week."

"I explained that."

"I know, but—"

"Dutch, you deserve so much better than me."

Glaring up as hard as I could, I said, "You either have an inflated opinion of me or a distorted opinion of yourself. I think it's both. I think the only way we are going to settle this once and for all is"—I shifted onto him, raised his shirt, and dipped my hands down his pants—"to work it out until we are too exhausted to argue."

I slid my hand down his rock-hard abdomen and wrapped my fingers around his erection. Every muscle in his body turned to marble. He clenched the hand at my back into a fist as I pushed all the way down to the base of his cock. I massaged and kneaded until I felt the familiar rush of blood beneath my fingers.

He took a fistful of hair and pulled my mouth onto his as I worked.

I leaned away. "But really, can I have a hint? Not even for both of your secrets. Just one will do. Wait, are they related?"

Without another word, he grabbed the edge of the Twister mat, pulled it over us, then rolled, locking us together like the contents of a burrito.

"Are you sure Cookie left? She didn't just go to the bathroom or something?"

He covered my mouth with his and pushed his hips into mine, his erection hard against my abdomen.

"If she's still here," I said, suddenly winded when he sought an ear, "she is about to be severely scandalized."

Completely ignoring me, he flipped me onto my stomach, his movements rough, hurried, and pressed into me from behind. And as he wrapped his long fingers around my throat from behind, he asked, "What was it you were saying about erotic asphyxiation?"

"I was mostly kidding—" I gasped when he tightened his hold with one hand and pushed my pants down with the other. Cool air rushed across my skin a microsecond before his flames blistered it.

Then his mouth was at my ear again as his fingers unfastened his own jeans. "Spread yourself," he said, his voice low and smooth and demanding.

But my jeans were only down to my knees. I couldn't spread my legs.

When I didn't obey immediately, he sent a hand up my shirt and under my bra. At first he only fondled Danger, but then a sharp sting sent goose bumps erupting over my skin as he squeezed the delicate crest between his fingers.

He straddled me and locked my knees closed with his. "Spread yourself," he repeated at my ear, his fingers growing tighter and tighter around my throat. He buried his face in my hair and breathed in my scent. His cock lay against the small of my back, hot and hard and ready.

I reached back, put my hands on my ass, and spread myself for him.

"Good girl," he whispered before gliding his fingers seamlessly into the slickness there. He moaned into my hair. "You're so fucking wet," he said as he pumped into me.

I just wanted it to continue. Wanted him to continue. Until I couldn't see straight.

Then he pulled his fingers out and rubbed my clit softly. Luring. Coaxing. The movement sent waves of pleasure spiraling through my body, lighting every dark corner, kindling the most dormant parts of me with tiny, glittering earthquakes.

That time, I moaned, and it excited him more. He slid the length of his erection over my skin and positioned himself for entrance, his heavy cock pressing into me, struggling to be loosed between my legs like a racehorse seconds before the gates open.

But he paused, caught my earlobe between his teeth, nipped hard enough to wrench a gasp from me, then whispered, "Let's hope I fuck the right one."

The right one? My eyes flew open, and I stiffened, fearing anal sex like a Roswellian fears probes, but in one quick move, he buried his cock in my cunt.

A spasm rocketed through me, and I almost came the moment he entered, but he held fast, entombed deep inside me, waiting for me to calm. Waiting for himself to calm. I started shaking, and my fingers slipped. He tightened his hold to the edge of oxygen deprivation.

"*Vous ne devriez pas taquiner, mon amour,*" he said, his French as strong and fluid as his movements. "You should not tease," he repeated in English.

Even though he was still, the beginnings of an orgasm resurfaced in the distance, rippling through me in hot, pulsating waves. The tighter his hold, the deeper his cock, the closer it came. I struggled beneath him, luring it even closer, begging, but he held fast. His weight too much. His hold too strong.

He kissed my jaw. My neck. The corner of my mouth. Then, without warning, he slid out, but only an inch or two before he plunged back inside. I gasped as he held me down again. Tightened his hold on my throat. The constraint caused a flood tide of pleasure. It spread like wildfire, and I squirmed underneath him. Wanting that again. That pang of desire, sharp and erotic and fierce.

He clamped onto me, rendering me completely immobile, and did the unexpected. He slowed time as he pulled out and plunged inside again. Short, quick bursts. Sharp jolts of arousal causing the sweetest ache deep in my belly. My climax rocketed closer, but he tightened his hold and whispered, "Don't let it go."

His labored pants came in bursts as quick and short as his strokes, and I knew he was as close as I was.

"Don't let it go," he whispered again, his voice hoarse, his hands shaking as he pumped even faster. But I couldn't hold it.

His breath fanned across my cheek and, without slowing his stride, he pressed his mouth to my ear. "Now."

Time crashed into us, heightening the pleasure that exploded inside me. Every muscle tensed as the raw energy of orgasm spiked and pulsed and shook the world around us. A low growl erupted from his throat, and he clutched the plastic beneath us as his own climax shuddered through him in great, powerful waves.

He whispered a few choice expletives from between clenched teeth, and I couldn't have said it better myself. By the time he collapsed on top of me, only the shimmering remnants of pleasure remained, like tattered pieces of a forgotten star.

He slid his weight off me to lie by my side. His lashes resting on his cheeks. His mouth swollen and sensual.

"So, was it good for you?" I asked him.

He shook his head. "I faked it."

"Really? So did I. I guess we'll have to try again."

A slow grin spread across his face. "Okay, but the tarp has to go."

"Deal."

19

I'm one step away from being rich.
All I need now is money.
—MEME

We talked all night. And ate Reyes's amazing bourbon chicken. And discussed . . . everything. He answered anything I asked, and though I had no idea why he was opening up now, I was never one to look a gift horse in the chops.

We'd gone from the Twister mat to the sofa to the bathroom sink—long story—and finally ended up in bed. Bed was a massive four-poster of rustic gray woods and smooth, tasteful lines.

He asked a lot of questions, too. I explained about Heather, the homeless girl who'd been cursed, I'd mentioned in my drunken stupor at Satellite. Told him where we were on that case. And then I told him about my actual case.

Since he didn't work for the police in any way, I told him who'd hired us, mostly because I wanted to explain the other remark I'd made while inebriated about how Nick Parker has a file on us and Beep. How he was currently using it to ensure my cooperation on his case, but that it wasn't necessary, because Fiske truly was innocent of the charges against him.

But Reyes's interest snagged on the fact that Parker had a file on us. The apartment almost exploded around that time. I was forced to take Reyes's mind off Parker by flashing him Danger and Will. Totally worked. My girls always came through in a pinch.

But I knew Reyes well enough to know that he would not let that one drop. Not for a minute. And he could make things very sticky for us and our extremely delicate situation. The last thing we needed was a full-blown investigation into something that could get us both thrown in prison. I was pretty sure falsifying birth records and giving your child away was illegal.

I tried to feel him out as delicately as possible about the whole god thing. It was one thing for me not to know I was a god, but for Reyes, who'd been Rey'aziel in hell and then Reyes here, who'd been alive in his current state of mind for centuries, to have no clue. He was either playing that one very close to the bulletproof vest, or he really and truly didn't know.

It was getting late, but sleep was the furthest thing from my racing mind. Apparently that was not the case for Mr. Sugar Buns. He lay back, closed his eyes, and threw an arm over his forehead, his favorite sleeping position.

I could hardly have that. So, I crawled on top of him and started chest compressions. It seemed like the right thing to do.

"What are you doing?" he asked without removing his arm.

"Giving you CPR." I pressed into his chest, trying not to lose count. Wearing a red-and-black football jersey and boxers that read, DRIVERS WANTED. SEE INSIDE FOR DETAILS, I'd straddled him and now worked furiously to save his life, my focus like that of a seasoned trauma nurse. Or a seasoned pot roast. It was hard to say.

"I'm not sure I'm in the market," he said, his voice smooth and filled with a humor I found appalling. He clearly didn't appreciate my dedication.

"Damn it, man! I'm trying to save your life! Don't interrupt."

A sensuous grin slid across his face. He tucked his arms behind his head while I worked. I finished my count, leaned down, put my lips on his, and blew. He laughed softly, the sound rumbling from his chest, deep and sexy, as he took my breath into his lungs. That part down, I went back to counting chest compressions.

"Don't you die on me!"

And praying.

After another round, he asked, "Am I going to make it?"

"It's touch-and-go. I'm going to have to bring out the defibrillator."

"We have a defibrillator?" he asked, quirking a brow, clearly impressed.

I reached for my phone. "I have an app. Hold on." As I punched buttons, I realized a major flaw in my plan. I needed a second phone. I could hardly shock him with only one paddle. I reached over and grabbed his phone as well. Started punching buttons. Rolled my eyes. "You don't have the app," I said from between clenched teeth.

"I had no idea smartphones were so versatile."

"I'll just have to download it. It'll just take a sec."

"Do I have that long?"

Humor sparkled in his eyes as he waited for me to find the app. I'd forgotten the name of it, so I had to go back to my phone, then back to his, then do a search, then download, then install it, all while my patient lay dying. Did no one understand that seconds counted?

"Got it!" I said at last. I pressed one phone to his chest and one to the side of his rib cage like they did in the movies, and yelled, "Clear!"

Granted, I didn't get off him or anything as the electrical charge riddled his body, slammed his heart into action, and probably scorched his skin. Or that was my hope, anyway.

He handled it well. One corner of his mouth twitched, but that was about it. He was such a trouper.

After two more jolts of electricity—it had to be done—I leaned forward and pressed my fingertips to his throat.

"Well?" he asked after a tense moment.

I released a ragged sigh of relief, and my shoulders fell forward in exhaustion. "You're going to be okay, Mr. Farrow."

Without warning, my patient pulled me into his arms and rolled me over, pinning me to the bed with his considerable weight and burying his face in my hair.

It was a miracle!

"But are you?" he asked, the question part promise and part threat.

I giggled as a strong hand slid into my boxers. "No," I said breathlessly. "Never."

And as he slid inside me again, my body clenching around him in reflex, I believed it. I would never be all right again. And somehow I was good with that.

"You know," he said at around three in the morning, "there is one secret we've never talked about."

I tried not to get too excited, but . . . "Is this one of your two?"

"No," he said, then he laughed when I pursed my mouth in disappointment.

"So there's another one?"

"Kind of."

"You had three?"

"It's not really a secret. You've just never asked."

Intrigued, I scooted closer. "Well, then clearly I should have."

"You've never asked about the money."

"The money. Your money?"

"No, the government's," he said with a chuckle.

"Are we going to talk about the national budget? Because I am so there."

His gaze dropped to my mouth, his long lashes standing at half-mast over his dark, shimmering eyes. "You've never asked how much we have."

"We?" "We," he said sternly.

"I've never asked because I've never needed to. I already know."

One shapely brow inched up. "Do you?"

"Yep. Kim told me. I know exactly how much you have."

"We."

"Or had. That was almost a year ago, and we both know you've been burning through the stuff like crude oil."

Kim was Reyes's nonbiological sister. They grew up together, fighting side by side just to survive the horrors of the man who raised them, Earl Walker. He would do anything for her, and she for him. She proved it when she'd started burning buildings down about a year ago, all to hide evidence of what Earl did to Reyes. It was the sweetest misguided act of love I'd ever known, but she was on the verge of being a wanted woman, so Reyes set her up somewhere remote. I hadn't seen her since.

"So, what did she tell you?"

"Fifty big ones. Which was kind of hard for me to wrap my head around. I mean, fifty million? Who the hell has fifty million dollars?"

"Kim was talking about her money. Not ours."

"Yeah, she said that. But she doesn't touch it. You know that, right? She only takes a little of the interest to live off of. She told me she would never touch your money."

"I know." The muscles in his jaw jumped as he bit down in frustration. "She can be hardheaded that way. Like someone else I know."

"I wish I could get to know her better. I wish we could hang and share stories about you and talk behind your back like real sisters-in-law."

"Oddly enough, I wish that, too. I hope you still can someday."

I felt a current pass through him. A disturbance, though I couldn't identify it.

"Is something wrong? She's okay, right?"

He rolled onto his back and threw an arm over his forehead. "I'm not sure."

I rose onto an elbow beside him. "What do you mean?"

"I can't find her."

Alarm rushed over my skin. "She's missing? I don't understand. When was the last time you spoke to her?"

"Couple of days ago. She was setting up safe houses for the Loehrs. Scouting locations. Making the buys."

"Safe houses?" I asked, surprised. "How many safe houses are we talking?"

"At the moment, ten. She was working on number eleven."

"Ten?" I tried to stop my jaw from dropping. I failed. "We have ten safe houses?" Before I could stop them, tears amassed. "You bought ten houses? For, I don't know, just in case?"

"Of course." He said it like I'd grown another head.

"Reyes—"

"I told you. I'm doing everything I can to keep our daughter safe."

I blinked and turned away. The depths of this man's convictions astounded me. "I'm sorry. I got sidetracked. Kim?"

"Yes. She was looking at a house on an island south of Mexico. She was supposed to fly out today and get back with me, but she never texted me to let me know she'd made it."

My shoulders stiffened. Kim and Reyes were close. If anything were to happen to her, I didn't know how he would take it.

"I'm sure it's okay," he said, lying through his teeth. But I got the feeling he wasn't lying to me so much as to himself. "She probably lost her charger. She does that."

"Have you, you know, searched?" Meaning, had he searched for her incorporeally.

"Not yet."

"We could send Angel."

"We could, but I have him on another assignment."

"An assignment? Like what kind of assignment?"

He draped an arm over me. "It pertains to one of those secrets I told you about." He waited a moment and then said, "Go ahead. You know you want to."

"Okay, seriously, can't you just tell me one? It'll be like opening one present on Christmas Eve. Then I'll be satisfied and can sleep at night knowing that your secret isn't that you're really into women's underwear or that you like Howard Stern or that you watched a snuff film once. If I just had those three things out of the way . . ."

"Fine." He shifted to face me again. "You tell me one, and I'll tell you one."

I growled and buried my face in a pillow. "I can't. Not yet. But soon."

"Same here." When I started to protest—an act I had zero right to do—he raised an index finger in warning.

I leaned forward. Wrapped my mouth around it. Sucked softly before sliding off it.

Reyes's gaze didn't waver. He watched with great interest, and I felt his pulse accelerate.

"Oh, wait," I said, "what were you saying about money?"

It took him a moment to recover.

"That's what I wanted to tell you. I'm out. I've gone through all of it redoing the building and buying the safe houses."

"Oh, Reyes," I said, now worried for him. "It's okay. We have the restaurant and my business. We've never actually been in the black for longer than five minutes, but I can turn that around." I thought about it and cringed. "Or, you know, I can try. I'm always getting lawyers who want to hire me. But they usually want me to get their scumbag clients off the very legit charge of drug trafficking or spousal abuse or cannibalism, but that was only once." I looked at him, positive we'd be okay. "We can do this. I may have to sell out and get some creep off a couple of human trafficking charges, but we can do this."

"You would never sell out. And I was fucking with you. I need you to know where everything is should anything happen to me."

"What?" I scrambled up and sat cross-legged on the bed, the sheet covering my vitals since I'd recently lost my jersey and boxers. "What do you mean? Is something going to happen?" I gasped. "Is that one of your secrets?"

"No. This is just a precaution. We don't live the safest lives. In general."

"Oh. Okay, well, what do you mean where everything is?"

"Our money. Our lawyers. Our accountants."

"You have more than one accountant?"

"*We* have more than one accountant. Seven, in fact. And one general manager. Basically you need to know how to get to any and all our resources. You have full access to everything, of course, so you can get anything you need anytime."

"You have seven accountants?"

"We. And do you have any clue how much money we have?"

"Yes. I told you."

He shook his head. "That's not mine."

"Right, so you have more?"

He held up a thumb and index finger, indicating a tiny amount.

"Oh, wow." I lay back down again. "A little over fifty million." I let that sink in. Or tried to. It wouldn't. It was so very far beyond my comprehension. "So, if you stacked all your money in a pile, how big would the pile be? I need a visual. Like, could it fill a Dumpster?"

"Depends on the bills, but we don't have a little over fifty million."

"You just held up your fingers."

"I know, and I also know you don't care, but you need to."

"This sounds ominous." I slid a thumbnail between my fingers.

"Okay, just so you know, we have a little over thirty billion dollars."

I tilted my head. Blinked. Frowned. Looked up. Mumbled something incoherent. Bit my bottom lip. "So, two Dumpsters?"

"Everything you need, if anything happens to me, is in the filing cabinets in our closet."

"Oh, you mean that room the size of my old apartment? That closet?"

"Yes."

"Gotcha." I nodded and tried to absorb what he'd just said. "Just so I have this straight, you have over thirty billion dollars?"

"We have over thirty billion dollars."

He gave me a moment. It didn't help. Mostly because numbers were not my forte. I didn't math. Mathing was never on my list of favorite things to do, but it did make a strong showing on my list of things I'd do only if the other option was having my toenails removed by a man from El Salvador named Toro the Magnificent.

Yeah, no. My brain shut down after around three million. Couldn't think any higher.

"So, are you the richest man in the world?" I asked in awe.

"Not hardly. Not by a long shot."

"Bummer." I let all the possibilities rush through my mind like a movie on fast-forward. "I'm married to a billionaire like in all those books I read where the superrich guy falls in love with the poor chick who may not have much in the way of money but is wealthy in vivacity and sprightliness and is really into bondage?"

"Why not."

"And she may or may not need a heart transplant."

"Story of my life."

"Dude, I am so getting a Vespa. And a signed first edition of *Pride and*

Prejudice. And a pair of Rocketbuster boots." I looked around our exquisitely decorated apartment. "And, yep, an elephant."

"Okay, but you're cleaning up after it."

I scoffed. "I don't know if you're aware of this, but I'm married to a billionaire. I can hire a pooper-scooper. Wait." I tilted my head again as another thought hit me. "Isn't there like a club you have to belong to if you have that much money? Shouldn't you have, like, paparazzi and reporters following you around? And *Forbes* calling wanting interviews? And rock stars on speed dial? It's impossible to have that much money without being hounded by the masses."

"Not necessarily. You just have to be smart about it."

And he had smarts down to a science.

"And *Forbes* wouldn't call me, anyway."

"Why? Offshore accounts or underground bunker?"

"Something like that. Let's just say I am very good friends with our banker in Switzerland."

"We have a banker in Switzerland?" I leaned back and stared at him. "Dude, who are you? Who has that kind of money?"

"You do," he said, pulling me back down and into his arms.

20

Money may not be able to buy happiness,
but it's more comfortable to cry in a Mercedes than on a bicycle.
—MEME

I dwelled on the money thing, mentally making a list of all the boots I was going to buy. But I'd stop there. Just because one's husband was loaded was no reason to spend it all on boots. I'd just spend a very small percentage on boots. Each week.

But reality came creeping back in. He was right. What if something happened to him, heaven forbid, and I had to go on the run with Beep? I really needed to get my powers under control. Starting with . . .

"There actually is something else I need to know. For me and for Beep."

"Name it."

"I need to know how to dematerialize."

He chuckled. "You already know how to do that."

"Yeah, but not on purpose. I only do it when I have a meltdown or I'm in danger. You can do it on purpose. How?"

He took my hand in his. Laced our fingers together. "If you can't do it, there's something stopping you."

"Like what?"

"What stops us in almost everything?"

I shrugged.

"What is the universal reason for almost every human action?"

"Ah, right," I said, when it hit me. "Fear."

"Exactly. So, what are you afraid of?"

"I don't know. Nothing."

"Then do it." He watched our hands. "Slip away from me."

"If I could do it, Obi-Wan, I wouldn't be asking for your help."

"Then you're afraid." He took my chin and turned my face to his. "What are you afraid of?"

"I don't know. Maybe—" I shook my head. "No, that's stupid."

"Tell me."

"Maybe shifting onto the next plane entirely? The last time I did it, when I was running away from you and Michael in New York?"

He nodded, his expression suddenly severe.

"It burned my skin. It was so hot, like acid. And I ended up miles away in a matter of seconds. I'm afraid . . . I'm afraid I'll melt."

He gave me a sympathetic smile. "The supernatural plane didn't burn you."

"Damn sure did," I argued, remembering it so vividly. "It peeled the skin right off my bones."

"But when you materialized, were you harmed?"

"No. It was so strange."

"Again, it didn't burn you. But it is hot. And cold. The rules of this plane don't apply, like a human in space who is exposed to the solar winds. Except, we are no longer human, and it's still our plane, and we can navigate it at will."

"Then what happened, because my skin was being burned away like someone had taken a blowtorch to me."

"That wasn't your body reacting to the heat and cold from the other dimension. You did that yourself. It was a physiological response to what your mind perceived as reality. In that state, not much can harm you."

"Okay, then, speaking of space, what if I accidentally materialize there? I'll just be floating in the vacuum of space. Body swelling. Blood boiling. Skin turning an unappealing shade of blue and freezing. Then, knowing me, I'd explode. Even if I managed to make it back to the planet's surface, I would've been exposed to all those subatomic particles. You don't come back from that."

"Dutch," he said, talking me off a ledge, "you control where and when you go. And how fast. You can even, to some degree, control the time there. Hell, since you're a god, you could probably, I don't know, navigate time." His mind was suddenly racing. "There's just no way to know what you're capable of until you do it."

"Okay, but maybe we should start small."

He chuckled. "Sorry. You're right. Okay, concentrate." He held up our hands again. "Shift as far onto the other plane as you can."

I dropped my hand. "You don't like it when I shift."

He didn't agree, but he didn't argue.

"It's like you can't look at me when I shift. Like I'm monstrous."

"What?" he asked, dumbfounded. "You are still you when you shift, Dutch."

"Then why do I repulse you when I do?"

He focused on the ceiling. "It's not you. It's me."

"Seriously? You went there?"

He pinched the bridge of his nose.

"Reyes, what? Why don't you like it when I shift, even just a little, to see onto the other plane?"

He turned away from me and practically whispered what came next. "When you shift, you see the real me. The dark side. It's disturbing to know you can see that part of me."

"Reyes, it's fascinating." I turned his face back to mine. "I'm amazed.

It's like you're covered in a cloak of black mist. It cascades over your shoulders and down your back. I want a cloak of black mist. How cool would that be?"

He deadpanned me.

"Wait, if I'm still me and not some monster, how do you know when I shift? You know instantly."

"Your eyes. When you shift, your gold eyes almost glow. They sparkle like glitter when you see into the other realm. Talk about fascinating."

"So, it's a good thing?"

"That part of it is, yes."

"Because sometimes the way you react . . . you're positive I don't look like a monster? Like, maybe, a Chucky doll?"

"A Chucky doll?" he asked, baffled.

"Yes. I always had a fear growing up that I looked a little like Chucky. Something about the jawline. And you are, too, by the way. A very good thing. Okay, I think I'm ready."

He repeated the instructions, telling me to shift as far as I could. I did, and I watched as the scene before me turned from the soothing neutral colors of our apartment to the raging colors of the otherworld. The storms swirled around us. Lightning struck close by, and I jumped.

But Reyes wasn't watching the intangible world. He was staring at me and continued to do so a long moment, gazing into my eyes as I took him in. His smooth skin. His dark lashes. The otherworld intensified everything about him.

"Now, imagine you're floating away one molecule at a time."

I tore my gaze off him and focused on my fingers.

"Start at the tips." He brushed his thumb over my palm. It caused a quake deep in my belly, like they were connected by a string. "Let the molecules go."

He opened my hand, leaned forward, and blew softly on my fingers. His warm breath penetrated my skin and whispered through it.

"Let the molecules go," he repeated, and slowly, atom by atom, my body began to dematerialize. It started with my fingertips. He blew again, and they flew into a gold vapor around me until Reyes's hand slipped through mine completely.

Astonished and terrified—mostly terrified—I snapped back to the tangible world, the weight of my body taking shape again.

"That was amazing," I said. I glanced back at him, and his brows were drawn into a severe line. "What?"

He blinked back to me. "Nothing. Sorry."

"Oh, no, you don't. We said no more secrets. What's wrong? What did I do?"

"You're right. It's just . . . your color."

"Now you're racist?" I teased.

"No. It's just—"

"Is there something wrong with it?" I asked, alarmed.

"No, not at all. I've just never seen it before. Anyway, you did it. And you can do more, as your recent trips would suggest."

"Reyes, how do you not just fly around all the time, checking shit out?"

He laid his head against the headboard and laughed. "I do sometimes, but my life is on this plane." He brushed his fingertips over my palm again, studying me. "I love every inch of you."

My heart melted, and I hoped it hadn't dematerialized and rematerialized somewhere else. That couldn't be good. I turned in to him. "I love all your inches, too."

He bent to kiss me but stopped halfway to my mouth. "I almost forgot."

Before I could ask what, he rose from the bed and walked out of the room, flashing me his ass. I fought the urge to sigh. And snap a few photos.

I lay back and listened as he walked into the kitchen. If he pulled out the utensils again . . . But he came back with a bottle of champagne. The view this time was even more spectacular.

"I almost forgot. It's our anniversary."

"What?" I asked, bolting upright. "We've been married a year already?"

"Not that anniversary."

"Oh, whew. So, on this day however many years ago we . . . kissed for the first time?"

"Nope," he said with a smirk, opening the bottle with a loud pop.

"We . . . celebrated the first spine you'd severed in my defense?"

"Nuh-uh." The bed dipped with his weight as he eased back onto it, turned me over, and poured champagne in the small of my back.

The icy liquid stole my breath and sent a shock wave rocketing through my system. I squealed and buried my face. "Cold. Really cold."

But his tongue was already on my skin, warming me as he drank the sparkling wine. Then he poured it between my shoulder blades, and it ran straight down to pool in the small of my back again. I shivered and then sighed as his mouth lapped it up.

"The first time we drank champagne together?" I asked.

"No," he said, concentrating.

"The first time we landed on the moon?"

"Nuh-uh." He nipped as he drank, causing spasms of pure delight.

"Wait, is it my birthday?"

"No."

"Is it your birthday?"

"No," he said with a soft chuckle.

"Oh, thank God. Can I have a drink?"

"I think you've had enough to drink for one night."

I turned over, but he only continued the assault there. Pouring. Kissing. Lapping. Nipping. I grabbed a handful of hair when he dipped between my legs.

"The first time we had oral sex?" I guessed.

He shook his head as his tongue feathered across my clitoris. I sucked air in through my teeth as he deftly brought me to the brink of orgasm and then stopped. When he rose up, I whimpered in protest. He ignored me and took a drink from the bottle but didn't swallow. Then he started at my mouth, filling it with the bubbly wine, dripping it over my lips and down my neck. He took another mouthful and suckled a breast, the cold liquid hardening my nipples on contact. Then he gave the same rapt attention to its twin.

I squirmed under his ministrations. His mouth was blisteringly hot compared to the chilled champagne, and the contrast was almost painful. I gasped with each kiss. Clenched with each suckle.

He bathed my entire body. My stomach. My hips. My legs. My ankles. My insteps, which caused way more pleasure than I could've imagined. Then he made his way back up to the apex between my lower extremities.

His dark hair fell over his forehead and became entangled with his lashes. His sculpted jaw worked with each kiss. His full mouth firm but smooth. I could've watched him forever, he was so beautiful. So darkly handsome. And so clueless about it all, which made him all the sexier.

Then he dipped south with a mouthful of the good stuff, and I almost bucked off the mattress. He let the liquid slip from his lips and run between the sensitive folds of my cunt before he lapped it up in a hypnotic rhythm, coaxing the flames in rapturous delight. Tiny bites of pleasure quaked between my legs and pooled in my abdomen.

I curled my toes in the air and my fists into the sheets as he dropped the bottle, spread my legs, and entered me in one seamless thrust.

Wrapping me into his arms, he pulled me up until we were both upright. I thrust my fingers into his hair and started to rock, wanting that sweet sting to wash over me again, but he surprised me for a second time that night. He held me close, looked into my eyes, and let the darkness envelop him.

He shifted, and I followed.

Suddenly, we were making love amid a mosaic of colors and winds and lightning. My hair whipped around us as the heat from the other-world scalded the skin along my spine. Then I realized it wasn't the wind, but Reyes. His heat had multiplied. His hands burning and scorching and causing the most delicious spasms to rocket through me.

He gripped my shoulders and pulled me harder onto his cock. I cried out but could barely be heard over the storms raging around us. Still, I wanted more. So very much more. I rose onto my toes and began riding him. He cupped my ass and helped me, lifting me off him to the very tip and then plunging me back down.

Arousal flared to life, hot and thick and full of need. Distant, yet rocketing closer. He drove it forward, the sting of orgasm, with each thrust of his hips. The length of his cock massaged me from the inside, milked me until the sensation grew to nuclear levels.

I clutched at his shoulders and cradled his neck as he took me into a vise grip and pumped into me.

"Rey'aziel," I whispered, and he growled and ground into me harder.

Until there was no more resistance. Until it surfaced and burst and spilled into every molecule in my body, flooding me with a sensual pleasure like nothing else on this plane or the next.

Reyes tensed as he came, too. Growled and shuddered as he held on to me for dear life. Pushing out the last remnants of desire. And then we were back in bed. Panting, we collapsed onto the mattress.

After a long moment to collect myself, I looked over at him. "So, what anniversary was it?"

He sobered and seemed to withdraw inside himself. He threw an arm over his eyes and then, almost inaudibly, said, "The night you saved me."

I stilled. Studied his profile. Basked in the beauty of it. "I wasn't aware that I had."

A sad smile slid across his face. "Now you know."

"And what night was that?"

His jaw muscle jumped in reflex. "You have to ask?"

I didn't. I really didn't. Only one night would bring him such sadness. Such regret. The night I lobbed a brick through a plate glass window to stop a man from beating a teenaged boy.

"Well, good," I said, knowing he wouldn't want to talk about it at length. Surprised he would even bring it up. "I was worried it was the night I lost my virginity."

"January twenty-seventh. You were fifteen."

I bolted upright. "What? How could you possibly know when I lost my virginity?"

When I pinched him, he laughed softly and pretended to be in pain. We both knew better.

"I felt it," he said at last. "I felt something wrong, so I went to you. I'd only just realized you were real. And I thought you were in trouble."

"Trouble?" I asked, thinking back. Freddie hadn't forced himself on me in the least. If it was anyone's idea, it'd been mine. But still, truth be told . . . "Yeah, I think Freddie had a lot more fun that night than I did."

He snorted. "I can guarantee you he did."

"I can't believe—you're a Peeping Tom."

"Hey," he said, sliding out of the melancholy, "you practically summoned me to your side. I was there in an observatory capacity only. You know, should you have needed me. Or wanted a threesome."

I lay beside him. "I didn't know you and the Big Bad were one and the same back then. I fell in love with you that night. The first night I saw you."

"So did I," he said, his face so impossibly handsome, his tone so impossibly sincere.

"I mean it, Reyes. I did."

"As did I."

I scoffed softly. "You didn't seem very in love." It had been such a horrible night when I threw a brick through Earl Walker's kitchen window to stop him from beating Reyes. A beautiful teenaged boy with shimmering brown eyes and thick, dark hair. It still broke my heart to think about it.

Reyes stiffened. "You're not feeling sorry for me, are you?"

"I'm sorry for what you went through."

"Water under the bridge."

"Reyes," I said, raising a hand to his cheek, "no matter what happens, I love you."

His brows knitted for just a moment before he answered. "I love you more."

"Nope. Wanna wrestle for it?"

"For?"

"The championship. Who loves who more?"

He glanced up as though in thought, then whispered so quietly I barely heard him, "You are so going down."

And before I knew it, I was pinned to the bed. For about the tenth time that evening.

"You cheated," I accused as he held me down.

"Son of Satan," he said by way of explanation.

He had a point.

Reyes and I were still talking and laughing the next morning when we heard Cookie rush into the apartment. Fortunately, I'd already made coffee, so she stopped for a cup while I hurried to the bathroom for my robe.

"I'm going to hit the shower," Reyes said as I walked out. He stepped in front of me, his sleek body shimmering in the low morning light. "Hopefully, your aunt will visit. Surely one Davidson is as good as the other."

I gasped and wrapped my hands around his hips. Caressed his ass. Marveled that it was mine.

"Does it bother you that I'm still going by Davidson? I mean, after we got married, there was just no time before we had to rush to the convent, to holy ground. And then we were stuck there for eight months, and I never worried about it. Then with Beep and the amnesia."

"You've been a little busy," he said, a playful grin tilting the corners of his mouth. "But, no, it's doesn't bother me. I think it's for the best for now."

"Why?"

"If we keep everything in your name, it'll be easier should anything happen to me."

I stepped back. "Reyes, you keep saying that. What the hell? Is there something I need to know?"

"No." He reached out, grabbed the lapel of my robe, and pulled me closer. "It's just, you're a god, Dutch. You *will* outlive me. My physical body, anyway."

Having just gotten an answer I'd been hoping for, I stood rather dumbfounded. He truly did not know he was a god.

What would it do to him, to learn he was created from one of the gods of Uzan? How would he feel knowing he, essentially, had caused the death and destruction of millions of beings on hundreds of worlds? My chest tightened around my heart with the mere thought, and I wondered for the thousandth time if it would change him. If he would revert back to his old ways like an addict who falls off the wagon.

And then something else hit me. "What did you say?"

"You'll outlive me."

"No. About everything being—"

"—in your name. Yes. Didn't I mention that?"

"Are you talking about your money?"

"Our money, yes."

"Reyes." I dragged him over to the bed. I needed to sit down. "Why on earth would you put everything in my name?"

His head tilted as though he didn't quite understand the question. "Why wouldn't I?"

"You can't just put money in someone else's name. What if something happens and you need to get to it? You said you put everything in both our names."

"No, I said it was our money and assets, not mine. I didn't say whose name it was in."

"But there's thirty billion at stake."

"Not enough?" he teased. "I can make more. I do, actually, on a daily basis. The interest alone is astronomical."

Cookie sat at our counter, and I heard papers shuffling. She had information. Was bursting with it. But even she drew the line at barging into our bedroom. Thank goodness, because I was going to have another meltdown.

"No." I stood and stepped out of his reach. "I forbid it. I refuse. You go to your seven accountants and you tell them to take it out of my name."

"If you're worried about the taxes—"

"This isn't about taxes." I could not believe this was happening. "It's about you getting and keeping what is rightfully yours. What you worked for and you deserve."

"Well, I am listed on the accounts. You're just the owner of said accounts."

This was not happening. This could not happen. "Reyes, I won't take that money. Any of it. It's yours. I can make my own living."

"You are the strangest most perplexing human I've ever known."

I let out a long breath. "Reyes, please, take my name off. It's yours."

"Dutch," he said, standing in all his naked glory. "I started making that money from prison."

"I know. You hacked servers all over the place and made a fortune on the stock market and other investments. You. Not me."

"What I'm trying to say is, it's always been in your name."

A gentle breeze could have knocked me over, I was so stunned. "What do you mean?"

"When I started all this, when I figured out how to hack the markets, I put everything in your name. Well, everything but what I gave Kim and Amador and Bianca. I was always going to take care of you one way or another."

I clamped my teeth together. He had never had anything growing up. He had been abused and exploited and framed for murder before he even got a start in life. He worked hard for what he had. He earned every penny. I would not take it from him.

"Dutch, I'm not changing the accounts. It's yours. It's all yours. And that's final."

He started for the bathroom again. I put my hand on his chest. He instantly covered it with his own.

"Please, Reyes, please take my name off."

He bent until his mouth was barely a centimeter from my own and whispered, "Never." Then he went into the bathroom and closed the door as I stood in the middle of our bedroom on the verge of hyperventilating.

After I was able to breathe without almost passing out, I rambled into the kitchen.

"Well?" she said when I took down a clean cup, having left mine in the bedroom. But, hell, I could afford a dozen cups. I could afford a thousand. No, I could afford thirty billion. "How was your night?"

I put the cup down, ran to her, and cried in her arms for a solid thirty minutes. One for each billion in my bank account.

21

Coffee
Debauchery
Madness
One down. Two to go.
—STATUS UPDATE

By the time Reyes came out, Cookie and I were at the kitchen counter drinking coffee. Well, I was drinking coffee and going over some articles she'd printed out. Cookie was staring off into space, in total shock. She had a bit of drool leaking from one corner of her mouth. I reached over with a napkin and sopped it up. She didn't move.

"You told her?" he asked, getting a fresh cup himself.

"Should I not have?"

"Not at all. If anything happens to me, she will be the one you rely on most. She needs to know this stuff just as much as you do."

He turned toward me and leaned back against the counter. He wore a dark red button down and his signature jeans. They weren't tight, but they weren't loose. They had the perfect fit around his hips. Over his ass. Through his crotch.

"Do we need to go back to the bedroom?" he asked from behind his cup.

I straightened and cleared my throat. Then I offered him my best pleading face. "Reyes, please take my name—"

"No." He said it softly as though it were a caress. "It's done. It was done over seven years ago." He stepped to me, lifted my chin, and brushed his mouth across mine. "No more crying. And I think she might need medical attention," he said before grabbing his jacket and walking out.

It took another three cups of coffee to settle my nerves. Once Cookie came to, we went over the papers she'd brought. It was all the news articles she could find on each death at the children's home.

"Charley," she said, still unable to wrap her head around what had happened, "he put your name on the accounts even before he met you? Before he got out of prison?"

I nodded and closed my eyes, trying not to think of the injustices that had been done to him all his life, including this one. "What would possess him to do such a thing? That's his money, Cook." Tears slipped between my lashes, and Cookie grabbed me up again.

"He loves you, hon. He's always loved you. Even if you'd never met, he was looking out for you."

"But I don't deserve it."

"Charley." She set me at arm's length. "He believes you do, and quite frankly, so do I. That money will come in handy. And if nothing else, Beep will be an heiress."

A hiccup of laughter escaped me. "Okay, that makes the whole thing worth it. But I'm still not comfortable with it."

"I doubt you ever will be. I can't even imagine that much money."

"Right? So, seriously, how many Dumpsters do you think that would fill?"

A knock sounded at the door.

"Come in!" I yelled. "It's your ball and chain."

"Ah."

Uncle Bob walked in, looking very masculine in his brown suit and tie. "Looking good, Ubie."

"Thanks, pumpkin. Court," he said by way of an explanation.

"Up for murder again?"

"Not my court. I have to testify in court."

"Oh, of course. Sorry."

"I just wanted to let both of you know, I'm going to ask you one more time who hired you before I get a warrant and/or have you arrested."

"Aw, thanks for the heads-up, Uncle Bob."

Cookie simply raised her brows at him, completely content in the knowledge that she would win in the end.

He let out a frustrated sigh. "I'll do it."

"I'm sure you will. But if Joplin is so worried, why hasn't he asked me himself? And if he's harassing you about it, why don't you tell him to fight his own fights?"

"Because I'm not in the third grade, and he's a control freak. He is very, very interested in who hired you and why."

"That's strange. Why don't you tell him to mind his own bees wax and ask him why he's so worried?"

"Because I'm not in the third grade, and he's a control freak. Are you even listening to me?"

"Maybe he doesn't want Team Davidson showing him up." Cookie and I high-fived, we were that good.

He shrugged. "He said something about you blowing the case."

"Sounds to me like Joplin is worried he doesn't even have a case and he's trying to blame it on someone else."

"You're probably right. Still, the two of you might want to pack an overnight bag."

"As if they allow those in jail."

He leaned down to kiss his wife, then walked out.

"See you later, hon," Cook said. "If I go to jail, don't forget to pick up Amber from school."

When she received nothing but a grunt and the sound of a door closing, she giggled. "It's driving him crazy that we won't give him a name."

"It's the little things." I thumbed through the papers. "The nurse at the home?" I asked, steering her back.

"Okay." She pointed at one paper in particular. An employment record for the nurse in question. "She's worked there for years, but check this out. She left for several months to take care of her ailing mother. While she was gone, there were no deaths. Now, I know what you're thinking," she said before I could say anything. "The deaths were spread out over years. But as soon as her mother died and she went back to work at the home, another child passed away of an asthma attack."

She showed me an article.

"She's the common thread. Well, one of them. The home still has the same director, a few of the house parents, and a groundskeeper that it's had since the deaths began. I just found it odd that a boy dies right before the nurse goes on leave, and then another one a week after she comes back."

"That is certainly worth looking into."

The article called the nurse heroic after she tried to save the boy by administering CPR on him for over an hour before someone found her and help arrived. The picture that accompanied the article showed the nurse, bereft and sobbing and falling into a coworker's arms, as an ambulance took the nine-year-old kid away. The caption read, NURSE COLLAPSES AFTER CHILD DIES DESPITE HER BEST EFFORTS TO SAVE HIM.

"Very dramatic," I said, finding all kinds of things wrong with the picture. "Exactly the kind of attention a certain type of person thrives on."

"I thought so, too."

"Well, looks like I know what I'll be doing today."

"Me, too. Figuring out how many Dumpsters it would take to stash thirty billion dollars in."

We high-fived before I headed for George. Reyes's shower. No. I closed my eyes and let happiness shudder through me. *Our* shower.

By the time I left for the office to check in again with Cookie, I was dressed quite spiffily in a black sweater, jeans, and ankle boots. Which was pretty much what I wore every day during the winter.

Reyes had texted me a thumbs-up, which had become our code for, "I've checked with Osh. Beep and the gang are okay."

Walking across the parking lot to the office, I noticed a familiar neon-green minivan parked down the alley. It was the bungling ghost hunters. The adorable ones that I wanted to adopt.

I resisted the urge to hightail it to their van and give them a piece of my brain. Partly because it would be bloody and painful and all I had in my bag was a box cutter, but mostly because I didn't care. If they wanted to waste their time, fine. I was actually surprised they'd stuck around after our chat. Hopefully, I'd scared the French crew off. They were the dangerous ones.

My phone rang as I headed up the outside stairs to the office. Pari's picture filled my screen, complete with bug-eyes sunglasses. She never rose this early. My mind immediately jumped to Heather. "Is everything okay?"

"Groovy. Are you okay?" she asked, her voice groggy and muffled.

"I'm fine. Why are you up? And where are you? Your voice is muffled."

"I'm in bed. It's muffled because I can't quite lift my head yet. And I called because you butt-dialed me ten thousand times last night. Did you get drunk?"

"What? No."

"Don't lie to me, Chuck."

"Maybe a little. Is Heather okay?"

"She's good. I think she's getting better. The doc put her on a lot of liquids to hopefully flush any toxins out of her system. I think it's helping."

"Pari, thank you so much for keeping her."

"Not a problem, but I will say that a tattoo parlor is probably not the best place for an impressionable twelve-year-old."

"I know. I'll try to come up with other accommodations today."

Her voice cleared instantly. "What? That's not what I said. I just meant, you know, she could be scarred for life, but really, she's fine here. I don't mind."

"Really? You sure?"

"Of course. She's sleeping right now. Or I hope she's sleeping. She took off with one of my regulars at around one this morning, but I'm sure she made it back."

I so didn't fall for that. "I'm so not falling for that."

"It was worth a shot."

"Totally. Call me if anything comes up. I'm heading to the children's home to do some interviews today."

"Ten-four. Over and out."

"Over and—bye."

With both Heather and Beep safe, I could concentrate on my cases. But before I could head out to the children's home, Parker called.

"How's the case going?"

"Sensational, but you may have been made. Joplin is trying to get a judge to force me to say who hired me. He's way too interested."

"Are you fucking kidding me?" His explosive temper exploded. Thank god I didn't have him on speakerphone when I walked into the office. A deliveryman was just leaving.

I waited for the door to close, *then* I put him on speakerphone. Expletives, the really colorful ones, filled the air around us like dirty butterflies. Cookie and I cracked up as we listened. When he finally got around to telling me why he'd called, I was having a hard time keeping a straight face. Or voice since we were on the phone.

"I need this done, Davidson. I would suggest you close this thing. Quickly. Isn't that what you do?"

"Did you call just to threaten me, Parker?"

"What? No. One of Emery Adams's coworkers called. She has some information that might pertain to the case. I need you to go talk to her."

"What's her name?"

I took down the information he gave me on the coworker and asked Cook to look a little more into the nurse's background. The one from the children's home. Specifically, look for a history of mental illness or a history of physical ailments. Both could be a sign of Munchhausen's. If she was killing those kids and taking the glory for trying to save them, that would be a form of Munchhausen syndrome by proxy. Either way, it's hard to detect and even harder to prove.

"We could have an Angel of Death on our hands," I said.

"Whatever works. We just have to stop her."

I hurried downstairs, made out with my husband for about three minutes, then went in search of one of Emery's coworkers named Cathy Neville. It was actually on the way to the children's home, so that worked out well.

The Presbyterian Hospital sat down the road from our offices. It didn't take long to find Cathy. She was on break outside the lab, sitting on the edge of a chair in the waiting area, punching buttons on her phone.

"That's her," another tech said.

She rose the minute I walked up to her. "Are you with the DA's office?"

"Of a sort. I'm working Emery's case."

She nodded and stuffed the last chip in her mouth before trashing the bag. "Sorry to drag you down here. I told them I could just talk to someone over the phone. Can you tell me how the case is going? I mean, do they have the guy?"

"There's been an arrest but, no, they don't have the guy."

She cast me a confused expression and then continued. "Well, I just wanted to let the cops know that I think Ms. Adams was in trouble." She rolled her eyes. "Obviously. But, I mean, I think she was in trouble before she disappeared."

"How so?" We walked down the hall toward the lab where she worked.

"I didn't say anything to anyone. I didn't want to insinuate anything, but I found her in the lab the other night after we'd closed. She was crying."

"Was anyone in there with her?"

"No. I'd forgotten my phone. I do that. So I had to have Estelle let me in."

"Estelle?"

"Custodian. Sweetest lady ever."

"Did Estelle let Ms. Adams in?"

"Oh no. She's the administrator. She has keys to the whole place."

"Right. Did she say what happened?"

"No, Estelle didn't even know Ms. Adams was in there."

"I mean, did Ms. Adams say what happened?"

She shook her head. "No. She apologized, grabbed her bag, and hurried out. But I know how she feels. Sometimes you just have to cry and there's nowhere private in this whole place. I couldn't blame her for coming here after hours like that."

"I agree. Did you notice anything else? For example, was Ms. Adams disheveled in any way like she'd been attacked?"

"I don't know. I really never knew her that well. But now that you mention it, I think someone might have hurt her."

"What makes you say that?"

"She had blood on her skirt. Not a lot. Just like a drop that she'd tried to wipe off."

"Okay," I said while turning in a circle and scanning the area for cameras. "Why didn't you tell the police this before?"

"Oh, I've been on vacation. Just got back. I had no idea what happened to Ms. Adams until I walked in the door today. And then I knew I had to tell someone."

"I appreciate that. Thank you." I shook her hand. "Can I call you if I have any questions?"

She brightened. "Sure. I will help in any way I can."

"Here's my card if you think of anything else."

"You're a private investigator?"

"I am."

"That's so cool. I would love to be a PI."

Her credibility was dwindling by the second. She was a *helper*. One of those who went out of her way to assist others for the attention even when it's not wanted. Still, her information could be crucial to the case.

I called Parker on the way out. "I need the camera footage for the evening of the nineteenth."

"Any particular area?"

"Every area. There was blood on Emery's skirt that night, and she was found locked in the lab crying. You need to get that skirt. If she was attacked, it could be on the camera footage."

22

*My decision-making skills closely resemble
those of a squirrel crossing the street.*
—MEME

I did a drive-by at Satellite Coffee and refueled before heading out to the children's home to interview the heroic nurse. I just had to come up with a reason for being there.

"You could be looking to adopt," Cookie suggested.

"Too cold. And I don't think it works that way."

"You could be a philanthropist looking to make a donation."

"Way too cold."

"Sorry. Okay, well, maybe you're a reporter and you want to do a story on her."

I thought a moment. "That might work. She's had articles written about her before."

"There's really nothing unusual that I've found as far as illnesses. She never married and has no children of her own."

"Okay, thanks, Cook. I'll call you if I get anything interesting."

"Be safe."

I stepped out of Misery and went first to the office to sign in and check if the nurse, Florence Rizzo, was even there. I didn't want to go with the reporter angle. They might not appreciate that. So, when asked, I said, "I'm a consultant with APD. I'm working a case that Ms. Rizzo might have information on." Neither of those were technically a lie. I was more implying that APD had hired me to look into the case. I never said it outright.

The woman behind the desk didn't seem impressed either way.

"She's down the hall and to the right."

That was easy. "Thanks."

Okay, I needed a clean read off her first, then I'd bring up the string of deaths. A girl about sixteen with dark skin and large exotic eyes the color of smoked glass told me the nurse was checking on a kid in the infirmary. Alarms rang in my ears. Another sick child in her care.

When she walked in, I stood and held out my hand. "Hi, my name is Charley Davidson. I'm a consultant for APD, and I've been hired to look into a case here at the home."

"My goodness. Well, have a seat," she said in a Northeastern accent. Florence Rizzo was a slightly overweight mid-fortysomething brunette who liked Red Bull and comic books, if her desk was any indication.

I sat across from her and waited for her to clear her desk.

"You have someone in the infirmary?"

"Yes. Poor babies." She tapped the comic books to straighten them, then stashed them in her desk. "The flu. It's going around, don't you know?"

"Yes. It does seem to be worse this year."

"I think so, too. No one is immune. Darned flus. Well, what can I do for you?"

I certainly wasn't sensing anything out of the ordinary off her, but I was just getting started.

"It seems that there have been several deaths at the home over the years, and I was hired to look into it."

"Heavens," she said, but instead of being distressed or taken aback, I got the feeling she would be more than willing to cooperate.

Unfortunately, that is the signature response of a person with Munchhausen by proxy. They want the attention. They want to be seen as heroic or distraught. Anything to put the focus on them. And, worse, they don't believe they've done anything wrong, so to get a guilty reading off them is almost impossible.

"We have had a few unfortunate incidents here at Harbor House, but they were all explained in our reports."

"Yes, I read those. It's just that, statistically, it looks very . . . unusual."

"It most certainly does," she said, nodding in complete agreement. Then, just like that, a lightbulb went off in her head. "But you don't think there was foul play involved, do you? Those poor kids all had previous conditions. The ones who were sick." She started ticking off names on her fingers. "And then there were the accidents. Thank the heavens for Mrs. Ochoa. If not for her, we might have had another tragedy just the other day."

"Mrs. Ochoa?"

"Yes. Our custodian. A stack of lumber fell and almost crushed little Rudy. Mrs. Ochoa saw it about to happen and pushed him out of the way. He's in the infirmary, too, with a banged-up leg. Otherwise, he's fine. And then there were the suicides. Two of those.

"You have to understand, all these kids come from broken homes. Sometimes it just gets to be too much, and they think the only thing left for them is to take their own lives." Tears sprang to her eyes. "I wasn't here when those happened."

"I thought you'd worked here for over ten years."

"Yes, yes. I just meant I wasn't on-site. Our first suicide ever rocked the halls of this establishment. Almost broke the director, she was so distraught. I was in Delaware for a family reunion at the time."

I knew her accent was Northeast.

"And then CC. Poor CC. I thought she was doing so well. She had come to us after a bad foster home situation. Didn't trust a soul at first. But she adjusted so well. I had the night off when she took her life. It was so tragic."

None of this made sense. There was no rhyme or reason to the deaths. Accidents and suicides and strange illnesses. There was no pattern. Not one that I could see, anyway.

"Can you tell me who found the children who committed suicide?"

"Yes, the first one, a boy named Givens, was found by his roommate, and the second, CC, was found in the downstairs girls' room by Mrs. Ochoa. She called me in that night, she was so upset. But there was a horrible snowstorm, and I barely made it."

"And what about the others?"

"I don't understand."

"Who found the kids in the accidents?"

"Okay, well, one was Matthew's friend Abby. And with Roberto, it was our maintenance man, Joey. And then there was another girl, beautiful thing when she wasn't wearing all that eyeliner, who fell ill and became unconscious so fast we barely had time to call an ambulance. And then . . ."

I let her go on, trying to piece together the facts. All my Spidey senses would suggest Ms. Rizzo was telling the truth. She seemed genuinely distressed. Could all this truly be a coincidence? Maybe there really was no foul play. Maybe this was just a home with a lot of bad luck. Maybe . . .

When the truth dawned, I closed my eyes, almost kicking myself for being so thick. I sat back in the chair. Accidents. Illnesses. Suicides in children who had exhibited no signs of depression.

"Are you all right, Ms. Davidson?"

"Yes." I opened my eyes. "Sorry. Ms. Rizzo—"

"Oh, Florence, please."

"Florence, this might sound odd, but did you notice any strange behaviors in the children before they died?"

"No." She thought back. "Not that I can think of offhand."

"I have." I turned to the girl who'd showed me in.

"Malaya, what are you doing?" Ms. Rizzo stood to shoo the girl out. "Get back to the infirmary." She turned to me. "She had a fever this morning, poor dear."

"They aren't them anymore," Malaya said before the woman scooted her toward, I would assume, the infirmary.

Bingo.

"Okay," I said, jumping up. "I guess I'll let you get back to your day."

"Oh, okay, then. Good luck with your case."

"Thank you. Can Malaya see me to the front door?"

"Oh, I guess it wouldn't hurt. But then right back to bed, young lady." She smiled. "Yes, ma'am."

We walked a few feet before I asked her, "What have you noticed, hon?"

"Those with the curse. They aren't them anymore. They change."

I stopped and sat on a chair outside an office and fiddled with my boot to buy us time. She sat beside me.

"How do they change?"

"It's real slow at first. They just kind of go crazy, and then they get sick a lot, and then something awful happens."

"How long after something happens does another resident start showing symptoms?"

"It takes a while. We all guess at who it will be. For a while, we thought it was Heather this time, but she's gone. She ran away. I wish I was that brave."

"You are, sweetheart. You're talking to me now."

"That's not being brave."

"I think it is."

She looked at a woman down the hall. The custodian, Mrs. Ochoa, I presumed.

"They don't see us. They pretend to, but they don't. We tried to tell them about the curse, but no one would listen."

"Well, I am all ears," I said. "You hit the jackpot of ears. If I had any more ears, you'd be calling me a stalk of corn."

She offered me half a smile with a side of sadness.

"Do you know who's cursed now?"

She nodded and pressed her mouth together to keep it from quivering. "Hugo. My little brother. He's in the infirmary, too. That's why I pretended to have a fever."

Son of a bitch. I put a hand on her back, then asked, "How do you pretend to have a fever?"

"You just recalibrate the thermometer and put a heating pad on your face before Nurse Rizzo gets there."

I laughed softly.

"I did it too much one time, and it said I had a temperature of 112. Apparently I should have been dead. Or in a coma."

"See?" I said, grinning at her. "Brave. You risked a lot to stay here with your brother."

"Not really." Her breath hitched in her chest.

"Can I see him? Like, incognito-style?"

"You mean, can I sneak you in to see him?"

"Yes."

Her expression morphed into one of determination. She nodded, told me to go to the bathroom and wait for her there.

"I'll be right here. Don't get into trouble for this. I can come up with all kinds of reasons to be lost in the wrong area of the building."

She hurried off. I thought about using the facilities since it was so close, but not knowing how long she'd be, I decided to hold it.

"Ready?" she asked about thirty seconds later.

I nodded. She quickly led me down one hall and then another, and I no longer thought I would need to make up an excuse that I got lost. I really was lost. My sense of direction was like my sense of moderation. Nonexistent.

"In here," she said, slipping inside a darkened room.

There were six beds total, and three of them were occupied.

"There," she said, pointing, but she needn't have bothered. I spotted her brother the second we stepped inside the room.

We walked quietly toward him, but before we got to his bed, he sat up and looked at us. At me. And my fears were confirmed.

A demon sat inside him. Twelve feet tall even though the boy was no taller than five. But as Reyes had said, the rules of this world did not apply. It fit. Somehow the demon, all black scales and razor-sharp teeth, fit into his small body. They always fit. Fuckers.

I sat on the cot beside him, but the boy only stared at me, his gaze empty. He had the same incredible eye color as his sister, his large irises smoky and shimmering and feverishly bright.

"Hugo, what's wrong?" Malaya asked her brother.

"You're right, love," I said to her. I took her hand into mine. "He has the curse, but I can get it out of him."

She threw her free hand over her mouth.

"You'll have to trust me, okay?"

She nodded.

"I'm going to talk to the curse inside him. Whatever I say, and I might be mean, is not meant for your brother." I looked back at Hugo, at the demon inside him, and placed her hand on her lap. She sat on the next cot over, gripping the edge of the mattress, her knuckles white. He was probably the only real family she had.

"You are not being very nice, are you?" I asked the creature.

One corner of the boy's mouth slid up.

I shifted a little farther onto the otherworld.

"I can snap its neck," it said through the boy, but it was speaking Aramaic. Though Malaya had no idea what he said, I felt her still.

I spoke back in the same language. "Leave now and never come back, and perhaps I'll let you live."

"You leave," it said as though this were a game. "And perhaps we'll let you live. Though I wouldn't count on it." It wasn't stupid like most of them. It knew the moment it left the protection of the boy's body it wouldn't stand a chance. I hadn't actually expected it to. I just took the opportunity to lower my hand toward the ground and wait until Artemis rose up into it.

She scurried under the bed and took up position. She'd bared her teeth, yet stood completely silent behind him, ready to attack. The boy tilted his head, wondering what I was up to, when I froze time and nodded. Artemis jumped through the boy's chest and dragged out the demon.

It was frozen in time at first, stiff and incoherent as it oozed out into the open, but the second my light hit its skin, it snapped to the current time zone and started to shriek and writhe in her jaws. It bucked and lunged forward to bite me, its teeth like rows of needles, razor sharp and deadly. It missed. Then it threw its massive head back, bending its spine so far I could hear it crack. Or that could have been Artemis's bite.

"Why?" I asked it.

It had started to dissolve. To dissipate. To scatter into thin air.

"Why would you do this?"

With one last effort, it looked at me again and said, "To live while we wait. There are so many more in the shadows."

"What?" I asked, but it lost its hold and evaporated like ashes on the wind. "Wait for what?"

Time bounced back, slamming into me, the noise deafening for a split second before the world settled around me.

"Hugo?" Malaya said. "Are you okay?"

He blinked and shook his head. "I already told you I'm okay. You worry too much."

She glanced at me expectantly.

I nodded. "He'll be fine. It's gone."

A dimple appeared on one cheek. "Really?"

"Really."

She jumped forward and hugged her brother. He patted her head, not sure what to do and probably a little grossed out. I got the feeling they didn't hug much, but what siblings did?

I gave Artemis a quick attagirl, then she launched off my legs like a torpedo—that was so going to bruise—and disappeared through a wall.

"What are you doing in here?"

We turned to see Florence walking toward us. And Flo was not happy.

"I wanted to introduce her to Hugo," Malaya said.

"I'm sorry." I stood to leave. "She didn't mean any harm."

"It's okay, Mrs. Davidson." She relaxed and turned to the boy. "Hugo is very special."

"Oh yeah?" I asked.

He grinned from ear to ear. "I'm an inventor. I'm going to invent a tiny machine you can carry in your pocket that turns salt water into drinking water so when global warming melts all the ice, we can still drink the water that we're swimming in. You know, so we don't die of thirst."

"And he'll do it, too," Ms. Rizzo said.

"I have no doubt," I said.

I told Ms. Rizzo and eventually the home's director that I'd found Heather and she was on her way back. They would've had to call the police even if Heather came back on her own accord because they'd already reported her missing, so I called Uncle Bob instead. I could explain what happened, and he could make sure no charges were filed against her. But he was out on an investigation, so they had to call in an officer.

Then I called Heather and Pari and gave them the news. The curse was gone and would not be back. I thought she would cry. Pari, not Heather.

Pari brought her back to the home, and I spent the next hour explaining to the responding officer about the curse and how Heather believed she had it and was going to die if she didn't run away. He laughed it off like I knew he would and said that once he filed the report and he took her off the missing persons list, he didn't think there would be any further questions.

It took a while to convince Heather she wasn't cursed. That she never was, and that the curse would never be back. "Pari told me that you aren't from this world," Heather said when we were alone.

"Part of me is."

"She said you're from another dimension."

"Part of me is."

"She said you're like a princess there."

I could live with that. "Kind of."

"I wish I could see your light like she can."

I shook my head, grateful that she couldn't. I thought of Beep, what she would go through growing up so different. While I'd never wished to be anything other than what I am, it was not easy growing up with such an ability. "I'm glad you can't. And Pari talks too much."

Heather's illness all came down to an unusual flu that had been going around. She would be fine, and I had to admit, the excitement Nurse Rizzo showed when Heather showed up warmed my heart. They did see the kids. Maybe not all the time, but they did see them.

I gave hugs all around, and then Pari and I went to our cars. "You look like you've been hit by the truck of despair," I said to her.

She shrugged. "I kind of liked having her around."

"Me, too. Hey, maybe they have, like, a Big Sisters program where we can come hang with the kids."

She brightened. "You think so?"

"Never hurts to ask."

"You're right."

Without another word to me, she all but ran back inside to talk to the director.

23

*I was ready to take on the world,
until I saw something sparkly.*
—T-SHIRT

I left Pari in the hopes of finding Osh'ekiel somewhere in the great vastness. But Cookie called before I got very far.

"Charley's House of Lederhosen."

"Can you talk?"

"I think so. I might slur my words a bit. Didn't get much sleep. Otherwise, I'm good."

"Gambling."

"Oh, hell, yeah. Vegas. Blackjack. Male strippers."

"Mr. Adams."

"I guess he can go, too, but he has to get his own room."

"That's why all his business ventures failed."

I stopped midstride. "Are you trying to tell me Mr. Adams has a gambling problem?"

"A huuuuuge one," she said. "He is buried in debt. And not the good kind."

Was there a good kind? And now for the $20,000 question. "Who does he owe?"

"All I could find out is that his bookie is Danny Trejo." When I didn't say anything, she said, "Sorry, I saw *Trejo* and got excited. His bookie is Umberto Trejo."

"No way. Surely that's not the same Umberto Trejo I went to school with. And where did you get this information?" I was totally impressed.

"I have my sources."

"Mm-hm. Uncle Bob?"

"Yeah. Seems they've been looking into Adams, too."

"I thought he didn't know anything about the case."

"He *hears* things. That's what he said."

"And he shared this with you after he threatened to have us arrested because . . . ?"

"I promised him a very special date night."

"Cookie," I said, sniffing. "You're growing up so fast."

With my plans to hunt down Osh thwarted once again, I made a couple of calls and headed to a dive on Mitchel called the Dive. According to my sources, that was where Umberto conducted his business. And if he conducted it there, I had a feeling I knew who he worked for, a seedy lawyer who had his hand in more mold-infested cookie jars than a corrupt congressman.

I walked in to find several men strewn about the place. Almost every man there turned toward me, their paranoia rearing its ugly head. It had to suck being a criminal and suspicious of every person you saw. There were less stressful ways to make a living.

The only person who didn't turn toward me was a short beefy guy who was going over notes in a memo pad. I strolled over to him, all cool nonchalance.

"If it isn't Zumberto." We used to call him that because he zoomed everywhere. Couldn't sit down for more than a few minutes at a time. He could have been the poster child for an Adderall ad.

Shocked, he looked up at me. "Charley Davidson?"

"All day, every day. How have you been?" I sat three stools down from him, closer to the door and freedom should I need to bolt. All eyes were still on me, way too tense, way too ready to torture me for information. Or to just torture me. This was a seriously paranoid lot.

He shifted, suddenly uncomfortable. "Fine. What's up? I heard you were working for the cops."

"And I can only imagine who you work for."

"No one. I own this place." He indicated the small building by lifting his chin in true gangster style.

"Let me rephrase. Who you keep books for?"

He pressed his mouth into a noncommittal smirk and shrugged. "No idea what you're talking about. And you might think about leaving—now."

I moved one stool closer. "I'm here on official business. I'd hate for this place to get raided." I tsked and took it all in. The dingy wood and dingier mirrors. The floor that sloped north. The pool tables in serious disrepair. "I'd hate to see you lose this gem."

"It serves its purpose. Why you threatening? We were cool in school, right?"

"Yes, we were." I dared to say we were friends. I always liked the class clowns. "But that was before you started keeping books. Do you collect on the debts, too?" That would explain the muscle hanging out at such an early hour.

"Davidson, what do you want me to say?"

I moved another stool closer. Umberto waved a man off who was coming over to strong-arm me. "You can tell me what the deal is with one of your clients."

"Do you talk about your clients, Miss PI?"

"So, you've been keeping track of me."

"Nah, man, I only know 'cause you helped out my cousin." He dropped the charade and softened. "He was up for kidnapping and obstruction or some shit. You proved that crazy-ass chick set him up. You an absolute badass, Charlotte Davidson."

"No way." I sat at the stool next to him. "You're Santiago's cousin? I used to have such a crush on him."

"Everybody did. Damn, that *pendejo* got all the girls in school." He nodded to the barkeep. "What can I get you?"

"Oh, just water. I . . . . had an interesting night. I'm a little dehydrated."

"I hear that. So, why you in my business?"

"I need info on someone you keep books for."

"Not sure I can tell you anything, but shoot."

I thought of how I could phrase the questions without seeming too obtrusive, but gave up before I got anywhere promising. "How much does Geoff Adams owe you?"

He was looking straight ahead. A slow grin spread across his face. "I don't know who you're talking about."

I knew that wouldn't work. "Then can you tell me if he owed you money?"

"I just keep the books. If he did owe, say, someone in the organization money, it damned sure wouldn't be me."

"Oh. Okay." He really didn't seem like the kingpin type. I decided to appeal to his sense of family. "Umberto," I said, putting a hand on his arm. "It's important. His daughter is dead."

He bit down, put his drink on the bar, and turned in to me. Then he moved closer. Put a hand on my hip. Leaned forward until his mouth was on mine.

There was no lust in his eyes. He had no intention of feeling me up. He was, however, feeling for a wire. He slipped a hand under my sweater, up my stomach, and over Danger and Will. Luckily, I wasn't prudish. His manhandling would've seriously flustered someone like Cookie. But me? He could feel me up all day as long as that's all he did. And he told me what I needed to know at the end of it.

When he'd felt around to my back and along the waistband of my jeans, slipping his fingers in a little farther than necessary, he used it to pull me across the stool until my crotch straddled his. As he did all that, he did have a niggling of lust, but just a niggling. He'd never been into me, and we both knew it.

I leaned in so he could press his mouth to my ear. The room had gone quiet. No one moved as they watched the peep show play out before them.

"I'm only telling you this because we had nothing to do with the girl's death."

"Works for me."

Testing me further, seeing just how far he could take the charade, he slipped a hand between my legs, stroking me softly with his thumb.

"He owed Fernando a shit-ton. The guy was a total fuckup, and he just kept fucking up again and again. Just kept getting deeper and deeper. Deep is not a place you want to be with Fernando."

"You could've stopped taking his bets."

"Hey, if Fernando says give him a marker, I give him a marker. Seems the guy's father is loaded, and Fernando had a plan."

"This sounds bad."

He let his lips caress an earlobe. The peach fuzz on his face tickled, and I almost laughed.

"Let's just say his last bet was big. Thought he knew something about a game being thrown, but it was going to put him at over three hundred g's."

"Holy shit."

"Fernando took the bet. Told Adams if he lost and couldn't pay one more time, he'd start killing everyone he loved, starting with his daughter."

"Umberto," I said, suddenly wondering what he'd gotten himself into. I curled my fingers into the sleeve of his jacket.

He pulled me tighter. "You don't understand. When the game didn't go Adams's way and the girl actually died, Fernando lost it. Like he came unglued, *querida*. He was so upset. Thought one of his crew did it without his permission, but trust me, that didn't happen. He . . . questioned everyone."

I leaned back to look at him. "Umberto, you're sure he didn't do it? Because that would be one hell of a coincidence."

"Go ask him yourself, *querida*. You'll see."

"Okay. Stay out of trouble?"

He let me go and spread his hands. "Always. I'm lily white, baby."

The men around us laughed as I stood to leave. He caught me and leaned in again. "I didn't really need the show."

"You and I both know that's not true."

Raising his hand to my face, he ran his thumb over my bottom lip and then licked it as though savoring the last trace of chocolate on his fingertips.

I was shocked. I didn't feel lust coming off him in waves like I did when a guy was usually interested. Then I realized why. It wasn't lust he felt, but something deeper.

He took my hand and pressed it to his chest. "You broke my heart once, *querida*. I have to guard it now. Get the fuck out." He winked playfully and then dropped my hand and turned his back to me. It took me several long moments to realize he hadn't been joking.

I walked out, racking my brain, trying to remember how and when I could possibly have broken Umberto's heart. To say we'd been friends was an overstatement. We were in the same class. I knew him. He knew me. But we'd never given each other the time of day.

Misery purred to life around me, her engine only slightly louder than a 747. I was just about to head back to the office for more recon, mostly on this Fernando character, when I got a text. It must have been from Umberto. It said Fernando could see me in two hours and had an address to meet.

I didn't text back.

Since I had some time and I wasn't going to have to hunt down Fernando, I drove out to Mr. Adams's house. I couldn't believe how wrong I'd been about him. I pegged him for a standup guy. A stellar father. A pillar of society. But even his own dad had only bad things to say about him.

Did Mr. Adams Sr. know that Mr. Adams Jr. was also a degenerate gambler, as cliché as that was? I didn't think so. He would have told me. But how can someone be that deep into gambling, to lose everything again and again, and no one know? No one I'd talked to, at least.

Cookie and I chatted on everything she'd found out about Mr. Adams while I was being molested. He'd had a colorful life filled with a lot of unfortunate events. A little too many.

Mr. Adams was home when I knocked. He was a shell when he answered the door. Pale and withered like he had every intention of just wasting away. The guilt was eating him alive. Umberto had to be wrong about his boss. Fernando had to have done this.

"Mrs. Davidson. Did you find anything to exonerate Lyle Fiske?" he asked as he held the door open.

"Not yet, but I'm getting very close."

We sat in his messy living room. Magazines lay strewn about the apartment. A laundry basket of clothes sat on one end of the sofa with dirty dishes punctuating the disarray. The cleanest part of the room was a tank with a turtle in it.

I resisted the urge to introduce myself to the turtle. "Mr. Adams, I am all for finding out what happened to your daughter, but I'll need your help."

"Of course. Anything."

"I couldn't help but notice you've had a few unfortunate accidents over the last few years. Strange things like a broken leg. A dislocated shoulder. And you lost two fingers in a construction accident?"

He folded his hands together. "Mrs. Davidson, what does that have to do with my daughter?"

"Sir, you promised to be honest with me." When he said nothing, I added, "I believe it has everything to do with her and a certain bet that you made."

I barely got out the last word when Mr. Adams broke completely. He sobbed into a towel he had sitting on the sofa. His shoulders shook so hard I thought he'd rattle his ribs loose.

"I took the bet," he said, his voice cracking on every syllable. "I didn't think he'd do it."

"A man who would break your leg? Who would take your fingers?"

"Fernando didn't do this." He held up his hand. His pinkie and ring fingers had been severed at the knuckle. "That was another bookie in another city in another time."

"How long has this been going on?"

"Since I was in grade school. I bet on anything. Used to get sent home for running craps games in the schoolyard. I'd go for days without lunch and use that money to make a bet of one kind or another."

"Didn't your father ever get you help?"

He laughed a long moment. It was bitter and full of pain. "Oh, I have never lived up to his pristine standards, and he doesn't let me forget it. Adams men don't need help. They stand on their own two feet."

"Is that why you did it? As payback to him?"

"I don't know. All I know is that I took the bet. I signed my own daughter's death warrant." He broke down again.

"I'm sorry, Mr. Adams. But this is all hearsay. It won't clear Lyle Fiske. The evidence against him is too solid. We need something more to get Lyle off. We need a guarantee."

And I might just have one. I couldn't wear a wire to the meeting with Fernando, but maybe I could get something that would help us. See some clue that would get Lyle acquitted.

Fernando had to have done it. Who else? Unless a member of his crew really did do it, possibly thinking it would endear him to Fernando. But when he freaked out and started questioning his men, whoever did it clammed up, scared for his life.

If the guilty party was at the meeting, I would be able to feel it. If nothing else, I could tell Fernando and bargain for the guilty party to turn himself in.

Just as I stood to leave, I spotted a shotgun in the corner of the living room, and I knew exactly why it was there.

"I'm sorry, but could I have a glass of water?"

"Of course."

The minute he left the room, I texted Parker. *At Adams's house. Get here now.*

In a meeting. Be there in an hour.

Wonderful. How was I going to keep Mr. Adams busy for an hour? I had a meeting to get to myself.

I couldn't put Cookie in the middle of this. Ubie was busy. I couldn't drag Pari into this, either. I'd just dragged her into the Heather case. I had no choice.

When he walked back in, I was pointing the shotgun at him.

"What's this?" he asked, alarmed. For good reason.

"Sit down," I said, indicating the sofa with a wave of the gun like they did in the movies.

He stood there, took a drink of the water that was meant for me, and resigned himself to his fate by opening his hands. Damn, I didn't think of that. Pointing a gun at someone who is suicidal is like Christmas coming early.

I never think ahead.

"I mean it," I said from between clenched teeth, hoping it would make me sound more authentic.

"Just do it. Please." Tears still shimmered in his eyes, and as angry as I was at him, my heart still ached.

I released a loud breath in defeat and started to put the gun down when I remembered the turtle in the tank. I grinned and pointed the gun in its direction. "Sit down."

Thank God Mr. Adams had no idea I'd sooner shoot him than the turtle.

24

My family's coat of arms is a wraparound and ties in the back.
Is that normal?
—MOSTLY TRUE FACT

After tying up Mr. Adams, I put his phone on the table in front of him. "You can call the police when I'm gone. Just use your nose. It works. Trust me."

"Why are you doing this?"

"Because, Mr. Adams, you are a danger to yourself. I've called Parker, too. Oh, and I'm going to meet with Fernando, so if you could wait to call the cops and have me arrested for about, say, twenty more minutes, I'd appreciate it."

"You can't meet with him," Mr. Adams said. "Mrs. Davidson, Charley, he is not a nice guy. Look what he did to my baby. Please—"

"Mr. Adams, this is the only way to get the charges against Fiske dropped. I need to find the real murderer."

He bowed his head, grief consuming him.

I left him alone like that, hoping there wasn't another gun in the house and Parker really would get there when he said he would. Just in case, I called Uncle Bob, told him I'd tied a man up for his own safety, and asked him to send a uniform in, say, about twenty minutes.

The last thing I heard before hanging up was "You did what?"

I pulled around a rather nice house in what was known to the locals as the war zone. The crime rates in this part of town were astronomical.

I knocked on the front door of the house, a nice adobe with flowers in window trellises and ivies growing up the sides. It wasn't huge, but it was nicer than most of the houses in the neighborhood.

"This way."

I turned to a man motioning me to go around the side of the house and through a gate to the backyard.

"Are you Fernando?" When he didn't answer, I asked, "Strong silent type, huh?"

When we got to the backyard, a man in his midfifties waved me over with a barbecue fork. I could only hope it would not be the instrument of my death.

"I'm Fernando."

Wait. According to gossip, I was immortal. He couldn't kill me with a barbecue fork.

He then raised an eight-inch boning knife.

But a boning knife?

"I'm Charley."

Desperately needing a shave, he wore his slightly graying hair in a ponytail and a bright Hawaiian shirt with an A-line tank underneath. The sun had made an appearance, but it was far from Hawaiian shirts and barbecuing weather. He was not what I'd expected.

"You're not what I expected."

He chuckled and turned a stack of ribs on the grill. Smoke billowed around him, and my mouth watered. Just a little. Not enough to openly drool.

"Are you going to check me for a wire?"

He chuckled once more. "I think Umberto covered that. I hear you think I killed Adams's daughter?"

"I don't anymore."

He eyed me from over his shoulder and then motioned for me to sit at a patio table. "Good, because I didn't. I threatened, of course, but only because he doesn't know me well enough to know I would never do something like that."

A group of kids ran out the door and past us, the girls screaming as the boys chased them with dirty hands.

"*Abuelo!*" one of the girls shouted. "Save me!"

"*Ay, mi' jita.* Stop that and get back inside." They raced past us back in the house. "Sorry."

I shook my head. "No problem. They're adorable."

"So," he said, wiping his hands and sitting down next to me, "if you believe me, why are you here?"

"I was wondering about your men. You questioned all of them?"

"I did. None of my guys did it, and why would any other crew?"

"Are they here? Your men?"

He took a swig of beer. "My most trusted are here, but we have a very extensive network. To get all of them here would take a while. Umberto said you have a gift for extracting the truth out of people."

"I do. Kind of."

He leaned forward. "I do, too."

I bet he did. "Would you mind if I questioned them? Your men?"

"All of them? Yes, actually. But only a handful knew what I'd said to Adams, and they would never speak of it outside the circle."

He motioned for his men to come outside. It was clearly a day off. They were dressed casual, and each had a beer or chips in his hands.

"*The Walking Dead,*" he said.

I glanced around at the group of about seven men. Most of them were

Hispanic, apart from one. "They look okay to me. Are you planning on killing them later?"

"The show. On TV. It's a marathon. We're celebrating."

"Oh." That made so much more sense than the scenario in my head.

"They're all yours." He said it with a smile that was about one-quarter smirk.

"Um, okay." I stood slowly and leveled a hard stare on them.

Most of them tried not to laugh. One of them failed and got barked at. He straightened up immediately.

"Did any of you kill Emery Adams?"

Again, most of them just stood there, but one shook his head. Vigorously. Totally making fun of the whole situation.

I walked from man to man, pausing in front of each for a second and asking the same question before continuing to the next. I was certain they thought I was crazy, but I was good with crazy. I'd been called worse.

After getting nothing from any of the men that would suggest they'd done it, I said, "I assume you're all captains."

The clown punched the guy next to him on the shoulder. *"El Capitán,"* he said, and Fernando glared at him. He shut up again, but I was surprised the guy was still alive.

"My nephew. What can I do?" he said.

"Ah. Can I ask, just to make sure, who of you heard the threat—"

"Alleged threat," Fernando said.

"—that Fernando made to Mr. Adams?"

After getting the okay from Fernando, two raised their hands. The other five had no clue. I dismissed them and then asked, "Are you sure you told no one? It's just a very big coincidence that Fernando made the threat two weeks before Emery Adams was killed."

"I don't think you understand how this works," one said.

He was the big one who'd shown me to the backyard. The other one was younger and had a humble and yet terribly handsome face. He probably grew into his looks and into his position with the family. He wasn't nearly as cocky as the rest.

"We don't go home and tell our girlfriends what we did at work that day."

"Neither of you are married?"

"Or our wives," he added with a grin.

The young one laughed softly, and I couldn't quite figure him out. His emotions were different from the others'.

"So, the only ones in the room when you made that threat—"

"Alleged threat."

"—were these two men? And that was . . ."

I trailed off as realization dawned. "Where did this conversation take place?"

"At his house," Fernando said. "We had to pay him a visit when Umberto told me he wanted to make such a large investment."

I sat down again, unable to believe what I knew had to be the truth. It was the only thing that fit.

"I'm sorry to have bothered you, Fernando. Your ribs are burning."

"Son of a bitch." He jumped up and ran over to them.

I started to walk myself out, but the big guy nodded to the younger one, and he escorted me all the way to Misery.

I was going to say something to him. Something supportive and cheerleader-y, but I was never good at pep talks, and if I let him know that I knew, it would only stress him more than he already was.

Instead, I thanked him and let him walk back. He glanced over his shoulder once, as though worried I knew, so I dropped my gaze to my phone.

He was an undercover cop. And he was good. I would never have suspected him in a million years, but officers who work undercover had a level of stress that one rarely found anywhere else. And they stressed out about the wrong things. It was like giving a Rorschach to a hundred kids and getting similar answers from all but one. The kid who sees the world differently.

Undercover cops see everything from about twelve angles more than the average Joe. They have to. Their lives depended on it. Never knowing whom to trust. If you'll be made. If you'll be joking with the guys one minute and then lying dead with a bullet in your head the next. I didn't envy him his position.

After he turned the corner, I called Parker. He was on the verge of exploding again, but I didn't have time for his hissy fit.

"Parker, did you get the footage of the surveillance cameras at the hospital?"

"You tied him up."

"He was going to commit suicide."

"What if he presses charges?"

"Pfft, he won't. He's got a lot more to worry about than my pointing a gun at him."

"So, you admit you did it."

"Parker, what the fuck? Do you have the footage or not?"

"Yes. Why? There's nothing on it."

"She was never attacked? Did she argue with anyone?"

"No. We have her whole day. She seemed upset all day, and she'd actually left for a while to grab dinner."

"So, she left and came back?"

"Yes."

"And did what?"

"She went into her office. No cameras. And when she came out, she went straight to the lab. It looked like she'd been crying. She was wiping her face."

I rested my head on Misery's steering wheel. "Parker, I'm so stupid."

He didn't argue. Fucker.

"I think I know what happened, but I need to check one more thing."

"What? Tell me now."

"I need to check something." If I was wrong, I was going to look beyond stupid, so I opted not to voice my suspicions.

"What if you die in a freak accident? Just fucking tell me."

"I will. Give me until tonight."

"Davidson—"

I hung up before he could threaten me again and called Cookie.

"You're alive!" she said, relieved.

"Yeah, Fernando and I totally hit it off. Did you look into Mr. Adams Sr.'s holdings?"

"Oh yeah. It's like he told you, he sold almost everything a couple of years ago and liquidated all his stocks."

"Almost?" I asked, not knowing if my heart should fly or sink.

This case was about to get very complicated.

Postponing my search for Osh again, I grabbed something that closely resembled chicken strips at a drive-through, hit another drive-through for a mocha latte, then headed for the great outdoors. My route would take a little over two hours, but if I was right, and I liked to think I was, it would be very, very worth the trip.

I hadn't even hit I-25, however, before I spotted a very familiar neon-green van behind me. I pulled into the parking lot of a truck stop and waited. Instead of pulling in, they pulled on to a side street.

I got out of Misery and marched toward them.

They panicked. The looks on their faces were worth the price of admission. When I was about ten feet away, they all stared straight ahead and tried to start the van. Like they didn't see me coming. And I thought I was bad at acting.

I knocked on the driver's-side window. They stopped and looked at each other, wondering what to do.

"Roll it down," I suggested through the window.

The van was old school, and Tristan, the only Ghostbuster without a brother in the gang, turned the handle. The window squeaked on its rollers. It was a long and awkward moment, and all I could do was stand there and fight a grin. I didn't want to embarrass them. Well, any more than they already were.

"Didn't we talk about this?" I asked.

Tristan had yet to look at me. When he did, my heart fell just a little more for him, his boyish face sweet and concerned.

"We—we were worried about you," he said. They all had the decency to look ashamed.

"Why?" I asked.

"The French team. They aren't very nice."

"And, no offense," one of the brothers said, "but one kiss is not going to scare them away."

I laughed. "It may not have, but I can handle myself. I promise."

"We saw that entity throw you around like a rag doll. What you are messing with is dangerous."

"Is it? Can I ask you a question?"

They all nodded in unison.

"Have you been experiencing any unusual activity?"

"All our lives," Iago said. "But mostly Tristan."

"Oh yeah? Since when?"

"Since I was about two. I can sense when the dead are near."

I fought another grin. "Can you?"

The departed that had attached itself to him was practically sitting in his lap. Big guy with crazy hair and a straitjacket. It glared at him. Unblinking. Unmoving. Unwavering. Just nonstop glaring.

I saw the departed all the time, and even I was a little creeped out.

"Anything more recent? Maybe something since you visited an insane asylum? Or an old prison?"

His face lit up as recognition hit him. "Yes. We had an assignment at an abandoned sanatorium in Kentucky."

"And ever since then," another chimed in, "we've been having some really weird stuff happen."

"Weird like how?"

"Mostly with Tristan. He feels cold spots and something brush up against him."

I leveled a hard gaze on him. "What did you take?"

"We never take anything," Isaac said.

Iago chimed in. "We're urban explorers. We leave everything the way we found it."

I raised a brow at the man closest to me. "Tristan, is there anything you'd like to share with the class?"

"Me? No. Not that I can think of."

"You took something from a site?" Iago said, believing him no more than I did. "Dude, that is not cool."

"It was a toy soldier," he said, defending his choice. "That was it."

"Let me see it." I snapped my fingers when he didn't get it immediately.

Reluctantly, he pulled it out of a pocket in his jumper. A jumper. They were wearing jumpers. I totally wanted to adopt them. True, they had seen *Ghostbusters* one too many times, but seriously, one just doesn't find that kind of dedication anymore.

Iago studied his friend like he was seeing him with new eyes. "You keep a toy soldier in your pocket?"

"That's what she said," Isaac said, then doubled over with laughter.

As I thought, the departed tracked the soldier as he handed it to me, his eyes glistening. I placed it in my palm and let him see it.

"Okay," I said, "you have two choices. You can go to the asylum where you found this and put it back, or I can lure the departed that has been following you for God knows how long to cross. Your choice, but you have to put this back either way."

"You can what?" Isaac asked.

Tristan shook his head. "The departed that has been doing what?"

"You have a shadow. My term. A departed has attached himself to you because you took his tiny soldier."

"Please tell me that's a metaphor for his virginity," Isaac said.

"You can see it?" Tristan's eyes glistened with wonder. "And, for the record, I am not a virgin."

"He is a large childlike man with crazy blond hair and a lazy eye."

"And you can make him cross to the other side?"

"Yes, I can. In fact, I probably should either way. He's so lost."

Tristan put both hands on the steering wheel. "You should. If it's better for him, then definitely. And can you tell him I'm sorry?"

"You just did."

I leaned into the van and put my hand under the departed's chin. I raised his face to mine, but his eyes were locked on the soldier. As carefully as I could, I pulled him forward and reached out with my energy. Right before he crossed, he looked into my eyes, his own eyes wide as though seeing for the first time in a long time.

I let my lids drift shut and braced myself. His life couldn't have been easy. But what I saw went beyond all expectations.

He was as happy as any child, before he ate the paint. He got sick, and they said he wouldn't live. He did, but he was never the same. The lead affected his brain and, like any disabled child, made him a target for abuse his whole life. An angry, domineering father. A timid, apprehensive mother who gave in to her husband's every demand.

From there all I saw was misunderstanding, frustration, and abuse. So much. So often. They didn't understand. They didn't understand. He would try to tell them that he was hungry or thirsty or in pain, but they didn't have the patience or the desire to deal with him.

Eventually, he grew so big and uncontrollable they put him on high doses of lithium and silenced his desires once and for all. They controlled him better than any straitjacket could have. He tried so hard to get out of the forest, but it was so thick. So suffocating.

He waited for his parents to come back for him. He never saw them again.

I emerged struggling for air and for balance. Leaning against the van before I fell, I let the sorrow take over.

The last thing I saw was him being loved by grandparents he'd never met. They'd been waiting for him. For such a very long time.

Tears pushed past my lashes as I tried to catch my breath. I put my fists on the van and buried my face in the sleeves of my sweater. My chest kept hitching as I tamped down the sorrow.

"Mrs. Davidson?"

It was Tristan. He stood behind me and, I realized, was holding me upright.

"I'm sorry," I said, my voice hoarse. "That doesn't usually happen." I turned around and saw the worry on all their faces. Mixed with heavy doses of amazement.

"What happened?" Isaac asked.

Iago hit him on the shoulder.

Holding out the soldier to Tristan, I said, "He wants you to have this. He's in a much better place than that hellhole they left of his mind." I put both hands over my eyes and let the sorrow overtake me for one minute more. It was so overwhelming. "He's in a better place." Drawing in long, cool bouts of air, I pulled myself together and pushed off the van. Tristan held me, and Iago came around and took my other arm. "Note to self. Prepare better when letting a man in a straitjacket cross."

25

*If at first you don't succeed,
destroy all evidence that you tried.*
—STEPHEN WRIGHT

I left them to their devices, realizing I'd just stoked a fire that was already blazing inside them. They walked me to Misery, tamping down the million and one questions they had burning inside them, and made sure I could drive before leaving me, but I had a feeling they'd be back.

After putting the address Cookie sent me into my GPS, I headed that way once again. I hoped it would still be light when I got there, but I doubted GPS would help me much where we were going, Misery and I. Thank the gods she had all-wheel drive.

The sun was just setting when I finally, after four passes, found the turnoff. Seven minutes and three miles of bumpy later, I spotted a small rustic cabin nestled at the base of the mountains. This was a favorite spot of hunters, so most of the cabins in this area had no electricity or running water, but knowing Mr. Adams Sr., this one did.

Smoke piped into the air from a woodstove, but the occupant of the cabin was sitting on a lawn chair, taking in the very last rays of the day.

Emery Adams rose up and cupped her hand over her eyes to try to see past my headlight. She must have had company now and then, because my arrival didn't startle her. She seemed only mildly interested until she realized I wasn't who she was expecting.

She jumped to her feet and wrapped her thick jacket tighter around her shoulders. Shoulder-length hair the color of brown sugar flew about her face. Her features were soft and pretty but wary. Schooled.

I stepped out and walked toward her. It made her nervous. She glanced around like she was going to bolt, but where could she go? She'd likely die of exposure if she ran into the forest. She'd definitely get turned around and have a hard time finding her way back.

When I was close enough to be heard without raising my voice too much, I introduced myself.

"Hi, Ms. Adams. My name is Charley Davidson. I'm here to tell you that your plan, while excellently executed, picked up a hitch along the way."

"I don't know what you mean."

"Lyle Fiske is about to go to prison for your murder."

Both hands flew to her face and covered it.

"And since you're still alive and all, I thought we might try to get the charges dropped."

"No," she said from behind her hands. She sat on the chair, but kept her hands over her face as though to block out the news I'd brought. "No. He was out of town. Why would they suspect him?"

"Because he never left town."

She looked at me at last. "Yes, he did." Her disbelief was palpable. "He was at the airport. I saw him there."

"The app?" I asked, picking my way through the brush to get closer. When she nodded, I said, "He went to the airport. Started to check in. But he felt like something was wrong, so he changed his mind and went back to town."

Her fingers curled into fists over her mouth. "No."

I kneeled beside her. "If you don't come back with me, he could go to prison for the rest of his life."

She squeezed her eyes shut. "I never wanted this. I never wanted to hurt him."

"So, you didn't think your murder would hurt him? Maybe just a little?"

"I mean, I never wanted him involved in this." She locked her gaze with mine. "I tried to just break up with him, but I couldn't."

There was so much wrong with that statement, but I decided to drop it.

"He had nothing to do with this. This is all on my father."

I figured as much. "If it helps, he's riddled with guilt. He's even contemplating suicide."

Her chin rose in defiance, refusing to feel anything for the man. But I could feel the pain well up inside her. She was only fooling one of us, and it wasn't me.

"He wouldn't have gone through with it. Suicide. He doesn't have the spine."

"He's heartbroken either way."

"In his eyes he's guilty of murder. I wanted him to feel what I felt when he placed that bet."

"You overheard the conversation between your father and Fernando."

She nodded. "They told him. They said that if he lost and couldn't pay up this time, they wouldn't bother coming after him. They'd kill me. They told him point-blank. And do you know what he did?"

I lowered my head, knowing all too well.

"He placed the bet." Her breath hitched in her chest. "He bet my life on a fucking game."

"I'm sorry, Emery."

She curled into herself and sobbed until the night was cold enough to freeze the tears on her cheeks. I led her inside the cabin and made some coffee old school.

After taking her a cup, I said, "It was pretty ingenious, how you did all this."

"Clearly not ingenious enough. You figured it out." She shook her head. Wiped her brow with the back of a hand. "I can't believe they think Lyle killed me."

"When he couldn't get ahold of you, he used the app to find you, but that was your backup plan, wasn't it?"

She nodded and wrapped her hands tighter around the cup. "I didn't know if anyone would find my car out there, so I had a plan for him to tell the police that he had an app to find me. I thought they would find the car. Not him. And certainly not on the same day I did it." She glanced up at me. "How did you know?"

"There were several clues. Your phone was in the charger in your car, for one. Lyle mentioned that it was the kind that kept charging even if the car was off. And he said it was your idea to get the apps. It took me a while, but I realized you did that on purpose."

Embarrassed, she lowered her head.

"The blood part was what threw me initially, until I realized where you were caught crying at the hospital. In the lab. You'd had a blood test two days earlier. A lab tech mentioned it in an interview, so why would you have been in there again? You weren't pregnant. Your white blood cell count was way high, but you didn't have an infection. You'd been seen almost fainting more than once, and you were taking iron."

She didn't refute anything I said.

"And if you were just crying, why was there blood on your skirt? Little clues like that. How long did you save your blood?" I knew she'd been saving her blood. The white blood cell count gave it away. When someone gives blood, they lose red blood cells that must be replaced. The blood. The fainting. The iron. It added up to only one conclusion.

"Two weeks. I knew exactly how much I'd need to make it look like I couldn't possibly have survived the attack. I didn't have quite enough, but I supplemented and made sure that blood was soaked deep in the seat cushions."

"So, you came up with this plan—"

"That night. When he made that bet, something inside me died. But that still doesn't explain how you got onto my scent in the first place. What gave me away?"

"It started with a conversation I had with Fernando. He said he'd made that threat two weeks before you disappeared. And before that, all your friends and family said you'd started behaving strangely at around the same time. I put two and two together. Also, there was no tissue in the car. No skin or hair or gray matter."

She closed her eyes. "I thought of that, but short of cutting pieces of flesh off my body or chunks of brain out of my head, I couldn't leave any behind. Even if I got some from the morgue, they would've known it wasn't mine eventually."

"By the way, you're going to want to sell that car."

"Oh, my god, I can't believe they arrested Lyle." She dropped her face into her palms. "He's going to hate me. I've ruined . . . everything. All for that man. That man wins again. Somehow he wins every time." Her chin quivered as she thought back. "There was this one time he got me a really nice CD player. I was maybe twelve. I knew I wouldn't have it for long. He'd lose money at the track or at the bar, and come to hock it. But I loved it. I wanted to keep it so bad, so I hid it in the crawlspace under our house.

"It's so stupid. I mean, I couldn't even listen to it. But I just wanted it, so I told him it was stolen. That someone broke into our house while he was at work and took it. I came home from school two days later, and it was gone."

When she looked at me again, the fury she felt deep inside her billowed in the depths of her irises. "He never even mentioned it. Neither of us did. We just went about our lives like I'd never had it. A CD player is one thing, but my life." Her voice cracked. "He bet my life like it was an object. Like it was disposable. Like I was disposable. He deserves all the pain he's experiencing right now."

I certainly couldn't argue that. I made bacon and eggs as she packed her things. She'd even thought that far ahead. She took nothing from her house. She bought all new toiletries and clothes. We ate in relative silence, both of us miserable.

"I ruined my life. I ruined my life for that man."

"Maybe not," I said, putting my thinking cap on.

"What do you mean? I'll be arrested. I'll definitely lose my job. Forget having any future with Lyle." She shook her head. "He was the greatest thing since sliced bread."

"So, when you tried to break up with him?"

"I was trying to keep him as far away from this as possible."

"I figured as much. What if we go about this whole thing a little differently? How good are you at lying? And how high is your tolerance for pain?"

Two hours later, the stage was set. I nodded to her. She nodded back. And I picked up my phone. "Parker," I said, panting and swallowing hard like I'd been running. "I was right. Get down here. Hurry! And bring an ambulance with you. She's alive."

I gave him a description of the general area and hung up. We waited in the dark.

"You're sure they couldn't really know if every single drop of that blood was yours?"

"They don't have the time or the resources to check every strand of DNA in that car. It would take a lot of work to figure out if it were really enough blood loss to kill me." She reached out her hand, her roped wrist scraping across the warehouse floor. "I don't know how to thank you, Charley."

"You can thank me by giving your dad another chance."

"Then I won't be thanking you anytime soon."

"I understand," I said sadly.

"But maybe someday. I'm going to tell Lyle, though. Not about you. I'll tell him I set up the whole thing and called you or something. But he needs to know what he's getting into."

"How do you think he'll take it?"

"I don't know. Not well, I'm sure."

We heard sirens in the distance.

"Just make sure he knows you did everything you could to make sure he wasn't implicated."

"I will."

We waited as cars slid to a stop in front of the warehouse. "Hey," I said before they burst through the doors with guns blazing, "want to grab a coffee sometime?"

"Hell, yeah."

We fist-bumped, then I hooked my arms under hers and stumbled, falling to the floor with her just as the first flashlight landed on us.

"Over here!" I called, praying this worked. Orange may have been the new black, but what it did for my complexion was barbaric.

Uncle Bob showed up on scene, and I knew he could sense something awry, but he disliked Joplin just enough to not give a shit. They whisked Emery away in an ambulance immediately, but they detained and questioned me for years.

If this worked, I promised to straighten my act up. To do good things and stop making fun of other people's choices in accessories. The one thing that could tip the scale in our favor was the fact that Emery had fallen down a ravine the day she got to the cabin. She'd already been sporting some nasty bruises and scratches and one rather garish gash across her leg where she'd been impaled by a broken branch. That would work in our favor magnificently.

I still had to rough her up a bit. Or I tried. She called me a wuss and did most of it herself.

"Tell me again," Joplin said, "how you just happened to stumble upon my missing person?"

We'd gone over it a gazillion times, but smelling something off as well, he wanted to trip me up. To give him a reason to arrest me. Wasn't gonna happen.

"I got a tip from a source that a lady was being held here against her will for her father's gambling debts."

Emery threw that last part in. She wanted to drive that nail home. And since Mr. Adams apparently had gambling debts at several locations, who was to say which bookie it was that abducted her?

"They wanted to freak out the father, so they threw her blood, along with someone else's they'd stolen from a blood bank, all over her car. I got here, scoured the area, and finally heard a soft cry coming from inside this warehouse. I broke in and found her. It's not rocket science, Joplin."

"You just keep that shit up, Davidson, and——"

"Are you actually threatening my niece?" While Uncle Bob's voice was smooth and even, his temper had busted through the roof. He was furious. "She did what you couldn't, Joplin. She found your missing person. And you're going to give her shit about it? Why? Because she did your job for you?" He stepped closer until they were toe-to-toe. "If you even talk to her like that again——"

"You'll what?" he asked.

Man, that guy hated us. I wondered what I did.

The captain strode up then, his anger spiking a bit, too. "Joplin," he barked.

Joplin practically jumped.

"Get over here," he said from between clenched teeth, sounding a lot like Clint Eastwood. It was quite manly.

While Joplin received a thorough ass whipping, I wrapped an arm around Uncle Bob's.

"You gonna tell me what really happened?" he asked.

How did he know? "I solve cases all the time. What makes you think this isn't legit?"

"Because I figured out what she did, too."

"Damn it." I gazed up at him.

"Not all of it, but I had my suspicions."

"Uncle Bob, she had a very good reason."

He nodded. "I know, hon. I have complete faith in you."

"Really? You're not going to rat me out?"

"What the hell kind of uncle do you think I am? Also, Cook would divorce me."

Laughter bubbled out of me. "You have complete faith in me? For reals?"

"Yes. Well, not your cooking. Other than that, absolutely."

I gasped. "I've cooked for you, like, twice."

"Two times too many, pumpkin. Two times too many."

They finally released me just as Parker pulled up. He'd been in some really big meeting, but when he got there I didn't know how he would react.

He didn't say a thing. Just gave me a questioning thumbs-up. I nodded, and he scraped his fingers through his hair in relief. Lyle Fiske should be out of jail within the hour. I did not envy that conversation Emery was going to have with him.

I climbed into Misery and started out of the maze of empty warehouses I'd come across during another case a little over a year prior, having no idea they'd come in so handy someday. As I turned right, my headlights caught the reflection of a big black truck. I drove slowly. Another vehicle pulled up behind it, and the truck roared to life, did a U-turn, and drove off. It was Garrett, and the person taking over was Javier, one of his colleagues. It was time to get to the bottom of this.

I followed Garrett all the way to his house, my blood boiling. Not literally, 'cause that would hurt. He pulled into his drive, and I pulled in behind him.

"Charles," he said, offering me his signature grin.

"Don't Charles me." I stalked up to him and poked his chest. "Why are you tailing Uncle Bob?"

"Whaaaaat?"

He turned and walked into his house with an angry woman hot on his heels. "Don't play dumb, Swopes. Why are you tailing him?"

"It's a job. I can't tell you. My client has asked to be kept confidential."

"Bullshit. If I were tailing your uncle, I'd tell you who hired me."

"Now who's bullshitting who?"

He was right. Damn it. Unless he was brought in on the case, I would never reveal my clients' names.

"This is Uncle Bob we're talking about."

"No, you're talking about him. I'm getting a beer."

Just then, Osh spoke out like an omniscient presence. "Grab me one, too," he said.

I walked around to Garrett's living room and spotted him playing video games. "What are you doing here? Why aren't you watching my daughter?"

"I check in every hour."

"Do you know how much could happen in an hour?"

"I had to get some things in order and go over the plans with Swopes here and your husband."

"But not me."

"Yes, you. You were on a case. We didn't want to bother you." He killed another bad guy. At least I hoped he was a bad guy. Osh was a demon, technically a Daeva, so he could be killing the good guys for all I knew.

"I'm not even going to argue with you." I ripped the band out of my hair and scrubbed my scalp. "I have had the longest day ever."

Garrett brought Osh a beer and offered to make coffee. These two men had been with us through so much, and the only person on this plane who might know about Reyes and his creation was Osh. They were two of my best friends. And they knew how to keep a secret.

I waved the coffee idea away—unusual, I admit—and sat on the coffee table, which tasted nothing like actual coffee, between Osh and the TV.

"I will suck the soul from your body," he threatened.

"Whatever. I have something very serious to talk to you about. Like, the-annihilation-of-the-world kind of serious."

"The world is going to be annihilated? Again?" He turned off the game and tossed the controller on the table beside me. "We just stopped one annihilation. Can't this wait?"

I pursed my lips.

"Oh, you *are* serious."

"I never joke about the annihilation of the world."

He took a long swig, as did Garrett, who'd unbuttoned his shirt and let it hang open while he sat, his legs stretched out and crossed at the ankles.

Such pretty boys.

I closed my eyes and dug deep for courage. "Okay," I said, opening them again. "I need to know everything you know about Reyes's creation."

He frowned. "You mean in hell?"

"Yes."

He sat back, his youthful appearance making him totally look like a gamer. "I guess I don't know that much. Lucifer created him from the energies of hell and the fires of sin. Or that's the rumor."

"And how does that work, exactly?"

"Not a clue. Why?"

I sat beside him and looked from one to the other. "I am about to tell you the biggest secret I've ever had in my life, and I've only had it for ten days. But there is so much I don't understand, and I don't know what to do and who to tell. I mean, I told Cookie, but I tell her everything. I need help."

"They have facilities for that," Garrett said. "And medication."

Osh laughed, and I let my brows slowly cinch together. "I don't get it."

"You're punking us," Osh said.

"Saw it from a mile away," Garrett agreed.

"No, I'm not."

Garrett rubbed his face with his free hand. "Okay, so what is this big secret that is going to annihilate the world?"

"Well, it's kind of a three-parter."

"Want another beer?" Garrett asked.

"I'm good, but do we still have chips?"

Oh, my god. They weren't taking me seriously at all. Maybe all those times I didn't take them seriously were coming back to bite my ass.

Nah.

"Guys!" I said, holding up my hands. "Quit with the beer and the chips shit."

"Isn't there a game tonight?" Osh said.

And I lost it. I grabbed Osh, put him in a headlock, and gave him just enough oxygen so he wouldn't lose consciousness.

"I think she's serious," Osh said through his crushed larynx.

Having finally gained their undivided, I readied myself to tell them the most startling news since we learned the earth wasn't the center of the universe, when Artemis jumped out of the floor and lunged right toward Osh and me. Carrying a demon in her jaws.

Because it was so unexpected, I screeched and jumped on the sofa like one would do to avoid a mouse. Osh scrambled back, too, as the demon hissed and howled from being burned alive by yours truly's brilliant light.

Garrett rose as well, but he had no idea why.

Artemis was so happy she had a play toy. She shook it and growled at it and shook it some more, causing it more pain that it was already in. All the while her stubby tail wagged a million miles a minute.

The demon began to dissipate and evaporate into the air. When there wasn't enough to shake anymore, Artemis jumped to me, her mouth open as she panted, proud of her work.

"Good girl," I said, stroking her head. Then I pulled her into a head-lock, too, for some playtime. "That's her second one today," I said to Osh.

"Artemis brought Charley a present," Osh said, explaining it to Garrett. "A demon."

"And it's loose in the house?" he asked, appalled.

"No, it's not." I scrubbed Artemis's fur and rolled with her over the coffee table and onto the floor. Sadly, she landed on top of me instead of vice versa. It knocked the air out of me, but that didn't keep me from talking. Not much does. "There's no demon in this house, huh, Artemisia? Well, there is one, but . . . you are such a good girl. Yes, you are."

"You look like a mental patient," Garrett said, sitting back down. "All I see is you rolling around, talking to my carpet."

"Did you hear that?" I asked her as she gnawed on my jugular. "He called you carpet. Bad Garrett."

Then she stopped and stared off into the great unknown. A low growl rumbled from her chest. Her lips pulled back to reveal a killer set of canines.

"What is it, girl?"

This only egged her on. I lay there trying not to giggle. This was very serious. Trespassers would not be given quarter. No mercy!

I'd shifted and saw nothing out of the ordinary, but in true canine fashion, the slightest noise set her hackles on edge. She lowered her head and eased toward the window. Then, like a bullet shot out of a gun, she leaped through the wall and was gone.

She was so entertaining.

I laughed and turned back to the two men watching me.

"There really is a game tonight," Osh said.

"This is bigger than a game." I scrambled up and sat next to him again. "It's bigger than—"

"We get it," Garrett said. "Total annihilation. But can't it wait until after the game?"

"No. I have a plan, but first I have to tell you what my secrets are, because if I tell you my plan first without telling you . . . never mind. Just listen." I cleared my mind and thought how best to tell them that my husband, their friend, was created from an evil god. I steadied my resolve and decided. "My husband, your friend, was created from an evil god."

Osh took another sip of beer while Garrett thought a moment, *then* took another sip of beer.

"Okay, let me back up." This needed more explanation. They needed to understand what it could mean for all of us.

"Do you remember in New York in the warehouse when the evil emissary Kuur tried to kill me?"

They both shrugged at the stupidity of my question and took another sip.

I bit my lip. Closed my eyes. Scraped up all the bits of courage that remained on the bottom of my courage barrel and swallowed them. I was about to reveal something to them that could change the fate of the world. The god glass had been buried in the 1400s for a reason. The monks who buried it meant for it to stay buried.

"He wasn't trying to kill me."

I felt, rather than saw, their interest pique.

"I'm a god. Apparently not just anyone can do that. But I can be trapped. He was trying to trap me, and that's what happened to the evil god Satan used to create his son Rey'aziel."

Osh was wearing his best poker face, the one where he barely looked like he was paying attention. But I felt something jerk inside him. Like a puzzle piece falling into place.

I continued. "Okay, the story goes like this. In desperation, God, the God Jehovah, created what is called god glass. It's an entire dimension, a hell dimension, inside a piece of glass. It looks like a jewel. Like an opal. It is absolutely indestructible and a hundred percent inescapable. Only the person or being who puts you in it can let you back out again. Jehovah created it to trap one god." I held up a finger. "To lock away one god and one god only inside a hell dimension. A vast nothingness that stretches on for an eternity."

"Which god did he create it for?" Osh asked.

"That I don't know. Kuur didn't tell me everything. I doubt he actually knew everything. He was working for Lucifer. Surely the prince of the underworld wouldn't reveal his whole hand."

"If Jehovah created it, how did Lucifer get ahold of it to use it to create Rey'aziel?"

"See, that's the thing. The details get fuzzy here. For some reason, this god didn't get sent into the god glass, but I have no idea how it ended up in the hands of Lucifer. Neither do I know how, but he used it to trap one of the gods of Uzan for the specific purpose of creating a son. Reyes."

I waited. Let them absorb the information.

When they didn't say anything, I added, "After he created Reyes, Lucifer gave it to one of his worshippers here on Earth who, as you might imagine, used it for pure evil. A group of monks finally captured him, sent him into the hell dimension then, because god glass cannot be destroyed, traveled across the ocean, found a spot, and spent months digging a hole deep enough to bury it for what they'd hoped would be forever."

"And Kuur dug it up?" Osh asked.

I nodded. "He found it and tried to use it to trap me. To get me off this plane so Lucifer could get to Beep. So he could kill the being destined to destroy him."

"This is like a supernatural soap opera," Garrett said, growing frustrated. "How the fuck does that shit happen? I thought gods were nice and benevolent and answered prayers and shit. But no. In this episode, the gods have all been possessed and are evil and plotting to destroy the world."

"Gods don't get possessed," Osh said.

"Right. Sorry. So there are actually rules?"

Osh frowned. "The gods of Uzan, at least the ones I've met, are so far beyond anything Lucifer could have thought up, it's unreal. And Lucifer used one of them to create the son."

Then he did something I'd never seen him do before. He paled. The blood drained from his face as he sat there, stunned.

I studied the carpet. "This is bad, right? I mean, I don't know. How much of Reyes is an evil god and how much is . . . Reyes?"

Osh's hands curled into fists as he thought. "Wait," he said. "Did you see it? The god glass?"

I pressed my lips together, then reached into my pocket and pulled it out. "I took it after I trapped Kuur inside."

Osh's jaw dropped. He didn't move. "You . . . you trapped him?"

"Don't act so surprised."

"Sorry. So Kuur told you about Reyes? About how he was created?"

"No." I went back to studying the carpet, resisting the urge to gaze lovingly at the god glass. It was like a drug. Mesmerizing. Pure. Beautiful.

And yet inside lay a hell dimension. "No, Kuur didn't tell me. My dad did."

Garrett's expression changed from frustration to concern.

"That's how I got my memories back. My dad—he crossed through me to force me to remember who I was. What I was. And to pass on the information he'd gathered while he was doing recon in hell. He learned a great deal." I looked at Osh. "You honestly didn't know any of this? You didn't know how Reyes was created?"

He shook his head. "But it explains a lot."

"Like what?"

"Rey'aziel. He was so different. So much more powerful than anything else Lucifer had concocted. Even more powerful than himself, which didn't make sense. No one could figure out why. The Dendour put him through hell, literally and figuratively."

"The Dendour?"

"Like . . . teachers. Trainers. Only worse."

"And they put him through hell? Why?"

"Who knows? Jealousy, maybe? But he overcame every obstacle they threw at him. They tried every way they could think of to kill him. They beat him. Starved him. Tore apart his—"

"Stop," I said, covering my ears. After a moment, I asked, "And Lucifer just let them?"

"He wanted his son to be strong, so yes. But now I know, they couldn't have killed him. No matter what they did, he wouldn't have died, so they got progressively harder and harder on him until—"

"Until?" I asked, almost desperate to know.

"Until he stopped them," he said matter-of-factly. "He'd had enough one day and killed every Dendour there. Snapped their necks like they were twigs. Then he went in search of others. Anyone who'd wronged him in any way. They call it *Auya s'Di*."

"Day of the Blood," I said. I sat back and tried to imagine it, but how does one imagine a child growing up in a hell dimension? It was beyond my comprehension.

"To get a better concept of what he did that day, imagine a ten-year-old attacking and killing an army of trained soldiers with his bare hands, then going to search for more."

"Are you saying Reyes was ten?" I asked, alarmed.

"Not at all. He was much younger at that time. If you're comparing him to human years."

Had he just been destined to be abused? First in hell from legions of demons and then on Earth with Earl Walker? My heart ached for him, but I felt something else from Osh that I couldn't quite identify.

"What?" I asked him.

"Nothing."

"Osh, I mean it. What are you thinking?"

"What if that part of him is still evil?"

"That's what I'm trying to decide."

We looked at the god glass in my hand. Stared at it.

"Who wants another beer?" Garrett asked.

It was a bit much to take in.

26

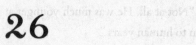

Don't borrow trouble.
Gotcha.
So, then, can I rent it?
—CHARLEY DAVIDSON

"So, your plan?" Osh asked me after they'd both downed a few beers. It was good for them. Let them relax. Take it all in.

Apparently they were ready for more.

"Yeah, about that. You both have to open your minds."

"Damn," Garrett said. "This is going to suck, isn't it?"

"Not for you," I promised.

"For me?" Osh asked.

I nodded. "Sorry. But first think of this. We know what area one, if not two, of the gods of Uzan are in, right? I'm assuming it's still there?"

"It's making its way east, leaving death and destruction along the way, but yeah. It hasn't caught on to the fact that we moved Beep and the Loehrs three days ago."

"I think that, since I know the general area where it's at, I can find it."

"And what are you going to do then?"

"Why, trap it, of course." I jingled the pendant, dropped it, scraped it back up, then held it up again, thankful it was indestructible.

Garrett laughed softly into his beer. Not because I'd dropped the pendant, but because of the sheer impossibility of our situation.

"Let me get this straight," Osh said. "You're going to walk up to it, open your little pendant, and tell him to jump inside?"

I snorted. "No. There is a process, and I know what it is."

"And we can tell none of this to Reyes?" Garrett asked.

"Nope."

"Not until we know where his allegiances lie," Osh said.

"I'm pretty sure we know, but what will happen if and when, like me, Reyes learns his true celestial name?"

"The name he had as a god?"

I nodded to Garrett. "Yes. Which part of him is the stronger? Which part will take over? The good news is that when I learned my name, I was still me. For a little while. Until I exploded, lost my memory, and vacationed in New York State. But I'm back, and I'm still me."

Osh shook his head. "That's a lot to hope for considering the alternative. But you're forgetting something."

"What?"

"You're forgetting that you are this bright-ass light any god within a thousand worlds can see. He's going to see you coming."

"Maybe not."

When I didn't explain, Osh questioned me with the quirk of a brow.

"This is where the open-mind thing comes in."

"It gets better?" Garrett asked.

"This is a prime opportunity, Osh," I said, trying to convince myself as much as him. "We can't let it pass us by and regret it later."

"Unless you have a better plan than walking up to him with your light beaming like a signal beacon and stuffing him inside that little necklace, I'd say we probably should."

This was going to get tricky. Very, very tricky. But I knew Osh's future to a minuscule degree. Could anything I do change that?

"But what if I could walk up to him undetected?"

Osh frowned. "Still a stupid plan, but how?"

I glanced at the carpet again. Thought about what I was doing. How many ways this could go wrong. Then I thought about Beep. I thought about her destiny. None of us mattered anymore. Not really. Not that we ever did. We were simply the foundation of what she was going to achieve.

"Charles?" Garrett said.

Whatever happened from here on out, this would change our friendship forever. I would be hated, and that was okay, too. If this worked, I would be saving my daughter's life. Giving her another chance to do what she was meant to do.

If it didn't . . . none of this mattered, anyway. I could not let this opportunity pass me by. I just hoped he would understand that.

I released a long breath. Slowed time. And attacked before he knew what I was doing.

Before Osh could react, I was on him. I lifted him off the sofa, threw him against a wall, and wrapped one hand around his throat.

He didn't even fight me. He just looked down at me, his face the picture of confusion. He still trusted me so much, he didn't fight back.

That would be his undoing.

"What the fuck?" he asked.

"You're going to do what you do best," I said. "You're going to ingest my soul. You're going to swallow my light so I can find the god and trap him in the glass while he's walking around in human form. It's the only time it can be done. The process requires blood, and gods don't have that unless they've hijacked a human body. I can't let this opportunity slip by. I'm sorry."

He finally started to fight me, but there are few things more lethal than a mother whose child has been threatened. Also, I was a god. He wouldn't have won. He must've known that because he stopped struggling almost the very second he began. Giving in. Sacrificing himself. The muscles in my chest contracted, tightened around my heart.

"It won't work," he said, panting with exertion and apprehension.

"I'm willing to take that chance."

"You don't understand." He lifted a hand to my face. Ran a thumb over my chin. "I could live off your soul until the stars burn out. I can't take you in one sitting. It doesn't work that way."

I tightened my grip on his throat, mostly for show. "Then make it work that way. I have to do this, Osh. It will never expect me if it can't see my light."

He bit back a curse. "You could've just asked."

"Not likely."

He closed his eyes a long moment, then nodded. "It'll kill me."

I moved my hand to his sculpted jaw. Pressed into him. Closed the distance between us until my mouth hovered just under his. "I know."

Then I put my lips on his, but in a surprising show of strength, he reversed our positions. He grabbed my throat, twisted me around, thrust me against the wall, slammed my head into it—twice—then lowered his mouth onto mine.

And he swallowed me. Siphoned the energy out of my body, the act painful and erotic at the same time. For both of us. He cupped my face with his free hand. Tilted his head. Deepened what boiled down to a kiss. Instead of slowing down, he sped up. Kissed harder. Pressed into me, wanting more and more of what I was offering.

His fingers dived into my hair, trapping it in his fist as he gorged on my soul. The act tapped something deep inside me. It curled inside me and then sprang taut. I dug my nails into the wall at my back. Pushed into him as it got closer and closer. Sharper and sharper. Until it exploded inside me.

I threw my head back, taking in air I'd never tasted before. Feeling drained and exhilarated like the atoms in my body had found a new playground.

Osh moaned. Fell against me. Buried his face in my hair a microsecond before he dropped to his knees. He clutched at his throat and curled into himself. His muscles contracted to the density of marble as he tried to hold all of me in. But he cracked. His skin splintered and broke, and the light that I'd carried around my whole life—a light that I have never seen—began to seep out of him.

He twisted around, his face a study in pain as he tried to hold in my essence. I kneeled over him.

"Hurry," he said, his voice hoarse. His fingers curled and his back arched, and more fissures cracked over his body, light shooting out of them.

I didn't have much time. My essence was too powerful for him to hold. It was like trying to contain a nuclear blast inside a lightbulb. It would explode sooner than later, shattering him as it did. He thrust his head back as another spasm of pain shot through him.

It would kill him. I knew that. I'd known it before I began. But it wouldn't kill him immediately. I had time. I could find the god, trap him, and be back before it ate him completely.

"What the fuck?" Garrett asked.

I rose from the floor, having no idea when time had bounced back.

"If I'm not back in fifteen minutes, call Reyes. Tell him what I did. Tell him to help Osh, but do not, under any circumstances, tell him where I am."

"What did you do?" he asked, staring at Osh in horror.

"No time. Give me fifteen minutes."

Then I closed my eyes and left this plane entirely.

I spotted the god instantly and zeroed in, materializing behind him in a matter of seconds. He was made of light, too, only his was grayer than mine. Murkier. And he was walking in a sea of people with lights flashing and music blaring and teens laughing and screaming.

I stopped and looked around to get my bearings. To my left was a giant red roller coaster. To my right was the ocean. And underneath me were wood planks.

A boardwalk? We were on a boardwalk?

Yes. The Santa Cruz Beach Boardwalk, to be exact, according to the sign by the roller coaster. I wondered why the god would be here of all places. Osh had said the North. New England? Since I had no idea where they'd moved her, I had no idea if he was closing in or not, but I was certain of one thing. He was enjoying the hunt.

Still a little astonished I could do it, I picked a spot in an out-of-the-way corner just beyond his line of sight and let my body take shape around me. Like a veil parting. Like a cloak settling around my shoulders and pooling at my feet. I materialized slowly, watching his every move and the moves of the people around me.

Homing in on the strange light, I followed it past the arcade to stop at a cotton candy stand. The human it had taken, the one it had hijacked, was a woman. According to Osh, she died the moment it entered her. Her arms were already discolored with yellow and purple bruises. She was painfully thin with long auburn hair that hung in messy strands down her back. Clearly it wasn't worried about keeping up appearances since it could only last for so long in that body, anyway.

It sensed me and turned, and time slowed to a stop as the world spun around me. I shook my head, speechless, and almost fell to my knees. A cry of surprise leaped from my throat, and I covered my mouth with both hands. Huge green eyes gazed at me in curiosity. A once pretty mouth, now covered in sores on one side, opened slightly as her head tilted to the side.

I feared I would crumple to the ground. I feared my mortal heart would stop and forget to restart. I feared for the world around me, because once Reyes found out this god had ripped his sister's soul out of her body so that he could inhabit it, the world would be a dangerous place to be.

"What are you?" Kim asked.

She had the same voice. The same gentle expressions. The same graceful mannerisms. But it wasn't her. It was the god.

Kim was supposed to be in Mexico. How did she get here? How did the god get to her?

I fought my urge to have a complete meltdown and feigned ignorance.

"Kim?" I asked, stepping closer. "Is that you?"

When I rushed forward, it didn't move. It didn't step back and veer away from me. It simply tried to figure out what I was. Without my light, I had no idea what I would look like to a supernatural being, but it clearly wasn't just like any other human.

"Kim," I said, throwing my arms around her and hugging. I knew she was just the shell, just the vessel, and that her spirit had probably already crossed, but I couldn't help it. I held her tight, wanting to apologize for not getting to know her better. I should've spent more time with her. We should've had coffee and lunch and gone to male revues together.

I pulled back, took her face into my hands, and kissed her mouth.

That's when the tears broke through. They streamed down my face as I kissed her hard and followed with a dozen tiny pecks.

It watched me, growing more suspicious by the second, so I quickly stepped out of its reach.

Then realization dawned. "Where is your light, little girl?"

"Why her?" I said, my voice breaking. "Why his sister?"

"How else to cripple him? He is almost as indestructible as I."

"Ah," I said, wiping my eyes. "Of course. Human life means nothing to you."

"As a gnat's life means nothing to you."

I nodded, beginning to understand him. It reached out and took a cotton candy from an elderly woman. When she began to protest, it turned to her.

"No," I said, starting toward him.

He chuckled and let her go. "Where is he? Rey'azikeen? I was hoping to see him before this body becomes completely useless."

"He's out. Which one are you? Which brother of Uzan?"

He threw his head back and laughed. "Brother? We are brothers, are we?"

I frowned at him, and how better to get the answers I needed than to ask? "I don't understand."

"What do you think Uzan is?"

"Your home dimension."

He seemed to become more confused. "I was under the impression you had learned your celestial name, Elle-Ryn."

"I have."

He stuffed another mouthful of cotton candy into Kim's mouth. The movement caused the sores to split. Blood slid down her chin, and I fought the quivering of my lower lip.

"Then why wouldn't you know . . . oh, my. Jehovah. He is a sneaky one, is he not?"

"Again, you lost me."

"Uzan, my dear, is a prison. One is not from there. One is sent there."

"A—a prison?"

"Rey'azikeen, Eidolon, and I were prisoners. It was supposed to be inescapable. Eidolon and I spent centuries there, rotting away much like this body. Until . . ."

Kim's eyes sparkled as he told the tale.

"Until?"

"Until Rey'azikeen was sent. Young. Rebellious. Absolutely brilliant."

That was Reyes, all right.

"And this is where the irony of it all plays a part. For you, Elle-Ryn-Ahleethia, are the one who sent him there."

"What?"

He was lying. How would that even be possible?

"You truly have no idea who he is. It is so lavish, so unprecedented, that you should fall in love with the very being you sent to rot in stink and decay. Into an agony that the seven original gods from your dimension, from Evuthwana, created."

"I didn't send him anywhere. I didn't know him."

"But you were, how do they say it? Tight? Yes, tight. You were tight with his brother. His real brother, for the day I am brothers with the likes of either of those two, I shall send myself back to Uzan."

"His brother?"

"You know. The older brother left with the burden of taking care of the younger one. But youth these days. He was too rebellious. Too stubborn. Too irresponsible. And his older brother worried for the world he had created."

"And what world would that be?"

"Why, you're standing on it, my dear."

27

Hearts are wild creatures.
That's why our ribs are cages.
—AUTHOR UNKNOWN

The world that I was standing on started to spin. He was lying. He had to be.

"I would remember."

"Ah, but Jehovah wanted you to reap his lost. You volunteered, yes, but not without some encouragement from the Man himself. And once you were in his realm under his laws, he must've plucked"—Kim acted like she plucked something out of the air—"the memory from your mind."

"Why would he do that?"

"To control you, of course."

"I don't believe you."

He took another mouthful of cotton candy. "Now that you know the memory is there, it will come back to you whenever you allow it to. But don't feel too bad. His brother created an entire dimension just for him. A hell dimension, though how it could be worse than Uzan, I have no idea. He was going to lock Rey'azikeen in it and throw away the key, as they say. But you talked him out of it. You begged Jehovah to just send his brother away until he came around. Until he understood Jehovah's vision." He gasped as a thought dawned. "Were you in love with him, even then?"

"The god glass was meant for Reyes?" Stunned would've been an understatement.

"Ingenious instrument. A vault. Absolutely inescapable. Then again, we are talking about the only god ever to escape Uzan. If it could be done . . ."

"This is unreal."

"Oh, don't wallow, my dear. It is most unbecoming. Besides, if it makes you feel better, I am the one who helped Lucifer trap him. It's like we're on the same team."

"You trapped him?"

"You did it first."

"Why would you do that?"

"He didn't exactly invite us to go with him when he escaped Uzan. We followed him. So, he went to big brother and begged for the god glass to trap us. To put us away like we were any worse than he. Well, that is a strong possibility, but it's all in one's perspective."

"He went after you?"

"He came after us both. Arrogant fellow, Rey'azikeen. So, we hid in the hell dimension of this realm and discovered that Lucifer was champing at the bit for . . . what do you call it? Payback? We devised a plan and used the god glass against him. Two and a quarter—Lucifer isn't the best fighter—against one? I like it best when the odds are in my favor."

"You ganged up on him."

"Of course. I'm not stupid. So, we trapped Jehovah's brother in the very dimension that was made for him. When we got back to hell with him, little Rey'azikeen wasn't quite his usual self. See, even a few seconds in that hell dimension is like years on this plane. He was so disoriented that by the time he figured out what was happening, Lucifer already had him in the rune. He didn't stand a chance, really."

"Why are you, a god, in cahoots with a fallen angel?"

"Boredom, mostly. It's been fun watching this little feud play out between Jehovah and one of his children. And don't get me started on the one between Jehovah and the boy. By the way, wherever is your light?"

"I lent it to a friend."

"Well, he won't live long."

"Longer than you."

He laughed, Kim's hair falling over her shoulders as her head fell back, and it hit me what he was doing. He was stalling.

I turned a full circle. Was his bestie from Uzan here?

"Why are you in cahoots with Jehovah?"

"I'm not," I said, watching the skies for another presence. I walked away from him, searching. Scanning.

"He's using you to do his dirty work. You're the hired help. And then he erases your memory? I'd find a better lot of friends if I were you."

Oh yeah. He was stalling. Only a god could kill another god, but maybe it was harder than it sounded. Maybe he needed backup. He'd already proved he fought dirty.

"When he remembers who you are," he continued, and I wondered if he ever shut up, "he shall not be happy. Rey'azikeen. You did send him to prison, one that your ancestors created. Do you think he will still love you?"

I tried so hard to remember. If I'd known Reyes way back when, maybe I knew this winner. Maybe I knew his name. Club God was bound to have a very small membership. I had to know his name. Then it hit me. Not his name but a plan. I was so good at those.

"You said you escaped with Eidolon," I said, keeping my gaze toward the heavens. "I thought you *were* Eidolon."

"It breaks my heart that you don't remember me. Not bad. Not like a complete break. More like a hairline fracture."

"Sorry. I'm horrible with names."

"I'll give you a hint." He took another bite. "It's bigger than a bread box—"

I swirled around and smiled. "There."

"Ah. Did it come to you?"

I opened my palm where I'd stashed the god glass. I was worried he'd see it in my jeans so I held on to it. For dear, sweet life.

He stilled instantly, his gaze laser locked onto the locket. The second I opened the glass cover, thunderstorms and lightning bolts shot out around us.

He reacted immediately. He started forward, but I slowed time. He met it and kept coming. I slowed it more, so much so that the people around us didn't just stop moving, they started moving backwards, sluggish and surreal. I was rewinding time. But again, he met it and charged forward.

The pause was enough, though. Enough for me to press my lips to the top of the glass, the lightning bolts crackling around my face, and whisper, "This is for you, Kim." I glanced at him from beneath my lashes, and just as he reached me, just as his finger brushed the pendant, I said, "Mae'eldeesahn."

Rocket had given me the clue in that picture, the shake to rattle my memory. And the blood I got off Kim's mouth was enough. The god glass just needed a single strand of DNA from the host to capture the being inside.

It worked.

He stumbled back, his face a picture of shock and utter disbelief that he'd been duped. He'd been trapped this time.

I'd seen the god glass work before. I waited for it. Mae'eldeesahn did not. He turned and took off running, but that seemed to make the lightning bolt that shot out after him happy. It curled around him like a lover and ripped him out of Kim's broken body.

What came out was not what I'd expected. It was more light than anything. More smoke than substance. And it was beautiful. Utterly stunning and absolutely malevolent.

And then it was gone. Sucked into the hell dimension until I called it out. An undertaking that would never happen.

I snapped the locket closed just as I felt another presence. No way could I get away with that twice. I swung around to find Reyes materializing behind me in all his dark glory. Slowly. Lethally, because that boy was the poster child for failed anger management classes.

He glared at me from underneath his lashes, but his concern outshone his anger. He strode up to me, took my shoulders, looked me up and down to make sure I wasn't injured.

I pocketed the pendant and took his face into my hands. "Reyes—"

"Are you hurt?"

"No, sweetheart, listen—"

"What just happened?" He glanced around, confused.

"Reyes, listen."

"What was that?"

"Rey'aziel."

He finally focused on my words.

"Reyes," I said, and a sudden sadness gripped me so hard I could barely speak.

"What?" he asked, stilling in alarm. Bracing himself. "What?"

"It was one of the gods of Uzan."

All expression slid away from his face.

"His name was Mae'eldeesahn."

"Was he—? Did you kill him?"

"No. No, I trapped him. He's gone."

Relief softened his features, but only just. He was more confused than anything.

"But he—Reyes, he'd hijacked a human host."

"That's what they do."

"No, it's—honey, I'm so sorry." A sob broke my voice. I knew what this was going to do to him. "He took Kim."

A half smile curved his mouth for a microsecond as he studied me in disbelief.

I stepped to the side and showed him. Kim was lying facedown on the pavement, an arm thrown across her back, the angles all wrong. Her red hair fanned out over her head like a halo.

"I'm so sorry."

He pulled out of my grasp and walked over to her. Kneeled down. Turned her over and wrapped her in his arms so that her face was almost touching his. He pushed her hair to the side and saw the sores. The sunken features. The yellowing of the skin and darkening of the bruises.

He exhaled sharply, fighting a sob. Then another. And another.

I sank to my knees, knowing there was nothing I could do.

His fingers balled into fists and then splayed against her as he pulled her into a tight embrace. He held the back of her head. Buried his face in her hair. And exploded into a sea of flames.

I realized then that people had surrounded them. But they only saw a distraught man holding a woman.

Or so I thought.

When he burst into flames, it was both on the intangible plane and the tangible one. Kids screamed and adults covered them as they dragged them away. And everyone, every single person there, ran.

Rising to my feet, I realized I had to do something, but the fire was too hot. I couldn't even get close. I could no longer see him. I covered my mouth as I watched my husband set fire to everything in a twenty-foot radius. Then thirty. Then forty. The roller coaster nearby. The arcade. The cotton candy stand. The ice cream parlor. One attraction after another became engulfed in flames as people screamed and ran and stumbled over one another.

Smoke billowed around me as families darted in all directions.

"I have no choice," I heard a voice say from behind me.

I turned to see Michael, my favorite archangel, standing there.

Rage enveloped me. "This is not the time."

He drew his sword.

This was not the time. The rage I felt at what he was threatening, at what Jehovah had done, erupted like volcano inside me. I ground my teeth together but showed him my palms as though in surrender.

Then I turned my left palm down. Artemis rose into it, materializing beside me. She lowered her head and bared her teeth and let loose a growl from deep within her chest.

Then I turned my right palm up. My old friend and guardian of a sort, Mr. Wong, materialized beside me. He put his hand in mine for a quick squeeze before drawing his own sword. His armor glistened, and power—as much power as I felt radiating out of Michael—pulsed out of him in glorious waves.

Michael grinned. "Do you think I'd come to a battle unprepared?"

Through the swell and ebb of smoke, a dozen angels appeared behind him.

I lifted a brow. "Do you think I would?"

Behind us, twelve hellhounds rose from the ground. They snarled and snapped, pawed at the earth, begged to be given free rein. The angels readied themselves.

"I need to have a word with your boss," I said.

"Not today." He lowered his head as though giving a silent order, and legions of angels appeared behind him. Hundreds upon hundreds as far as the eye could see—but there was a lot of smoke—all ready to fight.

"Michael," I said as though disappointed. "This is getting embarrassing."

And behind me, thousands and thousands of departed materialized. Beep's army. I called forth every name Rocket had ever written, and they stood like a sea of warriors. Ready to fight for my daughter, because if she was going to survive, she needed her father. I needed her father.

"Like I said, this is not the time."

"He made a binding promise," Michael said. "All three gods of Uzan. Off this plane. For all eternity."

"You tricked him."

"I let Rey'aziel trick himself."

"But that's not really his name, is it?"

He didn't answer that. Instead he looked past me at the flames that were now a hundred feet high. "He will soon go nuclear and level this town, if not several more. We aren't in the habit of giving passes to those who would see hundreds of thousands die."

"Seriously? Do you even watch the news?"

"Humans killing humans. Not my jurisdiction."

"I know Jehovah may not care about his brother, but I damned sure do. And you will not take him."

He worked his jaw in frustration. Torn. Weighing the odds in his mind. In the end, he sheathed his sword. "When the time comes, Val-Eeth, you will not be able to save him."

"That's funny. I don't think he's the one who needs saving."

Another cloud of smoke billowed around us, swallowing us whole. I heard a rustling of wings, and when the smoke cleared, they were gone. Every angel had vanished.

I turned to Mr. Wong, his golden armor shimmering as much as his mischievous eyes. "I thought we were going to have a battle."

"I'm sorry."

"Don't be. It would've been good practice." He turned toward our own army. "They need to get in shape."

I snorted. "Can the departed get in shape?"

"I will leave you, Val-Eeth." He bowed over my hand.

"Charley, please." Being called a god was a bit much.

He bowed again and disappeared. A microsecond later, Beep's army evaporated, as did the hellhounds.

Artemis looked back and whimpered. Michael was right. Reyes had lost control. I dematerialized and stepped into the fire. He still held her tight, but he had incinerated her. All that remained of her body was an outline of ash.

He touched her face. It cracked like burned paper and flew away, the glowing particles floating around him. Then she crumbled in his arms and slipped through his fingers like sand through a sifter.

And the fire grew hotter. It burned. Even in the intangible world it scorched my skin. I realized he was lost. He couldn't control his powers.

Been there, done that.

Maybe he was just the opposite of me. Maybe if he learned his true name, he would be better able to control it.

What did I have to lose? I stepped closer, kneeled down to him, cupped his face in my hands, and whispered, "Rey'azikeen."

Nothing. The agony he felt scorched to the marrow of my bones. I said it again and again received no response.

This was not happening. Then I realized it didn't have to be permanent. I took out the god glass. If I didn't stop him, he truly would level the town and possibly more. He could sink half of California into the ocean.

The fire grew even hotter, the flames loud and relentless. I reached over to get his blood. I would only leave him in there for a moment. Just enough to calm him down. To disorient him and bring him back to me.

I put my nails on his wrist and scraped as hard as I could.

He finally looked at me, his gaze glowing and glistening. So I repeated his name. "Rey'azikeen. You have to stop. You're going to burn this town down."

He looked through the fire. He'd already leveled the park.

"You have to stop."

He furrowed his brows. Looked down at his sister's ashes. Bent down and covered his eyes with his fists.

That was when I saw them, rising over the god before me. I fell back and looked on in awe. He was covered in fire, his outline almost translucent. But the fire arced over him, too, and created the illusion of wings. Massive, angelic wings folded in and wrapped around him.

I forgot all about the impending nuclear disaster. I watched my husband as he sat back on his heels and laid his head back, trying desperately to get control over his emotions. He was solid muscle. Tense and combustible and so beautiful I ached. And he had wings. The fires licked over them, shaping and molding them. He dropped his head into his hands again.

Before I could snap out of it, another being walked into the fire. A departed. She laid her hand on Reyes's head, and he opened his eyes. Looked up at her. Almost collapsed when she kneeled down and folded him into her arms.

"He was trying to draw you out," Kim said, more beautiful than I'd ever seen her. "He knew that you've been following him."

"What?" I asked, appalled. I stood and walked over to him. "You were following him? An evil, malevolent god? Was this one of your secrets? Because I don't remember this coming up during our last conversation."

Kim laughed softly, stood, and hugged me. I hugged her back for a long time.

"I understand so much now," she said, then looked back at her brother. "I know how special you are. Both of you. I knew you were, but not like this."

"Kim, I wish we could have told you more," I said.

Reyes stood and looked at her like she was the sun and he'd been raised in total darkness. His fire still billowed around him.

"You don't understand," she said. Her face brightened. "My name is on Rocket's wall. I was sent."

"Kim, that's amazing," I said, not sure what else to say.

She nodded and leveled a loving gaze on her brother. "I was sent here for a reason. I know it. And I promise to guard her forever." She put one hand on my face and one on Reyes's. "I'll be your eyes and ears. I will give you minute-by-minute updates on how she is. What she's doing. Her first words. Her first steps." She lowered her head and smiled. "I'm an aunt of the girl who is destined to save the world. It doesn't get any better than that."

"Oh yeah?" I teased. "Well, I'm her mom. That's right." I blew on my fingernails and polished them on my shirt. "You can be jealous."

She chuckled, but Reyes was still lost. The fire still raged. Her loss still cut.

I stepped forward, drew him down to me, and put my mouth on his. Then I tamed the fire. I cooled it with my breath. With the beats of my heart. With the pulse of my energy.

The roar of the fire was replaced with a crackling sound as ice spread from under my feet, along the boardwalk, and up walls and posts and amusement park rides. The fires around us died immediately, and black smoke rose in its place, the scent pungent and acrid.

I pulled back. Reyes's wings were gone, and his fire had calmed though certainly didn't disappear. He was made of fire, so it was no wonder.

"Only she can tame the beast," Kim said.

I looked at her in question. "It's something Rocket said to me."

"Ah. He's smarter than he seems."

She nodded and pulled us both into a hug. "Would you like to see her?" she asked us in the softest whisper.

"Yes!" I said before Reyes could say no. When he gave me a wary look, I said, "I don't even have my light right now. Just for a minute."

His head still not quite in the game, he nodded, and in the next heartbeat we were in a convenience store. A couple in front of us was oohing and aahing as they served themselves cups of coffee.

"Your light is not as visible," Kim said, "but you're still not really human. The supernatural world can sense that. You must be quick."

"I promise." I couldn't take my eyes off the carrier Mr. Loehr had set on the counter while Mrs. Loehr doctored their coffees.

They were chattering about what color curtains to put in Beep's room. And Mr. Loehr needed to call the gas company the second they arrived. They were on a trip, across country from the looks of it. Were they moving them again?

I glanced around and saw the outline of a hellhound nearby. It backed away when it realized who we were, as did the other three.

A coo sounded from the carrier, and my breath came out too sharp, too loud, when I heard her. The Loehrs tensed instantly. Mrs. Loehr scooped the carrier up while Mr. Loehr stepped in front of them. A barrier. A protector. And then they recognized us, and relief rushed through them both.

I smiled, put an index finger over my mouth, and gave a secretive wink. Surprised, they smiled back and pulled me into a group hug.

"Is everything okay?" Mrs. Loehr asked.

Reyes nodded and took his would-have-been mother into a fierce hug. He did the same with Mr. Loehr while I stepped closer to the carrier she'd put back on the counter.

I could see her essence before I saw Beep herself. Then I saw her. A tiny hand at first. A pudgy arm. And then huge, coppery eyes that dominated a round face. For the first time in over a month, I saw my daughter.

I put a hand over my mouth, she was so beautiful. She smiled at me, her dimpled cheeks bright pink and full of life. Her eyes sparkling.

Mrs. Loehr looked on proudly. She tipped the carrier so I could see her better. "They say it's gas."

"Gas?"

"That makes babies smile at this age." She leaned in and whispered, "They've never met Miss Elwyn Alexandra."

She beamed at me and then at her husband. They seemed so happy despite the danger we'd put them in. They seemed grateful.

Reyes came to stand beside me.

I laughed softly, the joy in my heart so overwhelming. "She's dark and powerful and fierce," I said to him. "And she's no more human than you or I."

He squeezed me to him and then bent over the carrier. Beep took hold of his finger, and he laughed, as amazed as I was.

Kim looked down at her, too, her face aglow. Literally. She was no longer the stressed, nervous, skittish woman she used to be. As painful as it was to think about, death suited her.

I looked back at the Loehrs. "Her soul is made up of a million sparkling lights. Of stars and galaxies and nebulas."

They exchanged fascinated glances, then I realized something else.

"Reyes, she's a portal."

He looked closer at her. "You're right. But to where?"

"I guess we'll find out someday."

"May we hold her?" Reyes asked Mrs. Loehr.

I seconded the question with a nod, my brows raised.

She looked at us like we'd just escaped our padded cells and said, "Of course."

With Mrs. Loehr's help, we gathered her up, certain we would break her, it'd been so long. I pushed her into Reyes's arms and then wrapped my own around them both.

"How did you find me?" I asked him.

He touched her tiny chin. "I asked Osh."

I tore my gaze off my daughter. "You asked?" My voice rose an octave. "Osh?"

He nodded.

"So, you saw him?"

"You mean in the fetal position you left him in?"

He saw him.

I knew I had to get back sooner rather than later. But I just kept thinking, one more minute. One more minute.

"And he just told you where I was?"

"He didn't want to, but I applied pressure," he said. "He was already in a lot of pain. It didn't take much."

"Reyes," I said, appalled and feeling more than a little guilty. "Is he okay?"

"Define 'okay.'"

Kim put her hand on my shoulder. "It's time."

I panicked. "Just one minute more."

She only smiled at me, and that was all the convincing I needed. She was right. We were risking our own daughter's life by being here. Not to mention the Loehrs'.

A painful sigh shuddered through my chest as Reyes handed her back to Mrs. Loehr. And then something amazing happened. Beep looked at her as though she recognized her. She looked at her lovingly. There was no mistaking it, and I almost cried.

"Thank you so much," I said to her. "You will never know how grateful we are."

"No, thank you," she said. "You don't know what this means to us."

I hugged her to me again, deeper this time, and I could smell Reyes in her clothes and on her skin and in her hair. A part of him truly was human. The good part. The loving part. The important part.

She bounced Beep in her arms. "We owe you everything."

They both watched us go, Mr. Loehr with his arms wrapped around his girls, and I could only hope Mrs. Loehr didn't drop Beep when we dematerialized before their eyes.

28

The fact that there's a Highway to Hell
and only a Stairway to Heaven
says a lot about anticipated traffic numbers.
—MEME

By the time we got back to Garrett's apartment, seventeen minutes had passed, thanks to how much we'd manipulated time. Osh lay on the floor, writhing in agony, his head thrown back, his teeth welded together. The fissures in his body had cracked open and were leaking vast amounts of light, the unimaginable energy melding the molecules in his body together. It was like watching a nuclear reactor in a meltdown.

Reyes was right. Osh had only seconds.

I straddled him, pulled him upright, grabbed his jaw, and placed my mouth on his. Taking back my light, my energy, was comparable to swallowing a hydrogen bomb. I drew it out of him as quickly as I could before it killed him, and the atoms in such an excited state burst inside me. It was like brain freeze times a billion.

I wrapped him tighter in my arms. Held his head as he went limp. Took as much of me back as I could. I kept drawing out energy, sucking venom as though he were a bite victim, but he didn't wake up.

"Dutch," Reyes said, placing a hand on my shoulder. "You're killing him."

"No," I said with a sob, pulling him to me and placing tiny kisses on his face. "I'm sorry, Osh."

My light was out of him, but what was left was much worse. He was covered from head to toe in deep gashes, long lesions where the light had crackled across his body, trying to escape. His face, his skin normally so perfect, was a garish replica of the original as though an artist had decided to sculpt what he would look like in a horror movie.

And yet he was still so beautiful. So intrinsically handsome. So supremely broken.

I held him for a long time, rocking him.

"Dutch—"

"We need to get him to a hospital," I said, cursing myself for not having thought of it before. "Hurry."

Reyes kneeled beside me. "Sweetheart, look."

The wounds were already beginning to heal, the skin closing at the tips of the lesions, leaving dark red trails in their wakes.

I looked at Reyes. "He'll be okay?"

"Unfortunately."

I laughed softly, knowing he didn't mean it. They'd started out as enemies but had become very close. Like prizefighters who were friends outside the ring. Fair-weather friends, but friends nonetheless.

Pulling Osh to me again, I held him close, reveled in the heat of his body because that meant he was alive.

"There'll come a point," Garrett said from a few feet away, "where this will be considered a form of molestation. I might have to call this in."

I looked at him. "How many beers have you had?"

He grinned and raised his current bottle of Corona in salute. "Don't ever do that again."

"I'm sorry, Garrett. I didn't even think of what this might do to you."

He shook his head. "All's well that ends—"

"I didn't particularly care at the time, but looking back . . ."

A throw pillow hit me square in the face. I giggled, almost giddy with relief that Osh would be okay. Or at least alive. He may never be the same again, but he'd live.

"We need to take him back to the apartment."

Reyes shook his head. "I don't want to risk anyone seeing us carrying an unconscious body into the building."

We both turned to Garrett.

"I don't exactly have a guest room."

We looked at each other and nodded.

"Ready?" I asked.

We gathered him into our arms, and I was surprised at how gentle Reyes was with him. But carrying an unconscious Daeva was like carrying a limp lion made of spaghetti.

"By all means," Garrett said. "Take my room."

"Gawd, he's heavy," I said, grunting.

"You know, I could get him myself."

"No, I got this," I said, right as I slammed his head into the doorframe. "Shit. You think that'll bruise?"

Reyes fought a grin and lost.

We got Osh settled in Garrett's bed. Swopes wasn't nearly as annoyed as he pretended to be. He was concerned. He was traumatized. Cookie was on her way over to help watch over him. We'd agreed to take shifts until he woke up.

Reyes and I took first watch as Garrett went out for sustenance.

I lay beside Osh on the bed, touching the lines that were getting lighter and lighter. Only a few gashes remained. We'd stripped him and bandaged the worst of them.

Reyes was sitting in a chair across the room, his shirt unbuttoned and open, a beer in one hand and resting on a knee. He was so fierce. So powerful. And he was just sitting there drinking a beer. Eyeing me as though trying to figure me out.

"How did you do it?"

I tucked a strand of hair behind Osh's ear. "It's called god glass."

"That's what you had in New York?"

"Party favor. Kuur brought it, but he didn't know the rules of the game. He didn't bring enough for everyone."

"And how does it work? How does one trap a god, for instance?"

"They must be in a form where you can draw blood. You put one drop on the god glass, say their name, their true name, and presto. They are trapped until you decide otherwise."

"You've had it for over a week?"

I cleared my throat. "Yes."

"And you've known that I was a god for over a week?"

"Yes. My father . . . let me know. He told me you were created from one of the gods of Uzan."

"Why would you not tell me about this?"

I closed my eyes. Lowered my head. Whispered the truth. "In case I had to use it on you."

He went completely still. After what seemed like an eternity, he asked, "And why would you have to take such drastic measures?"

"I didn't know how much of you was . . . you and how much was an evil god from a prison dimension." The irony that he'd been in prison in both his celestial and his human forms was not lost on me. "I didn't know if you'd be a threat to Beep or not."

"That was good thinking."

I looked over at him, surprised.

"I'm not worthy to be a father. I never was. It just took Satan going to the convent, possessing me, reminding me who I was, what I was, to force me to come to my senses. I am worthy of neither of you. I wouldn't trust me, either."

"Reyes, that's not what I meant." When he said nothing, I asked, "How much do you remember about being Rey'azikeen?"

His irises glittered under his lashes. "You mean, do I remember you sending me to prison?"

I glued my lids shut.

"Do I remember my own brother creating a hell dimension just for me?"

I said nothing. His pain washed over me. Or perhaps that was mine.

"No. Not really. I remember my brother being so frustrated with me, so worried for his little dolls here on Earth, that he created a world where he'd hoped I would grow and learn something. I remember a god from another dimension, a god so beautiful the stars would sooner burn out than turn away from her, begging my brother to send me to her dimension. To a kind of prison, yes, but to a place where I wouldn't be left so utterly alone. A place where I would not slowly go insane."

My lids parted. Just barely.

"I remember her sacrificing her life to my brother. Bartering with him. Offering to be the reaper of his world if he would give me, a selfish piece of shit who wouldn't give her the time of day, another chance."

He closed his eyes and tried to wrest control over his emotions.

"I remember being so full of piss and vinegar, I studied and studied until I found a way to escape the dimension the beautiful god locked me in so that I could wreak havoc across the universe and, in turn, allowed Mae'eldeesahn and Eidolon to escape in my wake."

He was gripping the beer bottle so hard, I thought it would explode.

"To call Uzan a prison was a fallacy of the greatest measure. It was a paradise that your ancestors created for souls that were somehow lost. Somehow disoriented and adrift. But all I could see was the fact that I was locked there against my will." He laughed under his breath. "I don't deserve you or Elwyn."

"You don't think that perhaps you've paid for your sins a thousand times over?"

"How so?"

"Lucifer? The Dendour? Earl Walker?"

He studied the bottle in his hands, scraping at the label absently. "Should I leave you two alone?" he asked, changing the subject.

"He's taken," I said, accepting the fact that forgiving himself was something Reyes didn't do. "Osh. By someone very special."

"And who might that be?"

This might be a little hard for him to swallow. Tact was definitely in order. Or I could just blurt it out and watch his expression go from content to disbelief to horror to a bristly, murderous kind of fury. I chose door number two. "He's destined to be with our daughter."

Reyes's expression slowly changed from content to disbelief to horror to a bristly, murderous kind of fury. "Oh, hell, no." He shot to his feet. "A Daeva? Are you fucking kidding me?"

Just like a dad.

"Yes, a Daeva. But I wouldn't dismiss him so offhandedly."

He whirled around and scowled. Not really at me. Just in general. "What do you mean?"

I pressed one corner of my mouth together in thought. "Okay, you know how I was the grim reaper all my life, then suddenly I'm also this god from another dimension? And how you're the son of Satan all your life, then suddenly you're a god from this dimension? Who does that? Our lives are so weird. I think that maybe Osh is something else, too." I traced one of the dark lines on his face. "I think there's more than meets the eye. I see greatness in him, Reyes. I see a power beyond our imaginings. I see him giving his life for our daughter."

"Oh." He sat back down, satisfied. "As long as he dies in the end."

I snorted.

"So, was that another secret?" he asked.

"Yeah, sorry. I forgot about that one. Speaking of which, would you like to talk about the elephant in the room?"

"I guess we could since he's unconscious."

"Not that elephant."

"Well, we already talked about how you sent me to prison, then tried to trap me in a hell dimension."

"I did no such thing," I said, then chilled when I realized he was teasing me. "No. The other elephant. I'm pretty much out of secrets." I crinkled my nose in thought. "Yep. I think that's the last of them. The big ones, anyway. Just don't ask me about that time I was in college and there was this thing that I thought was a fake eyeball. You won't eat for a month."

"You trapped a god," he said, unfazed by the eyeball incident. I tried to be glad one of us was.

"You're in awe of me, right? It's okay. It happens."

"You're fucking amazing."

Pride swelled inside me.

"Or insane. The jury's still out."

Figured. "You're not getting out of it. Whatever your two secrets are, they cannot, in any way, shape, or form, be worse than mine were."

"Okay, but how were my secrets an elephant in the room? I was perfectly content, sitting here drinking a brewski—"

I burst out laughing. "Did you just say *brewski*?"

"—watching my wife molest an unconscious nineteen-year-old."

"It's like you were speaking a foreign language."

"We're going to have to rebuild the park," he said, his desperation growing.

"I think we can afford it. And stop trying to change the subject."

He grinned, and I almost fell for it, but for the barest hint of a moment, it faltered. "How about I tell you tomorrow?"

I rose onto an elbow. "Or you could tell me today."

After a very long pause, he went back to studying his brewski. "I have another gift, if you'd call it that. I've always just accepted it. It's come in handy a few times in my life."

"Seriously?" That didn't sound so bad.

"I can—I can tell when someone is slated for hell. Marked, if you will, like you can do."

"Wow, that's cool. I think," I said, twirling a strand of Osh's hair in my fingers.

"I can see it the minute I meet a person. If he or she is or is not going to hell. If they've committed the act that will put them there yet or not. Because I can see exactly when it happens, exactly when they get sentenced to hell, to the very second they make the decision that will get them sentenced there."

I sat up and crossed my legs on the bed. "Are you saying I'm slated for hell?"

"Hon, you slate. You don't get slated."

"Oh, right. So that's good for me, because daaaay-um. I could be in trouble." After a moment of thought, I asked him, "Okay, so who is it? Who's going to the fiery pits to suffer in agony for all eternity?"

He rubbed one hand over his eyes and, again, I got worried. When he lowered his hands and his eyes were shimmering with a suspicious wetness, I got very worried.

"Reyes?"

"Before I tell you, I just want you to know, we're on it. We're being proactive and—we're trying to stop his murder."

I slowed my heartbeat to better hear him. To stop the sudden rush of blood to my ears. To still my heavy breathing. "Reyes?"

"It's your uncle Bob."

I couldn't move. I sat paralyzed on Garrett's bed, trying to remember how to restart my heart. I'd probably need that sooner or later.

"When he arrested me for murder, I saw that he was slated to go to hell for an act he would commit about nine years after I met him. An act he committed two years ago, while I was still in prison."

My mind reeled, trying to grasp his words, but they fell away before they reached me. I couldn't quite wrap my fingers, or mind, around them.

"But when I met him, I remembered him. I remembered that I met another kid when I was going to high school. Grant Guerin. He hadn't committed the act that would send him to hell, either, but I still saw it. He was going to kill a detective. He was going to kill your uncle Bob."

Garrett walked in then and could sense the atmosphere instantly.

"I'm telling her," he told him.

Garrett cursed under his breath. "I thought we were going to wait until we found the little shit."

Reyes shrugged.

"Charles, look, we'll find the guy. Guerin doesn't stand a chance. We'll stop him. We've been keeping a tail on your uncle, hoping there's some early interaction with the guy that sets off a chain of events, but nothing so far."

"Why can't you just find him?"

"They got him on tape making a drug deal. When they went to arrest him, he bolted."

"Why wasn't he slated for hell then?"

"It's not as easy to get into hell as one might think. It's all about doing harm unto others. Up to the point when he kills your uncle, he'd never harmed anyone but himself."

"Why can't you find him?" Panic was setting in.

"We will," Garrett said. "He went underground, but he'll resurface."

"When? How much time do we have? You said you know the exact second when it will happen."

Reyes bit down. "We have less than a week."

"Why Uncle Bob?" I crawled to my feet and started to pace. "Why does he kill him? What happens?"

"Your uncle finds him and is about to arrest him."

"And?"

Garrett stepped closer. "Charley, you don't want to know the details."

"I do, actually. Reyes?"

"When your uncle finds him, the guy ambushes him. He hits him over the head."

"And Uncle Bob dies from that?"

"Yes," Garrett said quickly. Too quickly.

"What happens?"

"He doesn't die, but he's unconscious," Reyes said. "So the guy panics and—" He closed his eyes and turned from me. "He finishes your uncle off with acid and bleach."

The edges of my vision rocketed inward. I reeled, and Garrett caught me. Sat me back on the bed. Went for water.

I couldn't talk for the longest. The image was in my heart and in my head, and it was there to stay.

Then it hit me. "Where does he find him? Uncle Bob?" I asked, my voice rising. "Where does he find the guy? Go there. He's probably there."

"We have people posted there. When he shows, we'll know."

"So, we can stop this." I nodded, calming a little. "We can—wait." I gaped at Reyes. "My uncle, Robert Davidson, amazing detective, wonderful human being, incorruptible cop, was slated for hell two years ago. Really? And how did that happen?"

"Dutch—"

"Don't. Reyes, just tell me."

"He killed someone," he said from between clenched teeth.

"In cold blood? No. Two years ago? That shooting? They investigated that. He was cleared. He was shot twice. He fired in self-defense."

"Not that one."

Garrett had come back with a glass of water, but he looked away as Reyes shifted in discomfort.

"Are you saying my uncle murdered in cold blood?"

"Yes. Ice cold. It was rather impressive, really. At the time, I—"

"Why would he kill someone in cold blood?"

He lowered his head. He had no intention of telling me.

I stepped closer. "I can make you."

He said nothing. Offered no argument. Or explanation.

I inched forward and gave him one more chance. "Why?"

"All you need to know is that he had good cause."

"Reyes, I swear by all that's holy—"

"For you," he said, the words barely a whisper on the air.

"What?" I asked, my voice just as faint. Just as airy.

"He did it for you. They were—they found out what you can do."

"Who?"

"A low-life drug gang from Colombia, trying to get in good with their boss. Your uncle got a tip from one of his CIs they were going to kidnap you, take you back to Colombia, and present you to him as, kind of, a gift."

I couldn't have been more shocked if he'd punched me in the stomach.

"So, he found their hideout. He had nothing to bring them in on. He didn't want to risk arresting them, anyway, and them, in turn, telling another member in their organization about you. So, he broke in, took them out one by one, and then set fire to the place."

"No way. Uncle Bob would never."

"Your uncle knew the drug baron, Dutch. He knew what he was capable of. He'd witnessed it firsthand when he was in the military. He knew he had to kill them all to silence them. If word got back of your abilities, the Colombian drug baron would come after you himself."

"Why?" I asked, questioning everything I'd ever known about my uncle. "What does it matter? What would a Colombian drug baron want with me?"

"He was a collector. Fascinated with the occult. He believed that if he took the souls of those who were gifted by eating their flesh, he would inherit their powers. He'd already killed several people in the villages surrounding his compound, searching for the gift of sight."

"A drug baron wanted to eat me?"

"He would have, if he'd found out about you. He would've considered you quite the coup."

"Why are people so batshit crazy?" I railed, pacing the room. "Uncle Bob did this for a good reason."

"Hell seems to think otherwise. It doesn't matter that he did it for you or that they were bad. It was lives taken on purpose when there were other options . . . it wasn't self-defense. It was a conscious decision."

"So, even if you do something bad for a good reason, you automatically get a reservation at the Fire and Brimstone Inn?"

"Actually," Garrett said, "you might be able to help us out. Seems the only person who might know where Grant Guerin might be is your new BFF Parker. He was Parker's CI back in the day, and some think he still is. But he's not talking."

"Parker was a cop?"

"He started out there."

"Parker certainly likes to play by his own rules, doesn't he?" My mind raced with all the implications. "Okay, first we have to stop this walking corpse from killing my uncle. Then I can worry about what to do with his sentence."

Reyes smiled. "That was kind of already the plan."

"Yes, but I wasn't in on it then." I started to leave to pay Parker a visit when I stopped and turned back to my husband. "Any more secrets? You know, while we're on the subject."

"None that I can think of."

"Good to know." I needed to catch Parker by surprise. And how better to surprise him than by showing up at his house at 3 A.M.?

I walked back to Reyes and pulled his mouth down to mine. He tasted like fire and salt and lime.

"Don't wait up."

Garrett called out as I stalked out and closed the door. "But I got taquitos!"

29

Would someone please poke holes in the lid of my jar?
—T-SHIRT

I pounded on Parker's door for ten minutes before he opened it, as furious as I'd ever seen him. He hadn't bothered closing his robe, and his light blue boxers didn't hide much. You'd think he'd be blond there, too.

"Nick?" a woman said from the dark room beyond him.

"Go back to bed. I'll be there the minute I have Mrs. Davidson arrested."

"You wear socks to bed?" I asked.

"What the fuck, Davidson?"

"I need to know where your CI, Grant Guerin, is."

"How the fuck should I know?"

"Fine. Educated guess. Where, in your humble opinion, *might* he be?"

"You have thirty seconds to get off my property."

"Come on, Parker. I just got your college buddy off a murder charge and saved your ass from prosecution for obstruction of justice and whatever else Joplin could've thrown at you. He would have nailed your ass, and you know it."

"I have no idea where Guerin is," he said.

I scooched my mouth to one side in disappointment. "Just when I think you're all noble and shit, you do something stupid. How do you think I'm so good at what I do?"

He shrugged, frustrated and tired.

"I know when someone is lying, and I need to know where Guerin is."

"So, you're like a human lie detector. Interesting. Is this about the warrant? That UC was dirtier than my CI any day of the week. Even if I did know, I wouldn't tell the likes of you."

"Look, we can continue to work together, or we can end our business relationship right here and now. Your call."

But that meant nothing to him, and I realized something as we stood there. He thought I'd killed my own child. How else would one explain the hostility? He really was noble in a messed-up way. He was willing to go to jail for his friend for a perceived imbalance in the world. He wouldn't tell the cops where Grant Guerin was because the whole thing was unfair and/or unlawful in his mind.

Then again, I didn't give a shit. Guerin was going to kill my uncle. A good man. And Parker knew where he was. This was going to take some doing. I stepped past him and into his not-so-humble abode.

"I'll have you arrested," he threatened.

"You already said that. Keep up, Parker." I wondered if I should just tell him the truth. Of course, after finding out a Colombian drug baron wanted to eat me, I figured I should reevaluate how many people we let into our little circle.

"Okay, I'm going to give you a choice. Tell me where Guerin is or I'll tell Joplin the whole story." It was a cheap shot, but I was willing to risk a dent in my rep.

Parker, however, came unglued. The man had issues.

He got in my face and jabbed an index finger at me. "How dare you come into my house and threaten me, you little bitch. You think I don't

know about you? You think I'm not going to nail you and your uncle to
the wall?"

"My uncle?"

"Way too much shade in your neck of the woods, Davidson. Shady
dealings don't get much more shadowy."

He was really good at metaphors.

"You guys are always finding shit, just out of the blue. Anonymous
tips, my ass. You are the most unethical, unprofessional PI I've ever met."

"I am. I really am. I know about your file, too, since we're on the subject of unethical practices."

He was livid. "I'm going to nail your ass if it's the last thing I do. You
had something so, so—" His voice cracked, and I stepped back to look
at him. "My wife and I have been trying for five years, and you just
throw it away?"

"Parker," I said, empathy washing over me. Still, he did call me a
bitch.

"I know Detective Davidson was in on it. I know he was with you
when the baby was born."

"He was actually kind of above me." I remembered his face as he stared
down the well at me. And the worried look on it.

"Then you admit it. You admit you had a baby and, what? Accidentally killed it? Sold it? Gave it away? What?"

Was he honestly so noble that he would nail me, in the nonsexual sense,
even after what I'd done for Lyle Fiske? That he would give up a friendship or the hope for a lucrative—in a prosecutorial way—relationship
because he thought I'd broken the law? Was he really the kind of guy who
would arrest his best friend for drug trafficking instead of trying to help
him cover it up?

"You don't know me, so let me explain," he said. "I'm the kind of guy
who would arrest my best friend for drug trafficking instead of trying to
help him cover it up."

Wow. That was spot-on. I liked him.

"If you think because we solved a case together—"

"We?"

"—that I'm going to step back from this investigation, you're wrong. I will find out what you did with that baby if it's the last thing I do."

Uh-oh. Wrong thing to say. "Now you're just pissing me off," I said.

"Good. I hope you and your corrupt uncle—"

"Corrupt?"

"—get everything that's coming to you."

"Corrupt?"

"Now that I have your confession that you did have a baby and you can't produce any birth certificate or adoption papers . . ." His smile defined smug.

"Is that really it?" I asked him, almost feeling sorry for him. "Is that what all this is about?"

"Not at all. I've been onto you for almost two years. There's just too much—"

"Shade. Yeah, I got that."

"So, how about it? Want to just confess all your sins here and now? I have a legal pad somewhere."

Parker was a hard one to figure out. He was more complex than most people. I could use someone like him on our side. But even if I told him the truth, even if I gave him a show of supernatural wonder to prove it, he was the kind that wouldn't care. But he'd been willing to break the law for his friend. He was a tough nut to crack.

"One more chance, Parker. Grant Guerin."

"Kiss my ass."

I slowed time and contemplated what I was about to do. Not for long, however. I'd pretty much made up my mind the minute he told me he was going to find Beep no matter what. Sealed his fate with that one.

I rose onto my toes and brushed my mouth across his for the briefest second. Then I let time bounce back as the truth poured into his mind like a bad LSD trip. Pictures and memories. Everything that had ever happened to me. Everything I knew, good and bad. Supernatural and mortal. He got it all in one, massive info dump.

He saw the stars being formed. Planets align from space. Supernovas explode. Red giants die. He saw the fall of Lucifer and the rise of Noah's ark. He saw war and famine and peace and abundance. He saw the otherworld in all its glory. The gods and demons and everything in between. And he saw Beep. How she was born. How she was almost killed. How we had to give her up to save her life. What that did to me. And what I would do to him if he even thought about pursuing his investigation.

"Oh, my god," he said as he fell to his knees, drool slipping from one corner of his mouth.

It was a lot to take in.

He clasped his hands and bowed before me. I'd never been worshipped before. Not since I'd become human. I did not like it.

"I would never try to find her. I'm so sorry. I'll get rid of everything." He started crying, sobbing into the carpet beneath him.

I bent down to him and lifted his chin. "Grant Guerin."

He could hardly speak, he was shaking so hard. "He's behind McCoy's on Girard." I turned to leave, but he stopped me. "Davidson, I—I had no idea."

"Nobody does."

He closed his eyes and buried his face. "I had no idea."

I went back to him and kneeled beside him. "You'll be able to father a child now. Side effect of my touch, I suspect."

When he looked up at me again, he had such gratitude in his expression that my heart reacted no matter how hard I tried to turn it to stone.

"You're welcome."

I stepped outside, closed the door behind me, and turned toward the presence of a supernatural being close by. The crickets stopped chirping, and the breeze stopped whispering through the trees. I straightened my spine and clamped my jaw shut, unable to believe Michael was paying me a visit. Another one. And at this hour.

He walked out of the shadows, his presence so powerful it made the hairs on the back of my neck stand on end. His massive wings folded into place as I readied my hand. Faced my palm toward the ground. Prepared to summon Artemis should I need her.

When he spoke, his voice was deep and smooth and clear. "You cannot stop what has been set in motion," he said. Even in the dark, his eyes sparkled like a swimming pool reflecting the summer sun. Their reaction to even the barest fragments of light mimicked Reyes's. His could shimmer in the lowest illumination.

"Stop the death of my uncle?"

He wore a long black coat that swept the ground as he took another step forward. "It's one thing to help Father's people, but you will be changing their history. Father made a promise. You've already upset heaven, Val-Eeth. If you try to stop this—"

I helped people every day. It was how I made my living. And now heaven had a problem with it?

I laughed softly, astounded at his gall. " 'Try' implies the possibility of failure." I gave him a once-over before adding, "I have no intention of failing."

When I turned to leave, he was by my side at once. He wrapped a hand around my arm. Not hard enough to hurt, but enough to make his intentions known. "They'll come for you."

He wasn't malevolent. I felt no disdain coming off him. No anger or contempt or resentment. In fact, if I felt anything, if I had to pinpoint an emotion swirling beneath the massive wings, I'd have sworn it was something akin to admiration.

I raised my chin. "Let them."

"You don't understand." He lowered his head, his face stunningly beautiful, as I supposed most angels' were. "*He* will come for you, Val-Eeth. This is *His* realm."

His realm. He brought me to His realm. Practically blackmailed me into coming here to be the reaper of this dimension. To save Reyes from an eternity of hell, I'd agreed. And now He dared to tell me what to do in it?

I leaned forward until we were barely centimeters apart, fought the wave of euphoria being so close to an angel of Jehovah's induced, and shook my head at the reminder of whose realm I was in. His realm?

"Not anymore," I said. Then I jerked my arm out of his grasp and went to see a man about his impending death.